RICHARD FORD hails from Lee[...] [...]
the first town on the Thames. His [...]
in 2011. *Herald of the Storm*, boo[...]
his epic fantasy debut and was hig[...]
the series, *The Shattered Crown.*

Praise for the *Steelhaven* series:

'A perfect example of tight, gritty, character-driven storytelling'
Luke Scull, author of *The Grim Company*

'A breath of fresh air'
*Drying Ink*

'Exciting and different'
The British Fantasy Society

'A great piece of solid writing, the prose is sharp and when you get
to the action sequences they really take your breath away . . . A series
that I can't get enough of'
*Falcata Times*

'Dark, gritty, funny and clever'
*Galaxy Books*

'You'll find yourself looking forward to what Ford dreams up next'
*SFX*

'Mr Ford, welcome to the world of high fantasy, your challenge for,
and to, the throne is legitimate'
*Mass Movement Magazine*

'*Herald of the Storm* brought us to the edge of our seats and now *The
Shattered Crown* tips the seats up a bit as he puts us where he wants
us to be'
*The Bookbag*

'Violent, vicious and darkly funny'
*Fantasy Faction*

'An excellent book with excitement and intrigue in every chapter'
*Robin's Books*

'Won me over [...] lively and dynamic'
*Th[...] Book Plank*

'Spectacula[...]
[...]*ing Fields*

*By Richard Ford*

*Steelhaven series*
Herald of the Storm
The Shattered Crown
Lord of Ashes

# LORD OF ASHES

## RICHARD FORD

headline

The right of Richard Ford to be identified as the Author of
the Work has been asserted by him in accordance with the
Copyright, Designs and Patents Act 1988.

First published in 2015 by
HEADLINE PUBLISHING GROUP

First published in paperback in 2015 by
HEADLINE PUBLISHING GROUP

Cataloguing in Publication Data is available from the British Library

ISBN 978 0 7553 9410 4

Typeset in Minion by Palimpsest Book Production Ltd, Falkirk, Stirlingshire

Printed and bound in Great Britain by Clays Ltd, St Ives plc

Headline's policy is to use papers that are natural, renewable and recyclable products
and made from wood grown in well-managed forests and other controlled sources.
The logging and manufacturing processes are expected to conform to the
environmental regulations of the country of origin.

HEADLINE PUBLISHING GROUP
An Hachette UK Company
Carmelite House
50 Victoria Embankment
London EC4Y 0DZ

www.headline.co.uk
www.hachette.co.uk

For Lynne, Josie, Hamish and . . . is it Paul?
I can never remember!

# PROLOGUE

I t was dark and quiet inside the hide-covered shelter, almost peaceful. Nothing moved but a single piece of animal skin come loose in the night, letting the dawn light flit into the tent as it flapped gently in the breeze.

Endellion took a deep breath, smelling the salt tang of moist flesh and stale sex. Surrounding her on a pile of furs were half a dozen Khurtic warriors, every one of them deep in slumber, every one of them worn out from their long night. She smiled at the memory. They had tried so very hard to keep up but she was Elharim, and not even a half-dozen had come close to satisfying her appetite.

The one lying next to her – she didn't know his name, had no use for any of their names – bore the mark of her nails on his back, raw and livid on his pale flesh. He was a pretty one, his skin smooth for a Khurta, his face unmarred by war and violence. That was unusual for one of his kind. It had taken her some time to find such boys, the Khurtas were a notoriously ugly race, but after much searching she had managed to take her pick of their youngest and strongest. None had refused her. None had dared.

With a single finger she traced the line one of her nails had left on his skin. The boy stirred at her touch but did not wake. The night before he had cried out as she marked him, as she dug her fingers into his flesh, urging him, stirring his lust. He had been

1

good; one of the best and most eager to please. It was fitting she should have granted him such a battle scar. And these Khurtas so loved their scars.

A noise from outside made her forget her parched throat and fuddled head. It was the sound of stone scraping steel.

Endellion rose from the piled furs, deftly stepping over the bodies that surrounded her. She found her clothes piled in a corner, quickly dressed and pulled on her boots, strapping her sword to her waist and taking one of the furs to wrap around her shoulders against the chill winter air. With a last amused glance back at the spent bodies lying in her tent, she pulled back the hide covering and stepped out into the wan morning light.

He sat not twenty yards away, and though the sun was hidden behind a gloomy bank of cloud it still seemed like he shone. Endellion couldn't suppress a grin as she walked towards him, watching as he honed that blade, scraping whetstone on Riverland steel. Even though they were a thousand miles from their homeland in the north, when she laid eyes on Azreal it was as though she had never left. He was home to her. All she had ever wanted.

Of course she would never have told him that. There was a time, years ago, when she would have professed her devotion to him; might well have pledged herself to him and him alone. But that time was gone. She was of the Arc Magna, a warrior born, dedicated to the blade and the kill. Azreal was of the Subodai, a silent watcher in the night, a messenger bringing the word of his lord and sometimes with it the gift of death. Any union between them was forbidden, but that had not stopped Endellion taking her pleasure with him so many years before. And what heady nights those had been.

She stood for some time, enduring the cold just to watch him at his work. The stone rang on steel, the blade calling out with each stroke as though singing its joy. How Endellion would love to have made Azreal sing out in joy once more, feeling his flesh against her flesh, hearing his cries of lust mix with her own. It was a temptation she could barely quell.

'Are you going to stand there staring all morning?' Azreal said finally, without looking around or pausing in his labours.

Endellion almost laughed. Of course he knew she was watching him. There was little that passed beyond the knowing of Azreal of the Subodai.

'I could stand here staring until Oblivion claims me,' she replied.

He only shook his head at that, moving the whetstone along his blade with one last ring of the steel. In a single swift motion he stood, spinning the blade in his grip with a flourish and deftly slotting it into his sheath.

'Unfortunately neither of us can wait for Oblivion, my love. Our master has summoned us.'

Endellion couldn't manage to suppress a pang of excitement as he called her *my love*, but she did not speak further as Azreal led the way through the camp. If Amon Tugha had indeed summoned them, it would be madness to keep him waiting.

She walked close behind him as he moved through the Khurtic camp. They had been here for almost a week and the place was beginning to stink of unwashed bodies and rotting meat. It was not good for these savages to spend so much time amongst one another with no one to fight. Though Amon Tugha had united the nine tribes, old rivalries still burned bright and there had been many a feud settled in blood over the past few days. For her part, Endellion relished the violence and had even been eager to join in the fighting, but her master had forbidden it. He would have no dissent amongst his ranks, at least not before the city of Steelhaven had fallen. For every man slain in anger another had been executed at her master's hand, but the threat of a swift and permanent reckoning had still done nothing to curb the killing instinct of the Khurtas. Almost three hundred heads sat atop spears, looking towards the city they had come so far to besiege.

Further through the camp, a vast wooden stockade stood, housing prisoners chained to one another in their droves. The stink from them was worse than anything the Khurtas could have mustered and they were indeed a pitiful sight. Endellion could not take her eyes from them as she passed by. They were a mark of her master's power, his victories since they had first come to these foul lands. Once proud warriors brought low, stripped of their arms and armour, humiliated, starved and beaten. Every day they suffered was a day her lord was elevated above them.

Each of them that died only served to raise her master's repute yet higher.

Azreal turned his head away as he passed by the stockade. It made Endellion smile to see his disdain for such treatment. Mercy was a rare quality amongst the Subodai, but Azreal had little time for the suffering of prisoners. He saw it as a needless indulgence, and did not appreciate its value. Some would have regarded such an attitude as weakness, but Endellion knew only too well how deadly he was. For all Azreal showed mercy for the weak and helpless, he had none for those who would oppose him with a naked blade.

As they moved through the camp there came the sounds of saws and hammers. Those Khurtas with the acumen for it had been selected to craft Amon Tugha's weapons of war – vast siege towers, ballistae, mangonels and the like. Endellion had been surprised at how well the savage Khurtas had turned their hands to such labours, but then she had also underestimated their prowess in other areas and been pleasingly surprised at their ability to adapt.

The two Elharim crested a ridge to see the land rise yet further. Atop the next promontory stood a windmill, lonely against the morning skyline, its sails burned to rags by the Khurtic scouts who had first reached this position. Beside the sad sight of the ruin awaited their lord, Amon Tugha.

He stood as still and solid as that mill, staring out over the bleak fields of the Free States towards the city that was his ultimate prize. At his feet were his two hounds, Astur and Sul, one chewing hungrily on the bone of some beast, the other watching vigilantly as Endellion and Azreal approached.

As they mounted the hill, Endellion saw that the rest of his generals were also present. Brulmak Tarr picked impatiently at the scarred flesh of his face, looking on furiously as though it were he the Elharim had kept waiting. Wolkan Brude also looked on with hate from behind a mass of beard and hair, though he was as unmoving as Amon Tugha. Leaning against the wall of the mill, almost hidden in the shadows, was Stirgor Cairnmaker, hands resting on the handles of the sword and axe at his belt. Endellion could read nothing on his features; as though he cared little for the killing to come, but she knew from seeing his skill in battle, the hunger for slaughter he showed on the field, that he cared a great deal.

Azreal was the first to drop to his knee before their prince. Endellion followed suit, feeling the damp of the grass soak into her leather trews. For some moments Amon Tugha stood and stared southward, ignoring his Elharim bodyguards and the Khurtic chieftains in his thrall. All the while one of those hounds stared as the other noisily cracked at the bone in its jaws. Endellion glanced up as she waited; noticing that the bone the animal dined on belonged to no beast, but was the thigh bone of a man.

'Rise,' said Amon Tugha, without turning around, his golden eyes still fixed on that city as though it were built from all the jewels of the Riverlands.

The Elharim both stood and Endellion glanced to Azreal, who gave no sign as to what was going on. Were they just to stand here admiring Steelhaven from afar? They all knew why they were here; they had watched the city for days without so much as a single arrow fired in anger. What now?

'My ships from across the Midral have arrived,' said Amon, finally. 'Their bombardment will begin at sunset. It will be our sign to attack from the north.'

'About fucking time,' growled Brulmak Tarr in the guttural Khurtic tongue. Endellion thought it foolish of him to speak unless spoken to, but it was clear Amon Tugha had learned to give his savage warriors some latitude to their behaviour in recent weeks. They were barbarians and would never adapt to the traditions and manners demanded of Elharim warriors.

Amon Tugha turned, and Endellion saw him smiling, the blond spikes of his hair all but shining atop his handsome face, the ritual scars and burns to his chest and arms livid against his bronzed flesh. 'I know you grow restless,' said Amon. 'All of you have fought hard for many days only to be stopped in your tracks when our goal is in sight. Tonight your patience will be rewarded. The waiting is over.'

Endellion could have laughed at that. Though they had been camped here for almost six days the Khurtas had done little waiting;

instead fighting and fucking amongst themselves as though their lives depended on it. It was rumoured Brulmak Tarr had already killed a dozen of his own men, such was his impatience for battle.

Amon Tugha looked to Azreal. 'How go our preparations?' he asked.

'We will be ready, my prince,' Azreal replied. 'The siege engines will be completed by sundown. The location to the west of the city has been found, our warriors are already making the preparations you ordered.'

Amon Tugha nodded. 'Good. It is important we begin our attack now. We can wait no longer. The Father of Killers has failed and the queen of this city yet lives. I will see Steelhaven fall and take her crown with my own hands.'

Despite his master's words, Azreal shook his head. There was something he wanted to say, something that Amon Tugha might not want to hear. For a moment Endellion almost reached out to stop him, but it was too late.

'My lord, I must ask,' Azreal said, his head still bowed. 'We have the advantage. The city is cut off from land and sea. This kingdom is riven by feuds and the other nobles within it will not come to the city's aid. So why attack? Why make such a sacrifice when we could wait them out? Starve them? Put them on the offensive or force their surrender?'

Endellion could hear one of the Khurtic war chiefs snort in derision at the notion they would starve their enemy rather than fight, but she was more concerned with Amon Tugha's reaction. It was rare he would allow anyone to question his wishes without repercussion, even Azreal, who he favoured above all.

The prince looked at his assassin for some moments, and Endellion feared the worst. Then a smile crossed her master's face.

'You speak sense, my brother,' he said finally. 'But it is not enough to starve this city and pick at the flesh that remains. I want it razed. I want it destroyed. I want to walk its shattered stones and wade through the broken bones of its slaughtered defenders.' Amon Tugha's voice rose as he spoke, and both his hounds grew unsettled at their master's anger. 'I want its queen to suffer at my hand. I want to tread her smashed crown beneath my heel.' Endellion could see the golden fire in her master's eyes now. His lips turned up in a maniac grin and spittle gathered at the corners of his mouth. 'And I will have it within the next four days, no matter the sacrifice. No matter if every Khurta in my service dies for it. No matter if *you* die for it, broken and beaten in the dirt.' He stopped then and stared at Azreal, who could only hold his master's gaze for the briefest of moments.

'Yes, my prince,' Azreal replied, bowing his head.

Amon Tugha said nothing further, just turned back to the city of Steelhaven and glared at his prize, so close but still out of reach.

At such a signal, Endellion and Azreal backed away, leaving their master to his thoughts. Before they turned to make their way back down the hill Endellion saw that Brulmak Tarr and Wolkan Brude were grinning at Azreal's cowing. How she would have loved to punish them for such an insult, but it would only have served to stir Amon Tugha's ire still further, and there was no way she would survive that.

'Pleased with yourself?' she whispered as they made their way back through the camp.

'It had to be said,' Azreal replied. 'Every doctrine of siege warfare states we have the advantage. Needlessly pressing to raze the city will cost us dearly.'

'And yet we will still follow him,' she said.

Azreal stopped at that, turning to regard her with those eyes she found so beautiful. He was angry, that much was obvious, but all she wanted to do was grab him and kiss his lips till they bled from the passion of it.

'Yes, we will follow him,' he said. 'Unto death if we have to.'

She could feel the smile slowly dropping from her face.

Back in the Riverlands, two years ago, when the man they now called Amon Tugha had been banished, it had seemed they had no choice but to follow him. He was their master and despite his betrayal of the queen, his own mother, they were still bound to their prince. They were sworn to him, loyal without question, but ever since they had left their homeland doubt had begun to creep into Endellion's mind. Now, so many hundreds of miles from home, she was beginning to question that loyalty. She was Arc Magna, a peerless warrior, respected and feared by her kith and kin. Here it seemed she was just another of Amon Tugha's horde. Expendable like all the rest.

'You follow him like a sheep,' Endellion said, trying to keep the anger from her voice, but failing. 'What have we come here for? We are as disgraced as he is, we owe him nothing.'

'He is still our prince.' Azreal sounded as though he was trying to convince himself as much as her.

'And he will lead us to our deaths. For what? An ugly, stinking city a thousand miles from our home? That's not a good enough reason for me.'

'That is not the only reason. We are here to regain what we have lost. To build his name anew so they will hear it echoing back into the Riverlands. So they will know it was an injustice to banish him so. He is a king, and those that stand at his shoulder are kings alongside him.'

Endellion could see the light in Azreal's eyes as he spoke, hear the vehemence in his voice. It seemed he had lost none of his zeal, whereas she had almost none left at all. How would she persuade him of his folly? He would never listen if she pointed out the truth Azreal chose to ignore. That the man they called Amon Tugha had tried to usurp the crown of the Riverlands from his brother, the rightful heir, in a failed coup. That the 'injustice' as Azreal called it was more a mercy. By all rights their queen should have taken her son's head rather than cast him into exile. But she knew Azreal would hear none of it.

'You're right,' she said with a smile, adopting a mask she hoped he would not see through. It would not do to argue with Azreal when he was in such a fervour. 'We made our vows and we must serve. Even if it means we will die.'

Azreal smiled back at her. 'You won't die,' he said. 'There's no one alive can match you.'

At that, he left her standing amid the camp with the smell of fresh lit fires in the bite of the morning air. As she glanced towards the city in the distance, grey and imposing against the dark iron sky, she wondered if he was right, or if there was someone waiting within who could finally best her and leave her body to rot alone and forgotten in this cold and bleak land.

# ONE

**B**reakfast had become a pitiful affair in recent days and Waylian Grimm wasn't sorry to miss it. Though it was unlike him to skip a meal, especially since his time in the Kriega Mountains when he'd almost starved to death, he just couldn't bring himself to eat. There was a fight coming, a fight that might see the end of everything he knew, and the consequent knot in his stomach was twisted too tight to allow room for watery gruel.

He stared north out of his chamber window, probably not the best thing to do under the circumstances, looking forlornly towards the horde that would come to destroy the city any day now. But what else was he supposed to do? Try and ignore them? Offer some tea and cakes? Run like the bloody hells?

That latter option was off the cards, at least. The last ship had sailed from port three days previously and in the night a huge fleet had arrived to blockade Steelhaven's crescent bay. The way north was barred by a mass of cutthroat savages, and who knew what lay in wait to east and west. Waylian couldn't go anywhere, even if he wanted to.

*Just have to sit tight and wait for the fighting to start, won't you, Grimmy.*

But when would the bloody fighting start? The Khurtas were just sitting there, lighting their fires in the night, singing their brutal dirges. They'd made a pretty good show of scaring the shit out of everyone in the city, but so far made no move to attack.

Perhaps Amon Tugha had got bored. Perhaps he'd seen the imposing curtain wall and barred gates of Steelhaven and thought better of it.

Waylian was pretty sure that was a wish too far.

Amon Tugha had come a long way to take Steelhaven for his own. There was no way he'd be leaving without a fight.

Waylian washed his face in a bowl of cold water and donned his robe before leaving the chamber and making his way down the vast stairway that wound its way through the core of the Tower of Magisters. The corridors had become all but deserted in the days leading up to Amon Tugha's arrival. Where before there had been aimless chatter there was now silence. The atmosphere of studiousness replaced by an air of steely determination that seemed to hang over the place now that his mistress, Magistra Gelredida, had mobilised the Archmasters to her cause.

It had not been easy. His mistress had brought the most powerful magickers in the Free States to heel through subterfuge and blackmail, and Waylian had helped her do it. He could only hope that when all this was over he wouldn't be the one who had to face their ire.

*Don't worry about that right now, Grimmy. You have to survive the forty thousand Khurtas about to rain all the hells on the city you're stuck in. You'll most likely be long dead before any of the Archmasters has a chance to seek vengeance.*

Making his way down the oak staircase, Waylian could hear the guttural shouts of combat and the clash of steel echoing up towards him. One of the floors had been cleared completely of desks and shelves and other paraphernalia and converted into a fighting gallery where the Raven Knights could practise. Their normal training yard in the tower grounds was being used by Archmaster Drennan Folds and his apprentices, where their inexpert attempts at magick would do less harm. Consequently, the Raven Knights trained inside, the clashing of their weapons making an almighty racket within the hallowed confines of the ancient tower.

Waylian paused on the staircase, watching them through an open archway as they went at one another with sword, spear and glaive. He could only marvel at their strength and skill – even fully armoured they fought with a speed and ferocity that almost made Waylian's head spin. He had watched the Wyvern Guard training on the way from the Kriega Mountains and had thought them a fierce and deadly bunch. The Raven Knights almost matched them for raw brutality, and surpassed them in finesse and vigour. Waylian wouldn't have liked to call which order of knights were the more proficient killers.

He stood and watched, almost mesmerised, until a figure walked from beyond the entranceway, blocking his view. Lucen Kalvor turned slowly, regarding Waylian with those dark arching brows of his. It was still unclear if Kalvor knew who had aided Gelredida in her plotting against the Archmasters. Whether Kalvor knew it was Waylian who had gathered proof that he'd murdered his former master to take his place as Archmaster was impossible to tell. It was clear, however, that he held no love for Magistra Gelredida, and by association it was doubtful he liked Waylian much either.

*He probably thinks you're her pet, like everyone else, Grimmy. People don't like other people's pets; always leaving their fur and the stink of their arses where they're not wanted.*

Waylian averted his gaze and hurried down the stairs. He could feel Kalvor's dark eyes following him as he went, not really wanting to know what the Archmaster was thinking. He was pretty sure it would be nothing complimentary.

Further down, the sound of clashing steel relented, only to be replaced by squabbling voices. The closer he got to the sound the more Waylian thought it reminded him of a gaggle of geese, pecking at one another over a scrap of food.

Again he paused when he reached the source of the noise, peering through the open door of a huge wood-panelled meeting room. In its centre sat Archmaster Crannock Marghil and surrounding him were more than a dozen magisters, all speaking at once, barracking the old man with their protestations.

'We will all be killed!' 'You should have bargained with the Elharim!' 'There's no sense in this, we should flee!' 'I'm too old to go into battle!' 'I can't fight, my sciatica's playing up!'

To his credit, Crannock soaked up the cacophony with a grim

11

defiance that belied his years, taking every panicked excuse on the chin like a seasoned pugilist.

Waylian remembered when Gelredida had given the old man the task of mustering the veteran magisters. At the time she had said they would follow Crannock, that they respected him. Looking through the open door into the room, Waylian could see little evidence of that. Nevertheless, the Archmaster seemed unbowed by the complaints of his fellow Caste members. It seemed they would have to join the fight whether they liked it or not.

When he'd made his way to the bottom of the vast stairway Waylian paused at the double doors standing open before him. He could hear the sounds of strict instruction coming from the courtyard beyond and he was in no hurry to rush out and let himself be seen by his fellow apprentices or their tutor. In the past few days Drennan Folds had put every apprentice left in the tower through their paces, assessing their abilities and training them rigorously in whatever area of the Art they proved themselves most proficient. It had been a harsh few days, and not everyone had survived. If there were any doubt as to the perils of tapping the Veil untrained then they had long been dispelled. The Veil held all the magicks of the world within its confines, and harnessing it was dangerous, even for experienced magisters. For an apprentice it could often lead to catastrophe.

Waylian had heard tell one lad named Mikael had choked on his own vomit after attempting a particularly tricky incantation. Another girl, he didn't know her name, had died screaming and clawing at her head, pulling out hair in huge knots until she had finally expired. Little wonder then that Waylian was out of favour with his fellows since he had managed to avoid being put at such risk.

Not that it was his fault. Magistra Gelredida had insisted he be spared the danger of premature training. There was no use trying to explain that to Drennan and his trainees, though. To them he was unfairly favoured. It mattered little to them that Waylian *wanted* to learn his Art, *wanted* to train alongside them so he might face the Khurtas with all the raging magicks he could muster and send them fleeing in terror back to their northern steppes.

12

*It doesn't matter. They all hate you anyway. You have no friends here, Grimmy. But then, you never had any friends here in the first place.*

When he knew he could wait no longer, Waylian stepped into the dim morning light and glanced out onto the courtyard. Gelredida would be waiting, and he knew he shouldn't be late.

His attention was drawn by the row of robed apprentices, each one standing and looking on as Archmaster Folds gave them their instruction. A line of mannequins stood opposite, their blank faces daubed with war paint to represent the savage Khurtas. To the far left one mannequin was burned and blackened.

Drennan held a block of charcoal, the dust of it having dirtied his robe at the front. 'You'll feel it grow hot,' he said, glaring at his students with one blue eye, the other as milky as the overcast sky. 'But don't worry, it won't burn your flesh. Just that of your target,' with a thick-fingered hand he gestured to the row of mannequins, smoke rising from the one on the left as though confirming the Archmaster's words. 'So who's first?'

Drennan looked expectantly at his charges but none of them seemed too keen to take him up on his offer. The silence wore on as Drennan regarded each of the apprentices with his mismatched eyes, one seeming to glare in disdain, the other peering right through them.

'I will,' said a girl Waylian didn't recognise. She took a step forward as confidently as she could but it was obvious for all to see she was afraid. She must have been older than Waylian, and better trained in the Art – *and who isn't* – but she looked tiny, her short cropped hair giving a boyish look to her face.

Drennan held out the block of charcoal and she took it from him, stepping forward to face the row of mannequins.

'Concentrate,' said the Archmaster. 'When you invoke, don't just say the words but feel them. Don't just focus your power but will it. Break the Veil. Take the magicks and make them yours.'

The girl nodded, staring ahead at the mannequins, grasping the charcoal so tight her knuckles went white. She closed her eyes for a moment, taking in several deep and calming breaths before she looked at the mannequins once more. Waylian could see the steely determination in her eyes, the strength in her boyish little face, the maturity, the knowledge that she would not, could not, fail.

As she spoke the invocation she closed her eyes and held out the block of charcoal. Waylian had no idea what the words meant, they were alien to him and sounded odd on the girl's lips, but as she spoke them the charcoal began to glow white. There was a hissing as smoke rose from her clenched fist but she didn't react to any pain. Her eyes flicked open and Waylian felt his heart skip a beat as he saw they burned as white as the charcoal in her fist, all the colour washed away by the powers she invoked.

There was a howl as the mannequin on the far right suddenly burst into flames, at first blue then a deep red. The heat was intense and Waylian had to shield his eyes from the conflagration as the mannequin took, but as quickly as they surged towards the sky, the flames died, leaving nothing but charred wood behind.

A smile broke on Waylian's lips. Perhaps they had a fighting chance after all. Perhaps they could beat the Khurtas if this was the power available to even an apprentice magister. But his optimism was immediately dashed as he heard the girl gurgling as though she were being throttled.

Drennan rushed towards her as she collapsed to her knees, her hand letting go of the charcoal which dropped to the ground and rolled across the courtyard. She began to shake convulsively. Her eyes no longer white, but blank and staring at the sky, white froth gathering at the corners of her mouth.

'Fetch the apothecary,' Drennan barked, as he held the girl close. Waylian could only watch, surprised at the Archmaster's compassion as he cradled the girl in his arms. It was a side of Drennan Folds he had not seen and Waylian suddenly felt a pang of guilt. Not so long ago, at Gelredida's order, Waylian had helped kidnap Drennan's son. It had seemed necessary then; Drennan would never have pledged himself to Gelredida's cause otherwise, but now he saw something different in the Archmaster that made him regret what he'd done. Where Drennan had previously seemed a ball of pent-up fury now he was all kindness and concern. It was enough to make Waylian feel sympathy for him.

'She clearly didn't bond fully with her prosopopoeia. The

resulting divagation from the Veil often leads to an abhorrent concomitant.'

Waylian turned at the voice, seeing another apprentice standing beside him. The youth was reed-thin with lank, greasy hair swept back from a prominent forehead, and a pair of eyeglasses on his pointy nose.

'Eh?' Waylian replied.

The apprentice regarded him curiously. 'You are aware of the transmutations undergone during preternatural importunement, aren't you?'

*Of course you're bloody not, Grimmy.*

'Of course I am,' Waylian replied.

By now Drennan had taken it upon himself to lift the girl in his arms and rush towards the base of the tower to find the apothecary for himself.

'I take it you're here for instruction like the rest of us?' asked the apprentice.

'Er . . . no,' said Waylian, glancing around for any sign of his mistress, but there was none. 'I'm waiting for someone.'

'Really? A little young to have mastered your Craft, aren't you?'

Waylian shook his head. 'It's not that. I'm just apprenticed to . . .' *Magistra Gelredida. The Red Witch. Who treats you like her handmaid. Who keeps you away from the rest of these apprentices who are learning to master their Art so they can be of use in the fight to come, while you run errands.* '. . . a magister with particular needs.'

'I see,' said the apprentice, though Waylian had no idea how he could possibly *see*. 'You'll be apprenticed to Magistra Gelredida then.' *Or maybe he could.* 'Which would make you Waylian Grimm.'

'It would,' Waylian replied, holding out his hand. 'And you are?'

'Aldrich Mundy,' the apprentice replied, looking down at Waylian's proffered hand as though it were a bloody knife. 'And there'll be no need for that. The hands carry a plenitude of bacteria. They're best kept to oneself.'

'Suit yourself,' Waylian said, disliking his new acquaintance more with every passing moment.

They stood for a while in awkward silence as Waylian thought desperately of something to say. For his part, Aldrich was quite content not to speak, seeming to enjoy the lack of conversation. Waylian opened his mouth to say something, not quite knowing what, when a familiar voice hailed him from across the courtyard.

'Waylian, come along,' said Magistra Gelredida, as though it were he who had kept her waiting and not the other way around.

'Anyway, have to run,' Waylian said to Aldrich, who acknowledged him with an insincere smile that never reached his bespectacled eyes. As he hurried to the Magistra's side Waylian could only hope their paths never crossed again.

The pair walked in silence through the gates of the courtyard and out into the city. There was a muted sense of urgency on the streets, the tension palpable amongst Steelhaven's city folk. Gelredida ignored them, and Waylian did his best to avoid anyone's gaze lest they look to him in hope – conveying a silent plea for him to use his magicks and save them from the horde that had come to smash down their walls.

He followed his mistress on her usual route. It was like a ritual she performed each morning since the Khurtas had arrived. Walk the streets to the wall at Eastgate and there mount the battlements. Then walk north to the Stone Gate, passing the archers posted there, the swordsmen and knights of every stripe, the auxiliaries and militia levies trading their banter, trying their hardest to take their minds from what was to come.

Again Waylian found himself avoiding the eyes of these men, not that any of them were interested in him. They were far too busy moving from the path of his mistress as she strode amongst them, her stern stare fixed far to the north, where the Khurtas were camped. When they reached the River Gate they would descend the stone steps down from the battlements and make their way back to the Tower of Magisters, but today was different. Today the Magistra stopped, placing her red-gloved hands gently on the merlon in front of her and letting out a long sigh.

Waylian watched her as she stared northward, starting to feel somewhat uncomfortable with the silence.

'You have been a loyal apprentice, Waylian,' she said suddenly.

'Magistra?' he replied, unsure of where this was going, or if he even wanted to know. Was she about to send him on another impossible mission? About to put his life in danger once more?

'I should have spared you all this. I should have let you leave this place days ago. Weeks ago.'

'But, Magistra, I—'

'There's no need to protest. I know you've hated your time here. Hated me. But you must know it was all for a reason.'

This wasn't right. She was unburdening herself. Confiding in him. In all the time he had known her she had never once imparted her feelings. He could only think it was a side effect of the virulent canker that infected her hands and body.

'Magistra, I will stay here as long as—'

She laughed. It lit up her face. Waylian was so taken aback he almost fell off the battlements.

'Yes, you will, Waylian. You'll stay as long as you're needed, you brave young fool. That's exactly the reason I should spare you the horror that's coming. But it's fools like you who may well save this city.'

He could only stare at her, wanting to tell her he wasn't brave. He was terrified. Had been terrified from the first day he set foot in the Tower of Magisters, but something told him she already knew that.

'I don't see there's anything I can do,' he said.

She regarded him with a look of sympathy. 'You might be surprised, Waylian. Courage isn't something that can be conjured like the magicks. You either have it or you don't. It's what makes people like you face impossible odds, when there is little hope.' She looked at him, gazing deep into his eyes. 'You'll fight here till the end. And chances are you'll die here like all the rest.'

He had to admit; the prospect didn't fill him with glee, but he knew she was right.

'Then it's settled,' he said. 'I'm not going anywhere.'

They stared at one another then, her eyes looking into him, assessing him. Whatever she saw deep inside was enough to satisfy her.

'Come then,' she said, continuing her route along the great curtain wall. 'There is still much to do.'

Feeling no braver, Waylian followed.

17

# TWO

**M**errick glanced at his reflection on the shield as he polished it. His cheeks had hollowed out in the past week alone, and he was leaner, hungrier than ever. It wasn't just the meagre rations that were turning him that way. He'd never experienced so much discipline, been trained so rigorously or punished so mercilessly, as he had since pledging himself to the Wyvern Guard.

At any other time in his life he was sure he'd have hated it; railed against it, run away or kicked up a storm. Now he had to admit he was thriving on every moment. That little sadistic imp that always sat on his shoulder was laughing its head off as he trained until he dripped with sweat, only to be rewarded with the soggiest gruel he'd ever had the misfortune to taste. It wasn't like him to take so much shit without complaint, but all he could do was relish the change.

*Change? You've been taking shit all your life, Ryder. Only difference is you now look better while you're doing it.*

That was true at least. He felt stronger and fitter than ever, and even in full armour he was fast as the wind. Whoever the forge master was back in the Wyvern Guard's keep, he was a peerless craftsman. Merrick now possessed the best sword he'd ever owned, its balance perfect, its edge keener than a kestrel's eye. Fully armed and armoured he felt all but invincible. Standing alongside his fellow knights it was as though nothing could match them.

*Fellow knights.* It almost made him laugh. Weeks ago he'd been scraping a living on the streets – no friends, no money, no luck. Now he was amongst the most dangerous bunch of fighters in all the continents of the world, if the legends were true. Strange how quickly fortune could spin you right round.

Looking across the courtyard he took in the scene of the Wyvern Guard in repose. They were polishing their armour, chatting idly or sparring on the square. Though they all looked relaxed Merrick could sense the tension. There'd be fighting soon. Vicious, dirty fighting that would see plenty of their number in the ground. A princely portion of these men would soon die in battle and each of them knew it. But if anyone could face death with a grin and a wink it was the Wyvern Guard. No one was ever eager to meet his end but Merrick could tell every man here was ready for it.

*And are you ready for it, Ryder? Are you ready to rush into the fray with a grin and a fucking wink? Or will you do what you've always done and run for the hills when the blood starts to fly?*

Despite the fact they were the roughest bunch of bastards Merrick had ever met, they were loyal to one another. Would die for one another. The Wyvern Guard was a true brotherhood; anyone with eyes in their head could see that. For his part, Merrick knew he was on the outside of that brotherhood. Some of the lads had taken to him, all right. He was liked well enough, even after such a short time amongst their number, but he knew he had a long way to go before they'd trust him like one of their own. It was no secret he was Tannick Ryder's son, but there didn't seem to be any antipathy because of it, but neither was he given any special treatment. Part of him was thankful for that. If he was ever going to gain the respect of these men he wanted to do it on his own terms, until they considered him an equal because of his deeds, not because he was son to their Lord Marshal.

Tannick had done a good enough job of treating him just like everyone else. The old man had shown him no favouritism, treated Merrick no different to the men he would soon be fighting along-side, and he could only be grateful for that. As a result no one showed him any ill will. Almost no one.

There was one among them that bore him no love. Cormach

Whoreson was even now staring at him across the courtyard with a look like he wanted to stroll right over and smash Merrick's teeth out. What he'd done to upset the mad bastard Merrick had no idea, but it was probably best to stay out of his way, at least until the fighting started. Then he'd want every one of these thugs watching his back. Whether Cormach would guard it or try to stick four feet of steel in it remained to be seen.

'Merrick,' said a deep voice. 'Horses need mucking out. Your turn.'

He looked up to see Jared motioning with his thumb. As the newest recruit it was only natural he'd get the shittiest jobs, even he knew that. It didn't make him like them any better, but it did make him stand without complaint and make his way towards Skyhelm's stables.

Merrick walked across the courtyard, giving a nod here and there to the lads he'd got to know. There was a nod in return from Lannar, the big shaven headed one, a quick wink from Stross as he polished a plate of his bronze armour. Their gestures were genuine enough but Merrick still felt on the outside. He liked to think he could talk to anyone, fit into any kind of company, but he had to admit the Wyvern Guard had been a struggle. Not that he was surprised at that. They'd been raised in the mountains and fed nothing but pain and hardship. He'd come from privilege, and although he'd fallen on hard times it was nothing in comparison to that of the men he now found himself among. Merrick had done his best to breach the gap. They had little in common on the surface, but every man was the same when you got down to it. Everyone wanted a laugh and a joke. All fighting men took the piss out of one another and the best piss takers often got the most respect.

If Merrick was good at one thing it was taking the piss.

It hadn't taken him long to work out who were the easy targets and who to avoid. Who he could push the furthest and who could take the harshest ribbing. Within a day he'd had some of these lads falling about laughing. He was just lucky that a man who could raise the spirits in a time of war was as valuable as the hardiest warrior.

When Merrick reached the stables he picked up the pitchfork

leaning against one wall and got to work. Wasn't long before he'd stripped down to his shirt, even in the cool morning air, and he'd got so used to the ripe stench of dung he could hardly smell it any more.

He had never been particularly fond of horses, and the troop brought down by the Wyvern Guard seemed an ill-tempered bunch. Still, he managed to do his job without one of them giving him a kick or biting at him, which was something to be thankful for at least. Within an hour he was sweating through his shirt. Within two he was feeling the ache of it in his shoulders and back. As he took a rest, letting his body cool a touch, Jared came with a cup of water.

Though Merrick wasn't especially fond of water – wine always taking preference to anything else wet – he took it gratefully and downed half the cup in one go.

'You've done a good job,' said Jared, glancing at the pile of steaming shit, oblivious to how condescending he sounded.

'Everyone has their particular skills,' Merrick replied.

Jared didn't seem to take up on his sarcasm. 'We'll need these destriers in tip-top condition for what's to come.'

Way back in the dim and distant, in the Collegium of House Tarnath, Merrick had studied the rudiments of siege warfare, and he was pretty sure cavalry wasn't a part of it.

'If we're defending a city what do we need horses for?'

Jared smiled knowingly. 'Not too familiar with the Lord Marshal's methods, are you, lad?'

'I suppose not,' Merrick replied, swallowing a comment about the fact his father had abandoned him years ago, so it was unlikely he'd be familiar with any such *methods*. 'Please enlighten me.'

'It's not likely the Lord Marshal's going to sit behind the wall and wait for the enemy to come to him. He'll want to use his advantage. Take his horse and run the bastards down.' Jared patted the rear of a destrier, whose flanks shuddered in response before it gave a whicker of annoyance. 'The Wyvern Guard have no match with sword and shield. But behind the wall we'll be as much use as any other man. On horseback, out on the field, we'll be bloody invincible.' He flashed Merrick a mad grin. 'Sounds glorious, doesn't it?'

*No, it sounds fucking insane.*

'Glorious indeed,' Merrick replied, imagining himself at the head of the column as they charged towards forty thousand Khurtas. How glorious it would be as he was hacked into tiny pieces. How proud he'd be of himself as his severed head stared gloriously from the top of a Khurtic spear.

Jared barked a laugh in his usual gruff tone. 'That's the spirit, lad,' he said, before slapping Merrick on the arm and walking back towards the barracks.

Merrick barely felt the sting of that slap as he stared at the row of stabled horses, wondering which one he'd have the pleasure of being killed on.

The afternoon seemed to pass a little slower after that as he began to picture all the ways he could die. By the time he'd finished mucking the horses and someone had arrived with their feed he could hardly feel the cold sweat on his skin or hear the laughter of the other men.

What was wrong with them? Didn't they realise what was in store? Did they really want to die that badly?

*Of course they do. They're looking forward to it. Haven't you worked it out yet that every single one of them wants to die in battle, serving the Wyvern Guard faithfully, obeying your father's every word?*

But that couldn't be true. Could it? Surely Tannick wouldn't have asked Merrick to join this mob if all that was in store for him was a certain death.

Slowly he made his way back towards the courtyard, looking for some water to wash in. The prospect of a cold bath wasn't a welcome one but it was preferable to stinking like a horse's arse.

When he made it back, the courtyard was clear but for a single figure sitting beneath the eaves to one side. Tannick Ryder rested his huge sword on one knee, rubbing oil into the blade with reverent care, his arm moving in long, careful strokes.

For an instant Merrick felt out of place. Over the past few days since he'd joined the Wyvern Guard he had spoken little with his father. He wasn't sure if now was the best time.

Nevertheless, he made his way across the courtyard, hoping Tannick wouldn't notice him, but deep down he knew that was futile.

'Been keeping busy, boy?' said Tannick without looking up from his labours.

'Er . . . yes,' Merrick replied, without wanting to go into too much detail about what he'd been busy with, though from the smell of him it was pretty obvious.

There was silence then, but Merrick couldn't just wander off. Part of him had to know.

'I hear we're to ride out and face the horde head on,' he said.

'That we are,' replied Tannick, still rubbing at that blade. 'We're the Wyvern Guard. We don't hide ourselves away behind walls. Besides, most of these lads have waited an age for a good fight. Wouldn't be fair to keep them from it.'

*It's so nice of you to take their feelings into consideration like that.*
'Won't it be a slaughter?'

Tannick stopped wiping at the blade and looked up, a wicked glint in his eye. 'That's what I'm counting on, boy.'

This did little to fill Merrick with any confidence. A mad charge into a mad enemy led by his mad father was nothing to look forward to.

'I can't wait,' he said, not wanting to show any reluctance, any weakness.

As Tannick looked at Merrick his mad-eyed stare softened and a smile crept up one side of his face. 'This must seem like lunacy to you. I can understand that, and I don't think any less of you for it.' *Oh, how good of you.* 'That's why I want you close. By my side, where I can keep an eye on you.'

'There's no need—'

'There's every need, boy. No harm must come to you. There'll be chance enough to prove your worth, but no need to risk yourself needlessly.'

'Then why ride out at all? Why risk everything for one strike at the Khurtas?'

Tannick went back to polishing his blade. 'We need to send a message – to the defenders of this city as much as the enemy. We need to show they can be beaten. That they're human. General Hawke and Farren and the bannermen of this city think the Khurtas are invincible. That Amon Tugha's already got them beat. I aim to prove them wrong.'

'I suppose that makes sense,' Merrick said.

'Do you? I doubt that. I reckon you think it's madness. That you'd be best served sitting behind the wall and waiting for them to attack like a peasant in his stinking hovel hoping the robbers lurking outside his door will eventually slink away.'

*Actually, that's exactly what I'm thinking.*

'No.' Merrick tried to sound as enthusiastic as he could. 'I think showing the Khurtas can be hurt will help boost morale amongst the city's defenders. And when we ride in to smash the enemy I want to be right in the heart of it.'

*All right, Ryder, steady on. He may well take you up on that.*

'I'm glad to hear it,' said Tannick, and for a moment Merrick could have sworn he sensed some pride in the old bastard. 'But no. As I said, I need you by my side. You're too important to risk.'

'How so?' *Because it's never seemed to bother you before.*

Tannick rose to his feet, holding his sword reverently between them.

'Despite what you might think, boy, I didn't just come back for this battle. I came back for you.'

It took a moment for that to register. Even when it did, Merrick found it hard to take in.

'For me? You wouldn't even speak to me for days. I had to get stabbed through the chest. I almost died defending the queen before—'

'I needed to know you were up to the job. That I could put my faith in you,' said Tannick. 'Because one day this will be yours.'

He held up the sword, the *Bludsdottr*, as though it were all the riches in the Free States.

*A sword? A fucking sword? You came all the way back here after all these years just to give me a huge bloody sword that I'll barely be able to lift?*

Merrick stared down at it, bewildered.

'I know. Beautiful, isn't it?' said Tannick, as though he held a new-born baby in his arms and not a hunk of cumbersome steel. 'And it will be yours when I'm gone. Only you can wield it. Only you can take my place.'

'Take your place? Why? Are you going somewhere?'

'Not yet,' Tannick replied, hefting the sword over one shoulder. 'But by the time I do, you should be ready.'

With that he walked inside.

Merrick stood in the courtyard for some moments, wondering what in the hells that meant.

*You should be ready.* Ready for what? To carry a ruddy great sword? He couldn't say that the prospect filled him with glee.

Not that it was worth thinking on too much. He had to survive the Khurtas first, and from the sounds of it that was going to be no easy feat. Then again, Tannick had told him he was too important to risk, so that meant he was in no real danger. That he'd be safe when the slaughter began.

Right?

All of a sudden the prospect of a wash in freezing cold water didn't seem the worst of Merrick's problems.

# THREE

In the days since the Khurtas came he had stood and he had watched. There weren't many who had summoned the nerve to disturb Nobul Jacks as he kept his vigil, standing there like a statue night and day – but then he was Nobul Jacks no longer.

They called him the Black Helm now, a name he'd not used for years. A name he thought he'd left behind him in the mud and blood of Bakhaus Gate. That had been a war against an invading army, just like now. Nobul had become the Black Helm to face the creatures that tore up from the south intent on destroying the Free States. He'd lived through it then by becoming more than a man . . . or was it less? When the Aeslanti beast men had rampaged across that valley he'd faced them as an animal himself . . . the undefeatable Black Helm. Now, as he faced north, at the horde waiting to invade the city, he wondered if he'd be able to become that animal again.

The rest of the men whispered behind his back, talking in hushed tones, spreading word of him along the wall like a plague. For some, Nobul knew that name would bring solace against the coming dark. For others it would mean little – they wouldn't know or care who he was, and reputations meant nothing if you couldn't back them up with grit and steel.

It didn't matter anyway – once the fighting started he'd have to prove himself all over again, and no reputation, no matter how renowned, was going to stop an axe or a blade from caving in your head.

And so he'd stood and waited and thought on whether the years had made him too slow, too weak, too dull in the head and the heart. Part of him didn't want to know. The other part could barely wait to find out.

Of course Nobul hadn't stood there day and night. He'd slept. He'd eaten. He'd washed and pissed and shat. Kilgar and the rest of the lads weren't far away and they were still looking out for him, though things weren't the same as they had been. None of them, not even Kilgar, thought to question him on what he was doing. On where the helm and hammer had come from. On why he was just watching the horizon instead of mucking in with the rest of the lads. But he was the Black Helm now and the Black Helm didn't take his turn handing out the gruel or mucking out the latrines with the rest of the lads. It might have pissed some of the other Greencoats or bannermen off, but none of them dared speak to him about it. There was something of the inhuman to Nobul now. Something that wasn't to be questioned.

One night someone had tried, though – one of the levies, drunk on ale and fear of the Khurtas, had come too close, started with the questions, and when Nobul hadn't answered he started to get his back up. He'd shouted and screamed and demanded an answer as to who Nobul thought he was. For his part Nobul had just gripped his hammer all the tighter until Hake and Edric came and ushered the bloke away. As much as it would have been easy to give the little bastard what for, it would prove nothing. He didn't need to demonstrate who he was or what he could do. Didn't need to relive old glories. Not yet anyway. There'd be fighting soon enough. Hard fighting where you'd either show your mettle or die trying.

They'd heard nothing from the Khurtas, though. Nothing but the occasional bit of shouting and the singing of dirges as their fires burned in the night. They must have been as impatient for the fight as Nobul was, but for some reason Amon Tugha made them wait. Were they going to try and starve the city? Nobul had to admit, that made him more fearful than anything. To get to this stage and then be starved to death wouldn't be much of an end to it all. He wanted to go out fighting – killing like he'd been born for. But he knew there was little need to worry on that score. Deep inside Nobul had a feeling Amon Tugha wouldn't disappoint. That the Elharim bastard was just biding his time, just letting the fear settle on the city like a dark cloud until he was ready to burn it down.

As the winter sun rose high in the clear sky, Nobul saw two riders coming from beyond the northern ridge. It was the first bit of movement they'd seen from the Khurtas in days and a swell of panic began to spread across the battlements as lookouts spotted the pair making their way across the flat plain. Nobul simply stood and stared as archers took their places and a serjeant barked for someone to fetch one of the generals.

The riders galloped to within a hundred yards of the main gate, whooping as they came, whipping their horses into a frenzy. Nobul could just make out the paint on their faces, the sharp yellow teeth in their grinning mouths. They wore furs, riding their horses without saddles, the steeds daubed with the same garish markings as the Khurtas atop them.

Once they'd reined in their mounts the two warriors waited, their excited horses churning up the ground in the shadow of the curtain wall. Neither was armed, and it seemed obvious they weren't about to attack. Nevertheless, the archers standing on the wall could contain themselves no longer. With the hum of a bowstring one of them loosed. The arrow fell to the right of the pair, and they duly kicked their steeds, retreating a few yards from the wall.

'That was shit,' said one of the archers, nocking his own bow as he said it.

Another hum and another arrow shot towards the riders, this time flying overhead and causing one of the Khurtas to duck. He yelled in delight, and again both riders kicked their steeds into action, retreating yet more yards up the plain.

'Volley this time, you useless bastards,' said another of the archers. 'On my count.'

From the corner of his eye, Nobul saw the gathered archers nock in unison, aiming at their targets despite how pointless it seemed. Loosing half a dozen times to kill two scouts was just a waste of arrows. There'd be easier targets soon enough when the Khurtas came charging forty thousand strong.

One of the archers counted back from three and there was a rasp of volley fire. The sound of their bows loosing as one was impressive enough, even if their aim was shite. Nobul could probably have done a better job, and he was about as good an archer as he was a milkmaid.

Though close, the volley of arrows seemed to hit everywhere but its target. This time both the Khurtas screamed in delight, moving their horses further away from the wall. It was then Nobul realised what they were doing, but before he had a chance to say so, someone barked at the archers to stop.

It was a deep voice, and old, but it carried enough command to make Nobul turn his head to see who owned it. A white-armoured knight was making his way across the battlements. His hair was down to his shoulders, moustache and beard drooping over his gorget. The armour that covered him from neck to toe was intricately gilded, making it look as though he wore a wolf's pelt, and at his hip sat a huge sword that no man so old should have been able to wield.

'Are you bloody stupid?' said the old man, snatching the closest archer's bow and rapping it over his head. The archer raised his hands to defend himself but gave no word of protest. 'Do you think they're offering themselves up as bloody target practice?' The rest of the archers looked at one another dumbly, none of them daring to risk an answer. 'They're testing your range. They're seeing how far the horde can advance before it's in danger of being hit, you bloody dullards!'

The archers could only mumble their apologies. Two of them slunk off back along the parapet and the old knight flung the bow back at its owner who was still rubbing his head.

Grumbling to himself about incompetent morons, the knight turned to leave, then stopped, thinking better of it. Nobul watched as he slowly turned and made his way closer, casually, almost as though Nobul wasn't there. Then he stopped at the battlements, resting his elbow on one of the merlons and looking out. The pair of them stood in silence for a while, as though the old man were

29

sizing him up, wondering whether it was worth starting a conversation.

'I remember you,' he said, finally. 'Or at least the man they say you are.' Nobul gave no answer. He knew there were those who doubted he was the real Black Helm. And who could blame them – it had been the best part of sixteen years since he'd fought at Bakhaus Gate. Surely the Black Helm would be old by now, long past his best. This couldn't be the real one, could it?

'Don't suppose it matters if you're the same man or not,' the knight continued, 'as long as you can fight like the Black Helm.' He looked Nobul up and down. 'You look the part, at least.'

Nobul would have liked to ignore the knight, to tell himself this old man's opinion didn't matter a shit, but there was something about him. The way the man carried himself, the way he spoke, made Nobul want his acceptance. Made Nobul need this old knight to believe him.

'I'm him, all right,' Nobul said, still staring out across the plain. 'Don't worry yourself on that score.'

The knight nodded. 'That's a relief. We'll need you, and no mistake. You fought like a daemon back then. Hope you've still got that in you.'

*Well, have you? Have you still got that fight? Can you still swing that hammer? You killed a bar full of naked revellers and kicked a dog to death in recent days, but these are the Khurtas. Savages. Killers to a man. And you're well past your prime – some might even say over-ripe. Have you really still got it in you?*

'Guess we'll find out soon enough,' Nobul said.

'That we will,' said the old man with a laugh. 'I'm Bannon.' He held out his arm.

Nobul knew the name and for a moment he paused before accepting that arm. The Duke of Valdor was standing next to him, striking up idle conversation about the past and what was coming from the north. Wasn't every day you got to mull over the old days with nobility.

'Nobul Jacks,' he replied, grasping Bannon's forearm in a warrior's grip.

'So that's the name of the Black Helm?' said Bannon. 'Can't say as I've heard of it. Would have thought a man like you would have made a name for himself in the Free Companies. Would have made himself rich.'

'There's also high odds in the Free Companies a man like that will make himself dead.' Nobul released Bannon's arm and went back to staring out north. 'I didn't fancy that.'

The old man chuckled. 'That makes sense, I suppose. So what's changed your mind? What's made you pick that hammer up again? Chances are we'll all be killed standing on this wall. You could have made a run for it like so many others but instead you chose to stay and fight.'

Nobul had to think on that. Had to go over everything that had happened to lead him here, to this point. All the loss, all the grief, all the pain and death. He would have told Bannon all about it, and he was sure the old man would have listened. But then again Nobul had never been much of a storyteller.

'Sometimes there just ain't a choice,' he replied.

The duke nodded at that and stood beside Nobul, staring out onto the plain. With the archers having stopped their attempts to shoot them, the Khurtic riders had finished their milling and retreated back towards the distant ridge.

'You're right,' Bannon said, still staring north. 'Sometimes we just don't choose. Sometimes those decisions are made for us. I lost my son to those savages. To some bastard assassin sent by Amon Tugha himself. I don't have a choice at all. I'll fight and I'll die because there's a debt I owe.'

Nobul could sense the pain in him, the bitterness. He wanted to admit that he'd lost a boy too. That he knew the sting of it, deep in your heart where no amount of vengeance could ever ease it. He should probably have warned the old man that it wouldn't get any better no matter how many men he killed, but he guessed Bannon would find out in his own way.

'There'll be plenty more sons lost before this is over,' he said instead.

Bannon nodded in agreement. 'And fathers. And brothers. And if we don't stop them at this wall there'll be wives and mothers and all the rest too.'

Nobul continued to stare across the plain. He could just see the dark shafts of arrows in the grass, showing the Khurtas how close they could come to the wall without fear of being shot.

'And if they're gauging our range you can be sure they're coming soon.' Bannon looked at him, looked into the eyes behind his black helmet. 'Are you ready?'

Nobul didn't have to think on it. He already knew the answer to that one. 'Aye, I'm ready. I've been ready for these fuckers a long time.'

'Good.' Bannon clapped him on the arm. 'Then I'll be proud to stand beside you.'

For the first time in an age, a smile crept across Nobul's lips. 'Don't stand too close, old man. Wouldn't want you getting in the way.'

Bannon laughed as he turned and continued to chuckle while he made his way across the battlements. It seemed strange to laugh so long at such a thing, but Nobul knew it was the gallows humour that struck all men in the calm before battle. There was nothing to laugh about here. Death was no laughing matter – whether you were dealing it out, or whether it was coming for you.

And Nobul Jacks knew full well that when the Khurtas finally came he'd be the one doing the dealing.

# FOUR

Regulus and his warriors had been posted to the western wall, overlooking the vast river that ran in floods from the north. Crossing the river were three bridges, the centremost having long since collapsed, leaving only an impassable monument that reached up from the fast flowing waters like some drowning beast. On the other side was a vast, derelict city, crumbling and ancient, but still teeming with ragged Coldlanders. Even now they were marching into the city proper, fearing the onslaught that could at any moment descend from the north to consume them.

Even though these gates would soon be closed and barred with iron they still needed to be defended. There was nothing to stop the enemy moving through the crumbling streets over the river and crossing the two bridges that were still intact. Regulus knew he had been bestowed a great honour, been offered the chance he yearned for – to defend the bridge with black steel and tooth and claw, and earn himself a formidable reputation.

It was still not enough for Regulus Gor.

He wanted to be on the northern wall, where the enemy would most readily focus its strength. The vast plain in front of the city was the most likely place for the Elharim warlord to amass his mighty army. Regulus wanted to be where the fighting was hardest, where the killing was the fiercest and the glory would be bestowed on him in a flood.

Nobul Jacks had been posted to that wall. The honour of meeting the enemy in their greatest numbers would be his, and that stung Regulus deep. He owed Jacks a life debt and it would be difficult to repay while he was stuck here, watching the river run past and hoping the enemy were bold enough to try and cross the bridge. His chance to settle that debt seemed all but lost for now. He could only hope Nobul Jacks would live long enough for him to pay it. Deep inside, Regulus was confident he would.

In the last few days, the stern Coldlander had become something of a legend amongst the city's defenders. Once he had donned that helm of his he commanded a strange fear and respect amongst the city's warriors. Regulus had not realised just how formidable a reputation the Black Helm bore, and he could only envy Nobul Jacks for it.

Not only that, but the man had crafted the best armour Regulus had ever donned. It was black steel, to match the sword at his side, each piece crafted to fit his form like a second skin: light, manoeuvrable yet hard as granite. It made Regulus feel invincible. He could only hope that in the days to come he would be able to test its worth in battle. His greatest fear was that he would be needlessly stuck defending the western gate while his chance at glory was to the north.

The Coldlanders practised their swordplay in readiness for an attack. Below, on the street where ranks of warriors waited in anticipation, they fought one another in friendly bouts. Regulus could only smile at that. What could they possibly hope to learn in the next day or so before the enemy came for them? They would learn more in the first few moments of a real battle than they ever could in a hundred days of practice. Those who were quick enough to learn would most likely survive. Those who weren't would certainly be the first to die.

Regulus would have been happy to walk amongst them and impart his own wisdom, the evidence of which was writ in the myriad scars he wore proudly on his flesh, but he knew it would only fall on deaf ears. He and his warriors were still treated with suspicion, despite what they had done to protect the city's queen.

Not that Regulus cared. He was not here to make allies. He was here to kill.

The only men whose opinions he cared for were his own warriors. Even now they took the time to gather their thoughts, to polish their new armour and hone their new weapons. Hagama, Kazul – even the youngest of them, Akkula – were seasoned fighters. They did not practise their skills. This was a time to reflect on what was to come, to picture yourself victorious, to know that there were none who could stand against you. To fill yourself with anticipation of the slaughter. And his warriors knew how to slaughter all too well.

As Regulus looked out over the wall at the slow moving crowds he heard the sound of movement behind him – the clanking of armour, the slap of weapon against hip, the clumsy footfalls. He didn't have to turn to know it was one of the Coldlanders, they were always heralded by noise, never seeming able to tread lightly, but then these people were surrounded by stone. On the plains of Equ'un the Zatani had long ago learned how to tread lightly. Every tribe – whether Gor'tana, Kel'tana, Sho'tana or Vir'tana – had learned that it oftentimes meant the difference between life and death. Here such things seemed to matter little.

Regulus turned to face the man. He recognised him – 'Sargent', they called him – an honorary term, though what he had done to deserve it Regulus had no idea. The man was fat around the middle, his hair grey with age. Such a man would not have lasted long as a chieftain on the plains. His smell was rank, even from a distance, but Regulus had learned in the past days that the stench was nowhere near as offensive as the man's manners.

'Are you ready?' he said, keeping his distance. His voice was filled with disdain, but it was easy to read the fear behind it.

'We are of the Gor'tana,' Regulus replied. 'The most feared tribe among the Zatani people. We are always ready.'

The man frowned, but nodded with it, satisfied enough with the answer. 'Good. And remember who's in charge here. You may have been pardoned by the Crown but it gives you no special privilege. You're under my command, and so are your men.'

That almost made Regulus smile. He would have sorely liked to see this man try to command his warriors, especially Janto. That would have been a sight to see as the Sho'tana tore the man's head off with a gleeful roar.

'We are here to fight for your city,' Regulus replied. 'What other command could you have of us than to kill the enemy?'

The sargent looked thoughtful for a moment. Then, unable to think of any argument, simply nodded.

'Aye, well. Just make sure you and the rest of your kind are—'

Regulus caught something in the corner of his eye. He turned to the south, in time to see the sky turn bright. It was as though the horizon had caught fire, shooting a line of burning debris towards the heavens. Half a dozen burning spheres rose up, contrails of black smoke in their wake. At first there was no sound, but as the fireballs hit their zenith and began to hurtle back to the earth, a wave of noise engulfed the city. It was a roar, an unnatural scream that came from the sea. Regulus had never heard anything like it and it took all his will not to raise his hands and block his ears as they were assaulted by the cacophony.

Smoke, flames and debris were thrown into the air as the fireballs rained. The sound of it hit him a moment later, the roaring reaching a crescendo as though all the tribes of Equ'un had suddenly raised their voices in a furious howl.

The Coldlander sargent ran back towards his men in panic, shouting orders, though what they could do about the sudden conflagration was beyond Regulus. He could only watch in awe as the sound of screams began to peal from the south of the city. The carnage must have been devastating, the victims of the fire standing little chance, but Regulus could not bring himself to feel pity. There was little room in his heart for it.

No sooner had one row of flames rained down on the city than another was sent hurtling into the air. It was clear the gods would have no mercy for the city this day, or for the days to come.

'At least now we know what that blockade of ships was waiting for.'

Regulus turned to see Janto standing beside him, staring towards the south. He grinned as he watched, hands resting on the twin axes at his waist. In the armour Nobul Jacks had crafted for him Janto looked a formidable sight, easily the most impressive of the warriors that stood at Regulus' command.

'And we know it won't be long before the army to the north

comes for what remains,' Regulus replied. 'Amon Tugha has made his first move. Soon he will attack.'

'About time,' said Janto, and the relish in his voice was palpable. Regulus knew he, more than any of them, savoured the thought of battle. He yearned for the butchery, and he too had a life debt to repay. Whether he would stay loyal to Regulus after that remained to be seen.

They stood and watched the sky rain fire for some time. The sounds of panic from the south rising as Coldlanders ran in all directions, some to escape the flames, some to help quell them. All the while doom poured down on the south of the city.

Glancing down at the bridge, Regulus could see the sudden fiery assault had hurried the exodus from the derelict city over the river, and the last of its inhabitants were making their way inside.

He and Janto watched in silence. Regulus could sense the warrior's loathing of their cowardice, but was their flight not just the same as his had been so many days before? When he had fled the hunters of the Kel'tana and come north, almost leading them all to their deaths? At least this way they would live to fight another day rather than be needlessly slaughtered by the horde that at any minute might descend on the city.

Once the last of the crowd had milled its way over the bridge they could hear the turning of a gear and the clacking of chains as the great portcullis was lowered. The tower they stood upon rumbled as the gate was shut but Regulus couldn't bring himself to feel secure. He knew they were not safe in here, and part of him felt satisfied at that. For Regulus Gor this was the beginning of his ascension. Or at least it would be so long as their enemy chose to attack the bridge.

Regulus could only live in hope.

# FIVE

Janessa's city burned and there was nothing she could do to stop it. She had vowed to be strong, to lead her people against the scourge descending upon it, but as she watched the fire rain down from the Midral Sea all she felt was powerless. But then even a queen could do nothing against this. She was no god – just a girl thrust onto the throne and made to bear all the responsibility that came with it.

Amon Tugha had not yet begun his attack and already her people were dying. She took little solace in the fact the bombardment from the sea had abated somewhat since noon. Now, as the sun began to go down, the deluge from the fire ships was only intermittent, but the damage had already been done.

She watched from the palace as a ball of flame lit up the evening sky, soaring high over the burning city to land amongst the blackened ruins to the south, the sound of it echoing through the dead streets. The only solace Janessa could take was that she did not have to witness it alone. They were all there with her; her war council, watching and waiting in dumb silence as Chancellor Durket relayed the cost of the damage, the estimate of casualty numbers, the buildings destroyed despite monumental efforts to fight the flames. Janessa could only listen, her heart sinking yet further with every grim account of the destruction.

When Durket had finished, Seneschal Rogan stepped forward.

His face was suddenly lit from the south by another burning missile and Janessa thought he resembled a snake now more than ever. He had done nothing she could condemn him for, though, and if she had learned anything it was that a man should only be censured for his actions, not his appearance.

'Majesty, we are so far at a loss as to what can be done about the fire ships. Dockside has all but been destroyed as has the Warehouse District. The Temple of Autumn still stands by some miracle. I can only assume the Daughters of Arlor have been hard at prayer.'

Janessa glanced towards the south-east at the two great statues of Arlor and Vorena, she looking out to sea and he towards the open fields in the north. Steelhaven needed them both more than ever, but they had been dead for centuries. No venerated heroes were going to come to Janessa's aid now. She had to save the city herself.

'My lords, suggestions?' Janessa said, turning to her assembled council.

General Hawke stared down at his feet. Marshal Farren likewise glanced off as though he hadn't heard the question, his ruined left eye twitching all the while. That was fine, she had expected little from them, but when Lord Marshal Tannick and Duke Bannon glanced at one another uncertainly she knew there was little hope.

'Every ship that remained in port has been destroyed, Majesty,' said Bannon. 'The fire ships are anchored too far from the dock, beyond reach unless someone swims out there. I have my doubts about how effective that would be.'

'Not at all, I would guess,' Janessa replied. 'We will need to find another way. Seneschal, you will speak to the Crucible of Magisters. See who they can spare and what can be done to destroy those ships.'

Rogan bowed, obediently.

'There is one other point of business, Majesty,' said Durket. His voice quavered as though he feared to speak. Janessa found it strange, the man had never been shy about voicing his opinions for as long as she'd known him, but after the day Azai Dravos had tried to control her mind and murder her bodyguard, the Chancellor had been far from himself.

'And?' she said when he did not continue.

'The Rafts, Majesty. They will be a problem.' He paused again, cringing as the sound of an explosion echoed from the south.

'Do I need to guess its nature, Chancellor?' Janessa asked, fast losing patience.

'Er . . . no, Majesty. The Rafts was constructed years ago, a slum we have unfortunately allowed to grow across the mouth of the River Storway. Essentially it's a bridge across the river into the city. If the Khurtas decide to attack there they could charge right across and into the Warehouse District . . . or at least what's left of it.'

'Very well,' Janessa replied, glancing at the faces of her war council, assessing who might be best placed to deal with the problem. 'Chancellor, you will see that the slums are evacuated as best as possible. Marshal Farren, you will position trebuchets on the battlements and at the edge of the river and see to it the Rafts is destroyed by nightfall.'

'Majesty, what if we can't evacuate in time?' asked Durket. 'And many might refuse to leave their homes. Nightfall might not be—'

'The Rafts will be destroyed by nightfall,' Janessa said, feeling her anger rising. 'Make it clear that anyone remaining in their homes will die.'

Durket bowed low. 'Yes, Majesty,' he replied before making himself scarce.

'The rest of the city's defences are as strong as ever, Majesty,' said Rogan. 'Only there is one thing that has been planned in the city's defence that we are not all in agreement over.' He glanced at Lord Marshal Tannick, who for his part didn't even bother to acknowledge the head of the Inquisition.

'And what is the nature of this disagreement?' Janessa said, aiming her question at the Lord Marshal.

'I intend to make a gesture,' replied Tannick. 'I don't mean to sit behind our walls and wait for the Khurtas to come screaming at us from the north without bloodying their noses first.'

'You intend to take the fight to them?' From what little Janessa knew of warfare, this sounded like suicide, even to her.

'I do. My cavalry will charge them on the field, cut them down where they stand. The armies of the Free States have not scored one victory over this horde yet. Showing the defenders on the walls that these bastards bleed and die like any other man will only serve us well.'

'It's bloody madness,' said Marshal Farren. General Hawke nodded his agreement. 'And a waste of men, if you ask me. If you want to commit suicide, Ryder, feel free, but the men of the Wyvern Guard would be better placed on the wall.'

'It's fortunate no one's asking you then, isn't it?' Tannick replied.

Farren rounded on him. 'It's not just me, you mad bastard.' He pointed at Duke Bannon, and Janessa saw the doubt in the old man's eyes. 'Ask him. Go on, see if he thinks it's a good idea.'

'Enough,' Janessa demanded, feeling some sense of pleasure when her generals stopped their squabbling and turned to her expectantly.

She looked at them, standing there ready to obey her every word. When first she had met them Janessa had been fearful, unsure of what to do or say. Now there was no doubt in her mind these men were hers to command.

And it was clear she had a decision to make. A choice that would result in one of her generals losing face. Then again, it was clear the time for tact was well and truly over.

'I agree with Lord Marshal Tannick,' she continued. 'A gesture is indeed what's needed. The Khurtas need to know what they are up against. That we have teeth, and will not merely cower behind our walls and wait for the end. I can think of none but the Wyvern Guard better suited to relay that message.' She paused. No one argued. 'Very well. I'm sure the rest of you have much to attend to. Set to it.'

Her war council bowed their assent, moving off as another fiery explosion cut the darkening sky.

Janessa turned to take it in, hearing a scream rise up from somewhere in the devastated streets, but she could not allow herself to be broken by it. Neither could she bring herself to feel sorrow for the Rafts and the people in it who would soon be made homeless or worse.

She had a city to save, and she could not allow herself to be distracted by compassion if she was to succeed. Janessa had allowed herself to be weak, had allowed her heart to rule her head and she had suffered for it. Now, all that remained deep inside her belly was a pit of dark where there should have been . . .

*A child. There should be a child growing strong.*

Janessa gripped the edge of the balustrade until her knuckles whitened, thinking of what she had lost and what would never be. Her child, River's child, had been stillborn. Now she was empty, barren, and all she could think that might fill the space inside her would be the defeat of Amon Tugha. She thought of it, yearned for it, to the detriment of all else. It was the only thing that occupied her waking mind.

At first she had thought to save her city, her people, but now it was more than that. She wanted to defeat her enemy utterly. To stand against him and taste victory, even if it cost the lives of every soldier under her command. The thought was bitter to the taste, but no matter how she tried to persuade herself she was doing this for her people, she knew it was vengeance she really wanted.

A firm hand came to rest on top of hers as she gripped the parapet. Kaira stood by her, gazing at her, eyes calm, controlled, and Janessa felt the weight of her anger suddenly lift. The woman was Janessa's sworn protector, but in recent days she had become so much more than that. A rock to which she clung in the storm that raged all around her.

'Majesty, shall we?' said Kaira, gesturing towards the stairwell.

Janessa nodded and they both made their way back inside. Without Kaira, Janessa had no idea how she would have coped. Her bodyguard had been a constant presence since the night Janessa had lost her child. Always by her side, day and night. Always strong, always steadfast. Janessa knew in the days to come she would need Kaira more than ever.

When she eventually entered her chamber, what awaited brought a rare smile to her lips.

'The royal armourer has done well, Majesty,' said Kaira, as Janessa stood and stared.

The armour she had commissioned days before had been left in her room atop a wooden stand. Even in the wan candlelight it glimmered, each plate seeming to melt into the next, the crown and crossed swords of Steelhaven emblazoned on the breastplate. There was no helm – Janessa had told the armoursmith she would have no need of one. She would wear her armour with her head high, her hair about her shoulders, her face visible to all. Janessa was to be a symbol, an icon, and the defenders of her city would see her, rally to her as she helped them defend the walls.

Absently she traced her finger across the emblem on the chest plate; her father's seal. Thoughts of his past victories came to her, victories that ended when he rode off to face Amon Tugha. Somehow the immortal Elharim had managed to murder her father off the field of battle. That would not happen to his daughter. Janessa was determined the victory would be hers this time.

Beside the armour stand stood the Helsbayn. Janessa found her hand straying towards it. When her finger touched the cold steel of the pommel it tingled to the touch, as though the sword itself contained a daemon that only she could unleash. Ever since she had slain the sorcerer Azai Dravos with the blade it seemed to instil a vigour inside her. When she touched it for the briefest of moments the feelings of loss deep within her soul abated. She almost yearned to draw it from its scabbard, to march out alone and take the fight to Amon Tugha and all his minions.

'You should rest, Majesty,' Kaira said from behind her. 'There will be little time for it in the coming days.'

Janessa did not turn around, but gripped the hilt of the Helsbayn, drawing strength from it.

'The time for resting is over, Kaira,' she replied, feeling a strange smile creep across her lips. 'I think now it's time for me to don my armour.'

# SIX

Weeks ago, when Janessa had suggested it, Kaira thought bedecking her in armour was a foolish idea. Now as she looked at her ward, at the Queen of the Free States, she realised her mistake. Despite her stature Queen Janessa still cut an impressive figure. It did nothing to put Kaira's mind at ease, though. The enemy was at the gates. There were undoubtedly some within the city who were still plotting to kill her. No mere suit of armour, no matter how finely crafted, could keep her safe from every knife in the dark that threatened.

'How do I look?' asked Janessa, glancing at herself in the mirror as though she stared at a different person.

*You look like a fish out of water. You look scared half to death and I will have to watch over you like a hawk.*

'You look ready to lead your armies and defend your city, Majesty,' Kaira replied. There was no need to speak her mind on this. The queen needed confidence, not the truth.

Janessa rested her hand on the pommel of the Helsbayn, that sword she now wielded with such assurance. But it was more than that. The blade seemed to instil a power in the girl, seemed to make her that much stronger, that much more capable. When Kaira had tried to lift the blade it had felt little more than a hunk of poorly fashioned metal. In the hands of the queen it sang.

'I feel ready,' Janessa said, but the tight grip of her gauntleted hand on the pommel of the Helsbayn betrayed a doubt she didn't speak.

Kaira knew then that this was still the young girl abandoned by everyone she had ever known. Her mother and siblings dead from the plague. Her father killed by the warlord who even now threatened to raze her city. Her child stillborn, its father long gone. Despite how impressive she looked in her armour, Kaira knew this girl was still so innocent. Still so untested and alone. This was a child playing at being a queen and part of that tore at Kaira's heart.

'You must still stay by my side, Majesty,' she said. For the first time she spoke with authority over Janessa. She needed her to obey. All time for propriety was gone; it had to be if Kaira was to protect her ward. 'At all times, whatever happens in the coming days, you must stay with me.'

Queen Janessa frowned. Kaira could see anger flare behind her eyes. Was it the Helsbayn giving her such strength, imbuing her with such defiance?

'I am a child no longer, Kaira. I am a queen. I have a city to defend. I don't need to be—'

'You are not a warrior yet,' said Kaira, raising her voice more than she should have but much less than she wanted.

Janessa grasped her sword, pulling it a foot from the scabbard. Her jaw set, her eyes staring intently. 'I don't need to be,' she said in a measured tone, though Kaira could sense the girl was fighting for control. She had to admit, it frightened her a little – not for herself, but for the child she was sworn to protect. 'I have this.' Janessa shook the blade, then slammed it back in its sheath with an audible clack.

'That weapon will cut down your enemies,' Kaira said, trying her best to remain calm. 'But it will not protect you from every sword and arrow. It is more important now than ever that you survive. That you live so this city has someone to focus its hope on. Your life cannot be risked.'

'I will not die.' And when she said those words Kaira almost believed them, was almost convinced that Janessa would not, could not be killed. Almost.

'Confidence will serve you well, Majesty. But it will not turn a weapon aimed at your heart. It will not make you invincible, and neither will that sword.'

'It doesn't have to,' Janessa replied, the fire in her eyes dimming to be replaced by grave determination. 'It just has to keep me alive long enough to strike at Amon Tugha.'

Kaira shook her head. 'You cannot seriously think you could face him and live. He is Elharim and has most likely fought and killed his enemies for centuries. Do you think it would be so easy to defeat him simply because you carry a blade blessed by Arlor himself?'

'We will see,' Janessa replied, and Kaira could hear that confidence waver. Despite her determination, despite whatever strength that blade gave her, Janessa knew it would never be so easy.

Kaira made to speak, to tell this girl that the fighting had to be left to real soldiers. That she was not yet a warrior queen, but before she could utter a word Janessa held up a hand.

'No more. This is pointless. What will come will come. Just know that I am prepared. That I am not the helpless lamb you think I am.'

'That is not what I think.'

*But it is what you think. You would wrap this girl in armour and protect her from the world just when it needs her the most.*

'No matter,' said Janessa. 'I need to think, to prepare myself for what is to come.' She turned to the window of her chamber that looked out onto a night lit by fire from the south. 'I am sure we won't have long to wait.'

She said no more, and Kaira knew she had been dismissed. That almost cut as deep as the blade Azai Dravos had used against her, but she obeyed the unspoken order nonetheless, leaving the chamber and making her way down the corridor.

For the briefest moment Kaira considered waiting outside the queen's chamber, waiting there to protect her, despite the girl's stubbornness, but there was still much to do. Much to prepare if she was to be protected, despite the girl's determination to put herself in harm's way.

Kaira made her way down through the palace. Garret would even now be preparing the Sentinels for the city's defence and there was undoubtedly work for her to do. Raised voices made Kaira immediately forget any thought of preparations, though. The first voice she recognised was Rogan's and she was in no hurry to hear what was pouring from his silken tongue. But it was the second voice that made Kaira halt in her tracks – a voice she recognised. A voice she had once feared . . . the Matron Mother, her former mistress and the figurehead of the Temple of Autumn.

It struck something deep within her. That voice had been a constant presence from Kaira's past and for all the years she had trained in the temple to become a Shieldmaiden. Even now, when she was Shieldmaiden no longer, she still felt the respect due to the old woman.

As Kaira made her way down to the main entrance hall of Skyhelm she saw it was empty but for the two figures. Rogan, though only diminutive in stature, still dwarfed the old woman. The Matron Mother glared up at the Seneschal, her eyes fixed on the taller man. Kaira stood back in the shadows and listened, feeling somewhat ashamed that she lurked like some footpad in the dark, but she had to know what was being said.

'No,' said Rogan, for once some emotion in his usually insipid voice. 'The Shieldmaidens must stay within the Temple of Autumn.'

'Madness,' the Matron Mother replied. Her own voice was raised in anger, and it brought back fearful memories for Kaira. Rogan seemed to be somewhat less impressed as she railed at him. 'Any day now tens of thousands of Khurtas will throw themselves against the walls of this city. And you expect its best fighters to cower behind the walls of a temple?'

'The Temple of Autumn will be this city's last line of defence. If the curtain wall is breached where will we defend the queen? Skyhelm stands tall in the midst of the city, but it is not a fortress. The last of the city's defenders, the queen herself, must have somewhere to rally to.'

Despite her disdain for the man, Kaira could see the sense in his words.

'The Shieldmaidens are better suited to battle on the frontline, not as a reserve force. Put them on the wall and we will not need anywhere to rally to. The Khurtas will wish they had never ventured from their northern wastes when faced with Vorena's chosen.'

Rogan continued to argue, but Kaira's attention was diverted as she heard someone come to stand at her shoulder. She gave the briefest of glances, feeling a pull at her heart as she realised it was Samina Coldeye, her sister, standing there in silence.

When last they had met, Kaira had abandoned the temple and her sister Shieldmaidens. Had turned her back on everyone and everything she had ever known. The shame of it stung her now more than ever, though she still knew it had been the right choice.

As the Coldeye watched with her silently, Kaira barely registered what was said between the Matron Mother and Seneschal Rogan. All the while she was thinking about her closest friend standing there. The friend she had not spoken to for weeks since she had left the Temple of Autumn to make her own way in the city.

'It's been a while,' Samina said eventually.

'Too long, sister,' Kaira replied.

She heard Samina's whispered breath, a smirk perhaps? A snort of derision?

'Sister? You would still call me sister? After what you did? After your betrayal?'

Kaira turned, feeling the hurt of Samina's words like a knife to her belly.

'I betrayed no one. I was the one betrayed.' She kept her voice low as Rogan and the Matron Mother continued their argument. 'I was used as a tool, as a weapon. I served with honour and was treated no better than a chattel. A slave.'

'We are all slaves to the will of Vorena. Or have you already forgotten that?'

'I still serve Vorena. And I serve this city. Just because I no longer do it as a Shieldmaiden does not mean I have forgotten the vows I made. The vows we made together.'

Samina shook her head. 'You serve your queen, Sentinel. Not this city and not its people.' Kaira shook her head to deny it, but perhaps there was a shred of truth there. Perhaps all the while she had thought she was serving the tenets of the Shieldmaidens in her own manner, in reality she had become preoccupied with defending the life of one girl.

'Remember when we were children?' Samina continued, before

Kaira could think of what to say. 'Remember it was always you who would do the right thing. Always you who would lead us in prayer. Always you who would push to serve our goddess. To serve the Temple of Autumn. And now you have betrayed all that. Left it behind like so much dust in your wake.'

'No . . . I . . .' Kaira wanted to deny it. Wanted to explain it had never been her intention to abandon her sisters, to abandon Vorena, but she never got the chance.

Rogan and the Matron Mother had finished their debate. As the Matron Mother turned to leave she saw Kaira standing there. The look she gave betrayed nothing. At that moment Kaira would have preferred her scorn, her rage, anything. All she received was a look of blank indifference that stung more than a blow to her cheek.

Samina walked silently to the old woman's side, who in her turn never gave Kaira so much as a second glance as she turned and walked from the palace. Kaira stood at the edge of the hall for some time after they left. She didn't even notice where Rogan had gone.

Had it truly been a betrayal? Had she really abandoned Vorena and her sisters?

*Does it matter either way? In the coming days this city may well fall and then who will care? Do not dwell on it. There is still much to do before you must flog yourself over this.*

Kaira moved to the huge doors of Skyhelm, determined to make herself of use, but before she could, Captain Garret entered, two Sentinels at his shoulder. His brow was furrowed, his face stern, and Kaira stopped before him.

'Captain,' she began, but Garret held up a hand to silence her.

'Save it,' he replied without breaking his stride. 'Your place is beside the queen.'

'But there is still much to do before the Khurtas make their advance.'

Garret stopped and turned to her. 'If there's anything we haven't done by now, it's too late. The Khurtas are on the move.'

49

# SEVEN

It was busy as all the hells in the tavern. Rag stood to one side just watching as Bastian's men went about their business. They cleaned and sharpened their weapons like they was some precious trinkets, or played their card games in silence, swapping coins around like the money didn't matter a shit. Some made their food and drank their drink but didn't seem to take no joy in it, as though they couldn't taste a damn thing.

They'd come three days previous. Just walked in all bold as brass and not saying nothing to no one. Shirl, Yarrick and Essen hadn't known what to do or say, and luckily they'd decided on nothing. Even Harkas moved out of their way and let them get on with their business. Not even the big fella was gonna mess with these bastards.

Understandable, really, since these were Bastian's best men. He was head of the Guild; ruthless and deadly and only interested in what could make him some profit. You didn't get to be that powerful without surrounding yourself with the dirtiest cutthroats in the game.

Bastian had told them to 'be ready'. He'd told Rag there'd be a chance to prove herself, but so far all she'd done was stand here trying not to get in the way. Something was brewing, of that there was no doubt. Just a matter of what and whether she'd be stuck right at the heart of it. Way her luck had been going lately, chances were she'd definitely be right smack bang in the frigging middle.

'What are we even still doing here?' muttered Shirl from the shadows. 'We should be long gone.'

'Gone where?' Essen hissed. His annoyance with Shirl's constant griping had only grown more intense over the past days. 'There ain't nowhere we can go that Bastian won't find us. And in case you hadn't noticed, there's around forty thousand Khurtas camped just north of the city. I reckon they're hungry too, just waiting for some fat fuck to stumble past so they can have a good feed.'

Shirl shut his mouth, looking equal parts angry and fearful at Essen's dressing down.

Rag couldn't help but feel for Shirl. Couldn't help but think he might be right. Who was to say if trying to escape was any less dangerous than sticking around? There was every chance one of Bastian's men would stab them in the neck before any Khurta got the chance.

The back door to the tavern opened, not with a bang but a whisper of hinges. Still, everyone in the place went quiet. Rag saw some hands stray towards blades while others just froze. She half expected it to be the Greencoats come to arrest them all, but deep down she knew they were too busy with what waited outside the city's walls to be bothered about what lurked inside some backstreet tavern.

What walked in was scarier than any Greencoat, though.

Bastian had given her a chill ever since the first time she'd laid eyes on him. It was a chill that never left her, a cold spike down her back that was always there, lurking like a stray cat. Seeing him just reminded her that it was still there, that she was living on borrowed time and it was this corpse-looking bastard she was borrowing it off.

He walked into the centre of the room and his men went about making themselves look busy. Bastian's cold eyes scanned the tavern, and Rag felt her heart begin to sink as they passed over all those lean, deadly blokes until they finally rested on her. He stared at her for some moments, dead fish eyes glaring, and Rag knew it was her he'd come for.

*Best not keep him waiting, Rag. You should know better than that.*

She walked across the tavern so slow it almost hurt. Rag had watched a man hanged once. Watched him walk to those gallows at a snail's pace like he wanted every last moment on earth to stretch out and give him as much life as possible. As she walked across the tavern towards Bastian, Rag began to realise how that poor fucker had felt.

He stared at her all the while until she came to stand in front of him, regarding her like some giant bird about to eat a worm. She just stared back, not wanting to speak but needing to know what in the hells he wanted with her.

Then he smiled.

It looked horrible on that skeletal face; cracking his pale flesh and showing a set of teeth yellow as old parchment.

'I have a job for you,' he said in a voice that creaked like a coffin lid. Then he let that hang there so long she almost had to ask him what it was. But Rag knew better than that. Don't speak until spoken to if you want to keep that tongue in your head. 'Someone is waiting,' Bastian continued. 'At the other side of the Rafts. It's important they are relayed a message. I need someone sly. Someone no one's going to notice. Someone insignificant. Naturally, I thought of you.'

*Thanks a fucking bunch.*

'Yeah,' Rag whispered. 'No problem.'

'That's the right answer,' said Bastian, reaching into his jacket and pulling out a roll of parchment, sealed with black wax. He held it out to her and she took it in her hand. As she tugged on the parchment she realised he still held it in a dead man's grip. 'Don't. Fuck. This. Up.' He spoke each word so sharp it was like being stabbed in the ear with them. Then he let go of the parchment and let her take it.

'I won't,' she said, sounding all small and mousey, but then what in the hells was she supposed to sound like? 'But how do I know who I'm looking for?'

*Fuck, Rag, don't ask questions. Are you trying to get yourself offed?*

Bastian regarding her with those blank eyes, as though mulling over whether her question was important enough to answer. 'Don't worry,' he said. 'They'll find you. Just make sure you get to the other side of the Rafts and don't lose that message.'

'I won't,' Rag replied, and she bloody meant it. Right now she would rather have lost her own head, though if she fucked this up that's exactly what might happen.

Bastian didn't say nothing else. Didn't acknowledge her or wish her luck or none of that shit. He just turned and made his way out of there, with the hardest men Rag had ever seen moving out of his way like he was ten foot tall and covered in spikes.

Once he'd gone, Rag went back to the corner of the room, in no mood to get in anyone's way. She looked down at the roll of parchment still held in her hand. The black seal was blank, the paper crisp. For a moment Rag had a suicidal thought and almost considered breaking the seal and having a look. Who would know, anyway? When she eventually delivered it on the other side of the Rafts she could just say it happened by accident.

But what if Bastian found out? And she knew he would, he had his ways. Her life wouldn't be worth living.

'What's that?'

Rag turned to see Yarrick looking down at the parchment in her hand.

'Message,' she replied. 'Bastian gave it me to deliver over the Rafts.'

Yarrick raised an eyebrow, half impressed, but clearly half glad it wasn't him had been given the job.

'What's in it?' he asked.

'Dunno.' She held out the parchment to him. 'But you're free to open it and have a look.'

Yarrick held up his hands like he was surrendering. 'Not a fucking chance,' he said. 'Who's it for?'

'Dunno that neither,' said Rag. 'But Bastian reckons there's someone waiting over the other side of the Rafts and he'll know me when he sees me.'

'Sounds fucking dodgy to me,' said Yarrick, a hint of sympathy in his voice.

'Is there anything round here that ain't dodgy?' Rag gestured around the tavern, at the gathered crowd of maniacs sharpening their weapons and waiting for trouble.

Yarrick nodded his agreement at that. 'When you off?'

'Soon as, I reckon. No point hanging around.'

'Suppose I'd better come with you then.' Though even as he said it Rag could sense the doubt in his voice.

'Bastian gave this job to me. No need for you to take the risk as well.'

Yarrick shrugged. 'Looks just as risky hanging round here.' He looked fearfully at the tavern full of cutthroats.

Rag couldn't argue with that logic. Neither would she say no to the company. Maybe she'd be better suited to this alone, better able to move unseen and get the job done, but deep down she knew she'd feel better with someone watching her back, even if it was only Yarrick.

'All right then. Let's go.'

With that they made their way out of the tavern, neither of them daring to look any of Bastian's men in the eye, just in case. Shirl looked at her, opening his mouth with a question on his lips, but Rag shook her head and he took the hint, sitting back in his chair and keeping it shut.

Out on the street the sun was just setting and the smell of smoke and fire drifted up on the sea breeze from the south. It was eerily quiet, as if all the folk off the street were hidden and just waiting for the chance to jump out on her and yell 'Surprise' like they was throwing her a bloody party.

'What the fuck's going on?' asked Yarrick, also sensing something was amiss.

'Wait here,' Rag said, moving towards a derelict chapel building across the street from the tavern.

It was one of those old buildings, some place of worship for the Old Gods long since abandoned. They built them high back in those days, and Rag was hoping it would give her a decent enough vantage point to see what was going on.

The climb didn't take long; the old stonework provided enough handholds for her to reach the top in no time. On the roof she could see out across most of the city, from the blackened seawall to the south all the way to the River Gate and beyond to the north.

Rag's grip on the stonework tightened. At the curtain wall all along the northern battlements stood a mass of armoured men, all looking out to the plain beyond. Past them, filling the plain, was a massive horde moving towards the city. Torches shone in the night, showing their numbers, showing the mass of savages moving on Steelhaven. Amongst the horde were huge machines – catapults, siege towers, battering rams and things Rag didn't even know the names for – all moving south like there weren't nothing that could stop them.

She watched for as long as she dared before she realised her mouth was hanging open and her fingers were starting to hurt they were gripping the stone so tight. Almost as quick as she'd climbed she made it to the ground where Yarrick was waiting.

'Well?' he asked. 'What's happening?'

She stared up at him, hands shaking from the climb and the fear.

'We need to get a frigging move on, is what's happening.'

# EIGHT

Forty thousand screaming, braying Khurtic bastards were massed outside the city, making all the noise in the hells. Merrick sat on his horse facing the deathly racket they were making, with nothing between him and them but a hundred yards of dark, grassy plain.

He had to admit, he'd spent better evenings having the shit kicked out of him in Dockside taverns.

The horse whickered beneath him, stamping its foot nervously. Merrick patted it reassuringly but it seemed to do little good.

*You think you're bloody nervous? I had plans – ambitions. What did you have other than a nosebag in front and a pile of shit behind?*

Beside him, to the left, sat Tannick. They hadn't spoken but it was obvious the old man wanted to keep him close, maybe to look after him and make sure he'd be able to take that bloody sword one day, or maybe just to make sure he didn't bring shame on the Wyvern Guard and the family name. Either way, Merrick took some strange solace from the fact his father was nearby.

The Wyvern Guard had ridden out as the Khurtas arrived. A few hundred men on horseback trotting out to face a horde of forty thousand. The savages were arrayed against them now, just standing there screaming, four hundred yards from the city wall. Every now and again a Khurtic archer would take a pot shot at them, his arrow whistling overhead or clanging against a shield, but other than that they were happy just to stand and shout. Of the great Amon Tugha there was no sign, and Merrick took no small reassurance from that. Howling savages he could just about stomach – an immortal giant from the Riverlands might well have been a foe too far.

'See them?' Tannick yelled above the din. 'They've come to take this city. Come to prove they're the hardest, deadliest bastards in all the corners of the world. Look at them.' He pointed, his arm sweeping from left to right as he took in the whole Khurtic front line. As he did so an arrow whistled past the winged helm on his head, but Tannick never flinched. 'They've come south to prove their might. To prove they're the greatest killers the Free States have ever seen. And we're going to prove them wrong.'

This time it was the turn of the Wyvern Guard to howl. Merrick had to admit, his father's words stirred him a bit, but he still couldn't bring himself to join in with their cheering.

From within the mass of Khurtas a figure came forward holding aloft a banner. He pushed his way through and planted it in front of the Khurtic lines, as though taunting his enemies with his prize. Through the gloom, Merrick could see the banner bore a red dragon on a yellow field, despite how burned and grimy it was. The standard of Dreldun, there in the hands of the bastard enemy. Merrick had never considered himself a patriot; most of the time he couldn't care less about loyalty to kings and countries, but seeing that standard in the hands of some foreign savage made him want to spit his ire. They'd come down from their steppes to the north and raped and murdered and burned their way south. That standard was a symbol of the carnage they'd left in their wake, of the innocents slaughtered needlessly. Even Merrick couldn't let that stand.

Tannick spurred his horse, gripping his reins tight and riding forward a few yards. More arrows flew but missed their target.

'Whoreson!' Tannick bellowed above the din. Merrick saw Cormach look up, staring eagerly from beneath his helm as the Lord Marshal pointed at the Khurtic horde. 'Bring me that flag.'

Cormach said something as he drew his sword, along the lines of *about fucking time*, but Merrick couldn't make it out exactly. Then he spurred his horse. The steed reared then set off at a gallop, clear of the Wyvern Guard line and headed straight towards forty thousand Khurtas.

Merrick watched wide eyed. It was either the bravest thing he'd ever seen or the most insane.

*Never get you doing anything like that, would they, Ryder? You stay in the crowd; you watch your own back. Don't bother risking your life for anyone.*

Cormach galloped at the enemy, arrows peppering the ground at his horse's feet. The front line of Khurtas began yelling in a frenzy, as though they were shouting encouragement, waiting for the moment they could kill one of these defiant, arrogant Wyvern Guard.

*He's going to die. He'll be cut down in a hail of arrows or a storm of blades and you get to sit here and watch. But then, you never liked that fucker anyway.*

Merrick found himself gripping his reins the tighter, felt his hand straying to the hilt of his sword. Found his stomach begin to tighten with excitement as he watched Cormach Whoreson riding to the most glorious death he would ever witness.

*Don't even think about it, Ryder. You're not cut out for any of that bravery shit. You're a self-serving coward and everyone knows it. What do you think you'll prove by getting yourself killed?*

His sword rang from its sheath. It felt good in his hand. Felt hungry. *He* felt hungry. Before he knew what he was doing, Merrick had put spurs to his steed's flanks and was yelling at the top of his voice. What he said he had no idea, it could have been something about the glory of the Wyvern Guard, could have been unintelligible nonsense. Either way it pushed the fear aside as his horse hit a gallop and he pressed his heels down so as not to be bucked from the saddle.

Someone shouted behind him. Was it Tannick? Were they words of encouragement? More likely words of admonishment for being such an idiot. Whatever they were, Merrick ignored them as he galloped across that empty plain, riding after a madman and into the face of countless savage killers intent on mounting his head on a spear.

*What the fuck are you doing, Ryder? You're going to die!*

Merrick gritted his teeth, the shield on his arm slapping against his thigh, the sword in his hand pointed forward at the enemy.

Up ahead he could see Cormach had almost reached the line. The Khurta standing at the forefront with the flag of Dreldun was beckoning him forward, screaming from the bottom of his lungs. Cormach flung his shield over his shoulder, and Merrick could see the mass of arrows protruding from it. As he got within ten yards of the Khurtic line, a group of savages ran forward, spears at the ready. Cormach tore at his reins, turning his steed and halting its gallop right in front of the standard bearer. A swipe of his sword silenced the screaming Khurta, who dropped to the ground in silence. Before the standard of Dreldun could fall, Cormach snatched it up with his free hand.

Spears thrust up at him, but Cormach's sword arm seemed to predict every wayward strike, slapping them aside with a chorus of metallic rings. He kicked his horse and it backed away, seeming to obey its rider's commands instinctually.

Merrick continued his gallop. He'd stopped screaming now, his voice gone hoarse. It would have done him no good anyway; the noise echoing from the massed ranks of Khurtas had drowned him out several yards back.

The sword still felt eager in his hand. His need to strike – to prove himself to his father, the Wyvern Guard and most of all to this mad bastard Cormach – had overcome him completely.

Before Merrick could reach the enemy, though, Cormach had put spurs to his horse once more. It bucked, leaping away from the Khurtic spears, and raced back towards the city.

By now the Khurtas had bellowed for more archers to the front, and a hail of arrows followed in Cormach's wake. Merrick slowed his mount, raising his shield, as black shafts slammed down all around him. Two pierced the shield, another sliding off his horse's barding. When he looked up from behind the shield, he saw Cormach was almost upon him.

'Wrong way, you fucking idiot,' Cormach shouted as he galloped past.

Merrick reined his horse around and followed as best he could.

*Well done, Ryder. You've just made yourself look a complete prat. But don't worry, it's doubtful anyone has noticed.*

Cormach was yards ahead as more arrows rained around them. Over the bellowing of the Khurtas, Merrick suddenly heard an inhuman squeal as Cormach's steed went down, a black arrow protruding from its flank. Cormach fell rolling with his horse, the standard of Dreldun spilling from his grip.

Merrick pulled hard on his reins, halting his mount as Cormach stood groggily, his helmet lost as he looked around desperately for the standard.

'Come on,' yelled Merrick, holding his hand out.

Cormach ignored him, retrieving the standard from where it lay and glancing back to the Khurtic line. Two more arrows hissed into the dirt at his feet and he held the standard out to Merrick.

'Take it,' he said. There was no fear there, no doubt; as if he was ready to stand and die. As if a flag was more important than his life.

'Get on the horse,' Merrick yelled, unable to quell the panic in his voice. 'Before we're fucking shot!'

Cormach stared back at him as more arrows flew overhead. He looked up with contempt, like he realised Merrick was saving his life and would rather have let the Khurtas gut him than suffer that indignity.

Just as Merrick was about to kick his horse and leave the mad bastard, Cormach grasped his outstretched hand and vaulted up behind him.

The screams of the Khurtas grew louder as they saw their quarry riding away. More arrows slammed into the earth all around but it was clear they didn't have a decent archer among them. Merrick kicked his horse harder, desperate to put as much distance between himself and the Khurtas as he could until eventually he made it back to the row of Wyvern Guard, his breath coming as fast as his steed's.

He reined his horse in before Tannick, staring at his father who glared from beneath his winged helm. Up on the wall he could see men cheering, raising their swords and bows in victory, as if they'd just hacked the head from Amon Tugha himself. Merrick paid them little attention, too intent on his father's reaction. 'I want you close,' he'd said. 'No harm must come to you,' he'd said.

60

Well, Merrick had certainly done a shit job of paying attention to that.

Cormach jumped down from the horse and presented the Dreldunese banner to the Lord Marshal, who took it in his hand and regarded it reverently for a moment, before thrusting it above his head.

'Right, lads,' he shouted. 'I think that's proved our point.'

With that he swung his horse around and headed back towards the Stone Gate.

Merrick could feel his heart almost beating out of his chest, the blood pumping in his ears. As he followed his father he realised his hands were shaking and he tightened his grip on the reins of his horse to try and stop them.

*Pleased with yourself, Ryder? Now that you've proven you're as crazy as the rest of them?*

Despite feeling elated at what he'd just done, he was still relieved they were entering the city once more. Having almost come face to face with the entire Khurtic horde, he was glad there was ten foot thick of curtain wall holding them back. He might have proven his worth to the Wyvern Guard, might have risked his life for a flag on a stick, but he still didn't want to die just yet.

As he rode through the gate the cheers were almost deafening. Men chanted the name of the Wyvern Guard and for the first time Merrick could see the method behind his father's madness. News of their deed would spread across the wall and through the city. The Khurtas had been robbed of their prize. They could be beaten. And the Wyvern Guard hadn't had to charge valiantly into their ranks to prove it.

Before he'd realised it, Merrick had pulled his horse up to a halt beside his father's. Tannick glanced across at him, and Merrick saw that the old man looked none too pleased.

*But what were you expecting, Ryder? Hug and a kiss? For him to ask you if everything was all right? If those nasty Khurtas nicked you with their horrible arrows?*

'I told you to stay beside me, boy,' said Tannick. 'You just risked your life needlessly.'

'Yes, Lord Marshal, but—'

'But nothing. Defy me again and I'll have you flogged. No matter how short of men we are.'

'Yes, Lord Marshal.'

'Other than that, good work.'

Merrick let that hang there for a moment, almost failing to recognise his father's acknowledgement. 'Good work?'

Tannick barked a laugh. 'Of course, good work. Cormach would be dead if not for you. The banner of Dreldun lost. I'd have had to send more men if he'd fallen. You showed bravery. Initiative. You did well, boy.' Tannick leaned over on his saddle, his warm look disappeared. 'But never disobey me again.'

'I won't,' Merrick replied. 'But it was Cormach who rode to the Khurtic line. He won the banner. If anyone should be commended for his bravery it's him.'

Tannick shook his head. 'The Whoreson's not brave, boy. Bravery is born of fear. You have to overcome that fear to show courage. Cormach Whoreson fears nothing. And he obeys without question – something you could learn from him.'

Merrick nodded his assent, though how much he took his father at his word would remain to be seen.

Before they could dismount, Marshal Farren approached, flanked by several Knights of the Blood.

'You're a fool, Ryder,' Farren barked. 'Risking your men like that. And what have you done other than stir the Khurtas up into a frenzy?'

'They're not the only ones I've stirred up,' Tannick replied, flinging the Dreldunese banner at Farren, who snatched it from the air. 'Look around you. These men are now eager for the fight and that means this city has a glimmer of hope. I've proven there's nothing the Khurtas have we can't take away from them.' He gestured at the cheering men surrounding them. 'These men think they just might win. So make sure you mount that where everyone can see it. The day's first victory is ours.'

'You're insane. Endangering your men for a standard.'

'Only two men,' Tannick replied. 'Both of them unhurt. And one of them my own son.' Marshal Farren glanced across at Merrick, who tried his best to look impressive under that twitching glare.

'Then you're a family of madmen,' Farren replied before stalking away. As he did so he thrust the banner into the hands of one of his knights, mumbling curses to himself.

With nothing further to say, Tannick dismounted, a steward coming to take his stallion's reins. Merrick sat for a moment, relieved that the shaking in his hands had subsided. For now he was safe, and a veritable bloody hero, but he was sure there'd be plenty more opportunities to show he was an idiot or a coward over the coming nights. Maybe even tonight.

Merrick swung his leg over the side of his mount and climbed down to find someone was already holding the reins of his horse for him. Cormach Whoreson glared, as though Merrick had just smeared shit all over his shiny breastplate.

'Don't think this makes us fucking friends,' he said, still staring deep into Merrick's eyes as though daring him to take the piss.

'Don't worry, I don't,' Merrick replied.

Without another word, Cormach turned and left.

'And there's really no need to thank me,' Merrick said quietly towards Cormach's back.

Oh so quietly.

# NINE

He could see the city burning from beyond the distant horizon before the ship's lookout ever spotted land. A black cloud rose up in the clear, crisp sky, a beacon to be seen from miles across the flat ocean. It had been a tortuous journey, but he now felt some relief that it was almost over.

River should have never left Steelhaven in the first place. He had lost count of the number of times he had cursed himself for his folly. But he had been tricked. His brother Forest had lied to him; told him their Father would hold to his bargain and spare Jay's life. And so, like a fool, he had gone along with their plan; slaying more men than he could count to ensure Amon Tugha's artillery ships were sent north to the city of Steelhaven. But Forest and the Father of Killers had not held to their side of the bargain and his own brother had come to kill him once River had played his part.

When River had learned of their betrayal at Aluk Vadir pretending to be a mariner aboard this ship had seemed the fastest way to return to her side. Now as he neared his goal they seemed to be travelling slower than ever.

For every hour they'd spent at sea, River felt his heart sink further and further into his chest. What if he was too late? What if the Father of Killers had already slain his love? What if Amon Tugha had already sacked the city and cut out her heart in front of his baying hordes?

River gripped the prow, staring intently, almost willing the wind into the sails of the ship. It had only been a few days since he'd set off to sea but it seemed like months. Since he had infiltrated the supply ship at the harbour of Aluk Vadir, desperate to return to Steelhaven, every day stretched out longer than the last, and with each passing hour River felt more helpless. Aboard the ship he had busied himself with the work of a sailor. It had not been difficult to pick up, and no one seemed to realise or care that he was an unfamiliar face with little experience as a mariner. Not one of them had questioned him, and River could only assume that many of the men aboard were unacquainted with one another, having been hired en masse as part of this fleet.

'Don't worry,' said a voice behind him, and River turned to see the first mate staring out towards the city as well. 'We won't get close enough to be in danger.'

River had hardly spoken to a soul since boarding, considering it best to keep his own counsel rather than risk giving himself away, and he was instantly wary at the man's familiar tone. He had become acquainted with every face aboard ship but these men were not his friends. They had come to aid in the sacking of Steelhaven. Whether they knew it or not, they were still his enemies.

'I am not worried,' River replied. *At least not for myself.*

'Once we've delivered the barrels of pitch and fresh supplies we'll be on our way back,' continued the sailor, as though River hadn't spoken. 'Shame, too. It might be quite a show watching this city fall.'

River tightened his grip on the gunwale at the comment, but said nothing. He was not close enough yet to the city. He could not risk everything now on a simple pique of anger.

'How do you know it will fall?' he asked. 'Steelhaven is well defended. It will take more than fire from the sea to break its walls.'

'Yes, it will.' The man gestured casually with his hand towards the city. 'Amon Tugha attacks from the north. Even now he will be mustering his Khurtas for an attack, if he isn't already assaulting the front gate. I imagine that's quite something to see.'

River watched as they approached, saw another ball of fire light the darkening sky. It seemed the city was to be assailed from all sides and there was but one man responsible.

Amon Tugha. The warlord who held so much sway over the Father of Killers. The one who had ordered Queen Janessa's death. *Jay. Her name is Jay.* He wanted to raze this city and slaughter every soul within it. While River had breath he could never allow the Elharim to succeed. He had to focus, had to prepare himself. If he was ever going to save Jay it would take all his wits and skill.

Night fell as they made their way closer to the city. By the time they were in sight of the artillery ships, all that could be seen of Steelhaven was a dark silhouette against the skyline. Aboard each of the waiting vessels fire burned in iron braziers, each one stoked high so that they might set light to their pitch-soaked missiles.

Every supply ship made its way towards a waiting artillery boat and River stood his ground patiently, *as the fisherman at shore*. Hidden beneath his tunic were his blades, which he had taken such great pains to conceal these past days. He watched while on deck sailors went about their business, furling the sails and uncoiling ropes to secure to the artillery ships. This was the closest they would come to the city.

Now was the time.

The first rope was thrown and deftly caught by a mariner aboard an adjacent artillery ship, then another, which was swiftly tied to one of the vessel's cleats. River was already standing behind the pilot at his own ship's wheel. Some days ago River had been told his name, had watched as he laughed and gambled with his fellow mariners. The man had seemed harmless enough and River had even heard him tell tales of a family back to the south. Something in his head told him this was unfair, that he had done nothing to deserve what was to come. But River could have no mercy now.

Silently his blade slid across the pilot's throat and River pushed him aside to gurgle his last onto the deck. Grabbing the wheel firmly he spun it hard, directing the ship straight into the artillery boat it had come to supply.

Men shouted in panic as the ship veered sharply, but in the dark no one could see what had happened to the pilot at his wheel. A barrel rolled across the deck as the ship listed violently in the water. More shouting pealed out in the night as the crew of the artillery vessel realised they were about to be rammed.

'What's going on?' shouted a voice close by, and River saw it was the first mate he had spoken to so recently. A blade slipped between the man's ribs and River grasped him as he fell, lowering his body to the deck as he gasped blood into punctured lungs. Looking up he saw the prow of the ship had almost met its target, moving closer in what would be the most brutal of kisses.

'Brace yourselves!' someone yelled in the dark, but River ignored him, moving towards the prow.

The ship lurched as it smashed into the artillery vessel. Men cried out as they were thrown across the deck. River moved fast, feeling himself propelled forward, but his footsteps were sure as he broke into a run. Aboard the artillery ship men began shouting in panic as the braziers they had stoked so high spilled hot coals at their feet and the trebuchet on deck lurched violently, though it did not spill its already burning missile.

River leapt from the crumpled prow and onto the artillery ship's deck. A mariner glared at him as he landed and made to speak, but River silenced him with a deft cut to the throat.

As River surveyed the scene of panic and confusion, the artillery ship slewed in the water, turning on its axis to face along the row of other ships which had been bombarding the city these past days. He darted to the trebuchet and sliced the rope securing the twenty-foot throwing-arm to its frame. The counterweight swung down with a creak of wood, sending its flaming load soaring along the row of ships. River barely noticed as the missile smashed into one of the artillery vessels further down the row, exploding in a shower of burning debris.

Fiery embers still glowed on the deck of the ship and River raced to an open barrel of pitch, kicking it over and spilling it onto the waiting coals. Flames took immediately, spreading across the deck in a pool of molten fire, and he heard men crying out in panic all around him.

'What are you doing, you fu—?' River spun and silenced his would-be assailant with two swift slashes of his blades.

By now the two ships were in disarray, locked together and burning in the night as men rushed around in panic. River went unseen as he made his way to the gunwale, sheathed his weapons and dived into the black waters.

The cold engulfed him, but River fought against the shock of it as it threatened to freeze his extremities. He swam further into the dark, every powerful stroke pulling him towards the city. As the ships burned behind him all he focused on was the distant shore, moving through the water *like a fish against the current*. By the time he reached the quayside that ran in a great arc around the bay, the conflagration on the far-off ships had risen into a pyre.

River pulled himself from the water and breathed deep. The swim had been hard, he was already shivering and could barely feel the tips of his fingers. As he glanced up to the burned walls of Steelhaven, he knew the climb would be harder. Steam drifted from the charred walls – the result of days of bombardment. At least now, as the artillery ships recovered from the damage he had inflicted, their attack would abate . . . for a while.

Still feeling the cold numbing his limbs, River found a handhold in the blackened wall of the city and began his climb.

# TEN

The sun had gone down leaving a blank, starless sky, but there was so much light from both within and without the city that Waylian could see almost clear as day. On the flat plain the Khurtas waited, torches burning bright as they bayed to the hidden moon in their grim foreign tongue.

Waylian had to admit, it scared the shit out of him.

The scores of magisters that surrounded him did nothing to ease his rising panic. They were the most powerful magickers in all the Free States, gathered in one place to do battle, but Waylian could not see how they would ever defeat the overwhelming number of savages waiting to swarm over the curtain wall.

The Wyvern Guard had gone out to greet them. Waylian didn't really know what he'd been expecting – for them all to get slaughtered, more than likely. They'd trotted forward in a row, defiantly facing the thousands, just sitting there until the Lord Marshal had given his order to attack. Only two riders galloped forward to face the horde, though, and they'd both come back alive and with a standard of the Free States as their prize. It looked impressive enough, and had shown the Khurtas weren't the indomitable force everyone thought.

Yet Waylian knew they were still the deadliest of killers, intent on bringing this city to its knees. No number of captured flags would ever settle the fear in his guts.

'Hold your nerve, boy.'

He didn't need to look to know it was Gelredida, standing beside him. As much as he wanted to heed her words, holding his nerve was easier said than done. Even with his redoubtable mistress by his side, Waylian felt like a rabbit in its hutch waiting for the foxes to arrive. Easy for her to say *hold your nerve*; she was a master of the Art, feared and respected and deadly as a viper. He was Waylian Grimm; a nobody, a neophyte, and he was just as likely to manifest shit from his arse as magick from his fingertips. Mind you, Marshal Ferenz would probably have disagreed about that. Not that Waylian had any idea how he'd managed to crush a man's head with a word. Hopefully he'd work it out, and soon.

'Stay behind me,' Gelredida said. 'And try not to get in the way.'

*No need to worry about that! When the Khurtas came flocking over the wall the last thing Waylian Grimm would do was throw himself into the fray.*

The Khurtas were beginning to get restless now, winding themselves up into a frenzy. Their siege engines were being rolled implacably towards the city walls and soon enough they'd be in range. In response, Waylian could sense the unease all around him.

Drennan spoke constantly to the apprentices in his charge, his voice a low grumble, but Waylian could tell his words were more of encouragement than rebuke. The youngsters in his care seemed focused; under the tutelage of the Archmaster they looked strong, mature and more than ready to face the advancing enemy. Waylian could only envy them for that. Though Gelredida had stopped treating him like shit on her shoe, he knew she still considered him beneath her – he still felt like a child in her presence and could only dream of sharing the autonomy the rest of these apprentices had been granted. Perhaps there was more to it, though; maybe it was her way of protecting him. Maybe she did have a beating heart beneath that frosty exterior. Or maybe she just had her own motives for keeping him on such a tight leash.

Further along the wall stood Crannock Marghil with his coterie of venerable magisters. They squabbled and clucked like a shed full of broody hens, some panicked at the rising disquiet amongst the Khurtas, others raising their own ire, as though they would need it to tap the Veil and unleash all the hells on the enemy when it finally attacked. For his part, old Crannock stood silently in their midst, an island of calm amongst the sea of thunderous old magickers.

The last Archmaster paced along the wall in front of his Raven Knights. Lucen Kalvor's brow was furrowed as he stared out at the Khurtas, hands clenched behind his back, white fingers locked together, as if to unclasp them would unleash his magickal fury all too soon. The Raven Knights themselves stood like onyx statues, spears and swords gripped at the ready. If the Khurtas managed to scale the walls it was the Raven Knights who would stand between them and the magisters. A last line of defence. As much as Waylian had feared them during his time in the tower, he was grateful for them now.

Down below, the Khurtas had begun singing – a dozen different cants from their disparate tribes, some low and guttural like a funeral dirge, others ferocious like a last battle cry. It resulted in a cacophony that Waylian felt to the pit of his stomach, and it made him want to puke. To add to the din they smashed their weapons into their shields, the racket rising up and over the city, drowning out the serjeants and captains who were vainly trying to calm the city's bannermen, rallying them with speeches and songs of their own.

Then, as suddenly as they had begun, the Khurtas fell silent.

It left a ringing in Waylian's ears and he could only watch in fear as the echo of their clangour slowly died. From the centre of the horde a single voice cried out, shouting in their guttural northern tongue. There was no way of telling what he said, but it must have been bloody important, for every one of the forty-odd thousand savages stood and listened in silence. At any moment Waylian expected their ranks to break open and for the hellish form of Amon Tugha to come striding through their midst, but it never happened. That single voice just continued to speak, continued to cry above the silence as everyone stood waiting.

Though listening to that voice was like listening to his own funerary rites, Waylian didn't want the warrior to stop. He knew what that would mean, that the battle would begin in earnest. As it went on he felt himself trembling at the knee, biting his lip, willing the voice on and on.

Until finally it stopped.

And the Khurtas charged.

Waylian's hands began to shake. He glanced around, half wanting to see what the reaction of the other magisters was, half looking for somewhere to hide. Though there was a pall of fear all around, not one of the magisters moved from their spot.

*That's torn it, Grimm. You've not even got an excuse to run now!*

Siege towers were dragged forward by beasts of burden, armoured and shielded in iron plate. Ladders a hundred foot long were carried by scores of screaming Khurtas, their shields raised against the flights of arrows raining down on them as they charged. In the distance Waylian could see a ram being pushed and dragged by men and beasts. To the rear of the horde trebuchets were being positioned, their forty-foot arms already winched in preparation of the death they would unleash.

Squinting down the length of the curtain wall Waylian could see archers firing in volley. Masses of arrows rained down, cutting through the Khurtas, but for every savage that fell another would take his place. For a moment Waylian felt panic grip him. There were no archers at this section of the wall. Who would stop the Khurtas climbing and attacking the Raven Knights head on?

For a moment he wanted to rush forward, to peer over the edge of the crenellated wall and see how close his doom was, but Gelredida's order had been clear.

*Stay behind her, Waylian. Don't get in the way. Oh, and try not to get bloody killed.*

He could hear the clatter of ladders from beyond the wall, but none of the magisters moved. Neither did the Raven Knights, holding their formation and awaiting Lucen Kalvor's orders.

Waylian almost didn't see the massive boulder as it flew out of the night. Almost didn't notice it soar towards the gathered magickers like a silent meteor, ready to smash them all to pieces. Not that it would have mattered if he had; there was nothing he could have done about it anyway.

One of the senior magisters took a clumsy step forward, ducking his head and holding up an arm to the night sky. The boulder shattered at his unspoken command, splitting into myriad shards that landed all around them, peppering the platform like hail. A rock as big as a fist came to rest at Waylian's feet and he stared at it for a moment, wondering what it would have felt like if it had struck him in the head.

*Probably not much, you bloody dolt. Might have even knocked some sense into you.*

Waylian watched the edge of the wall, expecting at any time a grim Khurtic face to rise up over the edge. He glanced to the Raven Knights, hoping beyond hope that they were not filled with the same fear and apprehension he was.

Something writhed in the dark between two of the wall's merlons. At first Waylian couldn't make it out, then it thrust forward, like the tentacle of some vast sea beast. It shot out, wrapping itself around a waiting Raven Knight and hoisting him into the air. With a powerful flick, the squirming appendage flung the screaming knight over the wall.

Lucen Kalvor bellowed for his men to brace themselves as yet more flailing tentacles appeared over the lip of the wall. In the dim light Waylian could see that they were not the arms of some landborne leviathan but roots, as though the bowels of a tree had been animated and ordered to climb the wall. For a moment his mind flashed back to the arena days before, when that ancient tree had sprung to life intent on murder. Was this the same fell sorcery at work?

*Does it actually matter a shit? You may well be about to die!*

Branches battered against Raven Knight shields as the Khurtas began to seethe over the wall, their climb made easy by the vines and foliage that were even now growing up the sheer surface. One of the old magisters bellowed something long and loud and it wasn't until Waylian squinted through the dark that he saw the old man had been impaled on a spiked branch.

'At them,' Crannock croaked, his voice rising above the din.

As the first wave of Khurtas surged forward Waylian felt the atmosphere grow heavy, pressure filling his ears and a metallic tang washing the air as a hundred magisters tapped the Veil in unison.

73

The first charging Khurta exploded in a shower of sparks and blood, his ribcage splitting open as though torn asunder by white-hot gauntlets. A second simply unfurled in curling ribbons of gore while a third was slammed to the floor and crushed as though by an invisible foot.

The animated branches retaliated in an instant, reaching towards the old men and women who had just repelled the first Khurtic onslaught. Waylian covered his ears against the screams as the venerable magisters, who had lived and taught in the city for decades, were torn apart. The Raven Knights ran forward to aid their masters, hacking at the writhing mass of branches, but they were too few to make much difference. An armoured body was flung past Waylian like so much discarded metal, while another's head was torn from its shoulders like a doll in the hands of an angry child.

One of Drennan's apprentices rushed forward, hands contorting to trace magickal sigils in the air, lips moving in some ancient incantation. At first the branches reached out for him, then pulled back as though repulsed by the youth's presence. They began to wither, shedding bark and foliage, rotting before Waylian's eyes. Then the young lad screamed. He grabbed his head, blocking his ears as though they had been assailed by a sudden massive pressure. Waylian almost covered his own ears as the scream rang out above the sounds of battle. Then the boy's head burst into flames.

Waylian could only stare in revulsion before he suddenly girded himself against the horror. He darted forward as the youth fell, still on fire. The heat was intense as Waylian reached his side, but he grabbed the lad's robe nonetheless, vainly trying to subdue the flames that consumed his head. Fire licked at Waylian's arms, singeing the hairs as his sleeves began to smoulder. The lad's screaming had ceased now but he still writhed, half fighting Waylian off, half fighting himself as the intense heat consumed him. Waylian beat at the flames as best he could, barely able to keep his eyes open in the face of the heat. By the time he had beaten the blaze down he realised the youth had stopped moving, his head now nothing more than a blackened stump.

All around was carnage as Waylian stared at the treacherous consequence of tapping the Veil before being fully trained. He almost didn't see the Khurtas begin to flood over the wall. Almost didn't look up in time to spot a savage eyeing him hungrily, blade in hand, eager for the kill.

Almost.

In a daze, Waylian spotted him at the last moment and he glanced around in panic, all thought of using his own fledgling powers gone from his head.

*Well, you don't want to end up a burned and blackened mess like our friend here, now do you, Grimm!*

It was obvious from the look in his eyes the Khurta wasn't going to hear any pleas for mercy and he certainly hadn't come climbing over that wall for a chat about the weather.

He was going to kill Waylian without even breaking a sweat.

The Khurta grinned as Waylian began to move. He bared yellow fangs, sensing his prey begin to panic, feeling his blood pump the faster as Waylian tried to make his escape. But it was not escape Waylian was looking for. As the Khurta dashed towards him, sword raised, Waylian lunged for a spear dropped by a dead Raven Knight. His hands closed around the haft and he hauled it up, stunned at how heavy the spear was. He had seen such weapons wielded in the hands of the knights a score of times but could never have believed it would weigh so much.

The Khurta charged regardless, a scream of triumph baying from his twisted lips, just as Waylian levelled the spear tip. The Khurta rushed on, the last thing he expected was Waylian to defend himself. The impetus of his charge skewered him on the spearhead and it pierced his torso just beneath the ribs as he ran onto it a full two feet before realising his error.

His scream of triumph turned to one of dismay. All Waylian could do was stare into the Khurta's wide eyes as he babbled in that sick northern tongue, screaming insults Waylian could scarce understand, though he didn't have to be fluent to get the gist.

Still he gripped the spear as blood flowed down the haft. The Khurta weakened, dropping his blade and falling to his knees. His eyes turned hateful as he carried on his litany of curses.

'I . . . I'm sorry?' replied Waylian, not really knowing what else to say.

The Khurta spat a last insult from his lips before collapsing to the ground. Waylian just stared as the fighting raged around him. When he managed to pull himself together he found his nails were digging into his palms and his face was streaked with tears. Through salty eyes he glanced to his left in time to see a Khurta leaping at him. His charge had been silent. Waylian stood no chance against his axe.

The Khurta crumpled in flight, his neck twisting, his arms snapping and that wicked axe falling from his grip before he landed in a heap.

'I thought I told you to stay behind me,' said Gelredida, walking forward out of the night, glaring with a look of distaste.

'I'm sorry, Magistra,' Waylian replied. 'But I was just—'

'Never mind,' she said, turning towards the battle. 'There is still much to do. Stay close this time, and do try not to get in the way.'

Waylian nodded, but the Red Witch didn't see him. She was already making her way towards the enemy. And Waylian had to admit feeling a little sorry for them.

# ELEVEN

**T**o left and right were men stricken with fear. Someone further down the line had pissed himself and Nobul watched as it trickled past his boot in a steaming river. Whoever it was must have had a bladder like a horse.

Nobul gripped the hammer tight, not that it made him feel any better. His heart was thumping fast and hard, seemingly in time to the beat of the Khurtic drums. He looked down at those bastards, come all this way to rape and murder. They were a seething mass of ferocity, their screams thrown forward with more violence than a clenched fist. Nobul stared it down as best he could. He'd been here before, faced worse enemies, and he was still breathing. But then he was the Black Helm – he was fucking invincible.

*But are you? Are you the Black Helm or just broken old Nobul Jacks?*

Maybe there'd be someone out there who'd stop him. Someone hard enough, someone who was iron and steel and could bring him down. The thought made him scan the horde as they raged, trying to spot their biggest and best. He willed them to charge, desperate for them to stop their howling, impatient for the fight to start.

And then the Khurtas fell silent.

The air was filled with a calm deathlier than anything Nobul had ever felt. His skin rose in bumps and it didn't matter how hard he gripped that hammer, he couldn't stop the fear and doubt creeping into his heart.

A single voice suddenly rose from the mass of bodies, holding those Khurtas in its grip like it was holding back time itself. Though he couldn't understand the words, Nobul knew it chanted a litany of hate and he wanted them to attack now more than ever. He was ready for them, despite the fear, and he would match whatever fierceness they could bring with violence of his own.

The voice ceased as suddenly as it had begun, and from out of the black night air came a thousand whispers that rose into a howl. 'Take cover,' someone screamed, and Nobul had the presence of mind to duck his head behind one of the merlons as a massive volley of arrows fell on the curtain wall. More screams carried along the battlements as those not quick enough were struck by the black shafts. A lad fell silent at Nobul's feet, an arrow buried in his eye and another through his cheek. He'd been standing there all day but not once had Nobul bothered to ask his name. Bit too late now.

More silence fell after the huge volley, and Nobul glanced over the wall to see if the Khurtas were on the way. If he'd been a godly man he would have said his prayers right then as he saw, not more arrows, but huge fucking rocks flying at the wall, one right towards where he was standing.

'Out the bloody way,' he shouted, diving aside as the rock struck, smashing the merlon he'd been peering over a moment before. It shattered, spraying shards in all directions as Nobul went sprawling, hammer spilling from his grip. He shook his head, dust and grit spilling from him, and hauled himself up, breath coming hard. His hand scrabbled through the rubble, desperate to find his hammer, and he felt a stab of cold relief when his fingers found the handle.

As he pulled himself to his feet he heard a shout from down the line, 'Here they bloody come. Give it to 'em, lads!'

A row of archers moved forward, one struggling to push past Nobul's bulk. Their serjeant gave the order to nock and draw but his voice was drowned out by the deafening noise rising up from below the curtain wall. As one, the Khurtas howled their fury to the night sky as they charged forward.

Myriad arrows cut the air as the archers fired down into the charging horde but it was like throwing snowballs at the sun. There was nothing that would stop the mass of savages reaching the wall.

Nobul girded himself. This was what he'd been waiting for. Yearning for. A chance to fight, and maybe die, facing his enemies. But there was something else, a seed of doubt nestled in the back of his mind.

*You're an old bastard now, and no mistake. This ain't like it was at Bakhaus when you were strong and full of spunk. Who's to say you're not just a dried-up old man with nothing but memories of old glories to fuel him?*

Ladders began to clatter against the wall. Archers kept firing down; one lad leaned over with a block of masonry raised high over his head and got an arrow in the throat for his trouble.

With a noisy clack, a ladder came smashing against the wall, right where that rock had made a gap in the masonry. Nobul stood gawping at it. There was a young lad to his left staring too, unsure of what to do, but Nobul was fucked if he knew what to tell him. There were no rules for this kind of shitty business. When the enemy came you fought or you fucking died. Those were rules enough.

Further down the wall came the sound of screaming, of metal ringing on metal as the first of the Khurtas reached the top of their ladders. Nobul paid it no mind, keeping his eyes fixed on the top of that ladder in front of him.

From below came a booming sound that rocked the wall. Battering ram, most likely, but that weren't none of Nobul's concern either. Another boom, and Nobul tightened his grip on the hammer.

*Hold your nerve, you old bastard. You'll find out soon enough if you've still got it in you. And if not you won't be around long enough to give a shit.*

A hand reached up over the wall, then a face came into view, all carved up like a butcher's block and painted for war. It stared with hate and lust and violence, and Nobul stared back. But he didn't move.

*Because you're all dried up, Nobul Jacks. You're all twisted inside with fear and regret and you're gonna die here on this wall with a gutful of Khurtic iron.*

The lad at the side of him screamed, rushing forward and lifting his blade high. He wasn't quick enough with the swing, though, as the Khurta pulled himself on top of the battlement and leapt forward, curved blade sinking into the lad's chest as Nobul stared on.

*That's it, just fucking stand there. Watch while everyone around you gets slaughtered. Do nothing to help, like you did nothing for your boy. Like you could do nothing for Rona. Just stand there and fucking die.*

As the lad fell without a sound, the Khurta looked around for his next enemy, bloodlust in his face, battle frenzy upon him. Nobul watched as the Khurta locked eyes with him. Just stood with that hammer in his hand and waited for his reckoning.

The Khurta howled, racing forward, sword raised high. Nobul's hammer smashed a crater in his cheek, silencing his war cry and sending blood and bone and teeth and hair spraying in a filthy explosion. The impact jolted Nobul's fist, up through his arm right to the shoulder. It hurt – an old familiar pain that sparked an old familiar lust.

More Khurtas climbed up over the lip of the wall, eyes flushed with the need for death and killing. They had come a long way for murder. Who was Nobul Jacks to deny it them?

He stepped forward, taking the fight to the enemy, meeting an axe swung at his midriff. His hammer smashed the axe aside as though it were kindling, breaking the haft, carrying on through, ramming into the chest of the first savage. The Khurta's face was a picture, all wide-eyed disbelief as his sternum shattered and he was thrown back, the wind blown from his lungs.

Nobul didn't wait to gloat, hearing a scream from his left as another of the bastards charged in, big old sword raised high above his head. As the blade came down Nobul spun. He felt the weapon cut the air behind him as he brought his hammer around in an arc, smashing the Khurta square in the side of his head. His enemy's scream was cut short as he was battered aside, and this time Nobul couldn't help but see the mirth in it. The bastard had travelled miles, come far from his homeland for a shot at bringing this city to its knees, and there he was, dead, with a last scream of fury wasted on his lips.

As he looked down at that body, Nobul realised he was smiling

80

behind his helm. His lips were pulled right back – so far they almost hurt – and his teeth ground together in a rictus grin of triumph.

*You see! You've been waiting for this. It's who you are. There's no denying you're an evil bastard. Make no mistake, you'll most likely die here, but by the hells there'll be blood aplenty before you . . .*

His helmet clanged as it was struck. The noise rang in his ears like a temple bell and he didn't even realise he was falling until he hit the stone walkway. The blow had turned his helm and he couldn't see. On the way down he dropped his hammer, and as he tried to rise he desperately felt around for it, but it was nowhere near.

With a growl of anger Nobul wrenched the helm from his head, any moment expecting to be stuck with a serrated blade. He turned in time to see two Khurtas bearing down on him, one fat at the middle, the other wiry and old, both covered in filth and smelling of death. They were waiting for him to see them. Waiting for him to turn and look in their eyes and see what they were bringing – to see the murder they were about to do, to feed off his fear.

Nobul would be fucked if he'd give it to them.

He stared back, defiant despite being unarmed and flat on his arse. The fat Khurta carried a maul, most likely what he'd just used to rap around Nobul's head. The other held a spear, its head all serrated so that pulling it out would make even more of a mess than sticking it in.

'Come on, bastards!' Nobul screamed above the din of battle.

The smaller Khurta drew back his spear, ready to strike. A blade flashed out of the night, cutting into his shoulder, shattering the clavicle and coming to rest near the nipple. The Khurta dropped his spear and fell, taking the sword with him as his companion spun, raising his maul. Though Nobul's saviour had lost his weapon he didn't stop, rushing forward with a head-butt that rocked the Khurta back. Another butt of the head and the fat Khurta went reeling over the lip of the battlement, screaming as he fell the hundred feet to his death.

As the man stooped to pull his blade from the Khurtic corpse, Nobul recognised who it was through the gloom. Kilgar turned, his one eye staring down at Nobul, blood flecking his cheek.

'Bit rusty, lad?' he said, half a grin crossing his face.

'Looks like it,' replied Nobul, grasping his hammer and helm and pulling himself to his feet.

Before he could speak a word of thanks a noise rose up above the din of battle to the western side of the wall. Where the magisters had placed themselves to defend that section a mass of foliage had risen from below. It carried a horde of Khurtas with it, branches writhing forward to attack the robed magickers as they vainly tried to defend the city.

No words were exchanged as Kilgar and Nobul raced along the rampart. But then nothing needed to be said.

As he rushed headlong to face whatever sorcery the Khurtas had conjured, Nobul felt his stomach churn. He would happily fight any man or beast, but this was an enemy of a different kind. He'd never liked the notion of magick. Back in that arena days ago he'd seen it first hand, and it had terrified him from his throat to his balls.

But he'd beaten his fear back then. As he tightened his grip on the hammer in his fist he knew he'd be certain to beat it back now.

# TWELVE

Regulus could see men fighting desperately to the north. He could hear their cries of pain and anger, and the clash of steel. Could smell the fear and blood on the air. His fists clenched and a low growl emanated from his throat, but still there was nothing he could do.

Gaze as he might across the great river to the derelict city beyond, there was still no sign of the enemy. How he yearned for them to pour over the crossing and attack the gate he now stood watch over. How his hand itched to draw black steel and cut a bloody swathe through the screaming horde that attacked the wall just yards away.

'Hold your nerve,' shouted the sargent. 'We have our orders. This is our position and we'll bloody well defend it.'

The fear in the man's voice was unmistakable. It sickened Regulus to his stomach. They were useless here, defending a gate that was never going to be assaulted, while to the north their aid was sorely needed.

He turned to his warriors, and each one stared back with anticipation burning in his eyes like a hot brand. Akkula, Kazul, Hagama, Janto, each looking fiercer than the last. Each lusting for battle and ready for the kill.

Who was Regulus Gor to deny them?

They needed no words. Regulus drew his black blade and placed his helm over the locks that cascaded over the pauldrons of his armour. As he turned and made north, his warriors followed, donning their own helms and brandishing their weapons eagerly.

'You there,' shouted the Coldlander sargent. 'Where do you think you're going? We're to hold this bloody position.'

Regulus and his men ignored the weary cries of the man. His voice rose in pitch with every word but it was clear he could do nothing to stop them.

With every step Regulus increased his pace. Nobul Jacks the armoursmith had done his work well, and Regulus hardly felt slowed or restrained as his stride widened until finally he and his warriors were sprinting along the walkway towards the battle.

Coldlanders moved from their path, only too eager to allow the Zatani to run towards the fray. Janto roared his battle lust, and Regulus bared his teeth as the war cry filled him with excitement.

Ahead the city's defenders fought a desperate battle as the painted savages swarmed over the wall. Here and there loose masonry lay across the walkway, and Regulus dodged rubble and bodies as he searched for his first enemy. He didn't have to search for long.

Four warriors, tattooed and scarred and with an animal stench about them, were hacking at the corpses of men they had recently slain. Their frenzy filled Regulus with a hatred he had not felt for many days, and he welcomed it – embraced it – as he leapt forward, his black sword raised.

Two of them fell before the others realised Regulus was even upon them. To their credit, the remaining two raised their weapons to defend themselves before Regulus could cut them down, his blade hacking against their iron axes. One lifted a shield, and Regulus smashed his sword against it three times in succession until the Khurta retreated from the assault in desperation.

The other Khurta made to attack, but before he could strike, Akkula's spear tore through his throat. The young warrior whooped with joy as the Khurta staggered back, his weapon forgotten while he desperately tried to staunch the flow of blood.

Regulus saw the remaining Khurta look up with fear as he saw the formidable Zatani charging towards him. All thoughts of slaughter seemed to fly from his mind and he turned tail, leaping over the battlements to his death rather than face being hacked to pieces by the black-armoured daemons who charged at him.

'Look,' shouted Hagama, raising his blade towards the ramparts further along the wall.

Taking a step forward, Regulus squinted through the night. In the dark he could see not only the desperate sights of battle, but also fell magicks. A writhing mass had covered the wall and was assailing the magick users of the Coldlands. It attacked remorselessly, hacking apart armoured men and robed sorcerers alike.

Regulus smiled, baring his white fangs to the night. This would be the glory he had waited for. This was where he would earn his name.

With a snarl he raced towards the thrashing beast, his warriors at his shoulder. He hacked through the first squirming branch as he ran past, seeing it die in a shower of dried foliage. He ignored the screams from all around him. Ignored the sorcerers retreating in their panic, ignored the armoured knights as they vainly tried to fight back against the onslaught. His only thoughts were of the glory of the kill.

A screaming Khurta charged out of the night, and Regulus hacked him down almost without thinking. He ducked as a twisting branch of foliage swept overhead, knocking Kazul off his feet. Janto leapt in, hacking at the branch with twin axes, roaring above the sound of battle, his cries carrying over the curtain wall and down towards the Khurtas below.

As though seeing them as the greatest threat, the thrashing foliage turned on the Zatani, focusing its assault on the fiercest fighters. The five warriors roared in unison as they fought, hacking at the branches, sending white sap flying as they fought desperately.

Regulus felt something grip his leg, but before he could hack at it he was pulled off his feet and hoisted into the air. His helm flew off into the night though he managed to keep hold of his black blade. Before he could hack at the branch that held him, another wrapped itself around his arm, pulling tight and threatening to tear him in two. Regulus growled against the pain, feeling his muscle and sinew strain as the branches tried to pull him apart. The growl turned into a roar of agony as he was lifted higher. As he was hoisted up he saw out over the battlements, facing the horde that had come to take this city.

*So much for glory. So much for making a legend of your name. Just another rotting corpse for the carrion crows.*

There was a blinding flash of light, and Regulus felt the branches suddenly release him. He fell to the stone parapet, his armour clanging as he landed. The limbs that had tried so effortlessly to pull him apart fell dead beside him.

For a moment all he could do was heave breath into his lungs as the battle raged all around, and before he could stand a robed figure came to kneel by his side. At first he thought they might offer aid. Then he saw the face of an old woman, her expression bereft of sympathy.

'Find the wytchworker that controls the beast,' she said slowly, as though Regulus were some kind of simpleton. 'Kill him and it will destroy his conjuration.' At first he thought he should be offended that this old crone would talk down to him in such a manner, but as he gazed into her eyes he found himself strangely drawn to her, irresistibly compelled to do whatever she asked of him.

'Don't just sit there,' she said, and waved him off.

Regulus leapt to his feet, sword still in hand. 'To me,' he cried as he ran past his warriors, hacking at a branch as he went. The rest of the Zatani pulled themselves away from combat, following as Regulus ran blindly towards the lip of the battlements. He didn't pause as he reached the edge of the wall, leaping over the lip and grasping one of the limbs that had crawled up the hundred feet from the ground. With his warriors close behind he began to climb down the mass of foliage, jumping from branch to branch with the sure-footedness of a forest animal. He passed several Khurtas making their way up the wall as he did so but he paid them no heed – the words of the red-robed witch were still at the forefront of his mind. He had to find this 'wytchworker' and despatch him. That was all that mattered.

Ten feet from the bottom of the wall, Regulus could see a huge gathering of Khurtas making their way towards the base of the foliage. He paused, his eyes following the green mass of branches as they snaked from the base of the curtain wall and past the waiting Khurtas.

In the distance he could just make out a single figure kneeling in the dirt. He was surrounded by a guard of around a dozen huge warriors, bigger than any other Coldlanders Regulus had ever seen.

'There,' he said, pointing through the night, showing his warriors their target. 'Kill the shaman.'

Before any of them could move, Hagama gave a howl, leaping from the greenery and into the mass of bodies waiting at the bottom of the wall. Akkula was quick to follow and Regulus felt his heart begin to race before he also threw himself into the fray.

The last thing the Khurtas had expected was to be attacked at the base of the wall, and Regulus took delight in the fact he had cut down half a dozen of their number before they realised what was happening.

Though they fought with fury, Regulus could still see no way through to the shaman. For the most fleeting of moments he wondered whether he would die here, cut down in a flurry of Khurtic blades, until there was a tumultuous noise from above. Blue fire cut the sky from atop the battlements, searing a corridor through the Khurtas. It blasted them aside, cooking flesh and blackening the earth.

Now Regulus could see a path to his target.

Before he could move, Janto cut his way through the lightly armoured Khurtas, heeding Regulus' words and making for the shaman who still knelt in the dirt. Regulus was quick to follow, reluctant to allow Janto the glory of killing the wytchworker.

As Hagama, Kazul and Akkula vented their ire on the Khurtas, Janto and Regulus ran forward. The branches that ran along the ground from the base of the wall began to converge, pulsating with unnatural life as they snaked back towards the shaman.

As the Zatani warriors raced towards him, his bodyguard began to move forward. They lumbered into Janto's path, hefting their massive warhammers, their faces showing no emotion as they created a phalanx of bloated flesh and muscle.

Janto threw himself against them, howling as he charged, axes raised high. He ducked the laboured swing of a hammer, which thudded into the ground sending a sod of earth flying into the air, and buried an axe in the thick skull of the first giant. As it fell he wrenched his axe free, turning to face his next foe as another warhammer swung in at him. This time he was not so quick, and barely had time to dodge away as the hammer came in. He took a glancing blow to the shoulder but it was still enough to fling him back, sending him sprawling to the ground.

Regulus took advantage as Janto fell. The Sho'tana warrior could take care of himself; there were still enemies to slay.

As Regulus neared the shaman he saw his emaciated arms were buried deep in the earth. From where they dug in, foliage sprouted from the ground, running in a pulsating thread towards the curtain wall. Where his flesh ended and the branches began was impossible to tell, and something about it turned Regulus' stomach. He fought back bile as he raised his blade. The shaman didn't look up, so completely was he transfixed by his own sorcery. While Janto took on the bloated bodyguards the shaman was undefended. Regulus did not pause, hacking down and severing the shaman's arms at the elbow. The old man screamed, reeling back, raising his stumps high as they spewed white blood into the air. Another swipe of Regulus' blade saw the shaman fall headless to the ground.

Janto roared, and Regulus turned to see he had defeated another two of the gigantic Khurtas. His dark armour shone in the moonlight, slick with blood, and his sky-blue eyes peered from behind his helm as he searched the night for his next victim.

Already the branches that had sprung from the arms of the shaman were beginning to wither and die. They blackened, crumbling fast, and Regulus could see their way of escape would be cut off if the foliage that had grown up the curtain wall did likewise.

'We have to go,' he shouted, running past Janto. Regulus didn't wait to see if the Sho'tana warrior heeded his warning, but sprinted for the base of the wall where his other warriors still fought.

The Khurtas had massed now, and Regulus took solace in the fact their screams rose high. His own warriors only roared back in fury as they cut down the savages who swarmed all around them.

Regulus fought his way back to the wall and Janto added his bulk so they could push their way through the mass of bodies.

Those Khurtas that did not relent were hacked aside. When Regulus reached Akkula, Hagama and Kazul he turned, his back against the wall.

'Climb!' he bellowed. 'And climb quickly, we don't have much time.'

Kazul was the first to leap up onto the branches. Already Regulus could see that they were blackening, going brittle, and he knew they would not hold for long.

Akkula was next, climbing the wall like an ape, as the three remaining Zatani defended the bottom of the wall. The Khurtas were wary of attacking now after seeing so many of their kind slain, but still they jabbed in with their spears, eyes wide with fear and bloodlust.

Regulus turned to Hagama, about to bellow at him to move, when an arrow hit the warrior in the throat. Hagama fell to his knee, blade falling from his grip as he grasped the black shaft protruding from his neck.

Before Regulus could rush to his warrior's side, Janto grabbed the pauldron of his armour.

'He's gone,' growled the Sho'tana.

Regulus shook off his grip, moving forward to aid Hagama, but the Khurtas were already taking advantage of the stricken Zatani. One stabbed forward, finding a gap between the black plates on the warrior's torso, the curved blade sinking deep.

'We have to go now!' Janto cried, just as he sank an axe into a Khurtic skull.

Regulus knew he had to leave, had to make it to the top of the wall before his escape was cut off, but he could not drag his eyes from Hagama. They had grown up together. Hagama had been with him every step, never yielding, never faltering even when the Gor'tana had been brought low and they were forced into exile.

*And he would not want you to die here. He would want you to live. To avenge him.*

Regulus roared, long and loud, sweeping his sword left and then right in a last defiant display, before leaping onto the vines and branches that still held fast to the curtain wall.

He could see Janto above, making his way up the wall with ease.

Kazul and Akkula were further ahead, one of them, Regulus couldn't tell which, dragging a screaming Khurta off the ladder of branches as he passed. The foliage was becoming more brittle with every yard they climbed, and more than once a handhold crumbled in Regulus' grip. Over the sounds of battle, he could hear the foliage cracking as it dried, rotting with every passing moment.

An arrow hit a branch next to his head, which shattered into brittle shards. More arrows followed as the Khurtas saw the Zatani were vulnerable as they climbed.

A sudden volley rained down from above as someone, Regulus couldn't tell who, organised archers up on the wall to cover their climb.

The branch he held suddenly broke, and Regulus slipped several feet before finding his grip. He was near the top now, Janto had just made it over the wall, but he still had at least twenty feet to go and it looked as though the wall of greenery might collapse at any moment.

Regulus moved with more urgency, ignoring the sounds of battle raging around him. All that mattered was reaching the top, surviving, so that he might avenge his brother Hagama.

As the lip of the battlements came within reach, the wall of foliage moved, cracking and grinding like a beast in its death throes. It lurched backwards, and Regulus felt the cold bite of panic in his stomach as the wall slipped beyond his reach. To his left a mass of vegetation fell away, dropping to the earth far below. Regulus made to leap, but the branches at his feet gave way before he could. He reached out an arm, one last attempt to save himself before he plunged a hundred feet to the earth below. His hand gripped something hard, solid, and for a moment his fall was abated.

Looking up he saw a face he recognised. Nobul Jacks stood at the battlements, one hand gripping the wall, the other reaching out with his hammer.

'Come on,' yelled the Coldlander through gritted teeth.

Regulus leapt, still holding the hammer, hoping against hope that Nobul Jacks was as strong as he looked. The wall of branches collapsed behind him as he jumped and Regulus held his breath as he swung, hitting the wall, expecting to fall, but Nobul held him fast. Regulus scrabbled at the wall, clawed fingers finding purchase as Nobul hauled him over the edge. They both landed in a heap, Regulus heaving breath into his lungs.

Nobul stood, and Regulus glanced up at him. 'I owe you my life again, Black Helm,' he said with a nod.

'There'll be plenty of chances to pay me back,' Nobul replied. 'Of that I have little doubt.'

As Nobul walked back along the wall, now littered with dead, Regulus glanced across, seeing his own warriors breathing hard from their climb. From the corner of his eye he also saw the woman in the red robes who had compelled him so convincingly to fling himself at the enemy. She smiled, offering him a nonchalant wave of her hand, as though that would be reward enough for his efforts and the loss of Hagama.

Regulus thought little on it.

The glory of what he had done would be more than enough reward.

# THIRTEEN

The sights, the sounds, the smells were not what she had come to expect from battle. But then Kaira had never experienced battle on this scale before. She had never faced enemies in such overwhelming numbers, never seen them fight with such savagery. And neither had she felt so helpless as she sat astride a horse beside her queen. All she could do was watch as the city's defenders laid down their lives. How she would have loved to charge forward, to stand shoulder to shoulder with them. To smash the Khurtas back over the wall, to scream in the face of their hatred. Sitting back from the conflict in relative safety she felt powerless.

Janessa watched intently from her horse, and Kaira took no small amount of pride in the way the young queen faced her first battle. Kaira had seen seasoned warriors show more fear. Had seen grown men flee when facing more favourable odds, but Janessa merely looked on, seeming to take in every yell of pain or anger, watching silently as enemies were flung from the wall and her bannermen went down with arrows in their chests.

The more time that passed the more agitated Kaira became. This was pointless, and dangerous. They were of no use here, Janessa least of all. There was no way she could be allowed to make a stand on the battlements beside her army. She would never inspire any troops from here; she was merely putting herself in harm's way.

Before Kaira could order them to retreat back to the safety of the palace, her worst fears became manifest. A boulder the size of a cowshed smashed into the parapet in front of them, flinging men-at-arms from the battlements along with shards of masonry.

As the massive rock crashed into a nearby building, Janessa's horse reared. A Sentinel took half a merlon to the chest and was hammered to the ground. Men shouted in panic and Kaira desperately tried to steady her horse as she looked to the queen. But Janessa's steed had calmed and now stood resolute, the girl staring up at the battlements defiantly.

Kaira followed her gaze, seeing that in the wake of the giant missile a host of Khurtas had come crawling over the wall. Some smiled, licking their blades in anticipation of the kill. Others whooped with joy, falling on the stunned defenders like wolves on their prey.

Looking back, Kaira saw that Janessa's hand had strayed to the Helsbayn at her side. Her eyes stared intently. She wanted to join in with the battle. Wanted to defend her city and stand by her armies.

*But she is not ready. She is but a child and will be killed if you allow her to fight.*

'Protect the queen!' Kaira shouted, kicking her horse in front of the Sentinels. 'Get her back to the palace. Let nothing stop you.'

Janessa protested as the Sentinels began to change their formation and one of them grabbed the bridle of her horse, but her words were lost in the commotion. Kaira watched as they guided her along the cobbled avenue and back towards the Crown District but she did not follow them. Could not follow them.

She knew she should have gone along, should have been at her queen's side, but something kept her rooted. If Queen Janessa could not help the stricken defenders hold off the Khurtic horde at the wall, then it was Kaira's duty to do it in her stead.

She kicked her steed, feeling its eagerness as she rode towards the battlements and the Khurtas who flooded over the wall. She reined the horse in some feet from the foot of the stairway, hearing it snort in frustration when she leapt from the saddle. As she took the stairs three at a time Kaira pulled her sword from its sheath, feeling the ache in a wrist that hadn't quite healed from the wound Azai Dravos had inflicted.

*It is nothing. A mere trifle. It will not stop you from carrying out Vorena's will. You are an instrument of righteousness honed and tempered in the flames of battle, ready to strike down the enemies of your gods and your queen. Nothing can stop you.*

The first Khurta barely had time to acknowledge her before her sword cleaved his head from his shoulders. Kaira's blade rang as it cut the air and her muscles protested slightly as she overexerted in her impatience for the first kill.

*Take control. This is not a game. This is not the practice yard. This is real.*

She gritted her teeth as another Khurta came running. Stooping in a low defensive stance and clearing her lungs with a single breath. All emotion was gone in an instant, to be replaced by everything she had ever learned, from being a child in the Temple of Autumn to a woman grown.

*You are Vorena's will made manifest. A bright flame in the dark.*

The Khurta's attack was savage, unfettered. His limbs powerful, his expression fierce. He never stood a chance as Kaira ducked low, reading his first clumsy swing before it ever came and skewering him below the ribs. She braced her shoulder as his dead weight hit her, then let him drop, levering her blade free with a foot planted on his chest.

'On your feet,' she bellowed at a young soldier cowering in the crenellated shadow of the battlements. 'All of you. Fight!'

Another Khurta ran at her. A swift hack of her sword and he fell screaming.

Seeing her cutting down the enemy so easily seemed to instil some courage in the wall's defenders. Two men stumbled hesitantly to her side. The boy cowering beside her slowly rose to his feet, the sword in his hand held limply, but at least he still held it.

'Form rank,' she ordered, and the men obeyed, making a line across the parapet that guarded the stairway.

More Khurtas were already making their way over the wall. Kaira stooped to pick up a fallen shield, linking it with the three men that stood at her shoulders just as the first of the Khurtas came screaming at them. His attack was wild, flailing his axe against the shield wall. Kaira and the men beside her stood resolute as more Khurtas joined the fray. A break in the attack and Kaira struck out, the tip of her sword opening a throat. No sooner had one Khurta fallen than another took his place. Behind the attackers, yet more were making their way over the wall.

'Stand fast,' Kaira said through gritted teeth. The four of them were all that stood between these Khurtas and the city. They would not be allowed over the wall without a fight but, despite her courage, Kaira knew there was little she would be able to do to stop them. Eventually she and the rest of these men would fall under the Khurtas' superior numbers.

A sword hit the top of her shield, denting it. The man to her right suddenly screamed and went down. Kaira shouted at him to get back on his feet but her words were lost in the melee. Another blow struck her shield, knocking her back a step, and she had to fight the anger, not let it take control.

All she could hear was screaming, rage spewed at her in the night, but it was not just rage – it was pain too, and fear.

The assault on her shield abated. Someone called out from behind the attacking Khurtas but not in their foul northern tongue. The sound of battle drifted across the battlements from beyond the mass of Khurtas and one by one the savages disengaged to face this new threat.

As Kaira took a moment to help the man to her right find his feet, she saw that more defenders had come across the battlements to repel the enemy. There was a flash of steel, a glint of bronze in the torchlight. Khurtas fell from the walkway and down into the city. Some leapt back over the parapet. Kaira could not help but allow herself a smile of relief as she recognised men of the Wyvern Guard, hacking and slaying with abandon. They were emotionless in their labours, every sword stroke measured, powerful, deadly. Among the relief she felt was also a pang of envy. These were peerless warriors, dedicated to their art, slaying the enemy with abandon. For a fleeting moment she thought back to the Temple of Autumn – to her sisters. How she yearned to be standing beside them now, Shieldmaidens all, fighting the enemy to the death.

*But that can never be. Samina was right – you abandoned your sisters long ago.*

As the last of the Khurtas was defeated, Kaira took a moment to look along the wall. As far as she could see the Khurtas had been slain to a man. Parts of the wall were smashed to ruins and bodies lay all along the battlements. But they had won.

Far below on the plain in front of the city, a horn blew loud and clear in the night. At the sound, the horde began to retreat back to the north, leaving their dead and dying behind on the field.

Kaira stared out at the retreating mass as it moved out of bow range of the wall and realised her sword was held tight in her grip, her breath coming in short, laboured gasps. Loosening her grasp on the weapon she felt her hand begin to shake.

'You all right?'

Kaira looked up at the familiar voice, stifling a smile as she saw Merrick looking at her with concern.

'I am,' she replied. 'Just . . .'

'Yeah, I know,' he said. 'It's not what I was expecting either.'

He grinned, but Kaira could see beyond the smile. Behind his eyes were fear and pain. Despite the fact he looked every inch the warrior in his armour, he was just as scared as she was, and she took a step towards him.

'How have you been?' she asked. 'Since you joined your father?'

Merrick shrugged. 'I've been tattooed, shot at with arrows, chased by Khurtas, screamed at by sword-wielding maniacs and I think I just killed three men, maybe four. But there have been shit times as well.'

He smiled again, showing his teeth, showing some of the carefree Merrick of old, and for the briefest of moments Kaira smiled too.

Without another word he offered her a nod, and turned to join the rest of the Wyvern Guard.

After watching him go, Kaira glanced north one last time towards the enemy. They had been beaten back but not defeated. They would return soon enough. And she could only hope she would get another opportunity to face them with her sword in hand.

# FOURTEEN

Whenever she'd been able, Rag had avoided the Rafts like the plague. Calling it a shithole would have been generous to shit. Pinching from Eastgate, and even Dockside, was risky enough, but the Rafts was one place you never wanted to get caught with your hand in someone's purse. Not that there was much worth pinching there.

As she watched the last of the slum dwellers walking past, it reminded her what a good decision she'd always made in leaving this place well alone.

The Greencoats were herding them out now, and being none too polite about it neither. Men, women and children, all looking like they'd not seen soap and a flannel for far too long, were being beasted like animals into the city. Every now and again some ugly-looking bastard would try and argue, try and make a fuss, but they were soon quieted with the prod of a baton or an angry shove. It didn't look like the Greencoats were taking any shit, and Rag could hardly blame them. You didn't fuck about with the residents of the Rafts – not if you knew what was good for you.

As relieved as she was that there'd be no dodgy, robbing bastards waiting for her in the shadows of the Rafts, she knew it would be no easy job getting through now. For some reason the Greencoats were evacuating the whole district – if you could call it that – and she guessed they'd be none too happy with her just strolling on by.

She knew she had to get through, though, weren't no choice about that now. The rolled-up parchment with the black seal that pressed against her inside pocket was enough of a reminder of that. Bastian wanted his message delivered, and what Bastian wanted he'd bloody well get or someone would pay the price for it. Rag didn't reckon she fancied paying what he'd charge if she fucked this up.

'Need to keep our heads down,' she said to Yarrick. He just nodded his reply, looking on at the scene. He was nervous, fearful, but Rag doubted he could be any more scared than she was. They were delivering that parchment to someone at the other side of the Rafts and she wasn't looking forward to finding out who.

The pair of them waited as long as they could until the crowd that was moving out of the shanty town thinned down to a trickle. For their part, the Greencoats seemed eager to have this business finished, and it was obvious there was something going down. Rag could only hope she had time to finish her own business before it all kicked off.

'Let's go,' she whispered eventually, when it looked like there was enough of a gap in the bodies to make a move. The dark would give them cover enough to make it past the Greencoats but they'd still have to be careful. She didn't fancy getting coshed over the head for her trouble. There was enough to worry about as it was.

Yarrick followed close as she struck out from the wall they'd been squatting behind. None of the people being evacuated gave them a second glance. Luckily, none of the Greencoats seemed to take much notice of anyone trying to get back into the Rafts, so concerned were they with ushering people out.

There were a few yards of open ground as Rag padded quietly over the rickety wooden platform that had been built across the river. Further on was a jumble of shacks to hide in if they weren't quick enough to go unseen. Yarrick stayed with her every step, but he weren't quite as light on his feet. In the quiet of night, if she'd been on the rob, that might have been a problem, but there was noise enough to cover their tracks from all the complaining and shouting going on.

When they made it behind the first wooden hovel they stopped, breathing deep from the run and the fear. Rag peered round the corner, relieved that no one had seen them. She looked up at Yarrick to see he looked just as nervous as ever. This was work he was unused to, and Rag began to wonder exactly what Friedrik – poor, dead fucker that he was – had employed him for in the first place. He was too nervy for a pincher, too scared for a strongarm, and certainly weren't quick enough with his wits to be kept round for the laughs. Took all sorts, she supposed.

Patting him on the arm she moved further into the densely packed dwellings. The stink rose up and hit her nostrils – fishy and clammy and shitty all at once. Here and there the wood under her feet would creak and give a little, and more than once she thought she might go right through to the river below. Ignoring the fear rising in her heart with every step, they eventually made it to the midway point of the river.

Voices rose up here and there from within some of the buildings. Folk who'd ignored the Greencoats, no doubt; deciding to fuck authority and stay despite what they'd been told. Part of her admired them for it; she'd never been a fan of the Greencoats, after all. Another part of her thought they were just bloody stupid. There must have been some reason for the evacuation, even if it was just the threat of the Khurtas coming screaming across from the Old City. Either way, that weren't her concern right now.

As she and Yarrick made their way further on, there was light up ahead. A lantern dangled there off a stanchion and for a moment, while she stared at that light just swinging in the breeze, she got a thought in her head.

*Don't you do it, Rag. You know what tends to happen when you get those thoughts. They've got you in as much shit as they've got you out, and Bastian ain't the kind of bloke to fuck about with. When he's given an order and it's been disobeyed it never ends well for whoever's done the disobeying.*

Rag padded slowly towards the light until she was stood beneath it. She knew she was exposed here, but just couldn't get that mischievous thought out of her head. Absently, her hand strayed to the inside pocket of her coat and she pulled out the letter Bastian had given her. She looked at Yarrick, who saw what she was doing. She reckoned he was too scared to care, because he said nothing as she broke the seal and took a look.

Even as she read she knew it was wrong, and when she saw what was writ on that little bit of parchment she mouthed a silent curse. Cursed Friedrik for teaching her those letters. Cursed her curiosity. Cursed herself for getting mixed up in such a shit of a business.

But she'd seen it now, and there weren't nothing she could do about that. There just weren't any unknowing something once you knew . . .

They were going to open one of the gates. In her hand was a message to the Khurtas telling them when and where: the Lych Gate on the following night. Bastian and the rest of the Guild were going to open a gate and let the Khurtas wander right into the city.

Rag stared at those words, reading them through a third time, just to make sure she understood right. There was no mistaking it. Surely this couldn't be allowed to happen. Surely she couldn't be the one to deliver a message to the Khurtas that would see gods knew how many innocent folk get slaughtered because of what she'd done.

*So what you gonna do, Rag? You gonna lose that there message? You gonna pretend you delivered it and try to con Bastian into thinking the Khurtas are on the way? He'll cut your throat if he finds out. Hells, he'll most likely cut your throat just for the laughs, but if he gets a sniff you've gone against him he'll kill you surer than shit, and it won't be quick.*

Rag rolled the letter back up and tucked it in her shirt. 'Let's go then,' she said to Yarrick, before moving back off through the shacks.

The further they went through the Rafts the deader and darker the place got. There was no more chatting in houses, no more torches to light the way, and the wooden platform underfoot got slicker and more rickety with every careful step across the river they made. More than once Yarrick slipped on the greasy planks but to his credit he didn't cry out and give them away.

Before long they'd almost made it to the other side of the river. There the Rafts petered out, joining the Old City, and Rag slowed up, peering through the dark for any sign of their contact.

'What now?' Yarrick asked, breathing hard. Despite the lack of light she could see his head glistening with sweat, even in the cold of the night.

'How the fucking fuck do I know, what now?' Rag answered, her own fear coming out as annoyance, not that she felt even a bit guilty for it.

The pair of them stood in the dark, just listening. From the north they could hear the sounds of battle. The night sky was lit up with fire and alive with screaming and shouting. As scared as she was, Rag was not a little relieved she weren't stuck in the middle of that.

There was sudden movement from the Old City. Though they could hardly see in the black, it was obvious someone was coming. Rag froze, feeling Yarrick do the same as the figure walked close, not making a sound. She peered through the night but couldn't make out any features. It could have been anyone, maybe someone from the Rafts or the Town, desperate and alone. Maybe they'd come tooled up and on the rob.

As the night was suddenly lit by a mass of burning arrows, Rag saw it weren't no desperate robber.

The face was painted in a mask of black and white stripes, the eyes were deader than a fish's, hair all shaved and tied back in a knot. He was naked from the waist up, body lean and painted just like his face, and in the brief flash of light Rag was sure she saw the glint of a blade.

She held her breath as the night darkened again. Yarrick was next to her; she could hear him breathing hard and it was obvious he'd seen the Khurta too. She only hoped he didn't do or say anything stupid enough to get them killed.

Another flash of light, and this time Rag saw the Khurta had moved. He was standing right in front of her now, same blank expression but this time palm held out like he wanted her to pay some kind of toll.

With a shaking hand, Rag reached in her pocket and took out the rolled-up message. There was no doubt in her mind that handing it over was the wrong thing to do, but she'd be fucked if she was gonna try and double-cross Bastian now – not with this evil-looking bastard standing right next to her.

She pressed the paper into the Khurta's hand and felt him take it from her. Another shot of fire brightened the night, and in that light Rag saw the Khurta had disappeared, leaving her and Yarrick wheezing and trying not to shit themselves.

'Can we get the fuck out of here now?' said Yarrick, not even trying to hide the fact he was almost crying like a baby.

'Shit right we can,' Rag replied, turning back towards the city and padding off as fast as her feet and the slick wooden boards would allow.

The pair of them made good time back through the Rafts. Rag didn't give a damn about stealth now, she just wanted to be away from this place as fast as she could, and Yarrick certainly weren't complaining neither.

They'd made it to about halfway back when Yarrick grabbed her shoulder.

'What the fuck's that?' he asked, pointing up towards the wall that ran northwards.

Rag squinted through the gloom, seeing something glowing atop the battlements in the distance.

'Fucked if I kn—'

A bright ball of flame catapulted from behind the wall before she could finish her sentence. It soared towards the Rafts, and was swiftly followed by a second and a third. Rag could only stand and watch in awe as the first ball of flame went over their heads, smashing into the shacks behind them and exploding in an inferno of light and heat.

It reminded her of the mess those ships had made of the southern half of the city, but this time it weren't the enemy doing the burning.

'What the fuck?' shouted Yarrick, as the other two balls of fire smashed into the Rafts behind them, each one closer than the last.

'Move,' Rag yelled, not waiting to see if Yarrick had the sense to heed her warning.

Already there was more fire in the sky. Rag could feel the heat at her back – whatever they were using to burn the Rafts it was doing its job, and no mistake. Must have been oil in those burning missiles, and it didn't take a magister to work out what would happen if they didn't move sharpish.

She could feel the heat as more fire shot overhead. Sense the explosion rip through the shacks behind and the vibration of it shake the boards beneath her feet.

*You need to move that arse of yours, or you'll end up so much charred bone at the bottom of the Storway.*

Another explosion ripped up the ground behind her, knocking her over. Rag's head hit the hard wooden boards and she floundered for a moment, trying to regain her senses and get the fuck moving.

Something whined in her ears, something high-pitched that set her teeth on edge, and it wasn't until she stumbled to her feet that she realised it was Yarrick.

He was on fire, just standing there screaming. Rag took a step towards him but thought better of it. Weren't nothing she could do now anyway. She squinted, wanting to shut her eyes, but she forced herself to look as he dropped to his knees, the fire consuming him, burning hotter than the hells as the oil that had spilled all over him took flame. He tried to say something, maybe begging for her to help him, but she couldn't quite make it out as he began to choke and writhe. Rag felt sick to her stomach as she watched on helpless.

*You can't stand around staring at this all night or you'll be bloody next.*

Feeling a short sting of guilt Rag dragged her eyes away, setting off at a run before another ball of fire made ashes out of her too.

Up ahead she could see other people running – those too stubborn or frail to leave the Rafts when they'd been told, now doing their best to avoid their fate. She stumbled past an old man, thinking for a moment that she should help him but then quickly reconsidering. Helping him would most likely have meant both of them dying. Besides, this was the Rafts. He weren't living here because he was nice and kindly. This place had a reputation and there were plenty who'd say anyone burned to death here got what they deserved. Some might even say it was a fate *she* deserved for all the things she'd done.

Still, Rag wasn't gonna hang around and accept it.

She could see the edge of the city now. See the gap in the wall. Not far, only a few more yards and she'd be safe.

Keep running.

Don't look back.

The walkway to her right erupted in flame and Rag was knocked off her feet again. She could smell smouldering clothes and burning oil. The soles of her shoes were scorched, her hair smoking, but she wouldn't go down that fucking easy. If she had to sprint back into the city a screaming, burning lantern she'd bloody well do it.

With the world on fire, Rag picked herself back up and ran.

# FIFTEEN

The Helsbayn was heavy at Janessa's side. For so long it had fuelled her like an elixir but now it felt like a burden, as though not drawing it and spilling Khurtic blood had made it sullen at her hip. She gripped the hilt, feeling the cold of it on her palm and through her fingers, and it seemed to make her equally as resentful that she had not wielded the blade in battle.

How many had died on the wall today? A thousand? Five? It hurt her that she couldn't do more, but then she was a rallying figure. A shepherdess around which the defenders of the city must flock, must fight for, must believe in. There was no way she could be risked. But Janessa would not shy away from the fight. She was determined to face up to it like any warrior queen should.

'The Rafts,' she said, as she was guided back to the palace of Skyhelm.

The Sentinels surrounding her looked on in confusion. 'Majesty,' said one, 'we must get you back to the palace. The bombardment from the south could mean the streets are—'

'The Rafts,' Janessa repeated. Even she knew there was strength in her voice. She had power now and none of her bodyguards would make her repeat herself a third time.

The Sentinels led the way to the south-western extent of the city. Much of it lay in ruins, blackened and burned by the bombardment raining in from the harbour. Janessa felt almost moved to tears but she knew no amount of weeping would repair the damage or bring back those who had been burned alive in the onslaught. Besides, there may well be many more dead before sunrise – how many tears could she shed before she ran dry?

As they reached the wall to the south-west of Steelhaven, Janessa could see the row of trebuchets were already waiting to begin their deluge. A steady stream of bedraggled folk were making their way north into the city, and sallow faces glanced her way as they moved past. Though she had done her best to unify her people in the face of the Khurtic attack, she knew there was no love here. These people were the lowest the city had to offer. She could only begin to imagine what they had suffered over the years and yet there was nothing she could offer them but the destruction of their homes.

She watched for some time, seeing those faces file past, knowing what was to come was necessary for the safety of the city. The enemy could so easily flood over the wooden bridge the Rafts provided. Its destruction was a necessary evil – yet another she would have to carry on her already overburdened shoulders. Janessa knew there was no choice in this and the more she watched her people walk to the relative safety of the city the less she was moved. There was no time for lamenting. The Khurtas had to be stopped.

When finally the Greencoats had ushered the last of the people from their homes and taken their place some distance away, a serjeant shouted for the order to fire.

Three trebuchets up on the wall had their payloads lit. Even from such a distance, Janessa could feel the heat as the oil went up in flames. At the pull of a lever the arm of the first trebuchet swung up, unleashing a fiery ball upon the Rafts. She could only watch as it soared through the night, smashing into the shacks in the distance. The first missile was closely followed by two more and within quick moments the Rafts was up in flames.

Janessa forced herself to witness the act. Seeing the fire consume part of her city, no matter how rundown that part was, twisted her insides.

*You must let this feed you. You must put this loss with all the others and let it fuel the hate you have for Amon Tugha.*

The trebuchets were swiftly reloaded and the serjeant shouted again. More fire in the sky. More flames rampaging through the Rafts.

A scream went up from below, quickly followed by another, and Janessa felt her heart stop. She had known they would never be able to clear the place out completely, at least not in time, but she had not thought to witness anyone's death.

But she knew she must. What was it Odaka had said to her all those weeks ago? *For every decision you make there will be consequences.*

Another scream, so high-pitched Janessa wanted to cover her ears, but she didn't. She stood and watched, hand still on the pommel of the Helsbayn, though it gave her little comfort now.

Someone came running from the burning wooden buildings still in flames, but they collapsed before they could reach the city. And still she watched, drinking it all in. Feeding on the pain and the hurt.

It took a full hour for the Rafts to burn, the rotten timbers finally collapsing into the Storway to be swept off into the sea along with anyone still trapped inside.

As she stared across the river towards the enemy beyond, Janessa vowed there would be a reckoning for this. Vowed she would not be ushered away to safety again while her city suffered. When the Khurtas attacked once more she would take the fight to them.

She didn't speak as her Sentinels guided her back to Skyhelm. Her hand trembled at the reins and if she had spoken she might have betrayed some weakness, might have sobbed, might have given away some tremor in her voice.

When finally they got back, the palace seemed empty. Dead. And she stood helpless within it. The palace walls rose high and proud, its defenders fearless, but she knew they would be as nothing when the Khurtas came. There would be little they could do against the horde, even here in this place where she had felt safe all her life. But Janessa did not care. She did not fear the enemy, she only feared defeat.

'The Khurtas are repelled,' said a voice that echoed through the hall.

Janessa saw who it was and something soured in her mouth.

Baroness Isabelle Magrida stood in all her glory, formal regalia glinting in the torchlight. She had foregone any jewellery, though, and her face was stern. Where her son Leon hid was anyone's guess. Janessa could only hope he was cowering somewhere beneath his bed and would remain far from her sight.

How Janessa loathed this woman now. The Baroness had been given shelter here in the palace ever since the destruction of Dreldun. She and her son had accepted that shelter and shown their gratitude with nothing but arrogance and disdain. For a fleeting moment Janessa considered how satisfying it might be to turn the woman out into the cold and let the Khurtas deal with her, but quickly put the thought to the back of her mind. Besides, it was more likely the Khurtas would be the ones to suffer when faced with Isabelle Magrida.

'Victory is ours, for the night,' the Baroness continued. 'The defenders of this city have acquitted themselves with honour and courage. You should be proud.'

Janessa could only stare. What was Isabelle after now? Was she goading her? If she was, Janessa was struggling to discern the barb, but from what she knew of the woman there had to be one somewhere.

'I am proud,' said Janessa. 'Of them. Not of me.'

'Don't be so hard on yourself. There was little else you could do.'

'No? Little I could do other than stand and watch as my city burns?'

'You mean the Rafts? That was necessary. A pragmatic decision that had to be made. And remember, the city has been suffering for days. We are beset, my child. Do not blame yourself for this.'

Janessa felt fury rising within her. All the pain, all the misery of the past days rose within her like a well overflowing.

'I am not your child!' she screamed. 'I am no one's child. I am a queen and I have just watched my people die. Innocents who were killed on my order. I am to blame for that. Me!'

Isabelle nodded solemnly. There was no trace of malice in her expression, no deceit. Hers was a look of genuine sympathy.

'And that is your burden . . . Majesty. I have felt it too, as did my husband, Arlor rest him. But it is better that a hundred perish than a thousand. Than ten thousand. We must all do what is necessary.'

Janessa just stared into the woman's eyes, looking for some excuse, some trace of scorn, some trickery, but there was none there. Slowly she nodded.

Before Janessa could speak any word of thanks, the door to the hall opened. Kaira walked in; even from this distance Janessa could see the blood that spotted her bodyguard's armour. She could only hope that it was not Kaira's.

'Majesty, the wall stands. Victory is ours for the night.'

'Yes, I . . .' Janessa turned but Baroness Isabelle had already left the hall. She looked back to Kaira, whose eyes stared out with a fire from behind the blood staining her face. 'Victory is ours.'

Even as she said the words there was no thrill in it. No sense of triumph.

As though to confirm as much, Kaira stepped in close. 'They will be back, Majesty. As soon as they have regained their breath, they will attack again.'

Janessa nodded, resisting the temptation to grasp the hilt of the Helsbayn.

'And we will be waiting.'

# SIXTEEN

Waylian's ears were ringing so bad it hurt his head. There were bruises on his body but he couldn't remember for the life of him where they'd come from. He'd been in a fight all right, there was no forgetting that, but no one had struck him. Surely he shouldn't have been aching this much.

He sat in his small chamber, just remembering the horror of the previous night. He had tried to sleep since, but all he'd managed were a few minutes before the nightmares in his head jolted him awake. As if the Khurtas hadn't been bad enough, the magick of their wytchworkers had left an indelible imprint in Waylian's mind. That writhing, thrashing thing reaching over the wall. So swift, so deadly.

The horror of it had almost made killing a man seem insignificant.

Waylian could still see his face, still hear his voice screaming in anger and pain.

'I'm sorry,' he had said.

*Bloody sorry?*

It was too late for sorry now, but what did it matter anyway? It wasn't the first man Waylian had killed. Many more attacks like the one last night and it would most likely not be the last. Kill or be killed definitely seemed to be the order of the day – and Waylian was in no mood to be dead any time soon.

He opened his mouth wide, trying to relieve the ringing in his head. He made a sound through his nose. Stuck a finger in one ear and waggled it. That seemed to work a little as the noise changed from a ringing to a dull drone. It was almost as though someone were calling his na—

Something hit him over the back of the head. It cleared the ringing in his ears instantly and he turned to see Magistra Gelredida standing there looking none too pleased.

'Are you deaf, Grimm?' she demanded.

He scrambled to his feet. 'Er . . . no, Magistra. I was just . . .'

'Come along. There is much to do before the next assault.'

She turned and left the room, Waylian following obediently in her wake.

*The next assault.* The words filled him with dread. Part of him wanted to believe the Khurtas had thrown everything they had at them the first night, but he knew that was unlikely. They'd probably just been testing the city's defences and tonight would be even worse – more savage, more deadly.

Waylian was about as far from a battlefield general as you could get, but even he knew that first attack had cost the city dear. As he and his mistress moved through the tower he began to get an idea of just how dear.

Raven Knights and magisters filled the corridors and chambers. The dead and dying were strewn all around being tended by those magisters and apothecaries fit enough to offer them aid. One Raven Knight reclined against a wall, his eyes staring blankly, his leg missing below the knee. It had been hastily bandaged but blood still pooled around him. Beside him was one of his fellow knights, his breastplate removed, a hole in his chest. Waylian couldn't tell if he was still breathing or not.

More bodies were laid out on the next floor down. These were clearly corpses, their faces covered with sheets. The frail bodies of old magisters lay beside the hulking forms of knights in smashed and rent armour, protocol and hierarchy seeming to matter little in death.

Down another flight of stairs and more voices were raised in agony. Waylian expected more wounded, but instead he saw a young novice, her fingers gripping her knees so hard there was blood on her robe, her mouth moving, spouting unintelligible words as she rocked back and forth. Beside her stood a magister, uncertain of how to help the girl from her malady. Looking in the chamber as he passed, Waylian saw yet more figures, and not all of them young, babbling inanities, the horrors of battle and tapping the Veil having taken their toll.

Past all this Magistra Gelredida walked impassively, not sparing a glance for any of the dead or dying or insane. For a moment Waylian could only admire her callousness; he would have much preferred to ignore it himself. But as he thought on it he knew she could never be so pitiless as to feel nothing for these people.

*Or could she? Over the past weeks she's put you in danger enough times. Not given a shit whether you lived or died to further her aims.*

But they weren't *her* aims. It was never for herself that she had sacrificed those around her. Everything she had done, everyone who had died as a result of her actions, had done so for the greater good. To preserve Steelhaven. To keep it safe from the enemy, when everyone else would have shirked the hard choices.

Waylian knew that had it fallen to him to make such impossible choices he would have failed utterly.

Gelredida led them into the library. It had become the surrogate meeting room for the Archmasters; the Crucible Chamber obviously meeting with his mistress' distaste. Inside they waited for her patiently – Folds, Marghil, Kalvor. It was obvious that each man had been affected deeply by the night's slaughter and none of them seemed able to hide the fact.

Drennan Folds gripped his thick arms, his mismatched eyes glaring at Gelredida as she entered. Crannock sat at a desk, drumming his arthritic fingers against the table top, one lens of his eyeglasses broken in a web of cracks. Lucen Kalvor reclined against a bookshelf, feigning indifference as he always did, but the blood he had yet to wash from his face and robe showed he had seen as much death as any of them.

Gelredida fixed them all with her inscrutable gaze. If they wanted any sympathy from the Red Witch they were about to be sorely disappointed.

'Drennan?' she said. 'How do your apprentices fare?'

Drennan Folds held her with that glare, his white eye unblinking. 'How the fuck do you think they fare? Of twenty-eight, seven are dead. Four have been driven mad by the horrors they endured and the rest are scared so shitless I doubt they will be able to perform so much as a parlour trick tomorrow.'

Gelredida took this in with an understanding nod. 'I'm sure you'll be able to motivate them,' she replied. Drennan made to speak, but she had already turned her attention to Crannock. 'And our veterans?'

The old magister continued to drum his wrinkled fingers against the desk as though he hadn't heard her. Waylian began to feel a little uncomfortable at the prospect that his mistress might have to repeat herself, but slowly the old man looked up.

'We lost twelve,' he said. 'Twice that number are wounded, I doubt they'll be fit for tonight.'

Gelredida nodded at his solemn news. 'We will need—'

'I know we will,' said the old man, wearily. 'And I will do my best.'

'Yes. You will.' She turned to Lucen Kalvor.

'Around thirty casualties. Leaves us around forty fit for the fight,' he said without looking up. Kalvor didn't seem to give a damn that his Raven Knights had suffered the most, but then he didn't seem to give a damn about much.

'I know this seems bad, but on a positive note their wytchworker is dead,' said Gelredida. 'Last night was particularly bloody. From now on we should face no more magick. Nevertheless, there's every chance the fighting will get worse before the end.'

'Get worse?' spat Drennan through gritted teeth. 'How could it get worse? We are losing magickers by the dozen. And do you know how long it takes to train Raven Knights? By the time we get to the end the Tower of Magisters might be nothing but an empty shell.'

'And what would be the alternative?' said Gelredida, her voice even and calm as she refused to rise to Drennan's complaints.

'We should have taken the bargain he offered us. We should have stayed out of the fight.'

'You're still as blind as that left eye of yours,' said Gelredida. 'Still hiding your cowardice behind a voice of reason.'

'You fucking led us to this!' he screamed. 'You'll see us all dead. You'll see the Caste destroyed. The only thing holding the Free States together and it'll be gone because you refused to bargain.'

There was silence. Waylian felt like backing from the room before the real shit started to fly, but he managed to keep himself together enough to stay put.

'Have you finished?' Gelredida asked eventually. Drennan stayed silent, thinking better of venting his ire any further. 'Good.'

She made as though to continue when the sound of running feet stopped her. Waylian turned in time to see a boy, probably a little younger than he was, run into the room. His face was aglow from his exertions, his regalia marking him as holding no allegiance to any particular administrative department within the city and yet still he had been allowed into the Tower of Magisters.

The boy dropped to his knee before the Archmasters, bowing his head as though he might be turned into a mouse if he showed improper deference. In his hand he held out a sealed scroll.

Gelredida impatiently signalled for Waylian to take the message, and he swiftly obeyed. It was sealed with white wax that bore no marking. He stared at it for a moment, unsure of what that meant.

'Well, open it then.' Her tone seemed to stretch beyond impatience, if that were possible.

Waylian broke the seal and unfurled the scroll. He read with all the haste he could muster.

'It is from the . . . Inquisition, Magistra,' he said. 'Seneschal Rogan demands that the magisters do their utmost to resolve the problem of the fire ships anchored in the bay.'

Gelredida sighed a sigh that asked if she didn't already have enough on her quite considerable plate. 'Oh, he does, does he?' She directed the comment at the young messenger. To his credit the boy resisted the temptation to look up, and Waylian knew all too well that he must have been scared for his life at the displeasure of the Red Witch.

'Very well,' she said finally. 'Tell the Seneschal we shall do our utmost to deal with it.'

The young lad needed no further encouragement and scampered off, almost bowling Waylian over on his way out.

'Gentlemen, if there is nothing further,' she directed at the three Archmasters. 'I'm sure we all have much to be getting on with.'

She walked from the room, each of the men following her with eyes full of loathing. Waylian would have tried a smile before he followed her but he knew that was as dangerous as it was pointless.

Down she went, through the tower, and Waylian had to give silent thanks for the fact there were no more dead and dying lining the stairwell as they descended.

'What will you do, Magistra?' Waylian asked, unable to contain himself. He knew she had a lot on her mind but even he wanted to know how she proposed to destroy over a dozen artillery ships in the bay.

'What will I do?' she asked in return. 'Why, I will go and seek help.'

Waylian let out a silent breath. For a moment he had feared the worst – that she'd be volunteering him for yet another perilous mission, this one involving a rowboat and some flammable materials.

He couldn't resist. 'Who from, Magistra?'

'From the Wyvern Guard,' she replied. 'The Lord Marshal still owes me a favour or two.'

Waylian pondered that for a moment. There was something amiss with this plan and he just couldn't stop himself.

'But how can warriors manage to defeat ships anchored out to sea? We don't have any boats to transport them across the bay, and even if we did surely they'd come under fire before they can even reach the first artillery ship.'

'Very good, Waylian. You're thinking this through. I like that. But they won't be attacking the artillery ships by boat.'

Waylian couldn't help but furrow his brow. He had to know.

'So . . . how are they going to do it?'

Gelredida turned and flashed him an ever so rare smile.

'Well, my young apprentice. That's where you come in . . .'

*Oh. Shit.*

# SEVENTEEN

I t had been the longest night of Merrick Ryder's life. Thankfully most of it had gone by in a haze of blood and violence. The never ending screams, the hack and slash, the piss-filled undergarments. But strangely, despite the death all around him, Merrick had never felt so alive. Had never felt like he belonged as much as he did when standing amongst the Wyvern Guard, when raising shield and sword with men he almost considered his brothers.

Riding at the enemy with nothing between him and them but the night air had seemed insane enough, but standing atop that wall when they'd come to attack had been the maddest thing he'd ever seen. Even though he knew it was coming he could never have prepared himself for the slaughter. And the Wyvern Guard were oh so good at the slaughter.

And at their fore, raising his blade like a Sword King of old had been his father, inspiring them, leading by example. The old man had cut through the enemy like a slaughterman gone mad, the gleam in his eye never faltering, the grin on his face showing a glee in butchery no sane man should ever have borne.

Merrick should have hated that. Should have judged the old bastard for taking such joy in the killing. *Look at him,* he should have thought. *No wonder he abandoned us. No wonder I was left alone to fend for myself with this mad fucker as a father.*

But Merrick couldn't judge him – Merrick could only admire him for his battle lust. He was caught up in it like the rest of the bronze-armoured knights surrounding him. Had only wanted to race into the thick of the fighting and get himself bloody alongside them.

And he had done that all right.

All morning he'd been scrubbing his armour. Thick bits of gore were stuck in the fluted plates and Jared had been adamant that every man clean his armour to a mirror sheen before they face the enemy again. Merrick just wanted to sleep and rest his aching muscles, his sword arm in particular, but he had risen with the rest and obeyed the word of the Lord Marshal's second. It seemed almost normal to him now, to wash and eat and fight with these men like their equal. The Merrick of old would have laughed, but then the Merrick of old was long gone.

*Is he? Have you really got over being a self-serving coward? Might be a bit soon to start patting yourself on the back just yet, Ryder.*

He sat amongst the rest of the lads as they polished swords and lacquered shields. They chatted about the previous night as though it happened every week. As though putting themselves in peril were just another part of life. Some laughed, comparing their kills. Some went into graphic detail about how they'd slit a Khurta's throat or pierced a groin or hacked off a limb. Their chatter was casual, light-hearted, as though they were bragging about winning a hand of cards. Merrick listened long enough for it to seem almost normal. He was about to laugh along with a big knight named Garnar as he talked about how he'd crushed a Khurta's throat with the edge of his shield when he glanced over to the other side of the courtyard.

Lying in a row, hidden beneath the pennants of the Wyvern Guard, were their dead. Of the three hundred who had fought on the previous night, thirty-eight of them were now corpses. Merrick had got to know some of those men in his short time amongst their number. Terryl had made him laugh on more than one occasion. Barsa had in turn laughed at Merrick's shit jokes louder and longer than most. Now they were dead, but the rest of their brothers didn't seem to think on it too much.

They'd laid their fallen out solemnly enough the night before. Bowed their heads as the Lord Marshal had said his words about 'brotherhood' and how their dead were now safe in Arlor's embrace.

But now it was like they were all but forgotten. Just lying there in the cold morning, waiting for someone to come and bury them.

Merrick couldn't have given two shits whether Arlor wanted to give him a hug or not when he died. When his time came he was damn sure he wanted more than to be laid out in a cold courtyard and covered with a fucking flag. He wanted weeping maidens and a funeral procession strewn with fresh flowers and not a little gold.

*You can want all you like, Ryder. You'll be lucky to get a hole deep enough to fit you in.*

With that dour thought in his head, Merrick went back to polishing his armour, trying desperately to take his mind from the prospect of an early, and undoubtedly gruesome, death. He tried to think back to the night before, to the camaraderie, to the elation of victory as the Khurtas had fled. Deep down, though, he knew they'd be back, and soon. Knew that there were tens of thousands of the bastards, and less than three hundred Wyvern Guard. Thirty-eight gone last night. How many tonight? And how long until it was his turn?

A cry went up from the barrack room they'd converted into an infirmary. As well as the dead they had over three dozen injured. Most were walking wounded, minor cuts and bruises, but the rest would be lucky to walk or raise a sword again.

Merrick reckoned that would probably be worse than dying – wandering around as a cripple for the rest of your days, no use to man or beast. He doubted the Wyvern Guard suffered any hangers-on in their number either. They were a brotherhood, and no mistake, but a ruthless and brutal one. They would fight for each other, die for each other, but weakness certainly wasn't tolerated in any form from what Merrick had seen.

He could only hope his luck would hold and he'd survive with everything intact, or die a swift and glorious death. It would definitely be the former if he had any say in it.

As he continued to buff his breastplate a figure silently entered the courtyard. No one seemed to notice the red-robed old woman as she made her way across the training square; everyone continued their laughter and not one of the Wyvern Guard even so much as glanced in her direction. It was like she was invisible to all but Merrick.

When she reached the centre of the courtyard, he suddenly felt a pull in his chest, right where his wound was. That wound, the one that should have killed him but a few short days ago, seemed to recognise the old woman, even if Merrick didn't. He lifted a hand to his shirt, expecting to feel it sodden with blood, but it was still healed over.

Merrick stared at her as she continued across the square. Before she reached the other side, Lord Marshal Tannick walked out from beneath the eaves of a building to greet her.

The two regarded one another with familiarity, though Tannick seemed a little wary. The words they exchanged were brief, with Tannick nodding and shaking his head while the old woman spoke. All the while the pain in Merrick's chest seemed to intensify, burning a little as though the blade were still sticking in him and starting to glow with heat. After a final solemn nod from Tannick, the old woman turned. As she did so she fixed Merrick with a look he couldn't read. There was something about her he recognised, but from where it was he had no idea. It was like he'd dreamt about her and the memory of it still haunted him at the periphery of his thoughts.

She made her way back across the courtyard, still fixing him with that look, the corner of her mouth turning up slightly as though she were somehow relishing his discomfort. Merrick grimaced at the pain now, fighting back the urge to cry out.

As the old woman almost made it to the archway leading from the courtyard, she stopped. Sweat had beaded on Merrick's forehead now, and he was filled with sudden dread and panic.

The woman in red lifted a gloved finger to her lips. As quick as it had started, the pain in Merrick's wound subsided, and he let out a sharp exhalation.

With that, the woman was gone.

While Merrick's eyes were locked on the archway from the courtyard, a shadow fell over him. He looked up to see his father standing there, face stern as ever.

'I'd have words,' said the Lord Marshal, before marching off back to his quarters.

Merrick glanced around, bewildered. Still no one had noticed the old woman or Merrick's discomfort. They simply carried on with their bragging and polishing. He stood gingerly and followed his father across the courtyard. Though the pain in his chest had abated, Merrick's legs were still unsteady, the beads of sweat on his head now cooling in the morning air.

'There's a mission,' said Tannick, once they were both within the confines of his chamber. 'And it's a dangerous one.' *Here it comes, Ryder. A chance to prove yourself!* 'That's why, when I ask for volunteers, you'll keep your mouth shut.'

'I'll do what?' Merrick asked.

'You will stay silent, boy. I'll not have you put in harm's way.'

'Harm's way?' Merrick could feel his hackles starting to rise. 'What would you call last night? A gentle stroll in the evening air?'

'You weren't in any danger last night. I had my eye on you all the time.'

'I don't need—'

'Regardless of your needs, boy, you'll not be volunteering. Is that clear?'

Merrick had suffered about enough of this. His father had allowed him to join the Wyvern Guard, given him a chance at redemption, but all the while stopped him from showing his worth. If he hadn't ridden out to save Cormach the foul bastard would be dead, and the defenders on the wall would never have seen the Wyvern Guard riding back victorious with their banner. And besides, he'd more than held his own on the wall last night. More than shown he was as good a blade as any other man there.

*But what did he say to you yesterday, Ryder? Don't disobey again, wasn't it? Are you going to try it? Are you going to defy your father's wishes a second time? Go on, give it a go. See what happens.*

'Clear as crystal,' Merrick said, struggling to hide his disappointment.

As he followed his father back out onto the courtyard, all he could think was this might have been his chance to prove his mettle. To show he was a warrior equal to his family's reputation. That he was not riding in the wake of his father.

As much as he had been accepted into the Wyvern Guard he wasn't convinced he had the total respect of his brother knights. And at least one of them clearly hated his guts, but the less he thought about Cormach Whoreson the better.

'Right, listen up,' shouted Tannick as he stood in the centre of the courtyard. Immediately the men of the Wyvern Guard stopped what they were doing and stood, crowding in around their Lord Marshal. 'We have a mission. I need twenty volunteers. It'll be dangerous and it's doubtful most of you will survive it. Who's in?'

Merrick glanced around. Few of the Wyvern Guard looked worried at the prospect of dying.

'I'll go,' said the first voice. Merrick wasn't surprised to see it belonged to Cormach.

Immediately he felt a bristle of anger. Of course that bastard would be the first to volunteer. Any chance to show he was the toughest, hardest, maddest fucker in this whole damned city and he'd be all over it like a peasant on pie.

*Unlike you, Ryder. You're just Daddy's little boy. Can't have you getting your hair messed up. Can't have you playing rough with the bigger boys.*

Merrick counted as more men stepped forward to volunteer one after the other . . . four, five . . .

*And the Lord Marshal's told you not to volunteer. So you'd better do as you're bloody well told, otherwise you'll be in for a spanking.*

. . . eleven, twelve, thirteen . . .

*And why would you want to put yourself in harm's way anyway? You want to live through this, don't you? The Lord Marshal's just said it's doubtful most of the volunteers will survive.*

. . . sixteen, seventeen . . .

*Just keep your trap shut, like you've been told, and you might just make it through this in one piece.*

. . . nineteen . . .

'I'll go,' said Merrick, barging his way forward before anyone could take the last place.

Tannick glared at him, and for a moment Merrick thought the old man was going to chastise him, right in front of his brother Wyvern Guard.

'Makes twenty,' he said instead.

It was all Merrick could do not to whoop with joy. But then he remembered that he'd just volunteered for a suicide mission. Whooping definitely did not seem the right thing to do.

# EIGHTEEN

Regulus stared out to the north as night turned to dawn turned to day. His claws had gouged a four-ridged furrow in the stone of the battlements, his grief over Hagama cutting him equally as deep. He knew he should not have let it hurt him so, he knew it was more than likely he would lose more of his warriors, even his own life, but still the pain was like a knife.

Hagama had been by his side since they were children. They had played together, fought together, bled together for years. Hagama had been the first of the Gor'tana to pledge himself to Regulus after his father had been betrayed. Even before old, wise Leandran had offered his service, Hagama had stood by Regulus' side, unswerving in his loyalty. And now he was dead.

It wasn't the need for vengeance that moved Regulus so; there would be time aplenty for retribution. It was the fact they had lost his body. The fact the Khurtas had dragged him off back to their camp to do Gorm knew what to his corpse. They would never be able to convey his soul to the stars. Never be able to ensure the Dark Walker couldn't catch the brave warrior before he took his place with the other fallen heroes of Equ'un. It was not a fitting end.

Sacrifice, though – Hagama would have the honour of a sacrifice no Zatani had ever been bestowed. Regulus made a silent vow that Khurtic blood would flow, and he would taste every drop in honour of his fallen brother.

'You should eat.'

Regulus turned to see young Akkula standing beside him. The youth looked sullen and it was obvious he too felt the loss of Hagama, even though the older warrior had castigated his young counterpart many times. They had never been friends, but Akkula was a man now – a warrior grown – and he would fight for his brothers and mourn their loss as any Gor'tana should.

'I am not hungry,' said Regulus, though he knew he should have been. The night's killing should have made him ravenous but his stomach was filled with a lust for Khurtic flesh that no amount of horsemeat would sate.

'You will need your strength for the next attack. We all will.'

Akkula was trying his best to help, but Regulus was in no mood to be lectured. He shook his head, and Akkula understood immediately, leaving Regulus in his dark mood.

No sooner had he gone than another figure approached over the battlements. Regulus recognised the sargent, feeling his heart slump further at the prospect of talking to the man. He looked furious and Regulus almost broke a smile at the man's barely suppressed rage.

'You fled your post,' said the sargent. Regulus noted he kept a safe distance. 'You'll obey your orders tonight or you'll—'

'I'll what?' Regulus replied, not even bothering to look at him.

There was a moment's silence as the sargent pondered his next move.

'We barely have enough men for the wall as it is. You can't just go running off wherever you please.'

Regulus nodded. 'Yes, I can. Your gate was not attacked, was it? My warriors and I would have been of no use had we stayed. From now you will find us where the fighting is hardest. Where the killing is bloodiest.'

The man made to speak but thought better of it. What would he do? Seek to punish the Zatani for repelling the Khurtas? For killing their shaman and sacrificing one of their own in the act?

The Coldlander slunk off, rather than speak again.

Regulus turned from the north, tired of his vigil now. He had mourned enough for Hagama, and besides, there was something he had to do before night fell and the fighting started again.

As he walked the wall many of the Coldlanders who had seen hard fighting during the night gave him a nod of acknowledgement, some even words of praise. How different from days ago when they had been baying for his blood and that of his warriors. He was one of them now, had shed blood and sacrificed a brother, just as they had. War was always the best way to unite men – bringing them together in their grief and hate.

Up ahead Regulus saw the man he was looking for. Nobul Jacks – the Black Helm as he had become known – was sitting with his back to the wall, hammer gripped in one hand, helm in the other. Whatever legend he had built for himself seemed to matter little now. The warrior looked weary after the night's combat. He was a legend no more. Just a man in need of rest. Not that the other Coldlanders seemed to regard him as an ordinary man. Regulus had heard their tales of him – that he could not die, that he was one of their ancient heroes reborn. That was perhaps why they gave him such a wide berth, their awe of him striking fear into their hearts. Regulus Gor did not share such awe, though. He knew Nobul Jacks was simply a man and could be killed like any other. He was just more difficult to kill than most.

'You have my gratitude again, Nobul Jacks,' Regulus said as he came to stand before the Coldlander.

Nobul inclined his head in acknowledgement. 'And you're welcome. Again.'

Regulus could see the fatigue in the man's eyes, his shoulders slumped. There would be much more fighting before the end, and for a moment he wondered if Nobul would last even one more night.

'More than that,' Regulus said, 'I owe you my life. I am yours until that debt is paid. You have refused once, Nobul Jacks. You cannot refuse again.'

Nobul looked up. At first there was defiance in his expression, and from what Regulus could read, a note of annoyance. Then the man smiled.

'You're mine?' Nobul said. 'And what the fuck am I supposed to do with you? We could both die tonight and what would the point be in you owing me a debt? Best look to yourself and your men, Regulus. I can take care of myself.'

From what Regulus could see, he very much doubted Nobul's words. He looked fit to drop, his face showing its age now more than it ever had.

'You speak truth. We may well perish tonight. But until the debt is paid, my life is yours.'

'I get it,' Nobul replied. 'And if I need someone to die for me any time soon, you'll be the first to know.'

'Don't jest, Nobul Jacks. You may find you need me sooner than you think.'

Nobul nodded. 'I have no doubt. But for now all I need is a bit of quiet. If you think you can manage it.'

Regulus nodded his assent. 'If that is what you wish.'

He left the Coldlander at the wall. There was nothing else to say. It was clear the old warrior was a stubborn one. Only time would tell if Regulus would ever be allowed to repay his debt. He only hoped he had the chance before Nobul managed to get himself killed.

But then perhaps it didn't matter that much anyway. They might all be dead before long.

Janto, Akkula and Kazul were waiting for him when he returned. Akkula and Kazul looked eager for the fight to come. Janto reclined against the wall, hands resting on his axes, but Regulus knew when the fighting started he would be as ferocious as any of them.

'Are you all ready for the night ahead?' he asked.

Akkula and Kazul nodded. If they were apprehensive about the fighting to come they did not show it.

Janto presented his usual lack of feeling, but Regulus knew he would get nothing from him. The only time the Sho'tana displayed any emotion was when he was in a killing rage.

'Good,' said Regulus. 'For we have lost a brother. He is to be avenged. Last night was but a taste of Zatani fury. Tonight we will teach these Khurtas the price for killing a Gor'tana.'

Akkula and Kazul growled their assent. Janto remained silent, staring at Regulus with those blue eyes.

Regulus merely stared back. He knew deep down how much Janto hated him, how much he would have wanted to kill him had he not been bound by his own debt. They were of rival tribes, after all – Regulus of the Gor'tana and Janto of the Sho'tana – the dishonour of it must have cut Janto deep. But the fact remained, Regulus had saved Janto's life those months before and the warrior owed him. For a moment Regulus wondered if he had been wise to hold Janto to that obligation. If his life debt was ever paid the Sho'tana would most likely direct his fury at Regulus.

Then again, it might not matter any. Tens of thousands of savages also wanted him dead. If Janto wanted to kill Regulus, he would just have to get in line with the rest of the horde.

# NINETEEN

The city was like a different world as River made his way through its streets – or at least what remained of them. The south of the city was little more than a blackened wasteland, and it had taken him well into the morning to navigate the carcass of what had once been a thriving metropolis. The old entrances to the system of tunnels beneath the city streets were impassable, and he had to make his way far to the north before he could find a way in. The sounds of battle had echoed through the city all the while, the fighting clearly intense. River could only hope Jay was safe for now, until he could find a way to protect her.

By the time he located a way into the under-city the sun was rising, the sounds of combat now gone silent as the Khurtic horde retreated. When he made his way through the flooded tunnels he passed several bodies washed down through the sewer inlets, their flesh so pallid and waxy he could barely tell if they were the city's defenders or one of the savages come to besiege it.

As he came close to the sanctum, River drew his blades. The Father of Killers was most likely waiting, ready. The man who had trained him to be the assassin he was might already know River was on his way and be standing silently, waiting to kill his son. But let him. River had come to end his life. It was only fitting the Father should be prepared.

There was some apprehension in River's heart. Some guilt at

what he had to do. He had lived his life for the Father, after all. Had even loved him in his way. But the Father of Killers was in thrall to Amon Tugha and had sworn to kill the queen. River would not allow any harm to come to her, even if it meant killing the man who had raised him.

Though River knew there was little chance he would survive the encounter, he was determined that the Father of Killers would die, no matter the cost. He would not put Jay in danger. She would never know of River's sacrifice, but that meant nothing. All that mattered was her safety.

He eventually came out in the vast subterranean cavern in which he had grown to manhood. It was pitch black, the light from the lanterns that lit the wall long since extinguished. River paused to ignite one, striking flint on tinder and catching sight of his surroundings in the sparking light. At any moment he expected the Father to come at him in that flash of illumination, but as the wick took, he realised he was alone.

He raised the lantern, shedding light in the cavern. Everything was in its place and it seemed as though no one had been here for days. Of course his brothers would not be here, Mountain was already dead at River's hand and Forest was many miles away, if he had survived his wounds. There was just him and his Father.

As he walked through the cavern River tried to control his breathing, ears pricked for any sound, even though he knew that if the Father of Killers had wanted to attack him unseen and unheard he could easily have done so.

'Father,' he called into the dark.

No answer.

River stood for what seemed an age, just waiting, illuminated in that massive cavern, *a floundering fish waiting for the net to be cast*. But no one came.

With no other alternative, River lit more lanterns and the torches on the walls, brightening up the system of caves that made up the inner sanctum. In every new chamber he entered he half expected the Father to be waiting, but there was no sign. By the time the caves were lit, River had dropped his guard completely. If the Father of Killers were here surely he would have shown himself by now, would have struck from the dark and ended the life of his troublesome son.

There was one place he had not looked, though. One place he had never even entered in all his years in the sanctum.

River made his way to the inner chamber of the Father of Killers with trepidation. Neither he nor his brothers had ever been allowed within their Father's private refuge, and it was obvious what the punishment would have been had any of them encroached upon it.

It lay behind a plain wooden door. The latch was a simple iron affair and there was no keyhole or bolt. It had always lain open, just so. But what need had the Father of Killers for security? Had any intruder managed to make it past his sons he would have had to be a formidable warrior indeed to survive such an encounter.

Now, as River flipped the iron latch, he wondered if he would have to be that warrior.

The door opened at the slightest push. The room beyond was in darkness, and River raised his lantern, uncertain of what to expect as he entered. Inside he saw plain blank walls, skimmed to a sheer surface and washed with white. At first the square chamber seemed empty, with not even a pallet for the Father of Killers to sleep on. As the lantern bathed the interior of the chamber with yellow light, River saw there was but a single item in the room.

On the floor in one corner lay a plain leather wallet. River recognised it immediately as the wallet Amon Tugha's messenger had brought for the Father many weeks ago. He remembered the silence that had pervaded the sanctum as his Father looked inside. Whatever it contained was significant indeed.

River wasted no time, placing the lantern on the floor and crossing the chamber. He knelt beside the wallet and reached out a hand, but paused before touching it. This could be a trap. Perhaps the wallet contained Elharim magicks that would wither the flesh from his bones. Maybe the Father of Killers had known he would come all along and had laid a trap.

No. The Father of Killers had sent Forest to murder River. He had no idea that River would survive, let alone return for vengeance. For all the Father knew Forest had succeeded in his mission. This could not be a trap.

River grasped the wallet and gingerly opened it. What he had been expecting to find he couldn't say, but it was not the dried and flattened rose that lay within the folds of the leather wallet.

He knelt and stared at it for several moments. A single rose. Whatever significance it had for the Father of Killers, River had no idea. Perhaps it was some keepsake from the Riverlands. Perhaps some gesture of union from Amon Tugha. River could only ponder as he reached out a finger to touch one of the dried leaves . . .

*White light burned his eyes – a tunnel of blinding, searing fire through which he fell. River wanted to scream but his mouth would not open. Wanted to close his eyes but his lids would not shut.*

*Nails.*

*Two nails pressed against his lips, the metallic tang of iron teasing his tongue. He knew he would take these nails and make something of them, something deadly, something profane.*

*A lone tree standing in an ancient amphitheatre. A hammer. The nails. A sigil.*

*A smile.*

*Later this tree will act as a distraction. It will allow him to reach his mark. To commit the killing he has been tasked with. Ancient magicks will be invoked. Fell northern words for a fell northern spell.*

*The arena fills as he waits in the dark, unseen and unheard. He has had many faces over the centuries, many names, but for this work he wears the same one he has donned for decades – old and comfortable.*

*When the time is right, when the tree comes to life with all the hate and fury of his master, he strikes from the shadow, cutting down many men. They are as nothing to him, it is like murdering children as his blade slides between and through the plate armour they think will protect them.*

*There is confusion. Screaming. Carnage.*

*And finally she comes to him.*

*She is defiant, but not as defiant as the last one who protects her. There is something about this man, something special within his blood, but that is of little consequence. And so he strikes. More guardians who cannot be allowed to stand in his way.*

*More death. More killing. A pursuit.*

*Until finally he has them.*

*They stand atop a derelict wall and he cuts down the last of her protectors. Still she shows no fear. He knows he should strike swift but he cannot help himself. He must know.*

*'What did you do to my son, River, to turn him against me?'*

*She smiles.*

*'I offered him love.'*

*He has heard enough. But there is movement behind him. He senses danger . . . real danger.*

*An old woman, but much more than just that.*

*She flings something at him and he reacts out of instinct.*

*Foolish.*

*He is consumed by flame. Smashed. Burned. His arm is gone. The mask he wears now matters little.*

*He turns to see her standing there. Defiant again.*

*Something inside him admires her for it. He finally realises why River betrayed him for this woman.*

*She raises his blade.*

*He barely hears her words as she plunges it into his throat.*

River fell back gasping, the leather wallet falling from his hand.

All he could see was the white ceiling flicker in the dancing light. As he sucked air back into his lungs he began to realise what he had just seen.

The Father of Killers was dead.

And Jay had been the one to kill him.

For a moment River felt elated. Jay was safe from the Father of Killers.

*But she is not safe from Amon Tugha.*

He glanced down at the wallet, seeing the dried rose had spilled out to lie on the whitewashed floor. His head had almost cleared now but there was still a fug there from what it had revealed to him. Whatever magicks had shown him his Father's past, whatever this thing was, it held great power. Perhaps it could show him more.

River reached out, grasping the flower and crushing it in his fist . . .

*The northern air was clear. Mountains surrounded him, rivers of crystal. Spires soaring, entwined within the landscape at their root. It was breathtaking to behold and he was proud to call it home. But he had no time to appreciate the architecture.*

*Instead he learned the killing ways. The tenets of the Arc Magna were not easily learned. Many failed. Many died. But not him. He was a prince, tall and proud and invincible. He would have made a great king, but that honour was not his by right.*

*His mother was a warrior queen. Keeping the Riverlands protected through ruthless stewardship. His brother was heir by right of birth, destined for power. He was but a warrior, a weapon. He would never be a king . . .*

*. . . unless he took the crown by force.*

*He gathered about him other warriors of like mind. Those who would never accept his brother as their liege. He planned meticulously. Trained his body unceasingly. And struck ruthlessly.*

*His coup failed.*

*While his co-conspirators were executed, he was exiled. Cast to the southern winds. Banished forever. Only Endellion and Azreal remained by his side. His loyal aides. They would be rewarded with all the riches he could bestow when he returned to claim his birthright.*

*And he would return.*

*But first he had to prove himself in the south. Had to conquer. Had to destroy. Had to tear down everything these southrons held dear and then rebuild it in his own name.*

*The Khurtas had been the first. Barbarians for sure, but effective in their killing ways and vast in number. It took him less than a year to defeat their nine tribal leaders and bring them to heel. In honour of his victory over them they gave him the name* Amon Tugha, *and he bore it proudly.*

*Next would be the Teutonians. A trickier prospect, no doubt, but he knew this would never be easy. He could only hope news of his victories was carried north to the Riverlands where his mother could hear of them. Where his brother could begin to fear him.*

*King Cael had at first appeared a worthy adversary, but he had faced the Khurtas with hubris. It had been his downfall. The king's untimely death had been unfortunate. How much he would have liked to have taken that life himself, but it was not to be.*

*Still, with the king's army defeated and routed, it was only a matter of time before he plucked the jewel from the crown of the Free States – Steelhaven.*

*And it would all have been so easy had she not taken up her father's mantle. Had she not dodged his assassins and confounded his spies at every turn.*

*And there she still stood, defiant as ever. And that was why she had to die . . .*

River felt his vision blur, the story about to end, but there was something else. Something . . . someone watching at the corner of his mind while he saw another life play out before him. He tried to turn his head, but the eyes upon him had already begun to look into his own.

*Amon Tugha stared. Amon Tugha saw him and knew him and read his intent.*

'Come, boy,' he said. 'Come if you dare.'

River opened his palm, letting the crushed rose fall to the floor.

Bile had risen, stinging his throat and dripping from the corner of his mouth. His eyes stared, burning, as though the blood vessels within them had burst from the strain of witnessing Amon Tugha's past.

He ignored the discomfort. Ignored the effects of the magicks that even now tormented him.

River was struck with a new determination. Steeled into action by what he had seen.

Amon Tugha had come south for a kingdom, and only Jay stood in his way. The Elharim would kill her if it was the last thing he ever did.

Unless River killed him first.

# TWENTY

She walked in the back way, pausing for a second in the dark hallway as she breathed deep, glad she was still alive. Rag's jacket had a massive hole burned in it and her big toe was sticking out of one shoe. Her hair stank and was all crispy on one side, and she was filthy from head to foot.

*Nothing you ain't used to, though, is it, Rag? Just count your blessings you ain't a charred piece of coal like that poor bastard Yarrick.*

One more deep breath and she opened the door into the main room of the tavern. They were all still there, all milling around like they had been when she left. No one paid her much mind, even though she looked like someone had just tried to set her on fire.

'Well?'

The voice came at her like a black cloud out of the dark, filling her with that dread she felt every time she heard it. Bastian was sitting in one corner, surrounded by his men. He looked expectantly at her. She didn't need no telling, and walked towards him across the tavern.

'Did what you asked,' she said.

Bastian nodded. 'Good.' He looked her up and down like she was a carrot he was about to take a bite from but there was a big maggot sticking out of it. 'No problems, I take it?'

*Yes, there was problems. I nearly got killed and poor old Yarrick burned himself all to death. You could say there was pretty much all the fucking problems you could ever have thought of.*

'No,' she replied. 'No problems.'

Weren't no point in telling Bastian her woes. He didn't give a shiny shit anyways.

He stood up without giving her a second glance, walking to the middle of the tavern and just waiting there. Gradually the chatter that filled the room ended as his men saw he was stood there ready to say something.

'The message is delivered,' he said in a quiet voice, though everyone could hear him. 'Tonight we open the Lych Gate. The gatehouse should be clear for you to simply walk in, but be prepared. Your lives depend on it. When this city falls, and it definitely will, the Guild needs to have done its part. There's a new power coming to Steelhaven, and we have to pick the right side now, or we'll all be eating our own bollocks come the time Amon Tugha takes the throne.' The men in the room made agreeable noises, some looking gleeful at the prospect, others keeping their impassive expressions. 'You all know your jobs. When the time comes, make sure you're ready.'

With that, Bastian headed for the door.

Rag almost went after him, almost wanted to know what her part in all this would be, but thinking on it she knew she didn't want no part. They were gonna open the Lych Gate and let the Khurtas flood in. They were betraying the queen and every soul within Steelhaven's walls. Not that Rag gave a toss about anyone in the city other than her crew and her boys, but still. It just weren't right.

She made her way over to where Shirl and Essen were, looking all sullen and trying to stay out of the way in case they upset any of Bastian's boys. She sat with them and watched with a pang of sadness as Essen looked around for Yarrick.

'He ain't coming,' she said.

Essen seemed to understand, his eyes lowering to fix on the table. He saw the state of her; it was obvious what they'd been through to deliver Bastian's message. She didn't need to tell him any more. Shirl weren't so quick on the uptake, however.

'Why?' asked the fat man, brow all screwed up in confusion. 'Where is he?'

'He's dead, you fucking dolt,' Essen snapped before Rag had a chance to answer. 'Where the fuck do you think he is? Look at the state of her.' He gestured to Rag's tattered clothing and singed hair and face all stained with soot. 'Does it look like she's just been for a stroll in the Crown District? Yarrick's fucking dead, you stupid fat—'

Essen stopped, glaring back at the table, fists clenched. For a moment Rag wanted to give him a hug, or at least lay a hand on his to show she had some sympathy for him, but it wouldn't do to show that kind of affection. Not here. Not now.

Shirl seemed to get the message, keeping his mouth shut and not looking at anyone. For his part, big Harkas just sat to one side, not saying nothing or even giving any sign he'd heard. If he'd given a shit about Yarrick it didn't move him enough to show it.

As the afternoon wore on, the room emptied as Bastian's men went off to do gods knew what in preparation for the night. Rag just watched them in silence, thinking all the while that what they was up to weren't right.

*But what you gonna do about it, Rag? You had your chance to stop this by not delivering that message. Now they're gonna open that gate and the Khurtas are gonna be waiting to pour in. And that's all on you. Nice one, you stupid little fucker.*

The more she thought on it, the more her heart sank. She thought about the women and children and old bastards who would be slaughtered by the thousand. She thought about Amon Tugha and wondered whether he'd even hold up to his end of the bargain when he'd taken over, or just kill them all anyway. She thought about poor Yarrick and what a waste it had been for him to come with her and give his life to deliver that message. And most of all she thought about her boys – Chirpy, Migs and Tidge – and about what the Khurtas would do to them when they came running through that gate, whooping and hollering to their evil gods and hacking down anything that moved.

And she knew what had to be done about it.

When the room had emptied enough that Rag felt comfortable

she wouldn't be heard, she beckoned the lads to huddle in closer round the table. Even Harkas moved in so he could hear her.

'This can't be allowed to happen,' she said, waiting a moment for that to sink in.

'What do you mean?' asked Shirl. It was bound to be Shirl.

'We have to stop them opening the gate.' Her words were spoken so slow even Shirl would understand it.

'And why the fuck would we do that?' asked Essen.

'Because if we don't, the Khurtas are gonna come right through the side door and kill a lot of bloody people.'

'So what?' said Essen. 'They won't kill us. Bastian's made a deal.'

'Yeah, he has. With the fucking Khurtas. Do you think they're gonna give a holy shite who's friend or foe when they come in? And who's to say Bastian's even gonna let us live once Amon Tugha takes over?'

Essen shook his head. 'We don't know any of that for sure. But what we do know is if we try and stop them opening that gate Bastian will have our balls stuffed in our eye sockets faster than it takes Shirl to eat a chicken leg.'

'People will die if we don't stop them,' Rag said, sounding a bit more desperate than she'd have liked.

'People are already dying,' Essen replied. 'And I've no intention of ending up one of them. Yarrick's already gone. I ain't gonna be next.'

Rag stared at him, feeling her argument slipping away. If Essen didn't join her the other two would be lost. Or so she thought.

'I agree.'

Slowly, Rag, Shirl and Essen turned to look at Harkas, whose rumbling voice was rarely heard by anyone.

'Eh?' asked Essen, when they'd finally got over the shock of Harkas speaking.

'Rag's right,' he rumbled on. 'We can't let them open the Lych Gate.'

'Look,' said Essen. 'Leave the thinking to us, all right. Trying to stop them opening that gate is madness. We'll all be better off just leaving it alone. Bastian's done a deal. The Guild and anyone in it is safe. We just have to sit tight and ride this one out.'

'You can do as you please,' Rag said, feeling more confident for Harkas' support. 'But we're gonna stop them while we have the chance. You in, Shirl?'

Shirl stared at her. Then at Essen. Then at Harkas.

'I've still got family in the city. They won't be safe when the Khurtas come. I guess I'd best help.'

Rag turned back to Essen. 'That's three to one. You still out?'

Essen shook his head. 'I ain't having nothing to do with this and you can't bloody well force me.'

'Ain't no one gonna. But you'd best keep your mouth shut about what we're gonna do.'

Essen glanced at Harkas, who just stared, all silent and intimidating. Then slowly he nodded.

'Right,' said Rag, 'that's that then. We've got some planning to do. But first I'm gonna see if we can get more recruits.' She stood up, feeling the weariness of her night creeping into her limbs, but she pushed it back. 'You two meet me at the main square in Eastgate in two hours,' she said to Harkas and Shirl. Then she looked at Essen. 'You best stay the fuck where you are.' Essen didn't answer.

With that she was gone from the tavern and out on the streets. The cold crept into her bones, seeming that much crueller after the heat of the night before. Her big toe in particular, sticking out of her shoe as it was, seemed to feel the chill most of all.

She stopped in the street, kicking off both shoes and leaving them there. She'd spent most of her life padding round in bare feet, and she'd never liked the way the shoes made her feet feel anyhow.

As Rag made her way south through the city to Dockside she saw what the Khurtas had done to the place. She'd seen first-hand what fire had done to the Rafts. Now she saw what it had done to Dockside and the Warehouse District. Weren't a house on any street that had got away unscathed. Some were reduced to rubble, others to ash. Every roof had at least half the slates missing and by the time Rag reached Slip Street she began to think this was a fool's errand. When she saw the state of the Silent Bull, she slowly raised a hand to her mouth.

The tavern where Chirpy, Migs and Tidge made their home was flattened like cow shit. The buildings on either side were still standing, more or less, but the Silent Bull was nothing but a pile of bricks and smashed timbers.

Rag staggered forward, stumbling through the wreckage. All she could think was that her lads must have been on the roof, minding their business, when a ball of flame came and took them all out in an instant. At least it would have been quick. Or that's what Rag kept telling herself.

In the distance another ball of fire came flying over the wall, and Rag watched as it smashed into something on the other side of the district.

This had been stupid. No one was still in Dockside, and even the lads wouldn't have been dumb enough to stay here with those ships in the harbour raining all kinds of shit down on the south of the city.

She turned to leave.

'I told you it was her.'

Rag spun at the voice, glancing around for a sign of whoever owned it. At first she couldn't see nothing, thinking her ears were playing tricks on her, and then she noticed him standing there. Tidge, face and hair all black, standing at the edge of the wreckage. Chirpy and Migs came into view then, looking at her all suspicious, but she didn't care. She ran to them, grabbing hold of Tidge and Chirpy in a headlock and squeezing them till they started to struggle. She kissed their filthy heads, feeling the tears of relief flood her eyes.

'You gone fucking soft?' said Migs as she tried to reach out for him too.

Rag laughed. 'Yeah, I think I have. I thought you were all . . .'

'Yeah,' said Chirpy, looking pleased to see her. 'We would have been if we hadn't been out on the rob. Every house round here's left empty. Easy pickings.'

'Not every house,' said Tidge. 'Boris stayed in the Bull after everyone had left.' He gestured to the wreckage. 'He'll be in there somewhere, flat as a fucking fart.'

'He was always moaning about his weight anyhow,' said Migs. 'Don't have to worry about that no more, do he?'

'What about Fender?' asked Rag.

Migs shook his head. 'Ain't seen no sign of that cunt since before the Khurtas got here.'

Rag had thought that would be the answer. They didn't need him anyway. She was here now. She would look after them.

'What you doing here anyhow, Rag?' Tidge asked.

She smiled at him. 'I've come for you lot,' she replied.

'What?' asked Migs. 'Come to see if we're still living in the lap of luxury?' He gestured around at the carnage.

'No,' Rag said with a smile. 'I've come to see if you want to help save the city.'

# TWENTY-ONE

A moment of quiet reflection. It was all Janessa had wanted. Part of her felt selfish for it. There was so much still to do, so much planning, so much to know, to organise, but she needed a moment alone.

The gardens had been her father's sanctuary; there seemed no reason why they shouldn't also act as hers. Even though the shadows of dark memory lingered here – the sickening touch of Azai Dravos, when he had looked into her heart, into her belly and found her unborn child – she still took solace in the place. Besides, she had killed Dravos; struck the head from his shoulders and stood the survivor. That was a victory she could revel in.

Thoughts of Dravos faded as she stood within the winter garden. The chill of the air did not bother her. She had dismissed her Sentinels and Kaira was elsewhere, most likely taking some deserved rest after her labours during the night. Janessa was alone, the weight of her armour and her sword gone for just a brief amount of time.

She breathed deep, remembering what it had been like before all this. Before she had lost Graye to betrayal and murder. Before she had lost her father to the hand of Amon Tugha. Before River had abandoned her.

For that tiny moment, as the cold breeze caressed her face and swept through her red curls, she was carefree again. There was no city in peril, no savages at the wall.

Should she have taken her chance weeks ago and fled the city? It would have been so easy. A swift horse or passage on a ship. Enough gold to make a new start, a new life. All this would have been as nothing – a past she could have left behind. There had been a chance, when River had asked her to run away with him. At the time it had seemed a difficult choice but now, in that garden, with the weight of ten thousand lives resting on her, she could hardly believe she had hesitated.

That chance was gone, though. Now there would be no swift horse. There was no caravel to carry her to safer shores. So she would take this moment and savour it. Breathe it in, despite the stench of death and fire that was carried on the air. Who knew when she would get another chance? Who knew how long this moment might last?

'I also find the quiet moments are the best.'

Janessa turned, her daydream shattered. Leon Magrida stood watching her from beneath the naked branches of a willow. Baroness Isabelle's son smiled at her warmly but it did nothing to stifle the cold on her skin. He too had lived at the palace since the Khurtas had set Dreldun on fire but thankfully, unlike his mother, Janessa had seen little of him in the past days of strife.

Her eyes scanned the gardens but there was no sign of anyone else. How he had made it past her Sentinels she had no idea. He certainly had a talent for lurking unseen. The thought did nothing to put her at ease.

'Lord Leon,' she said. There should have been more. Some polite small talk as was traditional at court, but Janessa could think of no words. This was hardly the time for such pointless wittering. And what would she have said anyway? *Hope you are well. Are the palace rooms still to your satisfaction?* It hardly seemed appropriate while her people died by the hundred.

He walked towards her, the smile still on his face. As he did so he straightened the black doublet he wore and she noticed the dagger at his side, instantly dismissing the notion he might be a threat. This was the heir to Dreldun, she was in no danger here.

'My apologies if I startled you, Majesty. But it has become increasingly difficult to find a moment when you are not surrounded by guards. And it is important that I speak with you.'

No, it couldn't be. Not now. Was Leon seriously about to propose? Now, of all times, when her city was on the brink? Was he insane?

'Lord Leon, I am sure this is nothing that cannot wait.'

'Oh but it can't,' he replied, still approaching, walking with a steady yet purposeful stride. 'You see, I have wanted to tell you for the longest time, but have simply been unable. But now we are alone. And there is no time like the present, as they say in the provinces.'

His smile changed, the humour draining from it in an instant. His eyes looked dead. If he was about to profess his love for her he certainly didn't mind how unconvincing it would look.

'My lord, this is neither the time nor the place,' she said, feeling her anger rise. Who did Leon think he was? Her city burned and all he could think about was his ascension to the throne. A throne that might well be rubble in a few short days.

'Oh, but it is,' Leon replied. He was within touching distance now, gazing at her with those dead eyes of his. She had never noticed before just how emotionless they were, as though he were dreaming with his eyes open. 'I have waited for this moment for what seems an age, Majesty. And so have you.'

'My lord—'

He reached out and took her hand before she could think to pull away. His flesh was cold and pallid like the dead. Like young Lord Raelan's flesh had been when he was laid out, waiting to be carried back to Valdor by his father's men.

'The time for talking is over,' said Leon, a smile playing on his lips. He looked at her with a hunger now – his dead expression replaced with one of need. The smile grew as his lips pulled back from his teeth. His eyes glared.

Janessa tried to pull away but he held her tight within his grip. She made to speak but he shook his head.

'Don't say anything. This should be a dignified moment. It is only fitting that there should be an aspect of formality to this. My prince, Amon Tugha, must have his due.'

Janessa felt ice run from the back of her neck and down her spine. She couldn't move as his words filled her with dread. As she stared at those dead eyes she suddenly felt sick.

All this time Leon had been under her roof and every day of it he had belonged to the warlord who wanted her head.

She saw his hand move to the dagger at his side, but her eyes were still fixed on his. Her Sentinels were only scant yards away but she couldn't cry out – he would simply cut her down, and from the look of zeal in his eyes it seemed unlikely that Leon would care when they came running to kill him, as long as he had succeeded in murdering her first.

'Shhh,' he said softly. 'This will take but a moment.'

The knife slid from its sheath.

Janessa's hand shot forward before she had time to think what she was doing. The heel of her palm struck Leon beneath the chin and she felt a momentary snatch of satisfaction as she heard his teeth clack together. He staggered back, the knife dropping from his grip to clatter on the garden path, but he still held her wrist.

She tried to strike again, balling a fist this time, but he raised his arm, catching her hand before she could hit him. For a moment they stared at one another, and she saw the anger in him, the madness. He was going to kill her and cared nothing for the consequences. Perhaps something had happened to him; perhaps his mind had been twisted by Elharim magicks. Perhaps he was simply insane.

None of that seemed to matter, though; if she didn't find help he was going to kill her.

Janessa took a breath in, to call for help from her Sentinels, but as she was about to let out a scream Leon hit her in the stomach. The blow doubled her over, and before she could fall he had her by the throat.

She grasped his wrists, digging her nails in, panic gripping her tight as she felt his strength. Her eyes darted around for any sign of aid but there was no one there. Leon shook his head.

'They're not coming,' he whispered. 'Not in time to save you. I realise this is becoming a habit, you being placed in mortal peril in your own palace, but I am not Azai Dravos. I do not want to control you. I want to kill you.' She felt him tighten his grip, squeezing her throat shut so she couldn't breathe.

On the floor lay the knife; she could just see it, but it may as well have been a thousand leagues away. Her vision began to haze. As it did so she saw Leon was smiling again, one of his teeth chipped where she had struck him below the chin. As she drifted off, Janessa got a strange sense of satisfaction from the fact she had wounded him, no matter how little. Still, it was a poor substitute for her life.

'Leon!'

The voice cut the silence of the garden, bringing Janessa back from the brink.

Leon's grip on her throat relented somewhat but he still held her fast and unable to speak.

'Mother, what are you doing here?' he said. 'You can't be here.' His voice wavered and Janessa saw that the look in his eyes, which had a moment ago been so focused, was now filled with doubt.

'Let the queen go, Leon.'

He glanced to where Baroness Isabelle stood. Janessa could see her now, calm as she always was, but her eyes were fixed firmly on her son.

'Why are you here?' Leon asked. 'You weren't to be involved. We have plans. I have made a bargain. We will be all powerful. We will rule the Free States. Dreldun will rise from the ashes stronger than ever.'

He turned back to Janessa, his grip tightening once more.

'How will you do that when you're dead, Leon?' said Isabelle. 'You have been made a fool of. If you kill her you'll be dead before you set foot from this garden.'

'I cannot die,' Leon spat.

'Of course you can, idiot boy!' Isabelle screamed.

Her voice seemed to snap Leon from whatever spell he was under. He loosened his grip enough for Janessa to pull herself away and drop to her knees gasping. She glanced towards the garden entrance but no Sentinels came running at the sound of Isabelle's raised voice.

'Amon Tugha has promised me,' said Leon, as much to himself as his mother. 'He is powerful beyond words. I have seen it. He has shown me.'

Isabelle moved forward, her eyes filling with sympathy. 'He has

145

cast his spell on you,' she said gently. 'He will hold to no bargain. He is using you.'

Leon shook his head. 'No, he has shown me the future. I have seen it. I will wear the Steel Crown. Dreldun will be the new power behind the Free States.'

Isabelle was close enough to lay a hand on his arm now, soothing him. Leon smiled as his mother shook her head.

'He will share no power with us, my sweet boy. He has turned your mind. But it's not your fault. You were always so easy to lead, gods, I know that more than anyone.'

Leon shook his head now, the fight he waged in his mind writ large in his eyes. 'No. I will be king. I will rule in his name, but I will be king.'

'Do you think Amon Tugha has come all this way with tens of thousands at his command to let you rule?'

Leon looked down at Janessa. A tear welled in the corner of his eye and for a moment she felt sympathy for him. He had been bewitched. By magick, by the promise of power, perhaps both.

'He swore to me,' he said gently, as though he didn't believe it.

Then he struck his mother across the face, his fist balled tight.

As the old woman fell his expression contorted. Janessa saw all the hate and loathing she imagined Amon Tugha bore for her. In that moment she could hold no sympathy, no mercy.

Leon came at her, his hands outstretched for her throat once more, but she was faster. As he grasped for her she lunged for the knife he had dropped on the garden path. Her fingers closed around it as Leon managed to grab a fistful of curls, hauling her up. His other hand took her by the throat just as she plunged the blade into his eye.

His grip went slack and he made no sound as he fell backward, the knife still protruding from his socket. Leon hit the ground like a discarded doll. Janessa stood and stared at his lifeless form as Baroness Isabelle began to scream, her voice rising in a forlorn wail that murdered the quiet of the garden.

Janessa stared on as her Sentinels came running.

# TWENTY-TWO

There were bruises and scratches all over him but thankfully nothing needed stitching. He couldn't remember where half his wounds had come from, but then you never could when you were in the thick of it. Nobul knew it wasn't the cuts and scrapes would be the worst of it, though. He was tired, almost ready to drop, and if this went on for as long as he thought it might, eventually he would fall and not get back up again.

Still, he wasn't in as bad a state as some of the other lads. It had only been one night, and the fighting had been relatively brief, all told, but some of the boys had been asleep all day. A few of them looked like they might not wake.

For Nobul the sleep never came easy after the fight. He was too alive with it, too needy for the killing. It had started now and he was filled with the anticipation of it. His hammer hand itched to be used. Besides, sleep had never been very kind to him. The shit he dreamed of was never pleasant. Memories he'd rather forget, too many deaths brought back all too vivid.

Yet still he yearned for it, fed on it like fresh cooked meat straight off the spit. Even now he could hear those bastard Khurtas winding themselves up for the night ahead. Singing their songs in the distance as the sun fell.

*And they'll be here soon, Nobul Jacks. They'll be flooding to meet you, falling over themselves to taste that hammer of yours.*

Nobul raised the weapon and looked at that metal head. It was the most finely crafted piece he'd ever made and it had taken him all day to clean the blood and brain and bone from the etched surface. His hammer was a thing of beauty, made for dirty, ugly work. The irony wasn't lost on him.

'Bet you sleep with that thing beside your pillow at night, don't you?'

Hake was stood beside him. Nobul had been so wrapped in his daydream he hadn't even noticed. The old man was bruised about his right eye and there was blood on his green jacket. There would more than likely be a lot more before this business was done with.

Nobul cracked a smile, a rare one at that. 'I always like to sleep beside someone I can trust.' He lowered the hammer, but didn't put it down.

'Reckoned you might need a bit of company. With the fact that the rest of these boys are too shit scared to talk to you.'

It was true. His legend from Bakhaus, and what he'd demonstrated the night before, meant most of the lads who stood beside him were as frightened of the Black Helm as they were of the Khurtas.

'And you're not scared, old man?' Nobul asked, half joking, half wondering.

'I ain't scared of much these days. Even if the Khurtas don't get me, the Lord of Crows ain't that far away. I reckon you're just about the least of my worries.'

'I reckon I am,' said Nobul, turning to look out through the waning light. To the north there was movement, but it was too far to make out.

Hake came to stand beside him at the battlements. 'Last night was just a taster, I'd have said. All Amon Tugha's young and inexperienced throwing themselves at the wall to soften us up. The ones he didn't mind sacrificing the most. Tonight'll be bloodier.'

'I know,' Nobul replied. He'd had the same notion himself. The Khurtas who had attacked the night before had charged in too fast and died too easy. It was obvious a lot of them were unblooded. Tonight Amon Tugha would most likely send his best.

Nobul glanced up and down the wall. They'd taken a lot of

casualties. Whether those who were left would be up to the job remained to be seen, but if they were still alive after last night's fighting, chances were they'd give it their best tonight, despite how tired they looked.

Over to the north a cluster of torches made its way towards them, bobbing through the dark like bright spirits floating in the night. The closer the torches got the more Nobul could make out – a massive group of Khurtas were moving with purpose, but they weren't alone. They dragged prisoners with them, men captured in the weeks of fighting their way south, and maybe even some dragged off the wall the previous night. The closer they got the more he could hear; brutal, guttural language and pleas for mercy. Nobul could only imagine the horrors these men had seen during their time as Khurtic prisoners. He doubted their plight was about to improve.

'What the fuck's going on?' asked Hake, looking anxiously towards the north.

'Nothing good,' said Nobul.

He walked east a way along the wall, hoping to get a better look. By now more of the wall's defenders had heard the commotion and were staring out towards the gathered torches. When the Khurtas and their prisoners had reached Dancer's Tree they stopped.

They set their torches around the base of the oak. Within moments they'd also lit a fire that illuminated the great tree so everyone could see it clear as day. Every man who stood on the wall was staring north and Nobul could feel their dread. They knew they were about to witness something terrible, but couldn't turn their eyes away yet.

Dancer's Tree stood just beyond the range of their archers, it was obvious the Khurtas knew that. As they watched, each of the savages bared his arse and his cock, screaming and taunting and laughing. And there was nothing anyone could do about it.

Then the slaughter began.

The Khurtas took pleasure in hacking limbs and eviscerating the soldiers of the Free States. Screams crossed the short plain to the wall as every man watched with growing dismay. Prisoners were hung from the great branches of Dancer's Tree, much like the days of old, only this time the guts of the condemned hung loose below them and their executioners roared with glee at every death. Some were nailed to the vast trunk, their screams rising over the sound of hammer blows.

Nobul could hear the despair in the rest of the men who stood to either side of him. Hake just stood there with open-mouthed horror, unable to speak. The Khurtas were doing their job well – before long the men on the battlements would be ready to turn tail and flee, allowing the enemy to surge up and over the wall with no one to stop them.

For Nobul, it only made his anger burn. Not because he felt sorrow for those men being slaughtered, but because under that tree he'd buried his boy only a few weeks earlier. Markus, who'd never done anything to anyone. Who'd been shot dead by accident because he was in the wrong place at the wrong time. Under that tree lay Nobul's son and those Khurtic bastards were treading all over the grave like he didn't mean a shit. It burned in Nobul, it cut him deep, and for every man on the wall who covered his eyes so as not to see it made his fury grow.

When they were done with the torture and hanging, the Khurtas took their burning brands and gathered their kindling and they set fire to that oak. Dancer's Tree had stood there more than a hundred years and it took them no time at all to set it aflame.

A lad to Nobul's right dropped to his knees, hiding his tear-streaked eyes from the sight. All along the wall were men with their heads bowed, trying not to weep at what they'd seen, shoulders slumped, all the fight beaten out of them, every man turning his eyes away as the prisoners, some with a bit of life still in them, burned on the tree.

It was about as much as Nobul could stomach.

He leapt onto the battlements, forgetting the hundred-foot drop behind him as he did so. Slamming his helmet on, he raised his hammer high.

'Listen to me,' he yelled. When only a few men looked his way he raised his voice higher. 'Listen to me, you fucking bastards.' More men looked to him; word began to pass down the line as men saw the Black Helm standing atop the battlements, hammer raised to the night sky.

*So what now, Nobul? Rousing speech, is it? Most of the time you can barely string a sentence together. Best not fuck this up or you'll only make things worse.*

Nobul let his anger burn for a moment. Feeling it inside like a swollen fist, all bloody from the fight. It throbbed inside of him and for a moment Nobul knew he had to make words of that anger like he'd never done before.

'Don't turn your eyes away,' he cried. 'Don't hide your fucking faces from them.' He thrust his hammer out towards the plain where the great oak tree burned. 'Look. Look at it and don't turn away. Eat it up till you can't eat no more. Fill your bellies with it. Fill your bellies with hate!'

Men were looking out to where he pointed now. And for anyone who didn't look, there'd be a man next to him who'd strike him on the shoulder or turn his head and make him watch.

'See what they are,' Nobul cried. 'They're fucking cowards. They'll torture and they'll murder, but we've already shown them our steel. They're gonna come again. They're gonna come flooding over this wall and there'll only be one thing to stop them.' He struck the head of his hammer against his palm. It fucking hurt, but it hurt good. It hurt like the hate within him and made him grin that dead man's grin. 'I'll be here. I'll face them till I'm dead. Who'll stand with me?'

Hake and some of the men around him shouted that they would, but it wasn't enough.

'Who the fuck will stand with me?' screamed Nobul, raising that hammer again like it was a banner for them all to flock to.

More men shouted their support and now everyone on that wall had eyes on him, had heads raised and not an ounce of fear between them.

'We'll fight. And we'll die. But not without taking our share of those bastards with us. For Steelhaven!'

'For Steelhaven,' one of them shouted. And the cry was taken up, at first a few, then dozens, then scores along the wall, all taking up the chant of 'Steelhaven, Steelhaven' till it rang out from the battlements and across the plain to drown out the Khurtas below.

Nobul stood there and drank it in, standing like he'd seen old

King Cael stand at Bakhaus Gate all those years ago. There'd been speeches then, speeches aplenty, and all better than his, but in the end the words didn't matter a shit. If what you said helped a man's hate win over his fear then it was speech enough.

He jumped down as they chanted on, and Hake smiled at him. There was a strange look of approval in the old man's eyes.

'Do you think that was enough?' asked Nobul.

'Think we're about to find out,' said the old man, gesturing back over the wall.

Nobul turned. Through the dark, the Khurtas were coming again.

# TWENTY-THREE

They came roaring across the plain once more. This time Regulus and his warriors refused to be banished to the periphery of the battle but stood to the fore, above the main gate. They watched in silence as the Khurtas hit the wall, bracing their ladders and racing up to be met by a hail of arrows and rocks. The ram was also brought across the great plain once more, pushed by burly savages under the lash of their taskmasters. When one fell to a well-placed arrow, another would quickly be whipped into place, his fear of the scourge outweighing his fear of the artillery raining down. When it was finally in position, the great ram was smashed against the gate, shaking the entire wall beneath Regulus' feet.

The noise from below was deafening, the roaring sound of forty thousand men all bent on bringing the city to its knees. Young Akkula could not contain himself, stepping forward and roaring back down over the battlements, the cry echoing from within his helm and rising above the cacophony of guttural rage.

All the while the rhythmic boom of the ram served to mark out the beat of battle. Regulus stood watching; waiting for the first of the Khurtas to come crawling over the battlements looking for death, but the Coldlanders fought them back with a zeal he had previously not seen. Nobul Jacks had earlier made a spirited speech – stoking a fire within them that Regulus could only admire. As a result the Khurtas did not even make it to the lip of the parapet before being repelled. He was beginning to think he might have to leap over the wall and into the fray as he had done the previous night.

Then the gate gave way.

With a mighty crack of timbers the gate splintered inwards. The wall shook, and Regulus had to steady himself as the iron portcullis buckled beneath them. The head of the ram smashed through the gate one last time, sending sparks of burning wood and metal flying. The face of the ram was visible for a brief moment – a magnificent beast's head crafted from iron – before it was pulled back through the flaming gap where the gate had once stood. There was a roar of triumph from the Khurtas and panicked shouts from within the wall as the men below realised they were about to be overwhelmed.

Regulus spoke no orders, rushing to the stone stairwell that led down to the foot of the bastion. His warriors followed eagerly, Akkula and Kazul almost falling over one another in their keenness. Janto took up the rear but Regulus knew he was far from reluctant for the fight.

They reached the bottom, positioning themselves in front of the fallen gate. Coldlanders began to gather all around, their war chiefs barking orders. They were organised into rows, their shields raised, but Regulus wanted to hide behind no barrier. He had come here for glory – the honour of the first kill would be his alone.

'Get behind the bloody shield wall, you mad bastards,' someone yelled from behind them, but Regulus paid him no heed.

As they watched, a group of Khurtas came screaming through the gap they had made ahead of the horde, eager with bloodlust, desperate to slake their thirst with Coldlander blood. But Janto Sho was thirsty too.

With twin axes held at his sides he walked forward as half a dozen enemies came at him. Regulus could barely contain himself as the Sho'tana warrior hacked his way through the screaming savages, taking the honour of first kill for himself, but he let Janto carry on – there was sure to be plenty for everyone.

As Janto cleaved the head from his final foe a strange silence fell over the men behind. They knew what was coming through the gap where the gate had once stood.

Regulus almost gave a roar of challenge but he kept silent instead. Better the Khurtas didn't know what waited for them within the city. Better he greet them with black steel instead.

They came running through the open gateway, heedless of the arrows fired at them in a hasty volley, screaming their rage. Regulus felt a flicker of admiration – for a moment he was back on the plains of Equ'un, facing the Kel'tana one final time, their roars rising above the grasslands. Then he too was running, crossing the ground to the Khurtas, flanked by his warriors, black armoured killers all. The Khurtas did not take a backward step, and Regulus was glad of that. He would have hated to chase down fleeing men – better to face an enemy head on, better the taste of victory when defeating a worthy foe.

His sword rang and he roared as he slew. Beside him Akkula and Kazul did likewise, their ecstasy in battle sounding out for all to hear. In the press he lost sight of Janto, but neither did he care, so caught up was he in his own lust for slaughter. And for every Khurta he killed another took his place, screaming his rage, bellowing his hate. Regulus could only thank them for it – he would not grow fatigued, his breath would not grow short. He had a vigour that could not be sated, not by a dozen dead enemies, not by a score.

Behind them, Regulus heard one of the Coldlander war chiefs bellow the order to attack. The shield wall moved forward, spears jutting forth to take on those Khurtas who had slipped past the Zatani. More savages charged through the gate to join the fray and Regulus almost lost himself, almost raced right through the flaming breach to take the fight to the Khurtas outside.

But the second wave of barbarians did not attack alone. Amidst the charging savages Regulus saw two warriors treading with more care. They both wore black, a man and a woman, but even from a distance he could tell they were more than human. She walked with the confident gait of a warrior, her head uncovered, blond hair falling about her shoulders. He wore a hood, a mask across his face, and held a straight silver blade loosely at his side. Both surveyed the field with golden eyes that seemed to catch the firelight and burn of their own volition. In this pair Regulus saw more than savages attacking in fury.

He saw his chance at glory.

'Kazul. Akkula,' he barked over the din of battle. Both his warriors dragged themselves away from the fray and attended him at his order. 'There.' Regulus pointed his blade across the melee, towards the black-garbed warriors. A smile crossed young Akkula's lips and Kazul growled deep in his throat as they caught sight of the warriors and recognised what Regulus had seen – their chance to face a worthy enemy.

Janto was still lost in the battle, his roars audible over the din, leaving Regulus and his two fellow Gor'tana to cut their way towards the two Elharim, hacking aside the Khurtas in favour of more deadly enemies. As the pair came into view, Regulus saw a smile cross the lips of the woman, her eyes burning with lust as she seemed to revel in the prospect of facing him. He would not disappoint.

'Take him,' said Regulus, pointing to the hooded killer. Kazul and Akkula obeyed, eagerly charging forward to face the man, who merely stood waiting, sword held at his side, making no attempt to defend himself.

Regulus strode forward to face the woman as the battle raged all around. She continued to smile, regarding him with those golden eyes. There was no fear there, only anticipation, yearning.

With a roar, Regulus leapt at her. Her sword came up to meet his, blinding in its swiftness. His black blade clashed against her silver and they were locked together for a moment. Still she regarded him casually, and her strength belied her frame. Regulus stood a full head taller, dwarfing her with his thickly muscled bulk, but she did not relent under his attack. In that instant he realised it would be foolish to underestimate her.

With a grunt she pushed him away and he stepped back in time to avoid her counter, the silver blade moving with such deft speed it almost took his head off. Regulus knew he could allow her no respite and attacked once more with a growl, his black sword clashing against hers. She spun before he could press his attack, moving to his flank. Before she could strike he lashed out with a claw, rending her leather jacket at the shoulder.

The woman growled in pain, skittering back from his next attack, and glared briefly at the wound he had left. Now Regulus could see the look of amusement was gone from her golden gaze. Her brow was furrowed as she looked at the claw marks ripped into her shoulder. He took pleasure in that expression of anger. Gone was her arrogance. Now she would take him as seriously as he took her.

They ran at one another. Regulus' lips had slipped back from his teeth now as he charged, a snarl issuing from deep within him. The woman was silent but there was furious concentration on her face. Her sword spun as they clashed. The black blade in Regulus' hand jarred violently as their weapons met. She was fast, almost too fast, as her sword hacked a divot in the shoulder plate of his armour.

Regulus fought with all the animal fury of the Zatani, his blade and claws swiping the air, but he could not land another blow on her. As they fought he got the ominous feeling he was being toyed with, that she knew she was too fast, too skilled for him. It only made him angry, almost made him sloppy, and might have cost him dear.

The woman's blade caught his hand, hacking at his gauntlet and sending his weapon spinning from his grasp. Her foot came up, lightning fast, to strike at his knee, throwing him off his balance. He went down, slipping to the soft earth, and in an instant she was on him, sword raised. In that moment Regulus saw everything clearly; her eyes locked on his, the corner of her mouth raised in amused triumph.

He had been so eager. Now he was dead.

Janto roared. He was covered in Khurtic blood, his helmet gone, his face a mask of red rage. The woman barely had time to turn her attack into a parry before his axes fell. Against the fury of Janto's assault she could only retreat, hard pressed to fend off his flailing axes.

Regulus staggered to his feet, scrabbling frantically for his fallen blade. As he picked it up, feeling the pain in his hand, he heard a scream of anguish from across the battleground.

Akkula fell as the hooded warrior stepped away from him, pulling his blade free of the Zatani's chest. Spinning with the grace of a dancer, he easily fended off a challenge from Kazul as Regulus began to move, covering the ground to aid his warrior. Before he could reach him, the hooded warrior's blade sang once more, slicing Kazul's spear in two and severing his head.

Regulus snarled, leaping forward, heedless of the pain in his hand and knee. The hooded man looked up with those golden eyes, a brief flash of alarm there as he saw the fierce Zatani bearing down. The Elharim brought his blade up in defence, and Regulus' black sword clashed with it but his right hand was already shooting forward, faster than those golden eyes could follow. He gripped the Elharim's neck in a clawed fist, spitting a snarl as he tore out the man's throat. Those golden eyes regarded him with confusion for the briefest of moments, blood spewing from where his neck had been, before he fell.

Regulus would have roared in victory but the surrounding Khurtas came at him, their attacks frenzied. It was all he could do to fend them off as he was put on the back foot, ceding ground to the enemy with every hack of their blades.

A horn blew, and Regulus looked up to see the Khurtas had been given the order to retreat, though some still fought on, unwilling to flee.

'Get behind the frigging shield wall,' bellowed a voice behind Regulus. His knee throbbed; he knew giving chase was futile and he grudgingly stepped back towards the Coldlanders.

Glancing across the field of dead he saw Janto had retreated too, allowing the Khurtas to run back beyond the shattered gate. The blonde woman knelt beside her fellow Elharim, glaring intently at Regulus. Before they could flee she ordered three Khurtas to retrieve the corpse but all the while she stared at Regulus. When the last of the Khurtas had escaped through the open gateway she followed, walking back reluctantly, as though she was in half a mind to run towards the defensive lines and take her vengeance.

Regulus could only watch the woman as she went, hoping against hope he would have the chance to face her again.

# TWENTY-FOUR

Waylian could only imagine the battle waging to the north of the city. He had seen it first-hand the night before, had lived it in all its bowel-threatening glory. It was just a relief he didn't have to experience it now. He was almost grateful that Gelredida had spared him the wall and given him a different mission. In his gut, though, he knew this would be no less dangerous than standing there waiting for the Khurtas to come running at him. In fact, it was likely much more dangerous.

He stumbled through the blackened wreckage of what had been Dockside. Here and there buildings were still standing – islands amidst a sea of devastated property. Fires burned all around and it took all Waylian's concentration not to trip amidst the detritus. His companion was no more sure-footed either. If anything, Aldrich Mundy was clumsier than Waylian, if that were even possible.

What had his mistress been thinking to partner him with Mundy? The lad was clearly a little bit . . . challenged. If this mission was as important as it seemed then surely he should be accompanied by a senior magister. Or someone who wasn't mad, at least.

'Keep up,' said Waylian, as the bespectacled apprentice tugged on his robe, which had become snared on a blackened timber jutting from a pile of rubble.

He thought Aldrich might give him some petulant comment, using all the verbose language he'd been led to expect, but the lad merely did as he was told. For a moment Waylian felt guilty. Aldrich had obviously never seen devastation like this. Despite his obtuse nature he was most likely terrified out of his wits.

'We're nearly there,' said Waylian, stopping and waiting for Aldrich, who clomped through the uneven ground like a new-born foal. When he eventually reached Waylian's side, Aldrich looked up at the night sky, his eyes lighting up from behind his thin-rimmed spectacles.

'Fascinating,' said the apprentice.

'What is?' Waylian asked, but he needn't have bothered.

He heard the distant roar, saw Aldrich's face brighten with light and the lenses of his spectacles turn white, and spun around to look at the burning missile soaring over the sea wall.

'See how it maintains its structural integrity until the moment of impact?' Aldrich said, pointing up at the night sky. 'It takes a great deal of ingenuity to—'

'Fucking run!' barked Waylian, grabbing Aldrich's robe and dragging him away from where the missile was quite clearly going to land.

He stumbled, Aldrich clapping along behind in his sandals. Something scraped against Waylian's thigh, tearing his robe and lacerating his flesh. He growled but tried to ignore the pain, not daring to look up as the ground all around them brightened like the dawning of a new day.

The heat grew more intense against his back, the noise deafening. Waylian grabbed Aldrich by the shoulders, tackling him to the ground, as what was left of the street exploded behind them. Fragments of masonry soared all about as Waylian sheltered behind a broken wall. Flaming shards burst against the street and Waylian covered his head. He could hear Aldrich squealing beside him as the world seemed to break apart in a searing explosion.

When he could eventually open his eyes Aldrich was mumbling to himself, still curled up in a ball. Waylian was about to reassure the lad when he felt his leg burning. The hem of his robe was in flames, and he started to desperately beat at it with his scuffed hands.

*This is madness. You're going to die here. She's sent you to die again. You should run, Grimmy. Call it a day. You've done enough for her – surely this is a suicide mission too far.*

When the fire was out Waylian glanced at the devastation. Through the fires that raged all around he suddenly spotted something in the shadows of a collapsed building. Three sets of eyes peered out from soot-blackened faces. Waylian couldn't tell if they were children or adults, but the fear written in their features was easy to see, despite the lack of detail. Suddenly he felt a growing sense of urgency to complete his mission.

'Let's go,' he said, rising to his feet and pulling Aldrich with him.

'What a quintessentially stentorian experience,' said Mundy, his voice quavering.

The left lens of his eyeglasses was now cracked and he stared with a wild look to him. Waylian had no idea what help Gelredida had thought he'd be, but it was doubtful he'd be much use in a state of shock.

*You'd best pray for a miracle, then, Grimmy. It's not like you're going to be able to destroy that fleet of ships single-handed, is it?*

They pressed on south. The Sea Gate was easy to see over the plain of flattened buildings and Waylian was instilled with a sense of foreboding. This place was already like the hells. If they tarried much longer there'd be nothing left but cinders, and whoever else was left cowering in the rubble would be doomed.

Waylian and Aldrich picked their way further through the ruins and when they eventually reached the Sea Gate there were several Greencoats crouching beside the wall. Their green jackets were soot darkened, their faces black, but still they waited. Waylian could only admire their dedication. He doubted he'd have borne the same commitment had it been his job to guard this gate.

'What the fuck do you want?' said one of them as Waylian and Aldrich came to crouch beside them. The man's face was a broken mess and he glowered angrily.

Waylian glanced at Aldrich, but it was obvious he had nothing to say. On any other day he'd have taken that as the blessing it was.

'We have to get out there.' Waylian pointed through the blackened iron portcullis, the wooden gate that would have stood in front of it having long since burned down.

'No chance,' said the man. 'This gate stays closed. Those are our orders.'

'We're from the Tower of Magisters. We've been sent to take care of those ships.'

He could hear the fear in his own voice. Part of him wanted the man to listen, to appreciate what he was doing. Another part wanted the man to tell him to fuck off back to the tower where at least he'd be safe . . . for now.

'I don't give a flying shit if you've come straight from the queen's bloody bedchamber. This gate stays shut.'

Waylian glanced around at the other Greencoats. None of them looked in a mood to disagree with their comrade. None of them looked in the mood for anything but running, truth be told. From the corner of his eye, Waylian caught sight of a pile of charred bodies, still smoking in the cold night. He wondered for a moment if they were the bodies of more Greencoats, friends of those left here to guard the gate. These men had been through the mill, of that there was no doubt. Who was he, a young pup dressed in a burned robe and looking scared as a fox in a snare, to order them around?

Without another word Waylian took Aldrich's arm and guided him away from the gate. He glanced to the north and thought about whether to head back to the Tower of Magisters to report his failure. But then he'd reported enough failures to his mistress. He'd been given a mission and he would bloody well carry it out, even if it killed him. Not that very many of the missions she gave him were without life-threatening peril.

'Come on,' he said to Aldrich. 'There must be another way over.'

Aldrich followed obediently as they made their way along the base of the wall. Before long they reached the stairs leading up the parapet, and with no other option they both climbed up to the battlements. The pair of them crouched below the crenellated wall and carefully Waylian peered over the side. Under the moonlight he could make out the crescent bay, the still waters looking black beneath the night sky. In the distance the fire ships sat in a row, their decks lit by burning braziers. Had they not been so dangerous, had they not flung so much death and destruction on his city, Waylian might have thought them beautiful.

Leaning his head out further he looked down to the ground

below. He couldn't estimate the distance but it was obviously too far to jump.

'Think, Waylian,' he said aloud. He knew there was no point addressing Aldrich – he couldn't understand the lad at the best of times, and now in such a state of terror it was unlikely he'd make any more sense. 'There must be a way.'

He looked up and down the wall. Perhaps there'd be a rope somewhere. Perhaps a fisherman's net he could fashion into a ladder. As he moved along the walkway he realised Aldrich wasn't following. Turning he saw the apprentice was staring out to sea.

'We need to move,' Waylian whispered, though why he was whispering he didn't know. It wasn't as if the mariners on the artillery ships were going to hear him.

Without a word of reply, Aldrich clambered on the wall, gripping the merlons to either side of him.

'What are you doing?' said Waylian, panic gripping him.

He rushed to Aldrich's side, reaching out to pull him back, but with unexpected speed, Aldrich gripped his wrist and pulled him up onto the battlements.

'What the fu—' was all he had a chance to say before Aldrich leaned back and pulled them both over the lip of the wall.

There was no time to scream. No time to try and stop himself as he fell into the darkness. The air rushed in his face, his stomach lurched violently. As they fell Aldrich gripped him around the arms and Waylian squeezed his eyes shut, girding himself for the impact.

When he opened them again they were both standing at the base of the wall, Aldrich still holding him in a surprisingly tight grip. They looked at one another as the sea breeze brushed their faces. Aldrich didn't say a word, letting go and leading the way down to the dock. Waylian stared for a moment, not quite able to believe he was still alive, then followed, on legs like jelly. He had no idea what magicks Aldrich had used to halt their fall but he was thankful for them anyway.

'Next time, bloody warn me,' he whispered. If Aldrich heard him he gave no answer.

They made their way down to the waterside and along the great crescent harbour, their shoes making barely a sound on the wood.

As they moved through the dark another flaming missile was fired from one of the ships, soaring past them and over the city wall to land with a dull explosion.

Waylian was following his fellow apprentice now, who seemed to have taken the lead. He should have been put out about the sudden change in their dynamic, but if he was honest with himself he didn't really have a clue what he was going to do when he got to the harbour anyway.

When they were level with the ships, Aldrich stopped, glaring out at the row of vessels anchored in the water.

'What now?' asked Waylian. 'I hope you've got something spectacular planned.'

Aldrich turned, smiling now, and he offered his hand to Waylian. 'Oh indubitably,' he replied. 'But your assistance is required.'

'How so?' asked Waylian, reluctantly taking Aldrich by the hand.

'You have tapped the Veil before, haven't you, Waylian?'

'Of course I have.' *By mistake, but I've still bloody done it.*

'Then let's try it together. It's quite the most quickening of experiences.'

Aldrich knelt beside the harbour, laying his palm on the wooden boards at his feet while still gripping Waylian's hand. At first there was nothing, no incantation, no magickal signs, only the pungent smell of the sea carried on the night breeze.

It was some time before Waylian realised his hand had turned to ice. A cold he'd never felt before crept up his arm where Aldrich gripped him, into his flesh and into his bones. He wanted to call out but he had no voice, wanted to pull away but there was no strength in his limbs.

He looked down to see that where Aldrich's other hand was touching the planks they had turned to ice, a solid sheet that spread from the young man's fingers and down the side of the strut on which the crescent harbour stood. The more he stared the more he saw the ice spread out from the base of the harbour and into the sea. Waylian could hear the ice cracking as the sea solidified and all the while he grew colder.

Just as he thought he could stand it no longer and would be turned into a solid block of ice, Aldrich released his hand. Waylian collapsed to the boardwalk, feeling heat instantly flood back into him. Aldrich merely stood, looking out to sea and at the pathway they had both made. Waylian saw it led out into the night, towards the waiting artillery ships in the distance.

'What now?' he mumbled through gritted, frozen teeth. 'Are we supposed to just stroll up and put their fires out?'

'No,' Aldrich replied. 'There is no way we would succeed with such a strategy. But they could.' He pointed back up towards the city.

Waylian looked, but through the dark he couldn't see a thing. Then, through his cold-numbed ears, he thought he heard a sound like thunder.

# TWENTY-FIVE

They rumbled through the streets on horseback. Twenty of them, fully armoured with shield and sword. This had all seemed like such a good idea at the time – and fact was, they were riding away from the battle that raged to the north – but now Merrick was beginning to see the error of his ways. Just twenty men against a phalanx of ships anchored south of the city. Just twenty men taking on an entire fleet. Granted, they were the meanest, hardest bastards Merrick had ever had the misfortune to meet, but still; they were only human.

The Lord Marshal hadn't said a word to him as they prepared their destriers for the mission. Merrick had half expected the old man to approach him, demanding that he change his mind, but Tannick said nothing. Maybe deep down he was proud. Maybe some part of him was glad Merrick had volunteered for the most perilous of tasks. Or maybe he just didn't want to lose face in front of the Wyvern Guard by chastising his son who'd volunteered for such a perilous mission.

Whatever the reason, Merrick was glad of it. There were enough things to think on without arguing with the old man. Things like not getting stabbed or burned or drowned were much higher on his list than worrying about the punishments Tannick Ryder could come up with for his disobedience.

As they made their way further south through the city, Merrick got to see first-hand what carnage the artillery ships had wrought, and for the first time he appreciated the importance of their mission. Dockside and the Warehouse District were in ruins. To the southeast the Temple of Autumn seemed relatively untouched, but that did little to assuage the devastation that had been wreaked on the rest of the city's southern quarters. Merrick only hoped there had been no one living here when the bombardment began. Deep down he knew there must have been. Deep down he knew most of these houses would have bodies in them, burned and black and clawing at the sky with dead hands.

*And that makes you angry, doesn't it? That makes you want to kill. That moves you and you don't fucking like it, Ryder.*

Merrick gripped his reins tighter, his jaw setting. He tried not to look, not to think, but it was impossible. This wasn't war, this was murder. For all his selfishness, for all his self-indulgence and arrogance and acting the jester for so many years, this hurt. There needed to be a reckoning for this.

*But you've never been the vengeance type, Ryder. You've never given enough of a shit. Revenge is a waste of time; it just gets in the way. What happened to Merrick Ryder the pragmatist?*

'He's dead and gone,' he said through gritted teeth.

*Only time will tell, Ryder. Let's wait and see, shall we? There's still plenty of time for you to prove you haven't changed.*

The twenty horses gradually made their way to the sea wall. Cormach led the way, the white pelt he wore across his shoulders bobbing in time to the stride of his warhorse. Just before they reached the gate a fireball cut the sky above them, smashing into a street a hundred yards away. It was an unnerving reminder of why they were here, but did little to curb Merrick's determination.

They reined in, their horses milling before the great portcullis. It was blackened and charred and Merrick wondered if the mechanisms that opened it would still work.

'Open the gate,' Cormach shouted.

Merrick looked at the base of the portcullis. In the dark he hadn't even seen the soot-encrusted men cowering there.

'What the fuck is wrong with everyone tonight?' said one of them. 'This gate stays closed. By order of the queen.'

Cormach trotted his horse forward, staring down from the saddle.

'Open the gate,' he said, his tone measured in that *don't fuck with me* way he had about him.

The gate guard looked up at him. Merrick could tell he wanted to argue, but a quick glance at the twenty Wyvern Guard, all armed and armoured and ready to kill something, and he quickly changed his mind.

The filthy Greencoat gave a nod at the rest of the men. Three of them scuttled into the small wheelhouse and within moments the gate started moving. It shuddered and creaked, soot and charcoal falling from it in great clumps as the three men wound the winch. Merrick could hear them gasping from inside the tiny building as they strained to turn the wheel. All he could do was stare through the gate at the harbour below.

The ships were waiting, sitting there like they were beckoning him forward. He was most likely going to die down there and he'd bloody well volunteered to do it.

*Remember those shattered houses? Remember the bodies inside them? What happened to vengeance, Ryder? What happened to the old you being dead and gone?*

Before he had time to think on it further, Cormach spurred his horse through the open gate. The rest of the Wyvern Guard did likewise, the sound of their hooves on the cobbles ringing out like bells across the harbour. Trot turned to canter turned to gallop as they headed down towards the crescent bay. Cormach's sword rang from its sheath, nineteen others ringing after it. The sound of the horses' hooves changed timbre as they galloped from the cobbled road and onto the wooden jetty.

Merrick could feel the wind in his face now, the thrill of the charge. There must be a plan to this, something he hadn't been told, because how they were going to ride across the bay and onto those ships was a question he hadn't been made privy to.

As they clattered along the boards he kept his eyes fixed on the ships, wondering if at any moment they'd send one of their burning missiles hurtling towards the Wyvern Guard. He quickly realised he needn't have worried. The artillery ships weren't designed to be manoeuvrable. They'd never have a chance to aim before the Wyvern

Guards' steeds reached the end of the jetty . . . and plunged straight into the water.

Cormach's horse pulled ahead and he raised his blade. It was almost impossible to see where they were going, their way lit only by the moon, but thankfully it was bright enough so that none of them rode off the edge of the boardwalk.

Just when Merrick thought they'd run out of pier, Cormach yanked his reins violently, steering his horse to the left and off the side of the gangway. Merrick felt his heart lurch at the insane manoeuvre, thinking Cormach would plunge headlong into the freezing cold bay, but he saw the horse was still running, its hooves clacking against a new surface.

Without thinking, without even considering how mad this was, Merrick followed, his horse snorting in agreement with the insanity of the whole thing. As he reined the steed after Cormach's he felt the difference under its hooves, heard the clacking and cracking as though he had just ridden onto a bridge of . . . ice?

The Wyvern Guard galloped down onto the sea, following Cormach as he rode towards the first of the artillery ships. They were approaching at the fleet's flank, the bridge spanning out before them, taking them right up to the gunwale of the first vessel. Merrick could hear the mariners aboard their ships, shouting in panic. They'd heard the approaching knights now, and could more than likely feel the rumble of hooves on the ice bridge.

As he followed Cormach up the slope onto the deck, Merrick was almost blinded by the fire still alight on board the ship. He just had time to see Cormach cut down a sailor, just had time to see another member of the crew trapped under a sheet of ice that had consumed the deck, his eyes staring up in blank terror, before he was off the other side, his steed leaping the gunwale.

Cormach didn't stop, and Merrick was determined not to let him get too far ahead. There were twenty Wyvern Guard, all eager for the kill. No use crowding the first ship when there were over a dozen more to go at.

The second ship was better prepared, sailors shouting, brandishing their billhooks and cutlasses threateningly, but Cormach's steed bowled past them as though they weren't there. They rode on, taking the third ship, the fourth. Merrick could hear the sounds of battle behind as the Wyvern Guard engaged those sailors still able to fight and not trapped in the ice. He began to think this might not quite be the suicide mission he had first anticipated. Maybe his righteous anger would be sated after all. Those women and children burned alive back in the city avenged by his hand. The hand of Merrick Ryder. Reborn as a divine weapon of—

His horse whinnied shrilly as it lost its footing on the ice bridge. It staggered then fell, and it wasn't until he had leapt from the saddle and rolled clear that Merrick realised the animal had taken a spear to its side. By the light of the fires on deck he could see the silhouettes of three sailors coming at him. Cormach had ridden off ahead and the rest of the Wyvern Guard were still hacking down survivors on the ships behind. He was on his own.

The three mariners surrounded him, their backs to a bright fire still burning on deck. In the glare Merrick could hardly make them out and only narrowly avoided the first thrust of a cutlass. He brought up his shield in time to catch another blow before gaining the wherewithal to counter. There was a cry from the dark and he felt the jarring of sword hitting flesh, but his relief at striking a blow was short-lived. His helmet clanged as something hit it from the side. Merrick slipped back, losing his footing on the deck. The shield fell from his hand as he was bowled backward, the gunwale hitting the back of his legs. He couldn't stifle a cry of panic as he was pitched back into the water.

His free hand grabbed out as he fell, for something, anything. Somehow he still kept a grip on his sword, fear of losing such a blade almost trumping his desire to survive. Something snagged his armour just as he hit the water. The black consumed him, the freezing dark. His helmet came off and he had to let go of that beautiful sword. To his relief he'd been caught in netting but his armour was still pulling him down, sucking him into the black depths. Merrick's arm shot from the freezing water, grasping the net. With titanic effort he pulled himself up, dragging his head out from under the sea, snorting salty water and gasping for air.

For a moment he paused there in the cold, breathing heavily, panting the life back into himself. Above he could still hear the sounds of battle. The screams, the whinnying of horses. Something plunged into the water nearby but he couldn't bring himself to look and see whether it was one of his brother knights or a mariner.

When he'd breathed enough air back into his lungs, Merrick pulled himself up. The going was slow, his armour seeming to weigh twice as much as it had before he'd fallen in the bay. Clapping both hands on the gunwale he dragged himself up over the side of the ship, flopping onto the deck like a landed fish. His breath came hard and he could have closed his eyes and slept if he hadn't been so bloody cold.

*No point lying here all night. What happened to vengeance? What happened to the new Merrick? You're just as lazy and useless as the old one.*

Merrick dragged himself to his feet. His sword was lost and he looked around in the gloom for a weapon, any weapon. One suddenly came at him from the dark – the blade of a cutlass, curved and sharp as fuck. On the other end of it was a scared-looking sailor, eyes all wide and desperate like he'd seen some murder he hadn't been expecting and was determined he wasn't going to be next.

'Why don't you calm yourself?' said Merrick, holding his hands up in surrender. The mariner didn't seem too impressed with that. In fact it seemed to make him angrier and even more desperate. 'There's a way out of this for both of us,' Merrick continued, hoping his mouth would do a better job of getting him out of the shit than his armour and weapons had. 'We can both survive this but you have to be cle—'

The sailor's head split down the middle. In the dark it looked like black gore had exploded from his skull. He stood there for a moment, staring in confusion as if he'd just been asked the meaning of life, before collapsing to the deck. Cormach was standing behind him.

Merrick let out a sigh of relief and leaned back on the gunwale, careful not to pitch himself backwards this time. Glancing up and down the row of ships he saw that the Wyvern Guard had already done their work. Fires burned on the deck of every ship and they were already reining their horses in, ready to leave.

'That makes us fucking even,' said Cormach when he'd finally managed to free his blade from the mariner's skull.

Merrick waved an arm nonchalantly, in no mood to argue. He was too busy thinking about what a monumental fuck-up he'd just made. About how he'd bravely ridden onto the ships and managed to almost die without knowing if he'd actually killed anyone. He doubted his contribution would be recorded in the annals of the Wyvern Guard.

So much for vengeance. So much for being the righteous hero.

*But at least you're still breathing.*

# TWENTY-SIX

Nobul watched the siege tower moving towards the wall. He didn't move, didn't speak, just stood and stared. Around him was a ruckus – arrows flying all about, men shouting for reinforcements. Someone was sobbing somewhere. Someone screaming. A dead body lay a couple of yards away, chest all opened up. The severed head of a Khurta was laid on its side in the shadow of the wall, staring at him angrily from the dark. Nobul had no idea what the savage head was so pissed off about – it hadn't been him that killed the ugly bastard. There were plenty of others he had killed, though. And when that siege tower got close enough there'd be plenty more.

'Come on, bastards!' someone shouted beside him.

Arrows flew past his head, clacking harmlessly against the armour of the siege tower. An archer inside the tower fired back, not quite as harmlessly, and someone in the line fell screaming.

Nobul gripped his hammer the tighter as the siege tower came to a stop. An eerie silence fell over the wall's defenders as they waited for what was about to happen. Nobody knew quite what was going to come screaming from inside but they were ready to kill it, whatever it was.

With a creak, the armour plates that made up the front of the tower fell forward on iron hinges, creating a bridge to the wall. The Khurtas were already running before the thing even landed.

Nobul wasn't about to let them set foot on the battlements without a proper greeting.

He ran forward, ahead of the rest. His hammer connected with a Khurta's sword, sending it spinning off over the battlements. The bastard was screaming so loud Nobul felt it ringing inside his helmet and his hand reached out on instinct, grabbing that warbling throat and cutting off any noise. Still with the first Khurta in his grip, Nobul swung again, smashing a shoulder and putting another down before he'd had time to step off the ramp.

More noise consumed him as the rest of the wall's defenders followed his lead, shields raised, spears and swords striking forward. Blood splashed on his arm, and he raised his hammer again, setting it to work, beating his way through the mass of bodies as they became crammed together. Men fell from the ramp to their deaths, the screams mixing with shouts of anger.

The feel of hammer on flesh and bone juddered through his arm, his shoulder starting to ache. In the press all he could see were screaming faces, lurching towards him, easy targets. A blade clanked off his helm. A Khurta fell in front of him and Nobul brought his boot down on the exposed head three times before the rest of him stopped squirming.

Deep in the back of his throat he began to growl, spitting his ire as more and more men fell before him and the press thinned out. Every Khurta that ran from that siege tower was met by blade or hammer or arrow. They came so eager for the kill and that's what they got. Before long Nobul was standing on his own, bellowing at empty air, with no one else to fight.

He looked over his shoulder and the rest of the city's bannermen were standing staring at him, their faces masked with shock and blood. Nobul breathed heavy, and it wasn't until he lowered his hammer that he realised the Khurta he had grasped by the throat was still in his grip, dead eyes staring, tongue lolling. As Nobul dropped the limp body to the ground there was a shout of alarm from the east.

'They've taken the fucking Stone Gate!'

Nobul saw it was a young lad, helmet too big for his head, face a mask of blood. He just stood there, not knowing what to do. As he looked around he could see everyone else was doing much the same.

Slowly Nobul walked down from the siege tower ramp, picking his way through the bodies.

'Make sure that burns,' he said to a couple of lads, pointing back to the tower. 'Rest of you, on me.'

With that he set off at a trot, looking through the dark to the east. He could see a press of soldiers ahead, a tight phalanx on the wall, and beyond them was the bastion of the Stone Gate. Nobul couldn't see much of what was going on but he could hear the Khurtas shouting in their language.

By the time he reached the bastion, the shouting had risen to screaming, but there didn't seem to be much fighting going on. Nobul pressed his way through the crowd, men all tightly packed, cowering behind their shields. As he reached the front he saw the Khurtas were waiting opposite the top of the gate tower. They were taunting Steelhaven's defenders, beckoning them to attack, and it was obvious these weren't just any savages. They knew throwing themselves at a phalanx of shields would be suicide. They wanted to get their enemy to attack in the open space of the bastion.

Who was he to disappoint them?

Nobul pushed his way past to the row of shield bearers at the front. When he tried to move through the shield wall one of them made to speak, most likely to tell him not to be a stupid bastard, but when he saw that black helm he shut his mouth quick sharp. The wall parted and let him through, out onto the roof of that bastion with nothing between him and the Khurtas but the fear and death on the night breeze.

When they saw him step out onto that platform the Khurtas quieted a touch. Maybe some of them recognised him or had at least heard of the black helmed daemon wielding his hammer on the wall, smashing back their countrymen like they were nothing. Nobul couldn't suppress a smile at that. For the first time he saw doubt in the faces of the Khurtas, and if any of them wanted to take him on they were none too keen about it.

'Who's first?' he shouted across at the savage mob.

No one moved.

Just when he thought he'd be standing there all night, there was a commotion towards the rear of the crowd of Khurtas. From the shadows at the back walked a warrior a head taller than the rest. He pushed his way to the front, massive axe in hand, beard bursting out of his chin in a black mass. The giant stood there for a moment, weighing up his opponent, and Nobul let him drink in a long look.

The Khurtas started to chant as the giant stared at Nobul. 'Wolkan, Wolkan, Wolkan,' they sang, gleeful at what was to come. Behind Nobul his own men were silent, which wasn't a great vote of confidence, but luckily he'd never needed to be cheered on in a fight. The killing was enough of a reward.

'He's a bloody big one.' Nobul glanced to his left and saw Hake peering over the crowd behind. 'You sure about this?'

Nobul wasn't sure, but he knew it had to be done. This Wolkan cunt needed killing. These Khurtas needed showing their champions could be beaten. Besides, no other fucker was going to take him on, so why not the Black Helm?

'Be careful of that axe,' Hake shouted as Nobul stepped forward.

'Thanks for the advice,' he breathed in reply.

Wolkan barked a laugh of disdain as Nobul came, waving that big axe around his head as though it weighed nothing. Nobul hefted his hammer, staring up, and the Khurta grinned wide, showing his missing teeth. He laughed again, then took a massive stride forward so they were no more than a yard apart. They looked at each other, axe and hammer held at the ready. Then Wolkan brought that axe down like he was chopping a log.

Nobul grasped his hammer at both ends and held it up to block the axe. The hafts of their weapons struck together and Nobul's arms almost buckled under the weight of the blow, the axe blade clanging against his helmet. The force of it knocked him back a few steps and he staggered into the shields behind. One of the shield men pushed forward, throwing him at Wolkan once more. Nobul was sure it was meant as encouragement but all it did was put him right within range again. Wolkan swung his axe and Nobul just managed to duck, feeling the weapon sweep over him, keen to lop him in half. He spun, bringing up his hammer, but Wolkan was faster, grasping the weapon by the haft and raising his massive axe one-handed.

The huge Khurta opened his mouth to shout his victory cry, proud of himself at so easily besting the champion of Steelhaven. Nobul smashed his helmeted head right in the bridge of his nose, jumping up to reach, feeling the jarring impact like he'd just head-butted a tree.

Wolkan loosed his grip on the hammer, staggering back, his axe almost dropping from his hand. Nobul had to press in – if he gave this giant time for another attack he'd more than likely be done for. Maybe he should have made a spectacle of it. Maybe he should have drawn out the battle to show those Khurtic bastards just who was the best. Then again, the longer this went on, the more chance he had of dying.

Nobul's hammer came down on the Khurta's shoulder. There was a dull crack of bone, but to his credit Wolkan didn't cry out in pain. He instead tried to raise his axe, but Nobul batted it aside with his hammer, sending it skittering across the top of the bastion. Another strike at the shoulder and Wolkan went down, his face a mask of bearded rage. He began to speak in the Khurtic tongue – a garbled rant of hate. Nobul's next hammer blow caught him in the jaw, shattering it and giving the giant's face an odd skewed expression. His next strike staved in Wolkan's head, the hammer embedding itself in his skull, eye popping out of its socket to dangle uselessly on that bearded face.

The Khurtas had gone quiet now. Nobul looked at them as he wrenched his hammer free and let Wolkan's body fall to the ground in a heap. He thought about shouting for someone else to come forward and take him on, to see if the rest of them had the stones for a fight, but all of a sudden he felt bloody tired. Not that he need have worried. The Khurtas were just staring at him, some in awe, others in fear.

Behind, someone shouted the order to attack. A score of men ran past Nobul, eager to take on the Khurtas, eager to show them as much grit and death as Nobul had just shown this Wolkan bastard. If they expected a fight they were sorely disappointed as the Khurtas suddenly routed. As much as he'd have liked to join them in the chase, Nobul didn't have the heart.

'Nice work,' said Hake.

Nobul looked to see the old man standing next to him with a wry smile.

'It wasn't so hard,' Nobul lied.

'No, didn't look it.' Hake knelt down by the huge Khurta's body. 'Not every day you get to bring down a Khurtic war chief.'

'Should I be pleased with myself?'

Hake shrugged. 'Yes and no. You should be pleased you're still breathing, that's for sure. How long you're breathing for is another matter. You just made yourself a target for every Khurta at this wall who wants to prove himself. Word's gonna spread. And when it does they'll all be looking to claim your head and the glory that goes with it.'

*Well done, Nobul. If you thought things were tough before you've just made them ten times worse. But you never were one for doing things the easy way, were you?*

'Let them come,' said Nobul, gripping his hammer the tighter.

Suddenly, despite the hurt and the fatigue, he had the urge to smash more heads.

# TWENTY-SEVEN

River had stood at the city's highest promontories countless times and looked out over Steelhaven's majesty with awe. He had looked out for miles at views no one else had ever been privy to and thrilled at the sight. Now, as he clung to what remained of a crumbling tower, he was only filled with sadness.

Men fought and died by the score defending a wall that looked almost ready to fall. Machines of war flung burning artillery as others trundled across the plain that sat to the city's north, delivering savage, screaming warriors bent on destroying what had once been a place of such splendour. The enemy teemed, sweeping forward in a wave of savagery, and yet the city's defenders stood fast against them, despite the odds.

How River would have loved to race down and join them in their fight. How he would have loved to add his strength and skill to protect Steelhaven. Not because it was his city, but because it was hers. But he knew that was folly. To fight and die with everyone else would be courageous, but ultimately he would fall. There was only one way he could end this. Only one way he could save the city, and Jay with it.

Amon Tugha had to die.

With their warlord fallen these savages would have no one to rally to. They would be headless, aimless, and would scatter back to the north. Or so he could only hope.

River moved down from the tower. The rooftops he had known so well were changed now. Bombardment from the north meant that many of the structures he had traversed for years were no longer there or had become perilous to move across. More than once he lost his footing as a strut broke beneath his foot or a hole appeared in a tiled roof, and when finally he managed to reach the outer wall he was breathing hard from the effort.

The Khurtas were concentrating their attack to the north. Here on the eastern side of the city it was relatively quiet but the wall was still heavily guarded. In the dark, River managed to slip past the vigilant sentries, aided by the fact that most of them stared pensively to the north or out over the wall to the east. He easily scaled the bastion of the Lych Gate and slipped over the battlement. The climb to the ground was harder as he slipped down the face of the gate tower, past the two carved figures – hooded warriors holding their swords aloft – and leapt the last ten feet to land deftly in the dark.

He wasted no time, sprinting northwards. The night was black beyond the ambient light of the city and he was aware that there could be enemies lurking in the dark. Though the Khurtas were attacking as a horde to the north it was more than likely there were groups of them lurking elsewhere, ready to fall upon anyone desperate enough to try and escape the attack on Steelhaven.

River gave the massed army a wide berth, running far to the east as the battle raged into the night and skirting a ridge almost a league north of the city. As he reached a crest in the hill River slowed, hunkering down and moving in silence. Beyond the hill he could see the radiant light of campfires and hear voices talking in an alien tongue. As he neared he drew his blades, focusing on his work. The mark would be in that camp somewhere. Amon Tugha was waiting.

A sentry walked idly by as River crouched in the shadows. The man paused, staring south, and in the moonlight River could see a look of yearning in his eyes, as though he envied his brethren. They were unleashing their barbarism on the city, and he lusted to join them, to die beside them as they flung themselves at the wall. River was happy to grant him a death of a different kind.

His blade moved in the dark, opening the Khurta's throat. The man fell silently, his head almost severed as River moved on, down the ridge beyond and into the camp.

Hide tents of varying sizes and shapes were erected all around, though there were few Khurtas left in the camp, making it easy for River to stick to the shadows, moving unseen as he searched. Surely Amon Tugha would be in the largest tent, the one appropriate for his station. All River had to do was find it amongst this mass of hide coverings.

He stalked towards the centre of the encampment, listening intently for the sounds of voices or footfalls on the soft earth, all the while steering clear of the fires that burned intermittently. Occasionally there would be cries of pain from the Khurtic wounded that lay amidst the tents. They had been left there with no one to tend them, abandoned to live or die on their own. It seemed a cruel practice but River cared little for the savagery of it. They and their warlord were without mercy, he understood that clear enough. He would show just as little mercy when he faced Amon Tugha.

When he was roughly at the camp's centre he saw a tent that stood taller and wider than the rest. No sentries stood outside it and it seemed all but abandoned. River waited in the shadows, sensing that this could be some kind of trap, but there was no one he could see or hear and no other way he could think to locate his mark other than searching the entire camp.

He darted forward, crossing the clearing to the tent entrance and moving inside in one swift movement, blades at the ready. The tent's interior was dark but a waning fire was bright enough for River to see. Across the floor, perhaps twenty yards, was a wooden chair and on it, lounging casually, one leg slung over the arm, was a warrior. He smiled at River as he entered, holding that smile even as River moved towards him. As arrogant and powerful as this warrior looked, he was clearly not Amon Tugha, but with luck he might know where River could find him.

The warrior made no move to defend himself, despite River's clear intent. He showed no fear, and River felt a rising anger. He would make this man fear him, as he had made so many others fear him.

As he trod the ground no more than five yards in front of the wooden chair his foot sank up to the calf. River cursed himself as he felt a noose tighten around his ankle. There was little time to lament his stupidity as the tent suddenly erupted all around, Khurtas with bows and spears suddenly appearing from beyond the hide sidings. River slashed at the snare around his foot, desperate to free himself, but there was already a spear pressed against his back and three Khurtas closed in to point-blank range, aiming their bows at him.

His desperation to find Amon Tugha had made him complacent and now he was cornered. He glanced around, looking for any chance to escape, but there was none; a dozen warriors surrounded him, their yearning to do him harm plain to see.

Calmly the warrior rose from the wooden chair, speaking in the Khurtic language, the words flat and even rather than spat gutturally as River had heard other Khurtas speak before. A knife was pressed to River's throat, his own blades taken from him swiftly, warily, as though these warriors knew what he was capable of. Swiftly, his hands were bound behind him and he was led unceremoniously from the tent.

They moved south through the camp. All the while River searched for his chance to escape but no opportunity presented itself. It was as though these savages had been warned of his skill, as though they had been handpicked for this task. Their leader was certainly wary, despite his pretence at nonchalance, his hands never straying far from the axe and sword at his hips, his eyes watching all the while for any sign that River might try and escape.

Eventually they came to a ridge. Beyond it was the city, the siege raging into the night, fires rising, arrows falling. Silhouetted there, huge against the distant light, was a figure River knew could only be Amon Tugha. He stood easily seven feet, his bulk massive against the night. Some distance away were two more figures barely visible in the shadows; one was lying prone and still on the ground, the other, a woman from what River could see, crouched over the body in silence.

River was led up the ridge mere yards from Amon's back. It would have been nothing to make his attack but his hands were bound, his weapons gone. All he could do was stand and wait.

'You are the student,' Amon Tugha said eventually, his voice deep as the ocean. 'The betrayer. The one who turned his back on the Father of Killers for the love of a woman.'

River said nothing. He owed this warlord no explanation. He had come to kill him, not curry words.

Amon Tugha turned and glared with golden eyes, bright in the darkness. 'I know why you have come. I have seen into your soul, assassin. You would kill me. Save this city and save its queen. You are brave, if nothing else, and that is to be admired. But bravery will not protect you. And it will not save her.'

From the shadows a Khurtic warrior brought forth a huge weapon, a spear made of steel, the head almost two feet long and wide as a man's hand. Amon took it in his grip as though it weighed nothing. He spoke swiftly in the Khurtic tongue, and two of River's captors came forward, a knife deftly cutting his bonds. Another Khurta brought forward his blades and River took them, almost in a daze.

'You have come to slay me, assassin. Now is your chance.' Amon Tugha held out his arms, as though presenting himself as an easy target. 'Spare your queen my wrath.'

River needed no further encouragement. He had known in coming here he would most likely die. At least he could take the Elharim warlord with him to the hells.

He rushed forward, wary of the huge spear in Amon Tugha's hand. He was ready to duck or dodge but the Elharim made no move to defend himself. River leapt, his blade arm stabbing forward to take Amon in the neck, but the spear came up impossibly fast, the flat of its blade hitting River's outstretched hand and swatting his weapon away into the night.

River landed, stumbling as he did so, his right hand numb. Amon Tugha had moved from his path and was walking nonchalantly, spinning the spear he held as though it weighed nothing. Those golden eyes regarded River without emotion.

'You are quick for a southron, assassin,' Amon said. 'Precise. Dedicated. I would have valued such skill. It is a shame you must die.'

River rushed in again and feinted to the right, just as the warlord swung his spear. He had intended to dodge but his enemy's attack was simply too fast, taking River's legs out before he could react. He hit the ground on his back, bracing himself for the killing thrust, but none came. Instead Amon Tugha stepped back, allowing him to rise and attack once more.

As River leapt back to his feet he saw Amon was smiling, and anger welled within him. Frustration forced him to press a final desperate attack. He struck in, expecting the spear to skewer him, but instead Amon released his grip on the weapon and let it fall to the ground. His other hand shot out, taking River by the wrist in which he held his remaining weapon. The warlord's grip tightened like a vice, forcing the blade from River's grasp as Amon's other hand took him by the throat.

'You knew you could not win,' said the Elharim. 'Yet you came anyway. You sacrificed yourself for her and for that you have my admiration.' Slowly Amon turned River's head to look at the crouching figure off in the shadows and the body she held vigil over. 'But you are not the only one to make sacrifices in this. You are not the only one to suffer.'

River could only stare helplessly, choking in the grip of the immortal Elharim prince. This was it; he would die here, throttled to death as battle raged hundreds of yards away.

His vision began to haze, his limbs growing weak, but before he could succumb to oblivion River felt his arms being grasped by the surrounding Khurtas. They dragged him to a nearby tree and lashed him to the trunk so he could only look out onto the city.

'I am not without mercy, assassin,' said Amon Tugha. 'You came here to kill me but despite your failure I will allow you to live. To watch as your city burns. Perhaps before I slay your queen I will allow you to look upon her one last time.'

With that the Elharim disappeared into the shadows, leaving the gaggle of Khurtas to watch over River.

All he could do was stare to the south as the city was attacked. As Steelhaven died and there was nothing he could do to stop it.

# TWENTY-EIGHT

Jerrol and the ten he'd brought with him, Bastian's best, made their way east through the deserted streets like rats on the hunt. Hands, faces and blades were blackened with pitch. Even if anyone had been about at that hour of the night no one would have seen them.

The noise from the north end of the city echoed down through the streets. Jerrol didn't envy the soldiers their job. Facing the Khurtas was a thing for brave men, courageous and true to the Crown. Luckily for Jerrol he was none of those things. He'd never been brave. *Stab a man in the back soon as look at him* – that's what they said about old Jerrol the Nick. *You wouldn't see him coming*, they said. *Coward and a liar and a thief*, they said. Jerrol couldn't argue with any of that. It was always best to know what you were and admit it freely.

Didn't matter a shit if they were brave, anyway. The bannermen of Steelhaven were wasting their time and their lives defending that wall. Especially since he and his lads were about to let the Khurtas come flooding in through the side door.

Jerrol had troubled himself with the rights and wrongs of it for all the time it took him to sink an ale. He was Bastian's man – had been for years now – and what Bastian wanted, Bastian fucking well got. Who was Jerrol to question it? Who was he to say whether letting the Khurtas in was a mistake? Bastian had never led them wrong before and there was no need to think he'd be doing it now. Best just to get on with the task and trust they'd all live through it after.

Eleven men for this job was probably overkill. They had a Greencoat – Platt, his name was – on the payroll who was posted on the Lych Gate. He'd make the way easy for them as it was, so the fact they'd come mob-handed was only a precaution. Always paid to be careful, though, Jerrol knew that better than anyone. *No use taking risks*, his old man had always said. Not that it had stopped the old fart taking a knife in the belly when Jerrol was only a young lad, but they were still wise words.

The gate loomed at the end of the street. Jerrol felt his stomach turn a little bit as they approached. Didn't matter how easy it seemed, this job still had to be done right. He would be careful, and no mistake, but there was always something that could go wrong. The consequences if he fucked this up didn't bear thinking about. You didn't let Bastian down – that was rule number one. Palien was testament to that. He'd been clever and strong and earned the Guild a lot of money but in the end it didn't matter a shit. One fuck-up and you were meat, nothing more. Jerrol had been the one to run his knife across that bastard Palien's throat. The last thing he wanted was to be on the receiving end.

He halted at the end of the street, crouching down and peering through the gloom towards the gate. One low whistle, the sound of an owl in the night, and he knew the other ten lads would stop and take up positions in the shadows.

The Lych Gate was in utter darkness. Jerrol stared through the night, hoping the moonlight would give him some sort of clue what waited for them, but it was no use. Every torch and lantern for a hundred yards either side of the gate had been extinguished. There was no sound from within the gate's bastion. No clue if Platt, their inside man, had done his job or not. The place was supposed to be clear for them to just walk in. It was silent enough, but Jerrol didn't fancy strolling straight into the middle of a bunch of Greencoats just waiting to cut him another arsehole.

He raised his arm, signalling for one of the lads to move forward and check out what was happening. If there was danger, he was damn sure he wasn't going to be the one running straight into it. Why have a dog and bark yourself?

One of the lads, Kurt, sprinted forward through the dark. Jerrol lost sight of him as he reached the base of the gate tower and there was silence as they waited, breath held in case something went wrong. If it did it'd be the flip of a coin whether or not he ran off as fast as he could or decided to take on whatever trouble appeared. He was scared enough of failure, but that thing was always there in the back of his mind – *stay alive, don't get killed.* Right alongside – *don't let Bastian down, it just ain't worth the death he'll give you.*

Before long Kurt came running back out. He knelt down beside Jerrol taking a moment to get his breath back.

'Ain't no one inside,' he said. 'Not that I can hear, anyway. Place is all blacked out.'

'So no one's guarding the winch for the portcullis?' Jerrol asked, getting a feeling this was far too easy.

'Not that I can see.'

Jerrol turned to the rest of his men, ready to give the order to move. They'd planned this to the letter. Two would wait in front of the gate, ready to open it when the portcullis was raised. Four would split into two pairs either side of the bastion to make sure no one came waltzing along the battlements to make a nuisance of themselves. Two would guard the door to the gate tower. The rest would head inside, one taking watch on the roof while the other two would pull the winch to raise the portcullis. Easy.

Or at least as easy as these things ever got in the Guild.

With a flick of his hand, Jerrol led them across the open ground to the base of the gate tower. Immediately four of them split off to left and right, heading for the stairs up to the battlements.

Kurt opened the door, leading them into the black inside. Jerrol followed. All he could hear was the lad's breathing as he let his eyes adjust to the darkness. Even after they had, all he could see was a scant bit of light from the stairway leading up.

Slowly they crept through the tower. At any moment Jerrol expected someone to come bowling out of the dark, and his unease only grew as they moved further through the building to the first floor.

'What was that?' said the lad behind.

They all stopped. Jerrol listened through the dark. He could barely hear a thing. There might have been something from outside. Maybe a whistling noise. Maybe the sound of one of his men signalling in the night, but it wasn't loud enough to hear properly.

Eventually he shook his head. 'Fuck this,' he breathed at no one in particular. 'We can't hang around all night. You. Upstairs.'

One of the lads did as he was told, moving up the stairs to the roof of the tower.

Jerrol crept through the dark, looking for the winch that would raise the portcullis. His leg struck something in the dark and whatever it was clattered across the floor, making enough noise to raise the dead.

'We need some fucking light,' he whispered.

At first, silence. Then the sound of Kurt's flint striking tinder. As light flooded the room from the wick of a lantern Jerrol caught something in the corner of his eye. For a moment he thought he saw a child staring up from the stairwell to the ground floor, but a blink and it was gone.

Jerrol stared at the staircase for some moments before shaking his head.

'Let's get on with it,' he said, moving towards the winch.

There was a noise from the roof before he could even grasp the pulley wheel. Kurt looked at him, eyes wide, face all deathly in the lantern light.

'Go see what the fuck that was,' said Jerrol.

At first Kurt looked like he wanted to argue, then he thought better of it. He placed the lantern down and drew a blade from his belt, taking the stairs up with caution. Jerrol watched as he disappeared, alone now in the dark of the tower.

There was a whistle, but from where Jerrol couldn't tell.

Something made a noise on the roof but he couldn't make it out. *Was that a scuffle?* Then nothing.

Jerrol stared up at the hole to the roof before whispering, 'Kurt,' as loudly as he could into the dark. There was no reply.

A knife was in Jerrol's hand now. He couldn't remember

consciously drawing it from its sheath, but doing things on instinct had saved his life more than once. He glanced at the winch behind him. Thought about pulling it. Thought about leaving it and running off into the night while he had the chance, but before he could make a decision either way there were footsteps on the stairs from below.

Jerrol just crouched there, waiting. He should probably have taken the offensive and run across the room to attack, but he realised he was too shit scared to move. *Better to admit what you are . . .*

An open-faced sallet appeared, followed by a green jacket, stark in the lantern light. Jerrol made to move, willing his paralysed legs into action, but stopped himself when he recognised the face beneath that helmet . . . Platt.

Jerrol breathed out a sigh. 'Where the fuck have you been?' he said.

Platt just shook his head. He looked scared. 'I've been doing my fucking job and clearing out the rest of the Greencoats. Speaking of which, did you come alone?'

Jerrol shook his head. 'Course I didn't. The rest of mine are outside.'

Platt shook his head right back, looking even more worried. 'There's no one outside. And why have you put out all the lights?'

'I didn't put out the fu—' Jerrol glanced at the stairs again, then back at Platt. 'We need to crank that winch and then get the fuck out of here.'

Before they could move Jerrol caught something from the corner of his eye again. Definitely a child's face, this time peering down from the trapdoor above where Kurt had gone and not come back. *What the fuck is going on?* Jerrol had no idea but he was fucked if he'd let it go unanswered.

'You make a start,' he pointed Platt at the winch, then made his way up the wooden stairs to the roof.

There was barely enough moonlight to see by, but when his eyes adjusted he saw two bodies lying in heaps on the roof. One was Kurt's, something pooling around him in the dark.

Jerrol gripped his knife tighter, looking about him for any sign of movement and getting ready to stick it with six inches of steel.

He didn't give a shit if it was a kid, he'd gut the little bastard whoever it was.

*A whistle.* Jerrol turned to see a young lad standing on the battlements some way off. He stared for a bit, all small and alone in the night. Then the little cunt waved at him.

Jerrol bit back a curse, taking a step forward before realising he had a job to do. Before he could go back down there was another whistle. He spun to see another lad, looking much like the first, waving from the battlements in the other direction. It took a brief moment for Jerrol to realise they were both stood where his men should have been.

He bit back the panic, retreating off to the trapdoor and back down to the winch room. His eyes darted between those two little fuckers as he made his way down. Once he was back in the room, panting like he'd just run ten leagues, he slowly realised he was alone – Platt had done a runner.

*Enough fucking about! Turn the winch and get the fuck out of—*

Another whistle, this one loud. It sounded like it was in the same room.

Jerrol turned to see another smiling little face beaming up from the stairwell.

*Little bastard!*

With a cry of rage he darted at the boy, screaming something unintelligible as he went. The little lad was quick, Jerrol had to give him that, but he wouldn't get away. He took the stairs three at a time, bursting out onto the street, ready to gut the little shit.

In the darkness outside he went running straight into someone, stopping dead like he'd hit a brick wall. Jerrol looked up, seeing a face he vaguely recognised looking down at him. Was it Barkus? Farkus? Big fucker. One of the crew he'd seen hanging around in the tavern.

He made to speak, but instead of words he spat a gob of blood onto his chin.

*Shit, that's not right.*

Looking down he saw he was skewered on a blade held in the big bastard's hand.

Jerrol wanted to strike out with the knife in his own hand but realised he'd already dropped it.

He staggered back, that blade sliding out of his body with a wet sucking sound. He looked around now, seeing other figures standing there looking at him in the dark. As his knees went out from under him he saw someone walking forward, another kid.

When his face hit the street she knelt down beside him. He recognised her – Rag, she was called, everyone knew her name. The one who'd survived Friedrik and Palien. The one Bastian trusted so much.

She stared at him, no emotion in those little girl's eyes.

'That's the last of them,' she said. 'Let's get the fuck out of here.'

Jerrol kept staring down that street, all skewed on its side, until eventually it faded to nothing.

# TWENTY-NINE

She sat all night by his side. The battle had raged on but Endellion barely even noticed. The Khurtas came limping back from the gates of Steelhaven once more, walking past her in sullen silence, and still she had paid them no mind. Even when the sun rose, bathing her and Azreal in a light that bore little warmth, she scarcely even raised her head.

Endellion shed no tears from her golden eyes. The Arc Magna did not weep over their dead. Let the southrons weep over their losses. Let everyone in that city weep as it was torn down around them. Let the dark giants she and Azreal had fought weep until the gates of Oblivion opened in honour of the vengeance she would have.

When she and Azreal had walked through the smashed gateway she had expected to meet little resistance. All that should have waited were broken men fighting with little heart in the face of such overwhelming odds. She could only regret her complacency. What they had faced were beasts, not men. Creatures of the southern deserts; half-men, monsters. Her shoulder still stung where she had been clawed. She should have sought attention in case it became infected but Endellion wanted none. The scars that were left would serve to show the folly of her ways. How foolish she had been to follow Amon Tugha, to obey him without question, to think that Steelhaven would be so easily conquered.

Endellion stared down at the body in front of her. Azreal's eyes were closed. His throat lay open, the blood having congealed into a torn and fleshy mess. She should have covered it up, it was wrong to see him like this, but she also needed to remember. Above all she needed the hurt to burn inside her, to remain within her heart until she had a chance to avenge him.

She had loved Azreal, that much was obvious now. For a century or more she had yearned for him to be hers. Had followed him wherever he led, but never let him know what lay in her heart. That was not her way, nor that of the Arc Magna. She had lived her life by the tenets of her creed and enjoyed all the pleasures it allowed, but she would have given it all up for Azreal. He would have given up nothing for her, though. He was loyal to the end and had ultimately given his life for his master.

Endellion knew now that she would never do the same.

This was all for the glory of Amon Tugha. He would sacrifice them all, every last one of his followers, to attain his goal. And what was that? Glory? Vengeance? To prove to himself he was worthy of his mother's crown?

It had seemed so simple at first, it had been an adventure. One Endellion had embarked on with her usual hunger. She had finally been freed of the Riverlands and its stifling edicts. Now, so long after they had embarked on their journey, it seemed like madness to have ever left. In the cold light of morning she would have given anything to be back in her homeland with Azreal at her side.

A shadow fell over her but she ignored it, continuing to stare at Azreal's face and the wound in his neck.

'Our prince demands your presence,' said a voice. Endellion thought she recognised it, though most of these Khurtas sounded the same. She didn't reply, allowing nothing to sway her from her vigil. Let Amon Tugha demand what he pleased. She was done with him.

Still the Khurta stood behind her. She could sense his unease.

'Please, we must go to him.'

Endellion continued to kneel beside Azreal, trying to remember what had been between them. What could have been had she told him all that lay in her heart.

The Khurta placed a hand on her shoulder.

'The prince will be angered if you do not—'

Endellion's blade was out of its sheath and buried in his gut before the Khurta could finish his sentence. She glared at him as he looked back at her with surprise, then fear. When he slumped to the ground before her she recognised him – one of her lovers. He had been a favourite; energetic, vigorous. As he fell dead she realised she had never even known his name.

Once the Khurta had breathed his last she knelt beside Azreal once more, not bothering to retrieve her sword from the corpse. Not caring any more if she raised her blade again. Endellion simply stared, the cold seeping through her clothes and chilling her to her core.

There was no telling how long she knelt until another shadow eventually fell over her. She felt herself anger again, reaching for her blade, but it wasn't there, still buried as it was in the Khurta's corpse. Slowly she turned her head, hoping to frighten away any more of Amon Tugha's lapdogs before she had to kill them too, but standing behind her was no Khurta.

'A sad day,' said Amon Tugha. 'A black day I will never forget. Azreal was my most faithful. He will be sorely missed.'

*And not only by you*, she wanted to say. *You will forget him in time as your thirst for power grows, but I will never forget.*

Endellion said nothing. Despite her grief, she had no desire to join Azreal in Oblivion.

'Come,' said Amon Tugha, walking towards the city. He paid no heed to the fresh cadaver Endellion had made but merely walked by as though she had crushed an ant rather than one of his Khurtic warriors. Perhaps he did understand her grief after all. Or perhaps he simply didn't care for the lives of those beneath him.

Endellion plucked her blade from the corpse as she walked by, wiping the blood from it onto her sleeve. As she placed it back in her scabbard she felt the sting of the wound in her shoulder again. The lacerations had stopped bleeding, her Elharim blood having long since clotted, but still the pain was there. A reminder that she was not immortal, perhaps? A reminder that any of them could be killed . . . even Amon Tugha.

And yet he walked ahead of her, through the plain filled with bodies. He walked without fear, as though nothing could touch him, as though they could fling all the rocks and arrows and fire from the walls of Steelhaven and it would pass him by as though he were a ghost.

For a fleeting moment she considered drawing her blade. Considered thrusting it into his broad, scorched and tattooed back and into his heart to prove he was just a man. In an instant that thought was gone, though. As hate filled as she was, as grief stricken as she felt, she had no desire to die. Not here on this southern plain, far from her homeland.

The two Elharim picked their way towards the city and in the cold light of day Endellion could see the havoc the Khurtas had wreaked. The battlements of the city were smashed and blackened. Here and there men cowered in the gaps. At the foot of the wall bodies were piled high amongst the debris. Arrows peppered the field to the north; burned siege towers and the husks of artillery weapons stood all about. The smell of burned wood and flesh was vile, but it was nothing she had not experienced before. Nothing she had not taken pleasure in. She took no pleasure in it now.

Amon Tugha stopped within a hundred yards of the wall. Endellion could see archers scrambling into position, levelling their bows as though the Elharim prince might try to besiege the city single-handed, overcoming the city's defences where his Khurtas had failed. Instead he merely stood and waited, watching as word of his arrival passed from one end of the battlements to the other.

When a large enough crowd had amassed on the smashed walls Amon Tugha drew in a deep and cleansing breath.

'Warriors of Steelhaven,' he bellowed, that deep voice ringing out across the plain. 'Sons and daughters of the Teutonian Free States.' He spoke the word 'Free' with just a hint of disdain, as though it were misplaced and irrelevant. 'You know who I am. You know what I have done.' He paused then, as though waiting for some kind of answer, but Endellion knew there would be none. The southrons would listen in silence; that was their way. 'You have been told I have come to slaughter. To destroy. To raze this city to ash and massacre all who cower here behind its walls.' Again, another pause. Endellion expected at any moment for a volley of arrows to come their way, but nothing did. Every man looked down in awe at Amon Tugha, most of them seeing for the first time what they faced – not a man, but a god.

'Lies!' spat Amon. His fists were clenched now, his eyes scanning the wall as though searching for someone to defy him, to call him deceiver, to question his word. If such a man existed he did not speak. 'I have not come to destroy you. I have come to liberate you. To save you from your bondage. I would not hold you in thrall with lies. I would ask you to be loyal to no gods or flags. Dedicate fealty to me and you will be free men. All of you. This butchery can end. Your inevitable destruction will be averted. Your women and your children spared. I ask only one thing. That you give me your queen.'

For the first time the men on the wall began to grumble. Amon Tugha had obviously touched a nerve. It seemed they were as loyal to their queen as they were stubborn in defence of their city. It did not seem to faze Amon, though.

'You have one night to consider my offer. Tomorrow there will be no chance of clemency. No mercy.'

With that he turned and made his way back to the Khurtic camp. Endellion expected jeers and insults to follow them but the southrons kept their uneasy silence.

'You think they will betray her so easily?' Endellion asked as they crested the ridge where Azreal still lay.

'No,' Amon Tugha replied, the trace of a smile playing across his broad mouth. 'But word of my offer will reach the queen as surely as if I had whispered it in her ear. And who knows what she might do to save her city and her people.'

# THIRTY

Janessa had learned of the Elharim warlord's offer. She listened to the story that he had walked to within the shadow of the wall and made his proclamation. Every servant and steward and Sentinel was speaking of it in hushed tones but Janessa could not help but hear them. But then the corridors of Skyhelm had never held their secrets well, she knew that better than anyone.

If she was given to him he would call off his siege. Her life in exchange for the lives of thousands within the walls of the city. But Janessa knew there was no one that would give her up. Even had an angry mob arrived at the gates of the palace her Sentinels would have defended her to the death. But no one had arrived. No crowd of fearful men and women, desperate for their lives and the lives of their children, had come demanding the queen be handed over. The cityfolk of Steelhaven were loyal to her – perhaps they even loved her, despite this time of strife.

No, she would never be surrendered by her people.

But she could surrender herself.

It had been a hard decision, one she had not made lightly, but at least the thought of surrendering herself had diverted her thoughts.

Throughout the day she had been plagued by the memory of the gardens, of Leon's hands at her throat, of Baroness Magrida's screams as her son lay dead. Where the woman was now, Janessa had no idea. Conveyed to her rooms, no doubt, to be consoled by handmaids and watched over by guards in case she sought to harm herself . . . or someone else.

Janessa could not bring herself to feel guilty for it. Magrida had brought her son to the palace. Had seemingly been unaware of his complicity with Amon Tugha. She deserved everything she got. Besides, a resentful noblewoman was the least of Janessa's concerns now.

She had a decision to make, and she had to make it quick. Could she trust the word of the Elharim? If she gave herself over to him would he really spare her city? Or would he simply allow his Khurtas their sport?

And if she did not go, was she condemning the city to destruction? Would it, could it, manage to stand firm against the hordes arrayed against it? Was it only a matter of time until the walls fell, until the Khurtas came flooding in to burn and rape and destroy all before them?

Surely there were enough dead already. Surely the walls of Steelhaven were littered with enough corpses. If there was any chance that her sacrifice could save the life of just one of her people then she should take it. She had a responsibility to this city and everyone within its walls. Just the barest chance that it could be saved if she surrendered herself to Amon Tugha was more excuse than she should ever need.

Janessa stared at the Helsbayn, and then at her armour on its stand. Inside she knew she should have donned them to face Amon Tugha; that she should appear every inch the warrior queen as she stood before him and presented herself to his mercy. But she knew she'd never be able to get out of Skyhelm that way. Instead she donned simple clothes and put a cloak about her as she had done a hundred times before.

The palace corridors were all but deserted as she made her way down to the kitchens and out through the servants' entrance. By now she knew where every Sentinel in her retinue would be. Everyone else was in their chambers, waiting for the outcome of the siege, or gone, run away to escape their fate. There was no one to stop her as she stepped out of the palace, cloak drawn tight over her head, and the Sentinels on the gate paid her no mind.

For a fleeting moment she felt sorry for Kaira. Faithful, dedicated Kaira. A woman who had devoted herself to Janessa's protection. She would bear this loss as a personal burden. Janessa could only hope her bodyguard would understand this was for the greater good. That any chance, however slim, to save the city was one that had to be grasped.

As evening began to darken into night, Janessa made her way north into the city and her determination to go through with this mad plan was only hardened. Steelhaven was in pieces. Buildings torn apart, voices weeping in the early morning, the wounded groaning for succour when it was clear nothing could be done for them.

She passed a group of weary-looking soldiers sharpening their blades, every one of them showing a wound of some kind, their eyes heavy from lack of sleep. Not one of them glanced at her as she walked past, biting back her tears. The stench of the unwashed was almost unbearable. The stink of sweat and death.

As she made it to what was left of the Stone Gate the sight became no less despairing. The portcullis was a mess of twisted iron, the gate a pile of blackened kindling. The defenders had done their best to build a rudimentary blockade from old carts and piles of debris, but it looked unlikely to hold once Amon Tugha's hordes attacked once more. A serjeant barked orders for more stone as exhausted-looking bannermen continued to fill the hole in the breach.

Just to the left of the gate several wounded soldiers sat beside one another, one of them leaning against his neighbour, his face a mask of blood and dirt. Janessa made her way towards them, her cloak pulled tight about her to hide her red curls. If she was recognised now the game was most definitely up.

A water bucket sat to one side and she picked it up, dipping the cup into it and offering it to the first wounded soldier. He took it gratefully, handing it back with a nod when he had finished. Janessa worked her way along the line, all the while glancing towards the open gate as she made her way closer. When she reached the last wounded soldier she put down the bucket and walked towards the gate. She resisted the urge to run; to do that would only draw attention to her. At first it worked, and she felt her heart beating faster as she made her escape. No one said a word until she was under the shadow of the battlements. Then a voice called out.

'Oi you! Stop!'

Janessa broke into a run, sprinting through the gate, ignoring the carcasses still lying outside, ignoring the stench and the smoke haze that cut through the night. She ran on into the dark as voices called after her, but no one followed. To try and escape with so many Khurtas surrounding the city was suicide and no one would risk their lives to come after her. For all they knew she was a frightened commoner, not the queen of the Free States.

She stumbled through the dark. To the north glowed the light from the vast Khurtic encampment. If she just kept going, if she demanded to see Amon Tugha, if she gave herself to him, this would all be over. Every corpse she tripped over, every arrow that snagged her skirts, reminded her that this was the only way. The fighting had to stop now, and only she could end it.

The bodies and detritus thinned out the further north she went. With every step Janessa expected to be assailed from the dark but there was no one waiting to attack. The closer she got the more she felt the dread growing within her but she never once thought to turn back.

*This is the only way. There is no other option than to gift your life to Amon Tugha.*

Khurtic voices pealed through the dark before she saw the sentries. They were silhouetted on the ridge above and Janessa only hoped they would see her coming and not skewer her on their spears as soon as look at her.

She let her cloak fall to the ground as she made her way up the hill, the chill of the night air raising bumps on her flesh. One of the sentries spotted her as she came, shouting a quick warning to one of his comrades. They stood side by side, their spears held out defensively. Whatever they had been waiting for to come from the night it was obviously not an unarmed woman. The first Khurta glanced to the other uncertainly as Janessa made her way into the light. They spoke again but she had no way to understand them.

'I am Queen Janessa Mastragall,' she said, trying to sound confident, trying to stay strong, but her hands were shaking so much she had to clench her fists. 'Amon Tugha is waiting for me.' Janessa gestured towards the camp.

The Khurtas barked at one another, one of them waving his spear threateningly, despite the fact he had no one to fight. Janessa held her hands out, trying to show she was no threat, that she had only come to surrender, but the face of the savage in front of her showed he was in no mood to accept.

He lunged forward with his spear, aiming at her heart, and Janessa had no time to move.

A shadow broke away from the dark, along with the sound of steel cutting the air twice in quick succession. Before she could draw breath, a figure stood in front of Janessa, one hand holding the severed tip of the Khurta's spear, the other a straight silver blade spattered with blood. The Khurta fell without a sound as the second sentry backed away in fear.

In the weak light Janessa could see she had been saved by a woman; blonde, beautiful, her shoulder rent and torn from a recent wound. As the woman turned, Janessa was startled by her golden eyes gleaming through the dark.

'Your Majesty,' said the woman with a humourless smile. She nodded her head in the mockery of a bow. 'My lord will be overjoyed that you decided to accept his offer.' With that she gestured towards the camp. 'If you please.'

Janessa followed the woman, all the while keeping her head raised, fighting the fear. As they made their way through the sea of tents, Khurtas gathered, some looking on with interest, others with a baleful hunger. On they went, wending their way through until by the time they had reached the midst of the camp there were hundreds surrounding them. Janessa could tell many of the Khurtas wanted to harm her, to fall upon her and do unspeakable things, but this woman with her eyes of gold seemed to have a strange power over them. They feared her, that much was obvious. As much as she knew the woman was her enemy she could only be grateful that she stood beside her now.

Eventually they came to a massive pyre in the centre of the camp. Khurtas milled around it impatiently, as though a night without battle made them agitated. As Janessa approached the fire one of them, a giant compared to the rest, glanced towards her, his face a torn and scarred mess. He grinned hideously and Janessa almost felt herself weaken under that gaze. For a moment she wondered if this was Amon Tugha, but as another figure stood up from his crouched position beside the pyre the Khurtas hushed.

He walked towards her and she knew this must be the Elharim warlord. His hair was spiked, the colour of it seeming to shift in the light of the dancing flames, and his bare torso shone, the thick sinews of his arms and chest glistening. He fixed her with eyes that sparkled gold and as he approached he greeted Janessa with a welcoming smile. It did nothing to put her at ease.

'Such bravery,' he said in a deep and thick accent. 'The Mastragalls are truly a courageous line. You have come to save your city?'

'You know why I have come,' Janessa said, in no mood to parlay. 'End this, and send your horde back from where they came.'

'Your father was not a man to bandy words either. I liked that about him. But you shouldn't be so eager for this to be over. Not before you have seen the parting gift I have for you.'

Amon Tugha gestured away from the fire. A group of Khurtas moved aside as he did so, revealing a wooden frame erected in a clearing. Lashed to it, his arms and legs secured with rope, was a broken figure.

Janessa took a step forward, squinting through the light of the fire. As the man lifted his head she gasped and moved towards him, forgetting all else as she did so. River tried to speak but his mouth was filled with blood, his face encrusted with it. Janessa ran to him, cradling his head in her hands, her eyes filling with tears.

'As you see,' said Amon Tugha, now standing behind her. 'I am no monster. I have reunited two lovers for the last time.'

Janessa tried to ignore him; all she could do was stare at River as he looked back from a beaten and bloody face. She could tell he was in pain but would not show it. Could tell he was trying to be courageous for her sake.

'You will let him go,' she said, turning to the Elharim warlord. For a moment she realised how ridiculous it was that she would make demands of this creature. He was a beast, there was nothing she could do to intimidate him, but it didn't seem to matter now.

'Doubtful,' said Amon. 'It is inevitable he will one day return to avenge you. And there will already be enough men out there ready to kill me once I have laid waste to your city and taken its crown as my own. Now come. It is time for this to end.'

'No,' she cried, but there was nothing she could do as the Elharim took her by the arm. She had never felt such strength, and bit back a cry of pain as he dragged her away from River. 'You promised Steelhaven would be spared. You made a vow.'

Amon drove her to her knees, staring down with those golden eyes, so cold in the firelight. 'Your city will surrender to me, as you have done, or I will raze it to the ground. Every last stone. Every man, woman and child will be crushed.' He held out his hand and one of the Khurtas brought forth a massive spear which Amon took. 'Now, bow your head with dignity.'

Janessa stared up at him. Through the tears in her eyes she saw that she was surrounded. There was no escape, nothing she could do.

A tear rolled down her cheek, but it was not for herself.

Janessa Mastragall shed one final tear of sorrow for Steelhaven.

# THIRTY-ONE

S he was no interrogator. Kaira had already proven that with her failure to infiltrate the Guild. It had taken a child to help her find Friedrik and then he had simply laughed in her face when she tried to question him. And yet here Kaira was, in a cold chamber beneath Skyhelm, alone with a grieving old woman.

Kaira's guilt bit at her but she pushed it aside. Janessa had almost died in the gardens. Leon Magrida's complicity with Amon Tugha had fooled them all, but Kaira should still have been vigilant. It was why she took this burden as her own and felt the need to question Isabelle herself.

Baroness Magrida sat in silence. The haughtiness was gone. Her arrogance evaporated with the death of her son. There was still steel there behind the cloudy eyes. Still an element of determination. She was strong, of that there was no doubt, but was she guilty of involvement in a conspiracy to murder the queen?

Janessa had said Isabelle tried to stop her son when he made his attempt at the queen's life. Whether that was enough to prove her innocence remained to be seen.

'You say you had no idea your son was in league with the enemy?' Kaira asked. As much as she felt sympathy for the old woman losing her only child, she knew she couldn't show it. 'How can you expect us to believe such a thing? You arrived here together. Were constantly at one another's side.'

Baroness Magrida glanced at Kaira, looking her up and down as though appraising this woman, this mere bodyguard who had come to judge her. She opened her mouth to speak but changed her mind. Perhaps she considered Kaira beneath her. Despite the grave situation she was in, she still considered herself a noble. But then Kaira supposed she still was. Even if she was guilty of a conspiracy to kill the queen of all the Free States she was still a Baroness of Dreldun. Still had bannermen. Still had her subjects.

'You understand I must be sure?' said Kaira. 'I cannot allow you to walk free until you can prove you were not a part of this. That there are no further conspirators within the palace.'

Magrida smirked, her fingers tugging at the hem of her dress. It no longer looked as regal as it once had. Now it was dishevelled, hanging off her shoulder. The sleeve was torn, though whether it was damaged during the attack in the gardens or the old woman had done it herself out of grief and anger, Kaira could not tell.

'My son lies dead,' said Isabelle. 'The only heir to the Barony of Dreldun. Its villages and farms have been burned. Its capital razed. Even if the Khurtas are defeated, the province will be plunged into anarchy and I will be the one who has to govern in the chaos.' She fixed Kaira with a stern look, fire in her eyes. 'Do you think I give a damn about the safety of your queen? Do you think I care if you think me guilty of treason?'

'I think you are still a noblewoman of the Free States. Protest your innocence or admit your guilt, but say something. It's better you tell me. Were Seneschal Rogan here with his Inquisition—'

'He can't hurt me and neither can you. I owe you people nothing.'

Baroness Magrida waved her hand dismissively. Kaira suddenly felt her anger rising. This woman had shown her nothing but contempt. Had shown the queen nothing but disrespect, despite being allowed to stay here and be sheltered from the roving horde. Her guilt in conspiring with the enemy may well have been in doubt, but she was certainly guilty of arrogance and conceit.

Before Kaira could press the woman further, a bell rang out from above.

At first she had no idea what it was until she heard the shouts of panic. Kaira ran from the cell, feeling her heart beat faster within her chest. Had the Khurtas breached the wall? Were they attacking the palace even now?

She rushed through the door to the cell block, past the two Sentinels who guarded the Baroness. Kaira took the stairs at a sprint, racing towards the sound of a commotion within the palace. Garret's deep voice rumbled through the corridors as he barked orders and it took Kaira no time to find him in the entrance hall.

'She's bloody gone!' he shouted as he saw Kaira.

She had no answer for him. He could only mean the queen. The horror of it sank its teeth deep. She had a hundred questions but inside she knew Garret would not be able to answer any of them.

The palace was in upheaval as every maid and manservant was raised from their beds to join the search. Kaira ran out into the front courtyard, trying desperately to think, to remain calm amidst the chaos.

*She has gone to face Amon Tugha alone. She has given herself to him in order to save the city.*

The thought would not leave. As much as it frightened her, Kaira knew it was the only option. If Janessa had been murdered by an assassin they would have heard of it by now. Amon Tugha would want it known throughout the city that the queen had been slain.

No, it was obvious. Janessa had heard the Elharim's proclamation that her death would save the city and she had done the noble thing. Foolish, but noble.

A single horse was tethered in the courtyard bearing the livery of a messenger. Kaira leapt atop it. As she pressed her heels to its flanks and pulled the reins towards the main gates she heard someone shout behind her, but there was no time to stop and explain. No time to lose at all. No one knew when she had slipped out of the palace. No one knew how much time their queen might have left.

Kaira galloped out of the palace grounds, the horse's hooves clacking against the cobbles. She drove the steed on through the Crown District, screaming at the Greencoats to let her pass. Thankfully they were in no mood to try and stop her, opening the gates in time for her to gallop through. In the waxing dawn light she could see the streets were empty and gave silent thanks to Vorena there was no one to stop her as she made her way north.

By the time she reached the Stone Gate the horse was already frothing. Kaira reined in, desperately searching for anyone who could help her. Men milled around looking dishevelled, most looked wounded in some way. She began to despair that she might have to gallop out onto the northern plain alone when she saw a glimmer of bronze armour amidst the uniforms of the city's bannermen.

She rode along the base of the wall, hoping against hope they would be ready for battle. Her heart leapt as she saw Merrick standing amidst a group of other Wyvern Guard.

'Ryder!' The group turned at her call. For a moment she thought that this should remain a secret. That if word was to spread that the queen had given herself to Amon Tugha there would be panic. But if they were not in time to save her there would be panic aplenty. The time for discretion was over. 'The queen is gone. I think she has fled the city to offer herself to the Khurtas.'

Merrick needed no further encouragement. 'Get to the fucking horses,' he shouted.

Before he could acknowledge her further, Kaira had already pulled the reins around and headed back to the gate. Men ran from her path as she rode through the vast archway and out onto the empty battlefield. The sun was only just beyond the horizon but there was little light yet shed on the plain to the north of the city.

As she urged her horse northwards she knew this was madness. If she was wrong, and the queen had not gone north to surrender herself, Kaira was riding alone into the heart of the enemy camp. She would be slaughtered before she even reached its edge. But if Janessa had indeed gone to give herself up to Amon Tugha, she still had to face thousands of Khurtas single-handed. There was no way this would end well.

*Arlor is strength. Vorena is courage.*

Those words, which had helped her so many times in the past, seemed to do little now. She was going to die and so was the queen, no matter what she did. The folly of it almost made her furious but she could not afford to be angered. She had to fight, to be in control. She had to die as a Sentinel of Skyhelm . . . as a Shieldmaiden of Vorena.

As Kaira reached the edge of the camp she urged her horse up a ridge, at any moment expecting screaming Khurtic sentries to come charging from the shadows, but there was no one there to guard the camp's southern extent. The madness of galloping straight into the enemy's maw filled her with determination. Her sword was in her hand now, and she was eager to strike.

The encampment was dimly lit but still Kaira could see no one. Even with the sun finally peeking over the hills to the east she could spot no enemies. Then, ahead, she saw the gathered crowd.

Her heart sank as she rode. Janessa could already be dead, could already have been executed by the gathered savages, but there were only murmurings amongst the horde, not the cheers she would have expected. A whisper of hope in the dark morning.

Her steed was no destrier but still she urged it on. The Khurtas to the rear of the crowd had enough time to turn and spot her as she galloped towards them, but no time to move from her path. The stallion rode them down. Kaira's sword flashed in the dawn light. There were screams from her horse, cries of pain and anger from the Khurtas. A roar went up that made her heart sink and then she was through.

In the clearing at the centre of the crowd, Kaira saw Amon Tugha for the first time. He was formidable, of that there was no doubt, but Kaira was undeterred. She had come to die. All that mattered was how she did it.

From the corner of her eye she saw Janessa kneeling on the ground at the Elharim's feet, her mass of red curls unmistakable.

But Kaira was focused on only one man.

She raised her sword, crying Vorena's name as she hurtled straight for him. The massive spear in the warlord's hand thrust forward, impaling the charging horse through the chest and halting its gallop. Kaira went down with the screeching steed, rolling clear as she did so.

She was on her feet in an instant. Her weapon lost. A Khurta ran from the crowd, attempting to skewer her on his own spear, but she twisted, wrenching the weapon from his grip and spinning it deftly, the spearhead taking him in the throat.

Kaira's eyes were wide to the danger now. Khurtas were crowded all around and they moved forward, their weapons drawn, hunger in their eyes.

Amon Tugha raised his arm, speaking in the guttural Khurtic tongue before hauling his weapon from deep within the dead stallion's body. He held out a hand and beckoned for Kaira to come forward. A silent challenge between warriors.

This was how she would die. At the hands of the Elharim warlord, defending the life of her queen, no matter how forlorn her chance of victory.

It would be a good death.

As she stepped forward, as though heralding her final battle, the ground began to tremble.

# THIRTY-TWO

**M**errick had no idea how many Wyvern Guard had leapt on a horse to follow him. It was too dark to see as they rode across the battlefield towards the Khurtic camp, but he hoped it was more than had ridden out to destroy those fire ships. The camp over the rise was full of savage madmen who would boil them alive and shit in their skulls given half the chance. There'd definitely need to be more than twenty of them if they were going to make it through this in one piece.

He tried not to think about it too much. The prospect of someone shitting in his skull, boiled alive or not, didn't fill him with any joy. Instead he thought about how good he'd look when he got back to Steelhaven carrying the queen. 'What a fucking hero that Ryder is,' they'd say. 'He must be the greatest swordsman that ever lived. Let's pour our adoration, and not a little gold, all over him. And maybe throw in a couple of dancing girls.'

*Don't be a fucking idiot, Ryder. You're not coming back from this. You're going to die in a horrific way and your head's going to end up on the end of a pointy stick.*

He'd always hated pointy sticks and made a vow to avoid them at all costs, just as his horse hit the top of a ridge and galloped into the Khurtic camp. In the light of the campfires he could see there was little resistance. He could also see that there were definitely less than twenty of them riding in to face thousands of Khurtas. But at least Cormach was here. If anyone was going to get killed before Merrick it was bound to be that mad fucker, right?

*Right?*

They galloped between the tents, maybe a dozen of them. Someone screamed over to the left and was instantly silenced. Merrick could only hope it was a Khurta on the receiving end of a Wyvern Guard sword and not the other way around, but he was too enrapt in finding the queen and Kaira to look.

A crowd came into view. There was a commotion in their midst but Merrick couldn't see what it was. He urged his warhorse on and it grunted as he dug his spurs in twice for good measure.

A storm of confusion erupted as he struck the mob of Khurtas. Men and horses screamed, and the jarring impact rattled his teeth. Merrick struck out with his blade and felt it hit something but he couldn't tell what. He kicked the destrier again, urging it through the crowd. To his left someone roared above the din as more of the Wyvern Guard joined the fray.

In a rush of clarity he burst through the mess of Khurtas. By the light of a massive pyre he could see Queen Janessa on her knees, Kaira standing with a spear ready to defend her and the biggest bastard he had ever seen watching like this was all some kind of sport.

His eyes glowed gold, his body gleaming in the firelight, covered in arcane markings, an enormous spear held in one bucket-sized hand. It could only be Amon Tugha. No other man on earth could have made Merrick want to shit himself so readily.

He had no time to think as more of the Wyvern Guard burst through the line of Khurtas.

'Protect the queen,' someone shouted.

In response Merrick urged his steed forward. He aimed at Janessa, intent on hauling her onto the back of his warhorse and riding off into the sunrise, but before he could reach her Cormach had spurred his own mount in the way. Janessa grasped his hand and leapt up.

Merrick almost cursed the bastard, looking all heroic, that white bear pelt making him stand out like some sort of legendary hero of old.

Then Amon Tugha made his move.

He raised that massive spear far too quickly for a weapon of its size. The warlord looked powerful, all right, but even a man with that much muscle should have struggled with such a weapon. With measured grace he drew back for a throw, aiming at Cormach as he attempted to flee.

Before he knew what he was doing Merrick stuck spurs to flanks again. His warhorse bolted forward as he moved to block the throw. The spear strike that was aimed at Cormach hit Merrick's shield, piercing the top and slicing a gash in his pauldron. His horse reared back as Amon Tugha wrenched the weapon back, pulling the shield from Merrick's grip.

'Get the fuck out of here,' he screamed at Cormach, who needed no further encouragement, spurring his mount and galloping southwards.

The rest of the Wyvern Guard had made it through now, and they flanked Cormach as he made for safety.

Merrick would have happily joined them, but he was too busy staring in awe at the seven-foot Elharim warlord who had him fixed in a gaze that would have wilted flowers. Amon Tugha drew back his spear once more. This time Merrick had no shield, not that it would have done him any good anyway.

*You wanted to be a hero, Ryder. Well, are you happy now? They'll be singing songs about how you died saving the queen for years.*

The Elharim suddenly ducked as a spear almost took him in the head, missing by mere inches. Someone jumped on the back of Merrick's horse, the panic of it almost making him squeal, but he quickly realised he was not under attack.

'Ride!' shouted Kaira as she gripped the buckles of his breastplate.

Merrick didn't need asking twice and neither did his steed as it bolted after the rest of the Wyvern Guard. They'd made a gap in the crowd and he headed straight for it. Broken and stunned Khurtas littered the way and Merrick's horse seemed only too eager to trample them further into the dirt.

'Down!' screamed Kaira, grabbing Merrick's head and pulling it to the side as Amon Tugha's massive spear careered through the air after them. It thudded into the ground some way ahead of their path and Merrick stuck spurs to horse again, more eager than ever to leave this place behind.

Their steed did its best to navigate the maze of hide tents as Merrick headed back towards the city, but they trampled several on the way. A Khurta came roaring at them but Merrick's blade was faster. He could hear screams all around and his heart leapt as he reached the edge of the camp, with only an open field between him and safety.

Arrows zipped overhead as they made their way down onto the plain. In front, Merrick could see the remaining Wyvern Guard carrying the queen back to safety. He counted only half of their original dozen.

When they'd galloped hard enough to beat the range of the Khurtic arrows, Merrick slowed his horse down to a trot.

'You all right?' he asked over his shoulder.

Kaira nodded, breathless. 'I'm unhurt.'

'If you'd wanted to take on the entire Khurtic army single-handed you should just have said. I would have stood on the wall and waved you off.'

She didn't seem to see the funny side.

The Wyvern Guard eventually rode through the Stone Gate. If Merrick had expected a rapturous welcome he was sorely disappointed; no one seemed in any particular hurry to ask them what in the hells they were doing charging out into the night. Janessa had already climbed down from Cormach's horse, her cloak drawn about her head.

'Get down,' Kaira ordered. Merrick didn't have the energy to argue, clambering down as Kaira beckoned for Janessa to join her on the mount. 'No one must know about this,' she said as the queen climbed up behind her. Then she kicked the steed and headed south towards the palace.

'Don't mention it. All in a day's work,' Merrick said under his breath, watching the pair of them go.

When he got back to the compound, close to the wall where the Wyvern Guard had been posted, he saw his father waiting. Each of the half-dozen he came back with were patted on the shoulder as Tannick commended them for their bravery. Even Cormach

Whoreson was given an approving nod. Merrick smiled at his father, expecting much the same. He should have known better.

'What the bloody hells were you thinking?' said Tannick, keeping his voice low.

*He doesn't want to embarrass you in front of the other lads, at least. Something to be thankful for.*

'I was thinking the queen was in danger,' Merrick replied, fast losing patience with his father's constant coddling. 'I was thinking that her life is a little bit more important than mine and it was probably worth risking to save her.'

*Not strictly true – if you'd had time to think you probably wouldn't have gone at all, but no one has to know that.*

Tannick nodded. 'Aye, well you're back in one piece at least. Well done.'

'Thanks,' said Merrick as his father walked away. It struck him that the old man hadn't seemed overly concerned about the men who hadn't come back, but over the last few days they'd lost plenty of brothers to the enemy. It was clear Tannick couldn't mourn them all.

Merrick took some water from a barrel, feeling it cool his parched throat. With all the arse-clenching fear he hadn't realised just how thirsty he was. As he looked around at the other lads he saw Cormach taking the stairway up to the battlements.

*He obviously wants to be alone. He has just saved the queen, after all. He wants to bask in his glory by himself. You definitely shouldn't interrupt him whilst he's locked in quiet reflection. He hates you as well, so you'd be a stupid moron if you tried to make conversation now.*

Merrick took the stairs after Cormach.

The Whoreson was waiting on the walkway, staring out over the battlements as the sun rose in the east. Merrick casually walked up and stood beside him, trying to appear as nonchalant as possible, like this was some kind of accident.

'I'm sorry for the brothers we lost,' said Merrick, unsure why he was even bothering with this conversation. 'I know you knew them longer than me. It must be hard that we've lost so many.'

Cormach glanced over at him, then back out towards the rising sun. 'Not as hard as you might think,' he replied.

*Not quite as unpleasant a reply as you were expecting, Ryder. At least he didn't call you a cunt.*

'But these are your brothers. Weren't you brought up with them? Aren't you all bound by blood and honour?'

Cormach looked at him now, and for the first time there was the slightest trace of a smile on his lips. 'Don't have any brothers, do you?'

'No, I, er—'

'And if you did would you want them calling you Whoreson all the time? The only reason they call me nothing worse is they know I could end every last one of them.'

'I see,' said Merrick, remembering well when he was on the receiving end of Cormach's swordsmanship and having no doubt he could do exactly what he claimed. 'So that's not a term of endearment then?'

Cormach barked a laugh at that. 'What the fuck do you think?'

'I thought it might be something to do with your prowess in the whorehouse. Maybe a curse all your enemies shout before you—'

'My mother was a cheap backstreet whore from Silverwall. It's no big secret.'

Merrick was a little taken aback by the candid answer, but not all that surprised. 'But how did you go from that to being the first sword of the Wyvern Guard?'

Cormach fixed him with an amused look.

'Your father didn't pick his recruits from the highborn. Did you think he trawled the provinces looking for little lordlings to join his crusade? Every last man of us is scum off the streets. Lads no one would miss. Tannick took us all when we were young enough to obey him without question.'

'And your mother was happy with that?'

Cormach's expression darkened. 'Lord Marshal Tannick bought me for ten copper pennies.'

*And you thought he was a bastard for leaving you all alone with your mother when you were nothing but a child.*

'I'm sorry,' said Merrick.

'Don't be. It was a generous offer. She only asked for five, by all accounts.'

'But still, I'm sorry. That's an awful—'

'What the fuck are you sorry about? Why are we even talking? You don't give two shits about me and I definitely couldn't give a flying bollock about you. We'll stand on the wall and we'll watch each other's backs and tonight or tomorrow or some other time soon we'll both be dead. We don't have to be cocking friends to do it.'

With that he turned and walked on down the battlements.

Merrick watched for a while as that mad bastard made his way along the wall, and for the life of him he couldn't work out why they had to be friends either.

# THIRTY-THREE

Nobul was exhausted but it wouldn't beat him. It was a matter of not giving in to it, of ignoring the aches and fatigue, but when you were dead on your feet all the ignoring in the world wouldn't do you any good. He'd slept at least, but that had probably been a mistake. When you woke, that's when all the hours of swinging a hammer and taking a beating would catch up with you. The stiffness would seep into your joints, the cuts would sting that much more and the bruises would be so sore you couldn't even touch them. Whatever mad rush of blood you'd had the night before that kept the pain away was gone and all you had to stop yourself weeping from the hurt was the power of your will.

A lot of the other lads had succumbed to it. He'd heard weeping aplenty over the last couple of days, in the early hours of dawn when the Khurtas retreated back north and all that remained was the aftershock of battle. When you took a look around and saw your mates lying dead in a pile of their own guts. When it was time to ask yourself why you'd been the one to live.

Thoughts like that could drive you mad. There was no fairness to war. Sure, you could tip the odds in your favour by being the meanest, hardest bastard on the battlefield, but when your time was up that was it. The Lord of Crows wouldn't give a shit how tough you were, he'd come for you just the same.

Nobul had never believed in any of that religion crap, but he could understand why men did. Especially when every day you were facing a painful end. Thinking there might be something waiting in the hereafter could well make the knowledge you were gonna die that much more bearable. It might keep you going when it all seemed lost. Nobul Jacks didn't need any of it, though. He had enough to keep him going. He had his hate.

No matter how much pain he was in, no matter what aches ailed him, that hate would keep him going until the end. Until he could swing his hammer no more. Until some Khurta came screaming at him with just enough fury to put him down.

But until then . . .

Someone was standing beside him breathing heavily. Nobul glanced up to see Dustin looking at him warily. He'd known the lad a while, fought with him over the past weeks, but there was a distance between them now, like Dustin had no idea how to approach Nobul since he'd seen the Black Helm in action. They'd never been the best of friends, never had a long, lingering chat over beers, but some part of Nobul felt sorry about that. He'd never revelled in being feared, but it just seemed to follow him round.

Couldn't be helped now, though.

'What?' he said rising gingerly to his feet, using the wall to help him more than he'd have liked.

'It's Kilgar,' replied Dustin, taking a step back as Nobul stood to full height. 'He took a spear to the guts in the last assault. They don't think he's gonna make it through the day. He's been asking for you.'

Nobul nodded, gesturing for Dustin to lead the way. There weren't many people he'd have taken the time to see, to sit by their bedside as they breathed their last, but if he owed anyone in this city then it was probably Kilgar. The one-eyed fucker had taken him into the Greencoats when he'd had nowhere else to go, and he'd saved his life on the wall. Sparing the bastard a few moments at the end was the least Nobul could do.

Dustin led them down to what they were using as a makeshift infirmary – an old storehouse and stables knocked through to make one big building. It was eerily quiet as Nobul walked in, there was no one groaning, no one crying out for the priest. Here and there a Daughter of Arlor was tending to a wounded man with a damp cloth but other than that there was no movement. It was almost peaceful.

Kilgar was in one corner, Bilgot sat next to him. The fat lad looked a bit leaner than he had done last time Nobul saw him. His face was ashen beneath the grime and it was obvious he was about ready to bawl his eyes out.

As Nobul approached, Kilgar waved Bilgot off then held out his hand. Nobul took it, feeling how weak the serjeant's grip was. He was stripped to the waist, the dressings round his stomach turned red and there was an unmistakable stink of infection.

'They can't do nothing for it,' said Kilgar, seeing that Nobul was looking at his wounded guts. 'Khurtas cover their weapons in all sorts of shit. If they don't get you on the battlefield, infection will get you later. This spread bloody quick, though. Must have been some dirty bastard kind of poison.'

'You comfortable?' Nobul asked. 'You need water? Food?' It seemed only right to ask. He didn't have anything else to say.

'No point wasting it on me,' said Kilgar with a grin. It turned into a grimace and he coughed, spitting a fleck of blood across his cheek. Nobul gripped his hand tighter until the coughing fit had gone.

'I always knew who you were, you know,' he said when he'd finally calmed enough to speak. 'From that first day you were stood in the courtyard of the barracks. I recognised you straight away. The fucking Black Helm. Here to be a Greencoat. I knew you must have been in some kind of shit, or times had gotten bloody hard.'

'I appreciate you keeping it to yourself,' said Nobul.

'Weren't nobody's business but yours, I reckoned. I guessed you had your reasons. And why was I gonna argue having the Black Helm as part of my watch? There was no one gonna mess with us. Not with you around.'

Nobul nodded, though he doubted the truth of it. There'd been plenty to mess with him over the past weeks. There'd been a lot of men almost done for him too, but he was still here and they were dead.

'She came, you know,' said Kilgar, his one eye drifting to the ceiling.

'Who?' asked Nobul.

'The Red Witch. She stood right where you are now.'

Nobul knew exactly who he was talking about. He'd seen her on the roof of the Chapel of Ghouls a few weeks previous but not known her name then. He'd seen her on the wall too, though he'd given her a wide berth. He wasn't ashamed to say she frightened the fuck out of him.

'What did she want with an old warhorse like you?'

Kilgar smiled. 'Me and her go a long way back. Not many people trust that woman, but for some reason she's always made me feel safe.'

Nobul had no idea what Kilgar meant by 'safe' but he wasn't about to ask. 'And what did she say to you?'

Kilgar looked at Nobul then. He fixed him with his one eye and there was some kind of peace in there. 'She told me I'd done enough.'

Nobul nodded at that. 'I reckon she's right.'

For a moment something burned in Kilgar's eye, something of the old warrior coming back. 'But you're not done, Nobul Jacks,' he said, gripping Nobul's hand tight. 'You're a long way from fucking done.'

Kilgar closed his eye, his hand going slack. Nobul couldn't say whether the serjeant was dead or passed out, but he placed that hand gently on the bed anyway and took a step back. With nothing left to say he walked out of the makeshift infirmary.

As he made his way back up towards the wall he knew Kilgar was right. The aches and the pains were still there, but Nobul wasn't done by a damn sight. He'd make sure he didn't die on no bed either. He was going down in the fight, screaming and roaring and spitting his last breath at the enemy.

When he got back to the wall he saw a crowd had gathered. Archers were congregated in ranks and the nervous silence told him something was wrong. Nobul ran up the steps, hefting his hammer, expecting the worst. The Khurtas hadn't attacked in the day yet, but he wouldn't put it past them to change their tactics.

He squeezed past some of the levies till he made it to the front, looking out between the merlons. Over on the plain, just beyond the range of their arrows, were about a thousand Khurtas. They didn't look ready to attack, they were just standing there waiting.

As they all watched, a single Khurtic voice rose up as it had done that first night. It was a loud call, something long and nasty in their ugly tongue, answered by a choral groan as the Khurtas fell to one knee, all one thousand of them at once. That voice continued to chant, and the thousand with it answered. They punched themselves in the chest all in unison, changing the tone of their cries as they did so, screaming their lungs out. Nobul could see why some of the lads would be terrified of that, but the Khurtas weren't moving. They were no danger from this distance.

'It's a war salute,' said a voice at Nobul's shoulder. He turned to see Bannon Logar standing next to him, his armour more dented and bloody than he'd last seen it but the old man's eyes were more alive than Nobul remembered. 'It's a tribute to one of our warriors.'

'Which one?' Nobul asked.

'You know which one, lad. The Black Helm killed one of their war chiefs. You've challenged for the tribe. They'll be sending their best to test you.'

As if the old man had heralded it, the Khurtas split apart, allowing someone to walk through their midst. At first Nobul thought it might be Amon Tugha himself. The prospect of fighting that Elharim bastard filled him with no particular thrill, but when he could finally see their champion he was even less keen to jump straight into the fight.

The Khurta was bigger than the one he'd killed on the roof of the gatehouse. From this distance his features were hard to pick out but Nobul could still tell he wasn't pretty. He stood at the front of his thousand and bellowed, just standing there with a war maul over his shoulder, shouting his shit in Khurtic like it might make the walls of Steelhaven crumble.

Nobul took his helmet and placed it on his head, then climbed up on the battlements as best he could without looking an old, tired bastard. As he pointed his hammer forward at the giant Khurta all the noise stopped. They looked at each other across three hundred yards until the Khurta hefted his own massive hammer from his shoulder and pointed right back. Then, as one, the Khurtas turned and headed back north.

There were audible sighs of relief as they went. Nobul watched for as long as he could before he climbed back down off the wall. Last thing he wanted was to fall – that would have been a fucking stupid way to go after all his posturing.

Duke Bannon gave him a nod, a wicked grin on his face. 'You show them, lad,' he said, before walking off with the rest.

At least Bannon was looking forward to what was coming. And Nobul reckoned it would be pretty humiliating if he couldn't live up to the old bastard's expectations. Not that it mattered much.

Humiliation didn't matter a shit if you were dead.

# THIRTY-FOUR

Sleep was threatening to overwhelm him, despite the bright sunlight and the biting cold. River would not succumb, though. He could not. A chance at escape might come from anywhere, and he could not be asleep when it happened.

*A chance at escape? You know there will be no escaping this. You will die here, bound to this frame, watching the city burn in front of your eyes. Watching your queen slain by the Elharim.*

But Jay had not been slain yet.

When she came to the camp and gave herself to Amon Tugha, River had wanted to cry out, wanted to scream at her to run even though there was nowhere for her to go. Everything had collapsed around him as she had knelt before Amon Tugha. Everything he had fought to protect for so many weeks suddenly shattered. But Jay was brave, he had always known. That she would sacrifice herself for a city of people she hardly knew, because she was their queen, was no surprise. He should have known that no matter what he did to keep her safe he could not protect Jay from herself.

He could only hope her rescue was successful, that the knights who had ridden into the midst of the Khurtas had managed to take her to safety. Surely they were victorious; otherwise Amon Tugha would have paraded her corpse amongst this camp of savages by now.

No, better that River think about his own escape. Though it looked almost hopeless, perhaps there was a way.

Two Khurtas sat by the embers of a fire, furs drawn tight about their shoulders. Maybe if he could goad them enough they might offer an opportunity for him to escape. Bound as he was, River doubted he had much chance, but there was no other way he could see to get himself out of this. And now more than ever he had to return to the city, had to be at Jay's side to protect her.

He stared, locking his eyes on one of the Khurtas. He didn't speak their language and doubted they knew much of his. The only way for him to taunt them was to show his defiance, that he wasn't beaten. Perhaps it would appeal to their barbarity.

One of the Khurtas stared back, his expression displaying his hatred. It was obvious he wanted nothing more than to draw the dagger at his side and open up River's flesh, but still he sat there by the fire, unmoving. It belied all River knew about these barbarians.

'They will not move from their fire.'

The words were whispered in River's ear. The voice of Amon Tugha was unmistakable. How he had managed to get so close without River sensing him was a mystery, but then the Elharim were mysterious in their very nature. Hadn't the Father of Killers been one of them? And River had grown up with the man. All that time he had known very little about his origins.

'The Khurtas are savage. Fearless,' continued Amon Tugha, coming to stand beside the frame to which River was bound. 'They respect only one thing – strength. And they are obedient to he who holds power. For all their faults – their savagery, their brutality – they can be relied upon to remain loyal to he who has proven himself worthy of it. And there are none more worthy of it than I.'

He moved to stand in front of River now, staring at him. The man exuded power, not just in his frame but in his manner. He was like an animal, at once calm and majestic, but with a feral edge that suggested he might explode with ferocity at any time.

'You should understand about loyalty, assassin. You were loyal once, or so I am led to believe. The one you called the Father of Killers put great store by your devotion to him. But you cast that loyalty aside. Only a man who has known betrayal, lived betrayal, can understand the true meaning of loyalty. I am curious . . . does it hurt that you betrayed the man who gave you everything? The man you called "Father"?'

River looked up into those golden eyes. Despite the difference in their appearance he saw something of the Father of Killers in the warlord's visage. Both cold, uncaring, ready to sacrifice anything and anyone for their own ends.

'He was no father to me,' River replied.

Amon Tugha smiled. 'Indeed. He was a son of the Riverlands. And you his southron pup. You were nothing to him in the end. You were right to betray him – he would only have led you to your death.' The Elharim looked to the northern horizon, a strangely wistful expression crossing his face. 'We were boys together, he and I. He became Subodai of my mother's House. She cast him out years ago but he remained loyal. For a century or more he remained devoted, yearning for the chance to return to the Riverlands with honour. Can you imagine how he felt when I offered him that chance? One last chance at redemption?'

River simply stared. He cared little for the hopes or dreams of the Father of Killers. Neither did he think much of Amon Tugha's nostalgia.

The Elharim looked back at River, fixing him in those golden eyes. 'But of course you also know of redemption. You seek it even now. A man born and bred to kill, brought low for the love of a woman.' A grin crossed Amon Tugha's lips. 'How many have you killed, assassin? How many innocents alongside the guilty? There will be no redemption for you. The only mercy I offer is for you to live long enough to see this city fall. I will rule these lands for a hundred years, long after you are dead. And then, when I have raised an army strong enough, I will return to the Riverlands and claim what is mine by right.'

River stared into Amon Tugha's face, straining against the ropes that held him tight. There was nothing he could do; no way he could stop this immortal warrior even if he was free. But perhaps one last show of defiance.

'Good luck,' River said.

Amon Tugha's grin widened before he turned away.

River could hear his laugh for a long time before it faded into the distance.

# THIRTY-FIVE

'So . . . that's it, yeah?'

Shirl had asked the question a half-dozen times now and it was starting to get right on Rag's nerves.

'Yes it is,' she replied. 'Now stop going on about it.'

'But—'

'Will you shut the fuck up!?'

She could understand he had questions. She got the fact that he was most probably shitting himself, but there was nothing she could say to put him at ease. Shirl's peace of mind was the least of her troubles. Fact was, this probably wasn't the end. Fact was, Bastian was going to find out it had all gone wrong. He'd already know that the gate wasn't open and the Khurtas hadn't come running in. He'd know that his men never returned with the happy news they'd succeeded in their mission. He knew right now, and was most likely trying to find out what had gone wrong.

Rag should have been hiding. She should have taken her boys and run off to some corner of the city and waited out the siege, for good or bad. But that would have given the game away sure as shit. Bastian would then have known beyond any doubt they were involved. No – she'd just have to blag it, like she blagged every other thing.

How long she could keep that up only the gods knew – and they weren't telling.

*Best just to sit tight and pretend like you don't know nothing. There's nothing to connect you to what happened. Bastian will think the Greencoats found out and killed all his men. There ain't nothing to worry about.*

But Rag knew there was plenty to worry about. She'd been in the shit before, though, and she weren't dead yet. She could always keep her mouth shut. It was just a matter of what the other boys had to say.

Harkas and Essen were sat playing a card game. The big fella didn't look particularly bothered about what he'd done, which was all of the killing. Rag and Shirl and her boys had helped well enough, causing distractions in the dark so Bastian's men had walked right onto the end of Harkas' blade, but it was him done the murders. Eleven men he'd slain in the night. Eleven corpses he'd left lying there for someone to find in the morning light. Rag had always been afraid of the big fucker but she'd never thought him capable of that. And now he sat there all normal, like it didn't mean a shit.

Essen hadn't been involved but he wasn't about to say nothing. If Bastian found out he'd known about their plan to stop the gate being opened he'd be just as dead as the rest of them. She was sure she could rely on them both to keep quiet; they were solid, she'd learned that well enough. In fact she'd have been playing cards right along with them if she had any idea what the rules were.

Chirpy, Migs and Tidge were in the corner, eating themselves stupid. Rag knew she should have sent them away to hide but they'd begged to stay with her. She'd abandoned them once before and she'd be fucked if she was gonna do it again. Besides, they'd been her crew for years. She knew she could rely on them to keep it shut. They might be little boys but they were tough as boot leather and loyal as hunting dogs. She'd take them over a grown man any day.

Then there was Shirl.

Rag knew he'd never be able to keep his mouth shut about anything. He was a coward and a dullard but at the end of the day he was part of her crew. As much as she wanted to get rid of him she knew she just didn't have it in her. Only time would tell if that was a stupid mistake.

As the back door to the tavern opened, Rag realised that time might come sooner rather than later.

Two men entered. They weren't in dark clothes but Rag knew they were part of Bastian's crew just from looking at them. They were lean, eyes moving constantly, either looking out for danger or trying to find their quarry. When those eyes fell on Rag she realised which.

'You Rag?' one of them said.

'Yeah, what about it?' Rag answered, even though she had a pretty good idea what.

'Someone wants to see you.'

'Well maybe I'm fucking busy.' It wouldn't do to go along too eager. She didn't want to look like a pussy and all frightened like a child. That might give the game away before Bastian had even had a chance to question her.

'I'm not fucking asking,' he said, taking a step forward all threatening like.

From the corner of her eye Rag saw Harkas move one hand down to the knife at his belt, even though he kept his eyes on the cards fanned out in his other. Almost without moving she splayed out her fingers for him to relax. She'd got this – no need for it to turn nasty.

'So who's fucking telling?' she said, giving it the tough talk. Wouldn't do to back down so easy.

'Bastian, you stupid bitch. Who do you think it is?'

Rag smiled. 'Well, why didn't you say so? Lead the fuck on.'

Both men seemed to relax a bit, though they didn't take their eyes off the other lads. Rag saw one of them give a lingering look over Chirpy, Migs and Tidge, who'd stopped eating now and were just looking on warily. Then they led her towards the door.

'Where you taking her?' Shirl blurted as they walked outside.

Rag didn't answer and neither did Bastian's men, though she had a pretty good idea where they were bound.

Night was drawing in out on the street. There was a chill in the air but that wasn't all. Sure as shit the Khurtas were coming again, and when the sun had dropped they'd be throwing themselves at the city like madmen. She could almost taste the fear along with the cold. Then again, Rag had her own problems. As she was led through the streets she almost envied those lads up on the wall. At least they knew what was coming and had a chance to defend themselves.

She might get a shiv to the neck at any second and not even have the chance to run.

Before long, Rag realised where they were. She could see the Chapel of Ghouls on its distant hill, sitting behind its brass fence. The entrance to Bastian's lair weren't guarded quite as well as the last time she'd been here, but then what was the point? Greencoats had a bit more on their plate than chasing after the Guild right now. If only they knew how much Bastian was in the Khurtas' pockets they might have taken a different view.

They walked down through the tunnels beneath the city streets, followed by the constant dripping from the damp ceiling, and into that central chamber. Rag stared at the floor right where Palien had been killed. If she'd expected to feel anything about seeing that spot again she was disappointed – that place where he'd had his throat cut made her feel pretty much nothing at all.

As her eyes adjusted to the light she realised Bastian wasn't gonna make no kind of dramatic entrance like he had before. He was already sitting in the shadows waiting for her. From what she could see he looked tired – like someone had just dug the bastard up and dipped him in skin . . . not that she'd have mentioned it.

Rag just stood there. Wouldn't do to speak unless spoken to – that kind of shit might get her killed – so she just waited while he sat and stared.

'How are you?' he said finally. 'Well rested after delivering my message? I see you're looking much less singed than when I last saw you.'

*What was this, some kind of trick? Since when did Bastian give a fuck about anyone's welfare?*

'I'm fine,' she said, taking a quick glance around for the punchline. No one was laughing, though.

'Good.' Bastian stood up, walking a little ways into the light. His dark eyes shone a bit in the torchlight like ink floating on water. She'd seen a dead shark once on the docks and it reminded her of that a bit too much. 'Did you have a pleasant evening?'

This was getting weird. Surely he must have known. Surely he was making her feel at ease so it would be that much worse when he stuck something sharp in her.

'It was okay,' she replied, wondering which direction the pointy metal was going to come from.

'That's good. Now ask me.'

'What?'

He turned to her, his voice lowering. 'I said ask me about my evening.'

Rag braced herself. 'How was your evening?'

She knew exactly how his evening must have been and she knew what was coming. Her shoulders tensed as she waited for his tirade, but it never came.

'Let me tell you,' he continued matter-of-factly. 'It was something of a disappointment. A disaster, you might say. It seems the Greencoats were a little more vigilant than I'd have liked, and my plans to open the Lych Gate came to nothing. As you can imagine, this has vexed me slightly.'

'I can imagine,' Rag said. The words just came out, she hadn't meant them to. He was just making her so bloody nervous.

'Can you?' he asked. 'Can you imagine how vexed I am?'

Rag stared up at him, trying to give him her best 'lost puppy' face. She knew it was pointless. He didn't give a shit about her and especially not about puppies. She tried shaking her head instead.

'No, you have no idea.' His face turned stern and he locked her in those shark eyes. 'I lost a lot of men. I didn't open the gate either, so essentially I've betrayed the man who's coming to level this city and everyone in it. Which is why that gate is going to be opened no matter what.' He looked down at her as though she were some kind of tasty morsel. 'And you're going to do the opening.'

That took a bit to sink in.

'I'm what?' asked Rag.

'You're clever. Resourceful. You don't have the muscle but I don't think you'll need it.'

'But how am I supposed to—'

Bastian leaned in close. 'You'll think of something, won't you?'

Rag looked back. For a moment she wanted to burst into tears. Instead she cracked the biggest smile she could muster.

'Of course I will,' she said. 'You just leave it to me.'

# THIRTY-SIX

Waylian stood in silence behind his mistress as she stared from the window of the Tower of Magisters. The mosaic glass was cracked where a missile flung from a Khurtic trebuchet had managed to strike the tower lower down. The pattern was still held in place by its lead frame but the picture itself, an Archmaster of old Waylian couldn't name, was skewed awkwardly, making it look as though he had been sliced in half.

Magistra Gelredida stood and watched as the skies darkened. It was some way off nightfall but a veil of black cloud had cast its shadow over the city, rolling in from the Midral Sea like a tide covering the sky.

Waylian dared not interrupt as she stood there, as though keeping vigil. He had so many questions, wanted to know what he could do to help, but couldn't find any way to ask. If she had one last task for him she'd have given it. It seemed as though all hope had fled.

Drennan's apprentices were beaten – half of them dead. Crannock's veterans had fared worse, only a handful remaining. Lucen Kalvor's Raven Knights had taken a beating but many still stood resolute, ready to protect their wards until the end, for all the good it would do them.

'The city is all but lost,' said Gelredida, putting voice to Waylian's thoughts. 'Things are going to get much worse. The next attack will most likely see the Khurtas breach the wall. If not this night then the next.'

She had never sounded so defeatist before, and Waylian had to admit it worried him.

'But, Magistra, there must be something we can do. There must be some task you could give me?'

Gelredida turned to him and Waylian saw she was smiling. That was almost enough to put him on his arse.

'I could ask you anything, couldn't I? Loyal Waylian Grimm. That's one of your virtues. You've always been dependable and I would rely on no one else.' She walked closer to him and placed a gloved hand on his shoulder. She'd never touched him before and he found it strangely reassuring . . . until her face turned stern. 'Be careful who you give your loyalty to, Waylian. If you survive this, by some miracle, you must trust no one. There will likely be no members of the Caste left to offer you safety or advice. If these walls fall, if Amon Tugha has his way, you will be alone. Your power will be sought after. Perhaps your very soul. Look to yourself, Waylian Grimm, and be the man you were always meant to be.'

She was talking now as though she wouldn't be there. As though he would no longer be her apprentice. It scared him a little, sparking yet more unanswered questions, but all he could do was nod in agreement.

Her stare lingered for a moment, and Waylian struggled to read what was going through her mind. Was she concerned for him? Was that compassion? She'd certainly never shown anything like it before. All she'd ever done was put him in harm's way. It was a bit late to be worried about him now, when the city was about to fall and they were all going to be slaughtered.

'What now, Magistra?' he asked, desperate to divert her attention.

'Now we do what has to be done,' she replied. 'The only option left open to us.'

Gelredida turned and headed for the door. Waylian didn't have to be asked – he knew he should follow wherever she led.

They made their way down through the tower, down below the entrance hall to the dungeons that lay beneath the tower's foundations. They passed the cells where Waylian had witnessed a man being tortured to death by Gelredida's own hand. The cold of the place suddenly made him shudder, or was it the memory? Either way he gripped the sleeves of his robe, pulling it about him tighter like a cloak.

Gelredida continued down through the tower, deeper than Waylian had ever gone before. He could barely find his footing in the scant light, desperately trying not to trip on the slick stairway and bowl into his mistress. Deeper they went, and as they did so the presence of Raven Knights seemed to increase. Two at the corridor entrance, two more in an antechamber, two others guarding a door that led through to a row of cells.

Waylian wondered what could be in those cells that would be such cause for concern. What could they house that would require six Raven Knights, men who were so sorely needed on the wall protecting the other magisters against the unstoppable enemy?

When he followed Gelredida through the doors and down the corridor he saw that every cell was empty. He counted nineteen in all, each one vacant until they reached the very last. By the dim torchlight Waylian could see little inside. As he looked and his eyes slowly adjusted to the gloom he realised there was a single body lying on a cot in one shadowed corner. The place stank of damp and rot and piss and Waylian had to grit his teeth rather than gag.

'It's time,' said Gelredida in a stern voice as she came to stand next to the cell.

At first the body on the cot didn't move, and Waylian wondered if she were talking to a corpse. Perhaps she had finally been unhinged by the pressure of protecting this damned city. Perhaps her last-gasp attempt to rescue every soul in Steelhaven was to rail at a rotting carcass.

Then the body moved.

Waylian peered through the dark as the figure sat up and stretched, dark, lank hair covering his face. Then the dishevelled form stood and slowly walked forward. There was something in his gait that Waylian recognised but he couldn't quite place it. As the figure reached the bars he shielded his eyes with one hand against the glare of the torch, masking his features.

Then Waylian saw him smile behind a mass of dark, wispy beard.

'Hello, Grimmy. It's been a while.'

Waylian felt his bollocks clench at the sound of that voice. It was a voice he'd never wanted to hear again. One that struck him with terror. With memories of pain and death.

*It can't be him. He's fucking dead. You fucking killed him.*

The figure moved his hand, pressing his face up against the bars and smiling that friendly, amiable smile. He was still handsome despite the mass of hair and beard.

He was still Rembram Thule.

# THIRTY-SEVEN

Janessa had not spoken since Kaira brought her back to the palace. She merely sat in her chamber, staring out to the north of the city, looking beyond the wall to where lay Amon Tugha's army.

Kaira had no idea what to say. It had been her duty to protect the queen and she had come close to failing, more than once. Not that Janessa made it easy for her. Kaira could never be blamed if Janessa gifted her throat to the enemy, but it wasn't blame she was concerned about. She had grown fond of this girl. Grown to love her, even. She had been thrust onto the throne, given the role of a warrior queen when she was no more than a child. No wonder she had taken it on herself to sacrifice everything to save the city. Kaira couldn't say whether she would not have done the same in the queen's position.

'I have failed,' Janessa said quietly.

Kaira moved to her side, placing a hand on the girl's shoulder.

'You have not. You yet live. The city still stands. While you breathe there is hope.'

Janessa shook her head. 'He will come and he will destroy this city. You should have let me die.'

Kaira grabbed Janessa by her arms, hauling the girl to her feet.

'No,' she said, staring Janessa in the eye. 'You are a queen. You are stronger than this. You have survived worse than this; every attempt on your life has failed.'

'And how many have died to protect me?' Janessa shouted back. Tears welled in her eyes. Kaira didn't know whether to be sorry or encouraged by the sudden fire inside the girl. 'How many more will die before Amon Tugha's victory?'

'Hundreds,' said Kaira. 'Thousands, maybe. But they will die on their feet, in defiance of him. They will not kneel before him and offer themselves like sheep to the slaughter.'

Janessa looked to the ground and Kaira sensed her shame.

'I'm not strong enough. I can't beat him.'

'Not on your own.' Kaira lifted the girl's chin. 'But you are not alone. You stand at the head of a loyal army. You stand queen of all the Free States. And self-pity does not become you.'

Janessa nodded. 'I know. You're right.' She wiped the corner of her eye. 'I almost destroyed everything. Almost gifted Amon Tugha the victory he seeks. I have to make it right.'

Kaira smiled. 'Your only mistake was naivety. To trust the word of a man with no honour. But you will make that right.'

'I will,' said Janessa. 'And I will do it now. My sword? My armour?'

'I'll see they are brought immediately, Majesty.'

She gave Janessa one last smile before leaving her chamber. Kaira was encouraged by the girl's sudden fire but also knew it did not mean they could win. Janessa may well have been right about not being able to beat Amon Tugha, but there were worse things than defeat. Kaira knew that all too well. She could only hope Vorena would keep them strong when the final battle came.

Kaira had not reached the end of the corridor from Janessa's chamber before she saw Seneschal Rogan waiting patiently. He smiled when he saw her and took a step forward.

'I trust the queen is well after last night's . . . excitement?' he said.

*How could he know so soon? But then he always knew. His eyes and ears were everywhere, within the palace and without.*

'She is quite well,' Kaira replied. 'And eager to join the fight once more.'

'Such a relief. The city needs her now more than ever.'

'And she will serve it as any queen would.'

'Of that I am sure. I trust you have enough men to keep her

safe? Should you require more I have servants of the Inquisition who would be only too happy to join her retinue.'

Rogan sounded genuinely concerned, and for a moment Kaira considered it. Janessa had been in enough danger, and it would only increase as the siege wore on. Perhaps Rogan's help was what she needed.

But no. It was Kaira's duty, and that of the Sentinels, to keep the queen safe. Only they could be trusted. Lord Leon Magrida had proven that beyond doubt.

Kaira shook her head. 'We have more than enough men, Seneschal. But your concern is appreciated.'

He bowed his head. 'I live to serve the Crown.'

'As do I,' she replied.

Kaira made her way down through the palace, on the way ordering a steward to have the queen's armour sent to her chamber. The Helsbayn was locked within its vestibule, and Kaira would trust no one else to bring the queen her sacred sword of office.

As she walked along an empty corridor towards the great hall, Kaira was sure she heard a mumbling. She stopped, alert to any danger. Perhaps she was being over-cautious, but the past days, and the inherent danger to the queen, meant she was immediately on edge. More mumbling, this time clear along the corridor and accompanied by a metallic clink. Chains perhaps?

Kaira slowly drew her sword and moved down the passageway, following the sound. It grew louder, more frenetic, and with every step she feared the worst – another assassin within the walls of Skyhelm? How many more before this was over?

She peered around the corner. An adjoining corridor led off into darkness but there was a door open to a large chamber. The voice was audible now, though spoken in hushed tones. Kaira couldn't make out any of the words; they were babbled as though by a madman. She waited, gripping her sword tight, feeling its weight, ready to strike.

With a jangle, Chancellor Durket appeared from the room. He carried a large leather pack over each shoulder, huffing under their weight as he staggered down the corridor. When he had moved close enough Kaira stepped out from her hiding place and he stopped dead, his eyes wide.

'Chancellor?' said Kaira.

'Er . . . yes?' he replied.

'Going somewhere?' Durket shook his head vigorously. Kaira guessed his gesture might not have been altogether honest. 'What do you carry there?'

'Nothing,' said Durket. 'I mean . . . nothing for you to be concerned with.' His brow furrowed in annoyance. 'Now, out of the way, I have to attend to the business of the Crown.'

Kaira didn't move, and he stared up at her trying his best to act defiant, but under Kaira's stern gaze there was little chance of that.

'I'll ask again, what do you carry there?' she said.

Durket merely stared at her, unwilling or unable to move. Kaira's patience had worn thin enough.

Her sword flashed out, slicing a leather smile from one of the packs. Gold crowns spilled out in a river, bouncing on the tiled floor, ringing the sound of Durket's guilt all along the corridor.

Kaira struck out, grasping Durket by the throat and slamming him up against the wall.

'Thief,' she spat. 'You think to abandon this place, your queen, in their hour of need. You would run away with the last of the gold in the palace coffers?'

Durket sobbed, shaking his head. 'It's not me,' he said. 'It not me. It's not me.'

Kaira felt a sudden sympathy for the man. They might all die here and Durket was certainly no warrior. He was weak and afraid but so was half the city.

As she released him he slid down the wall, tears flowing as he repeated 'it's not me' over and over through moist lips. She just stared down at him, sitting amongst his stolen gold, wondering what to do until he suddenly stopped his sobbing rant and looked up at her.

'Do you hear it?' he asked.

Kaira wondered if he had become unhinged through fear. 'I hear nothing,' she answered.

'I can hear it all the time. That voice in my head. It talks to me in the dark. Every night since . . .'

'Since when?' she asked, though why she wanted to decipher the ramblings of a man stricken with terror she didn't know.

'Since he came to take her. Since you killed his men and the queen took his head. I can hear him.'

'Who?' Kaira demanded. If she'd had to admit it, Durket's rambling was beginning to unnerve her. 'Azai Dravos? He is dead and gone. Nothing speaks to you but your fevered dreams.'

Durket laughed then. He laughed till the tears from his eyes and spit from his mouth ran free. 'No,' he said when his breath had returned. 'I know he's dead. It's the voice of his master I hear. The voice of Horas. He comes to me in the night. He calls to me.'

Kaira sheathed her sword. It was obvious Durket had been driven insane, but he was clearly little danger other than to the palace coffers. She reached down and hauled him to his feet.

'Leave the palace,' she said. Durket looked at her dumbly through red eyes. 'Leave this place and never return. If I ever see you again this Horas will be the least of your troubles.'

Durket nodded vigorously, then smiled. 'Yes,' he whispered, before stumbling off down the corridor.

Kaira watched him go, wondering if he wasn't the lucky one. Amon Tugha was almost within the city. Surely the insanity had only just begun.

# THIRTY-EIGHT

They had burned the bodies of Kazul and Akkula, the pyre lit bright against the ominous black clouds overhead. Regulus had said the words as best he could but how he missed Leandran and his wisdom now. How he yearned to have the words said right for the men he had brought north and who had died for him. Regulus knew he could not lament too long on that. They had known what they were fighting for. Yes, they had followed him out of loyalty, but they had also fought for their own glory.

Their pyre had been built high, but there were other pyres alongside. Pyres for the corpses of the enemy, pyres for the dead Coldlanders who had fought beside the Zatani and died in their hundreds. The stench wafted across the city, covering Steelhaven in the stink of burning meat. Regulus felt the sting of shame as his stomach rumbled at the smell. He took solace in the fact there would be time to gorge himself aplenty, either when these Khurtas had been defeated or when he was dead and returned to the earth as a warrior reborn.

For now he had to think about avenging his fallen. By rights there needed to be a sacrifice for both Kazul and Akkula. Regulus vowed there would be blood spilled in rivers for their loss. He could hardly wait for the next attack.

Night was already falling. It would not be long. He could see the enemy mustering to the north and the sense of unease washed across the wall, the Coldlanders girding themselves for what might be the final battle. Regulus felt no unease, only anticipation. This would be where he died or where his name would be remembered throughout the Coldlands and beyond. They would talk of his deeds amongst the Clawless Tribes for centuries. He could only hope word of it carried far enough south for Faro to hear. For Faro to know Regulus Gor yet lived. For Faro to fear him and his reputation before he travelled back to Equ'un to reclaim his birthright.

Janto sat some feet away, running a whetstone along the edge of one of his axes. The sound of it ringing out rhythmically was the only thing that broke the uneasy silence. It was ironic that of all the warriors he had brought north, Janto Sho would be the last to stand by his side. Of all the Zatani he had fought with, this was the only one who might turn against him. And now more than ever since his life debt was paid. Janto had saved Regulus from the golden-eyed warrior woman – they owed one another nothing now. They were equals once more, and from rival tribes no less. There was no telling what Janto might do next.

Regulus walked forward to stand beside him, listening for a moment to the ringing of whetstone on steel.

'There is nothing to keep you here,' he said when it was clear Janto was not about to stop. 'There is no need for you to risk yourself further.'

Janto remained silent, carrying on with sharpening his axe. Regulus waited until the ringing finally ceased and Janto stared out at the city thoughtfully, considering his answer.

'You think you are the only one with something to prove, Gor'tana? You think you are the only one searching for glory?'

'There may be little glory to be had. There may only be death.'

Janto barked a laugh. 'There is no glory without death. By risking our lives for this city, by destroying its enemies by the score, we will become legend. I think I'm in just the right place for that. There'll be enemies aplenty to build my reputation upon. A pile of skulls for me to stand atop and howl my name across the continents.'

'And when there are no more enemies to fight? Will you turn those axes on me?' Regulus took a step back, his hand not far from his own black blade.

Janto merely smiled, regarding Regulus with those blue eyes. 'Taking your head would be glorious indeed; I won't pretend I haven't thought about it. But look around you. These Coldlanders have tried to kill us once, and we came north to fight at their side. When we've defeated their enemies you'll be the only one left watching my back. I'd be a fool to kill you now.'

Regulus stared back at him. 'You'd be a fool to try,' he said.

Janto smiled, holding his gaze, not showing any sign of weakness.

'It may not matter anyway. Who knows, perhaps there is a warrior coming who can defeat us both. Then we'll never know which of us is the greater.'

'Perhaps there is such a warrior,' Regulus replied, looking out to the north. He drew his sword, and Janto quickly raised his own axes at the ready. 'If there is I think we're about to find out.'

He pointed to the north and Janto turned to see.

The Khurtas were on the move again.

# THIRTY-NINE

They came screaming across the plain and all of a sudden the hurt he'd felt over the past days was gone. Nobul stared down at them, gripping his hammer, wringing it like a cloth, teeth grinding together in anticipation.

He should have been at the gate, smashed in and useless as it was. That was where they'd head for, that was where the fighting would be most intense, but there were enough men there already. The Wyvern Guard, the Knights of the Blood, bannermen from Steelhaven and Valdor and Dreldun, all standing side by side, a steel wall that the Khurtas would smash against. Nobul didn't wear no steel – he was just flesh and a black helmet. He'd be more a hindrance than a help down there, so he stood on the wall and waited. There was sure to be enough fighting to go around anyway. Most of the Khurtic siege towers were smashed and broken down, the ram they'd been using was in pieces, but there were still plenty of ladders for them to scale the wall. Nobul could see them now through the night, a hundred Khurtas carrying each one.

The arrows started flying as he watched and he ducked under the deluge. Hake, standing beside him as he'd taken to doing, didn't move an inch. As the rest of the lads on the wall cowered beneath the volley of bowshot, the old man walked forward and spat a gob over the edge, chuckling to himself.

'You're a crazy old bastard, you know that?' said Nobul.

Hake didn't answer, just gave him a wink.

A ladder hit the wall some way down. Nobul wanted to walk down and wait for the first Khurta to pop his head over the battlements but he resisted.

*There'll be enough to go around, Nobul Jacks. Just you be patient.*

Sure enough, two more ladders clanked against the lip of the wall. Nobul glanced up and down the walkway, wondering if they had enough men left. Wondering if this was when they'd be overwhelmed.

Not while the Black Helm was fucking standing here, they wouldn't.

The first head popped up. Nobul crushed the top of it with his hammer and the Khurta fell silently. A second head appeared, raising a shield. This time Nobul went at it like he was hammering steel at his anvil. The Khurta managed to hold him off for longer than Nobul would have liked. All the while more ladders hit the wall – a dozen in all – and as they did more arrows came flying over.

Lads were screaming from further down. To the western side of the Stone Gate a boulder took off the top of the battlements. More screams over the pounding of his hammer on shield. Eventually the Khurta had nothing left, falling back. This one screamed all the way to the foot of the wall.

Something tamped down on Nobul's helmet as he took a step back, waiting for the next Khurta to show himself. It took a moment for him to realise it was raining, a few drops at first then more, big and fat and splashing down all around. The sound in his helmet was tremendous, and he thought for a second of taking it off when another Khurta showed his face. Before Nobul could smash him back over the wall another one came screaming from the left. There was barely enough time to raise his hammer to parry the fucker's curved blade. The weapons rang together and Nobul braced his thighs against the Khurta's attack.

Hake came in from the side, sticking the bastard in the ribs with his sword. The Khurta screamed, bounding away, and collapsed against the battlements, whimpering to himself as the rainfall soaked him through.

'Get back,' said Nobul, pushing Hake behind him as he turned to face more of the Khurtas coming over the wall. They both backed away as three more of the enemy edged forward.

'You take the two on the left,' said Hake. 'I'll have the big twat on the right.'

'Why do I get two?' Nobul said, though he was happy with the deal.

Before Hake could answer the wall exploded in front of them.

Nobul felt a moment of weightlessness, then something hit him hard in the back.

He blinked, once, twice, feeling the hard rain as it splashed against his face. His helmet was gone somewhere, his hammer somewhere else. As he tried to pull himself to his feet he groaned at the hurt, but it wouldn't keep him down, nothing would. Where he and Hake had been stood there was a massive gap in the walkway, rainwater now starting to piss down into the breach.

'Hake?' shouted Nobul. He could still hear men fighting further down the wall but in the dark and through the rain and smoke he could see fuck all.

'Here,' came a reply through the night.

Nobul staggered towards the sound, finding Hake sitting on a pile of rubble. He had a cut over one eye but other than that he looked fine.

'You all right, old man?' Nobul asked, pulling Hake to his feet.

'I'm still breathing,' he said, looking up at Nobul. 'You don't look too great yourself, though.'

Nobul reached up and felt a sting as he touched his nose. It was tender; his finger came away covered in blood.

'Does it look broken?' asked Nobul.

'You're still an ugly fucker if that's what you're asking.'

Nobul stared at Hake for a second, wanting to laugh. Wanting to slap his knees and bellow from the bottom of his lungs. Before he had the chance he heard howling from down the wall.

Hake stared back at him. 'That don't sound fucking good.'

'No it don't,' Nobul said, glancing around for his hammer. In the smashed rubble it could have been anywhere.

Up ahead, through the rain and the murk, he could see figures approaching and he doubted he'd last long if he had to face them with a piece of broken masonry.

'Here,' said Hake. Nobul looked up just as the old man threw him his hammer. Nobul felt relief wash over him as he caught it, feeling its reassuring weight in his hand. 'Now go bloody kill something.'

Nobul didn't need any encouragement. He was more than happy to do that. His boots splashed through the puddles that had gathered on the walkway as the rain washed blood down his face. His hands were cold but he knew they'd soon warm up. The first Khurta snarled at him as he came out of the rain but Nobul's hammer smashed the grimace right off his face. He swung free, all the aches gone, washed away by the downpour, every strike making a wet slap, sending the Khurtas reeling.

Hake was just behind him every step, the sly old bastard stabbing in here and there when he could but mostly making sure to stay out of the way. Wouldn't do the old fella any good to get in front of Nobul Jacks when his mad was up.

The swinging came to an end with a roar, but not one from Nobul's lips. It came from further down the wall, a feral cry; Nobul couldn't tell if it was animal or man. The Khurtas that were left backed away, not taking their eyes off him but moving as quick as they could.

Nobul stood watching, wondering what the fuck Amon Tugha had unleashed on the city as the weather beat down, soaking him through to the skin. Hake stood beside him, rain tamping off his helm, running off his beard. If he had any advice he was none too keen to share it.

A beast walked from the gloom. Nobul recognised the figure and tightened his grip on his hammer. He recognised it from the day before, from the Khurtas on the plain singing their war challenge. A challenge Nobul had accepted. Their leader had been scary enough from a distance, and now close up even Nobul felt the bite of fear. If this thing had ever been a man it wasn't any more. It must have touched nearly seven feet, face a mass of scars so gruesome Nobul could see sharpened teeth through its cheeks. Rings and chains and all sorts of other shit were pierced through its flesh and even its eyes had a hint of the animal about them.

Over one shoulder was slung the biggest hammer Nobul had ever seen and it gripped the haft in a hand the size of a keystone. It snorted from ruined nostrils, sending steam and spume out into the rain-filled night.

Nobul had come close before, on more times than he cared to remember, but he knew now, beyond doubt, this was where he'd die.

The twisted face bent into what Nobul assumed was a smile. The creature hefted the hammer, holding it in two hands, and beckoned Nobul forward.

He took a step.

'Sure you want to do this?' whispered Hake from the corner of his mouth. 'That's a mighty hammer he's got there. Makes yours look like a bell ringer.'

Nobul glanced at his own hammer, then at the one held by the beast.

'It's not how big it is. It's what you fucking do with it,' he replied, before walking forward to meet his end.

The giant's grin grew wider, the flesh of its face contorting, showing more teeth between lacerated cheeks. Its eyes opened wide, black as its soul, but Nobul didn't care for any of that shit. He'd stared into the hells before. They held no fear for him.

Nobul rushed in as the beast lifted its hammer high. At the last second he sidestepped, swinging his own hammer one-handed as the huge war maul crashed down. The maul smashed splinters from the walkway just as Nobul's hammer caught the beast in the ribs. It was a solid blow, bringing a grunt from the giant but no more. Its own hammer came up fast and Nobul had to duck to avoid having his head caved in.

Another swing and their hammers clashed. Nobul felt the jarring impact through to the joints in his shoulders, gritting his teeth against it, muscles screaming, back taking the strain. The giant Khurta held him with that grimace, leaning its head forward and gnashing its teeth. Nobul let go his hammer with one hand and punched the bastard in the jaw. It was like hitting an anvil but it did enough to put the beast off balance.

He pressed in, swinging again, managing a hit to the shoulder, but the Khurtic war chief just shrugged it off, lifting its massive hammer one-handed and bringing it down again. Nobul turned in time, feeling the ground quake underfoot as the huge maul struck.

Before the beast could raise its weapon again, Nobul planted his foot on the head of the maul, pressing his weight on it and striking out with the butt of his own hammer. It smashed into the beast's exposed mouth, shattering the front teeth and sending blood shooting onto his hand. The Khurta let go of its hammer, grabbing Nobul by the wrist. Its grip was tremendous, and he felt bone and sinew grinding together. He couldn't stifle a cry of pain as the beast forced him to drop his hammer.

The Khurta roared, making to bite his face, but Nobul reached out with his free hand, jamming a thumb in its mouth, grasping the flesh of its cheek and dragging it away. He pulled with all the strength he had left, bellowing in its face, clenching its torn cheek in his fist and feeling it tear in his grip.

Another roar, this time of pain, and Nobul was flung across the walkway, his head striking a block of stone. All he could hear was the beast's booming stride as it came for him and he desperately shook his head to clear the fug. He looked up in time to see two massive hands reaching out for him.

Desperately he scrambled out of the way, slopping across the rain-soaked walkway on his hands and knees. He knew how fucking stupid he must have looked but none of that mattered now. Seeing the massive war maul lying on the ground, he reached out, one hand grasping the haft as he rose to his feet. The beast was almost on him. Nobul roared as he lifted the maul . . . all of about three inches. Its weight was incredible, and he barely had a chance to realise he'd fucked up before the beast smashed a balled fist into his face.

*Black.*

His eyes flicked open. Everything was spinning but he was still alive. And it was still fucking raining.

*Move. You have to fucking move or you're dead.*

Nobul rolled aside as the massive war maul smashed a chunk from the paving slab he'd been lying on. He staggered to his feet but stumbled, the rain washing some clarity into his head, but not quite enough.

A hand gripped the back of his leather jerk, hauling him back. He could hear the scraping of that war maul on the broken pavement as the beast hauled it up for one last strike.

Nobul felt fury. He was going to die here. He'd expected it all right, he was going to die sooner or later, but now it had come he was fucked if he'd take it lying down.

The beast turned him around, wanting to look in his face as it killed him. Nobul's head struck forward, grasping its hand, biting into its thumb. Flesh burst and blood spurted into his mouth as the Khurta roared. Nobul's teeth ground on bone and he tore his head back, a massive thumb coming away in his mouth. The Khurta reeled back, fury in those black eyes as it raised its hammer, but Nobul's legs were already pumping. He grasped the haft of the huge war maul, throwing his weight behind it, putting the Khurta off balance. The giant stumbled back, losing its footing as Nobul came down on top of it, the haft of the war maul coming down over its throat.

Nobul gritted his teeth, pressing down as the Khurta stared up. All his weight was behind the weapon as he pressed it down, straining with all his might, spitting fury to the last. The war chief's face was furious but Nobul could see it weakening. That only made him push down all the harder, squeezing the life from the ugly bastard.

There was a choking sound as its tongue lolled from that torn mouth, the dark eyes glassing, and Nobul felt it go limp beneath him. He pressed down one last time, making sure the Khurta wasn't gonna get up again and he didn't stop until he heard his own victory roar in his ears.

Breathing hard, feeling the thrill of being alive, Nobul stood to see the Khurtas watching. Even when he spat the thumb of their war chief from his mouth they still looked at him with hate. There was no fear or respect here. These Khurtas were not about to flee.

Hake was at Nobul's side now, holding out his hammer.

'I think we're fucked,' said the old man, as Nobul grasped the weapon, feeling the rain washing over him, feeling his heart beat with the ecstasy of the kill.

'Come on then, bastards,' Nobul said, ignoring Hake's uneasiness and taking a step forward. 'Who's next?'

# FORTY

'But you told me he was dead,' Waylian said, looking in disbelief at Bram though his words were directed at his mistress.

'I told you no such thing,' Gelredida replied.

They stood in the entrance hall to the Tower of Magisters. Outside the distant roar of battle crept over the sound of the rain beating down.

Waylian could only stare at Bram, at his hollow, dishevelled features, at the arrogant smile he held despite his appearance. Hatred burned inside him along with the need to throttle the bastard, but he knew he couldn't. If Gelredida had released him she must have done so for a bloody good reason.

He could only think about how they had been friends. About how popular Bram had been with the other apprentices, but what a dark secret he had hidden. The murders he had committed and the evil magicks he had conjured that day within the Chapel of Ghouls. Had Waylian not managed to manifest some magick of his own and stopped Bram, the outcome would have been catastrophic. And here was Magistra Gelredida, unleashing him from his prison to roam the city once more.

'Why is he alive?' said Waylian.

Gelredida glanced over at Bram, who shrugged his reply, obviously as much in the dark about that as Waylian.

'He is the Maleficar Necris. He has power beyond imagining.

Power that perhaps no mortal should be allowed to wield, but right now he could be the only thing that will save this city.'

Waylian was about to say he didn't understand, but he stopped himself. He'd said those words far too often. Made himself look the dolt on too many occasions. He was damned if he'd do it again, especially with that murdering bastard Rembram Thule leering at him like some loathsome toad.

'If there are no more questions, we have work to do,' said Gelredida.

In the absence of further argument she led them from the tower. Bram followed, Waylian at the rear. Gelredida had seen fit to send the rest of the Raven Knights within the tower to the wall, so they had no further escort as they made their way out onto the city streets.

Two sets of manacles secured Bram's wrists; one made of iron and another similar to those Gelredida had worn in the Crucible of Magisters to nullify her powers. Waylian could only hope they would be enough. He had seen Bram's potency first-hand and it had almost killed him. The only reason he'd survived was blind luck and he was in no mood to push it any further. It was times like this he wished he carried a blade. Then he could see how dangerous Rembram Thule was with a knife between his ribs. He wouldn't be so fucking scary then, would he?

'How've you been, Grimmy?' Bram asked conversationally, as they made their way across the city. Screams rose above the sounds of battle and the rain had already soaked through their cloaks to the robes beneath. And now a man Waylian thought he'd killed was talking to him like they were strolling along a quiet beach. Of everything that had happened to him – from a near icy death in the Kriega Mountains, to facing a murderously animated tree in the amphitheatre – this was the most insane.

'How the fuck do you think I've been?' he replied.

'I don't know, Grimmy. That's why I'm asking. In case you hadn't noticed, I've been locked up in a dungeon for Arlor knows how many weeks. They didn't keep me apprised of how you were getting on and I've missed my old pal.'

'Fuck off,' Waylian spat. 'Fuck off, you fucking mad fucker.'

Bram looked genuinely hurt. 'Aw, come on now. There's no need for rudeness.'

'No need for . . . You tried to end the fucking world, Bram. What in the hells is wrong with you?'

Bram shook his head. 'There's no need to be hostile. I've just got ambition, that's all, Grimmy. It's not my fault you're happy to be someone's lapdog.' He nodded towards Gelredida. If she could hear she didn't acknowledge it.

'I'm no one's lapdog. And you're bloody insane. Don't talk to me.'

He dropped back a little, letting Bram and Gelredida walk ahead some distance. As much as he wanted to believe he was no one's lackey, he knew the truth of it. And he knew he'd let Bram get to him. Despite his former friend being insane he was clearly still a manipulative bastard. Probably best if they both kept their mouths shut.

They didn't have to walk on much further for Waylian to realise where they were headed. The Chapel of Ghouls stood ominously in the distance. Waylian felt a knot tighten in his stomach as they neared it, the memory of what had so nearly happened in that place making him feel sick. What made that sickness worse was the uncertainty about why Gelredida was taking them there now. Luckily Bram asked the question so Waylian didn't have to.

'Far be it from me to doubt the wisdom of the Red Witch, but why on earth are we returning to this broken-down old ruin?'

They had reached the gate now, with its fiendish brass carvings, each one in the shape of a ghoul or its victim. She drew her hand over the gate panel and whispered her quiet words. Waylian felt nausea engulf him as it had done the first time he came here, only now it was not so intense. This time he almost seemed to handle the experience with ease.

As the brass carvings moved in their silent dance and the gate opened, Gelredida stood and stared up the path to the Chapel of Ghouls. 'You wanted your chance at greatness, Rembram. And now you're about to have it.'

Bram glanced over at Waylian, both eyebrows raised as though the prospect excited him.

'Er . . . Magistra?' said Waylian. 'You can't possibly be thinking about what I think you're thinking about.'

Gelredida crossed the threshold and made her way up the path towards the chapel. Bram matched her long stride as Waylian stumbled along beside them.

'Magistra?' he said again.

'If you've never trusted me before, Waylian, you need to trust me now,' she said without turning towards him, her focus fixed on the ominous building.

'But this is madness. This is insane, you can't . . .' But Waylian knew she could.

*Of course she can, Grimm. She's the Red Witch; she can do as she pleases. How many people has she burned to get her way? How much has she risked to save this city? She was only too eager to put you in harm's way and you're her apprentice. Do you think she gives a shit about the lives of a few bog trotters swelling the city's underbelly if it defeats the Khurtas?*

Gelredida didn't lead them into the chapel itself, but up a make-shift stone staircase that twisted up the side of the building. Waylian followed behind Bram, mad thoughts of tipping the bastard off the stairs to his death flying through his head. But he knew he'd never have the courage for that, never be brave enough to defy his mistress, even when it seemed that she had lost all reason.

They reached the roof of the chapel and Gelredida walked around the perimeter with her hand held out, palm facing down. As she passed each stanchion set in the parapet that surrounded the rooftop, a torch burst into bright yellow flame. Despite the rain drumming down hard, the flames burned bright. In the light Waylian could see the roof was perhaps twenty feet wide, gaps in the flat mosaic tiles under his feet showing through to the chapel beneath. The pattern on the tiles was laid in some arcane design which Waylian didn't recognise.

Gelredida came to stand before Bram, staring him in the eyes. In return he regarded her with his usual arrogant expression.

'You will finish the ritual,' she said. 'You will unleash the ghouls on this city. Only you can do that. And only you can stop them.'

'What makes you think I'll do that?' Bram asked with a grin.

'Because if you don't, Waylian will kill you.'

*Waylian will bloody what?*

Bram glanced over at Waylian, who tried to look as brave as he could, and not like someone had just kicked him in the fruits. 'Him? He got lucky last time, you know that as well as I do, witch. He couldn't kill a crippled fly.'

'You would be surprised at what he's achieved since you were locked away from the sunlight.'

'You're right, I would. If he can conjure more than piss out of his cock I'll be fucking amazed.'

'You don't need to worry about him. You need to worry about you,' said Gelredida, staring into Bram's eyes. Waylian could feel the air turning, a metallic tang emanating from where his mistress stood. 'You will compel the undead of this place to destroy the Khurtic army. You will do your best to ensure they focus their assault on the enemy and spare the people of Steelhaven. Do you understand?'

Bram stared back at her, his arrogance gone now as he looked into her eyes. 'Yes, Magistra,' he replied.

'Now, prepare yourself,' she said, before removing the bracelets from around his wrists. Still manacled by the iron chains, Bram set about preparations for the ritual, mumbling some dark incantation as he knelt on the floor, tracing sigils in the cracked tiles with his fingertips.

Gelredida walked up to Waylian, regarding him warmly. She placed a hand gently on his shoulder.

'You are ready?' she asked.

Waylian nodded. 'Yes, Magistra,' he replied, though he knew he was anything but ready.

'At the first sign he is about to betray you, kill him.'

'But . . . how?'

Gelredida smiled. 'You will find a way, Waylian Grimm. You always do.'

As much as he appreciated the faith she was putting in him, he couldn't help but feel it was misplaced. How was he going to stop Rembram if the bastard disobeyed his mistress? And for that matter, where in the hells was Gelredida going to be?

'Magistra. I don't understand. Why is it down to me to control Bram? Why can't you do it?'

Gelredida smiled back at him, and he could see sadness in her eyes. 'My time is over,' she said.

Waylian felt his stomach lurch.

He opened his mouth to speak but found he had no words as she turned and walked away from him to kneel in the centre of the rooftop. Bram came to stand over her. His former friend was grinning once more. 'You really haven't told him anything, have you, old woman?'

She began to pull off her robe. 'I am sorry, Waylian. But this is the only way. I have been infected with the power of the Veil itself. I am already dead.'

Waylian could see the sickness that infected her hands had spread, covering her shoulders and chest in a web of black veins. Bram glanced over at Waylian as Gelredida handed him an iron dagger from her robe. 'You see, Grimmy, you can't achieve anything without sacrifice.'

'No,' Waylian screamed. 'You can't.'

Gelredida stared at him with genuine sorrow in her eyes. 'Remember what you must do. And do not hesitate.' She looked back at Bram. 'You neither.'

Bram gave her a wink. 'Oh, you know there's no chance I'll hesitate, old woman,' he said.

As he raised the dagger, a silent incantation on his lips, Waylian wanted to rush forward. He wanted to rip the knife from Bram's grip and plunge it into his heart. This was madness, this couldn't be happening. Gelredida wasn't thinking straight, the canker that had infested her body must have spread to her brain. But as the sounds of battle crept across the city, Waylian realised she was right. The Khurtas would soon overwhelm the city. This was the only way.

Gelredida closed her eyes as Bram plunged the knife into her chest. Waylian almost felt it pierce his own heart, clutching at his robe, tears welling in his eyes as he gritted his teeth against a cry of remorse. She made no sound as her head lolled backwards. Bram continued his incantation, seeming to gain in strength and stature as he mumbled the dark words.

Waylian could only watch through the torchlight as he saw dark magick seep from the blade of the iron dagger, spreading across the magistra's body. As it did so pressure began to build in Waylian's ears. He lifted a hand to his face to stem a trickle of blood from his nose just before the rooftop beneath his feet shuddered. One of the torches fell from its stanchion, and all the while Rembram mumbled his silent incantation.

As the dark sorcery continued, the air growing more humid despite the cold rain, Waylian took a step forward, heeding his mistress' words. If Bram betrayed them he would have to be killed without hesitation. The boy's eyes were shut tight now as he grasped the dagger in two hands, the blade still buried deep in Gelredida's chest. Her flesh had turned black, her body little more than a desiccated shell. Waylian clenched his fists, willing Bram to show him any sign of treachery.

The Chapel of Ghouls shook once more; this time masonry fell from the side of the building, shattering on the ground far below. Something cracked open within, like a giant egg breaking open with life, but Waylian knew there was nothing alive in there.

Bram's eyes suddenly flicked open, two black orbs staring up at the rainy night sky. At the same time something howled. Waylian felt it more than heard it. The noise seemed to clench his insides, tearing out any strength he might have had, replacing it with terror.

He staggered back, gripping the parapet of the roof. Below, in the wan light, he could see movement. Figures were creeping from the chapel, moving like animals though their limbs were unmistakably humanoid. From this distance Waylian could make out no details, and part of him was grateful for that.

After seven centuries, ghouls were abroad in Steelhaven once more, and all that could stop them running amok was an insane murderer.

And the only thing keeping that murderer in check was Waylian Grimm.

# FORTY-ONE

Rag had no idea how she was going to square this one off. She'd just got the lads to foil Bastian's plan to open the Lych Gate and now she had to tell them they was the ones had to open it. But what else was she going to do? Run?

*You ain't got no choice, girl. That's your only option now. You open that gate and the city's doomed. You don't open that gate then you're the one doomed.*

Everything had gone to shit. She'd thought she was so fucking clever, always one step ahead, but now it was obvious she weren't. Rag may as well have let Shirl be in charge. At least he'd be the one in the firing line when Bastian decided someone needed killing.

Time to call it a day. Time to get the fuck out of here before the shit well and truly landed. There was no other way. She'd never open that gate, it just wasn't an option. As much as her life depended on it Rag knew she'd never be able to live with herself if she helped the Khurtas come flooding in. There was only one course left – get her boys and get the fuck out.

Harkas, Shirl and Essen could come if they fancied. She wasn't in charge of them, not really. They could make up their own minds, but Chirpy, Migs and Tidge were her responsibility. She'd left them once and felt the guilt of it like a knife. There was no chance she'd be doing it again.

As she saw the tavern up ahead, sat all alone in the dark and the rain, she knew that there was no other choice. They could all disappear into the night. Four street kids fleeing the terror. Who'd even know? They'd spent their whole lives not being seen and staying in the shadows. She was sure they'd be far from this place before the Khurtas even noticed. Then they could just keep going. Let Bastian send his bloodhounds, let him put the word out that she was to be offed. It was sure as shite less dangerous than hanging around here.

Besides, weren't no guarantee Bastian was even gonna survive this. Who was to say Amon Tugha would keep his bargain and give the Guild a pass? Especially now Bastian hadn't kept his side of the bargain.

No, her and the lads would be far away by the time the dust settled. Once the fighting was done, if Bastian was out of the picture they could always think about coming back. There might even be rich pickings too. Lot of empty houses to hole up in. Lot of family heirlooms left abandoned. Lot of dead people wouldn't be needing any of their gear no more.

Rag walked into the tavern by the back door, wondering about the rights and wrongs of that last one, when she heard a ruckus from inside. She opened the door to the main bar to see the place was upside down: tables overturned, bottles smashed, tankards strewn about. Big Harkas was sitting silent, leaned up against the wall, bloody towel held to his face. Shirl was sat beside him like some kind of useless nursemaid. Essen stood in another corner looking scared half to death.

'What's goin on?' Rag asked, feeling a little sting of panic as she realised there was no sign of Chirpy, Migs or Tidge.

'Some of Bastian's boys paid us a visit while you were gone,' said Essen. 'Said you'd have some news for us when you got back. And—'

'Where's my lads?' Rag said, fighting back the dread.

Two heads popped up from behind the bar, and Rag let out a sigh as she recognised Chirpy and Migs. They both looked terrified but at least they was alive.

'We tried to stop them,' Shirl said. 'But they said Bastian wanted to make sure you knew he was serious.'

'What do you mean?' Rag said, glancing about the bar. 'Stop them doing what? Where the fuck is Tidge?'

'They took him,' said Essen. 'Said you'd have a job for us and taking him was to make sure it got done.'

Rag could only stare in between Chirpy and Migs. At the space where Tidge should have been stood.

*You've got a decision to make now, girl. Looks like all those thoughts of running away are gone on the wind like so much ash. Looks like you're gonna have to do exactly what Bastian wants or little Tidge is gonna get his little heart carved right out of his little chest. How you gonna live with that one?*

Rag knew she could never live with that one. But neither could she live with opening the Lych Gate and letting those Khurtas in. That would never fly, no matter how much danger her boys were in.

'What is it we're supposed to do?' asked Shirl, looking all mournful like he half knew the answer.

Rag looked at him, then to Essen and Harkas. Then to Chirpy and Migs.

'I'll tell you what you're supposed to do,' she answered, feeling her jaw tighten, her fists clenching. 'You and Essen are gonna get Harkas and the young lads and you're gonna hide down in Dockside. Those fire ships have been burnt to cinders and are sat at the bottom of the bay so it'll be the safest place in the city. You're gonna find the deepest hole and you're gonna hide in it and wait.'

She knew she'd said it like she meant it and none of the lads looked ready to argue.

'Wait for what?' asked Shirl eventually.

'Wait for me to come get you.'

'Why,' said Shirl, almost in tears. 'Where you going?'

'Where do you think I'm going? I'm off to get Tidge. Now enough talking and more fucking moving.'

Essen and Shirl picked Harkas up, who silently accepted their help. Chirpy and Migs followed them as they went for the door. Chirpy looked up at her as they made their way out.

'You are coming back, ain't you?' he asked.

'Course I am,' Rag said, tousling his greasy mop of hair. 'Now piss off.'

She watched them go, standing there for a minute alone in the tavern. She knew there weren't much chance she was coming back. If Bastian didn't do for her then the Khurtas would most likely come crawling over the city walls and do for her instead. There was no coming back from this. Up till now she'd always had some sort of plan, whether she thought of it in plenty of time or at the last moment. Right now she had no plan. No idea what in the hells she was gonna do.

No point putting it off, though.

Rag walked out of the tavern. The streets stank of rot and mud and smoke. Of war. Of death. She didn't care about any of those things, though. As the rain soaked her hair and her jacket through, she didn't think about any of it. All she thought about was finding Tidge . . . and maybe killing that bastard Bastian to boot. If only she was a killer. If only she'd taken to carrying a knife and learning to use it then maybe none of this would ever have happened.

As she saw the Chapel of Ghouls in the distance Rag knew it was hopeless anyway. She'd never have the stones to use a knife. Not on a living, breathing person. Getting someone else to do the killing for you, now that was easy enough. Sticking sharp metal in them until they stopped breathing was more than likely beyond her.

Once she'd made her way to the entrance to Bastian's lair she paused, squinting up the street, towards the chapel. Was there something moving up there? Something fucking weird through the rain and the dark?

*Focus, you stupid cow. Letting shadows in the night spook you is a sure way to get yourself killed.*

Rag shook her head, ignoring whatever it was – if it was anything at all. The fear was most likely addling her mind, making her sloppy. Being scared had a habit of doing that, and she knew she couldn't afford to let it put her off. Tidge was relying on her.

She slipped in through the entrance, relieved that there was no one guarding the door. Inside, the sound of rain echoed down the corridor to the underground passages and it weren't no trouble for her to move silent. There were a couple of fellas standing in the dark, hoods drawn up against the cold and damp, but Rag was by them without either even knowing it. She'd never had the best sense of direction but even she managed to make her way to the centre of Bastian's hideout without getting lost. There, in the shadows, she tried to think what in the hells to do next.

Light was coming in from somewhere, but from her hiding place in the dark Rag couldn't tell which direction. Before she could think of where to start looking for Tidge she heard a voice from down the corridor.

'It's true, I swear it.' The voice sounded firm but with an edge of desperation. 'I'd cleared the rest of the gate detail ready for your boys to go in and do the job. When I saw all the lights had gone out I went back for a look.'

Rag made her way towards the sound of voices, careful to stay out of the light where it was cast across the floor of the underground cavern.

'Then what?'

Rag almost froze at the sound of Bastian's voice, creaking towards her like a rusty door hinge. This was it, though; Tidge must be close by somewhere.

'Then I saw Jerrol. Asked him where the rest of his crew were and he said outside, but there weren't anyone outside. Then he got spooked. Went up to check out some noise on the roof. I could hear weird shit all around so I fucking hid. It was dark, no one was going to see me. Then Jerrol started shouting, ran out of the gate-house and into the street. That's when he was fucking murdered. Later on when it had gone quiet I had a look around and his whole crew was piled up in the shadows. Wiped out to the last man.'

'By who?' asked Bastian.

'I couldn't really make them out in the dark. But there were kids. Little kids running around in the night. One of them was a girl, I'm sure of it.'

Rag froze at the edge of the entrance. If Bastian wasn't going to kill her before, he sure as shit was now. Nevertheless, she peered around the corner, slow as you like, trying to see in. Bastian and two of his men were standing in the room, lit bright as day by a lantern on a table. There was another bloke with his back to her wearing a green jacket with the royal seal on it.

Bastian was smiling now. 'Let me get this straight, Platt. You mean to tell me a dozen of my dirtiest, meanest killers were done over by a bunch of fucking kids?'

The Greencoat held his hands up, trying to take a step away. 'I . . . I'm only saying what I saw. I swear it.'

Everyone was looking at the fella now, and Rag could sense they were wondering whether or not to shove their knives in him. She took her chance, stealing into the room, sticking to the wall where there was still shadows.

'What you saw?' said Bastian, as Rag skirted the edge of the room. There were crates and sacks in the way containing gods knew what but she wasn't here for no loot. 'Or what you want us to think you saw?'

Rag peered round the edge of a wooden box and her heart leapt. Sitting there like it was the most normal thing in the world was Tidge. He was listening to proceedings with a bored look on his face.

'Why would I make something like that up, Mister Bastian?' said the Greencoat with a hint more desperation in his voice. Rag waved over at Tidge, but he didn't seem to notice.

Bastian was silent, as though he were contemplating whether now was a good time to kill the Greencoat. Then one of his men leaned over and whispered something in his ear.

Rag waved at Tidge again. This time he noticed, but didn't jump or make a sound. Good lad, that Tidge. Lot brighter than he looked.

'You're right,' Bastian said. 'We do know someone who fits that description.' Something rumbled overhead, like a storm had just hit right on top of the cave they were in. 'Don't we, Rag?'

She froze. Tidge froze too, just staring at her. That was it, she knew there was no point creeping around any more, and slowly she stood up from behind the crate.

'Come to save your little friend?' Bastian said, just before there was another rumble. Part of the roof crumbled, dropping to the floor, though no one seemed to notice but Rag.

'What do you fucking think?' she said defiantly.

'I think you've come to get bloody gutted,' Bastian spat between his clenched teeth, signalling to one of his men with a bony hand.

Bastian's henchman slowly pulled a long dagger from his belt as the cave rumbled once more.

Rag came out from behind the crates, holding an arm out to Tidge. He moved towards her, taking her hand.

'You let him go,' she said. 'He ain't done nothing to you. He's no part of it.'

Bastian's lips curled back in a leer that almost made her sick. 'It's not him you should be worried about. It's y—'

The whole cave suddenly rocked. Bastian was almost knocked off his feet and the other blokes dropped down, covering their heads as the ceiling collapsed here and there.

Rag weren't about to hang around and wait for Bastian to finish his sentence and she tightened her grip on Tidge's hand before dragging him towards the exit. The rumbling calmed down as she ran into the dark and she could hear Bastian and his men coming behind, shouting at her and at one another.

As she ran she heard something through the corridor. It was a screech like she'd never heard before; seeming to carry with it all the fear she'd ever known in that one horrible noise. It echoed through the tunnels so loud Rag had no idea which way it had come from.

'What the fuck was that?' Tidge said in his little voice. Rag would have felt sorry for him if she hadn't been so shit scared herself.

'No idea,' she replied. 'And we're not gonna be down here long enough to find out.'

As she dragged him further through the tunnel she could only hope she wasn't lying about that.

# FORTY-TWO

Endellion watched beside Amon Tugha. He stood in silence, observing the assault from a distance, watching his Khurtas die by the thousand. The main gate to the city was smashed and artillery had blown a massive breach in the wall further to the east, but the warriors of Steelhaven defended it valiantly. She was almost moved by their sacrifice – surrender would have been the more rational response. If Endellion had learned one thing, these southrons were far from rational.

To the west of the city something caught her eye. A single flaming arrow was fired out across the river, soaring far over the derelict city that sat beside the new one like a corpse. It seemed strange; there were no Khurtas attacking from that side of the city, nothing that would require a flaming arrow to see.

Endellion might have dismissed it as a stray shot if Amon Tugha hadn't smiled beside her. His grin was wide, his expression almost gleeful.

'It is time,' he said, turning and heading back towards the camp.

Waiting for him was an honour guard of Khurtas. His best – warriors gathered from each of the eight tribes. The last surviving war chief, Stirgor Cairnmaker, also stood waiting. His demeanour was as arrogant as ever, hands resting on the sword and axe at his hips. His men, lean hunters all, warriors rather than savage fanatics, stood with him awaiting their orders.

'When the wall is finally breached,' said Amon to his one remaining general, 'you will head the final attack. You may take whatever spoils you wish.'

Stirgor smiled. 'There is only one prize I want. Wolkan and Brulmak were foolish to face him so brazenly. He'll not find me so rash.'

Endellion knew who he was referring to. The Cairnmaker earned much wealth and praise for his fighters in the Khurtic blood pits. Within the walls of Steelhaven was a warrior who would earn him renown throughout the steppes, if he survived long enough.

Amon turned to Endellion. 'You will join Stirgor in the final attack. It should be enough to slake your thirst for slaughter, my sister.'

Endellion nodded her reply, keeping her tongue firmly in check. She could only bristle at his words – at his expectation that now, after everything, after she had lost Azreal, that she would fling herself into the fray and give her life for the glory of Amon Tugha.

The warlord whistled and his hounds, Sul and Astur, were at his heel in an instant, their noses twitching at the prospect of being unleashed. Even they sensed the end.

Amon took up his spear and moved south towards the city, his warriors at his heels.

Endellion could only watch him go, half hoping that he was killed, or at the least that she never saw him again. The other half of her was envious of the slaughter, of the glory he would attain when he killed the southron queen and crushed her crown beneath his heel. A crown he had come south to claim. A crown that had cost the lives of countless minions and of the one man she would have gifted her soul to had he but asked.

She glanced over to where they had buried Azreal. He would be left here to rot under the cold ground, and for what? For the exaltation of Amon Tugha. His life wasted along with so many others.

Perhaps she should race into the city alongside Stirgor. Perhaps she should hunt down the black-armoured daemon who had slain Azreal and avenge herself.

*And what would be the point in that? You will most likely be killed and even if not, even if you are victorious, Azreal will still be dead.*

She had been a fool to come here. A fool to follow the prince. It had all seemed so simple, so valiant, so idealistic. But Amon Tugha had turned out to be far from the hero she had thought. He was selfish, arrogant, quite possibly mad. He had risked them all for this folly and now, on the corpses of his followers, he was about to claim his final victory.

*And you would allow that? You would stand and watch as he destroys this southron queen and her city for his own glory? Or perhaps you simply don't care?*

Endellion turned back towards the camp as Stirgor and his men checked their weapons, readying themselves for the final assault. None of them even acknowledged her as she moved northwards, passing the wounded and slain, picking her way past the embers of forgotten fires, past empty tents, their owners dead and rotting. As she reached the centre of the camp she saw him still waiting. But then where else would he be, tied as he was to that wooden frame?

His hair covered much of his beaten face but Endellion could still see him watching, staring as his city burned. Perhaps as his one love died.

But more likely the queen yet lived. Endellion could only envy him that, and in another time, another place, that envy would have seen him skewered on the end of her blade. But not tonight. Not in this place.

She stood beside him as he stared, watching his eyes, unblinking as they were, light dancing from them in the firelight. She could sense his hate, masking his despair. He would have done anything to be released. Anything to be allowed a chance at freedom, a chance to save his queen.

'I know your pain,' she said. 'I have felt it too. The loss. The help-lessness.' He gave no answer, merely continued to glare at the city beyond. 'To know that there is nothing you can do to save her.'

He glanced at her then, a fleeting look of sorrow before he turned back to the city with hate. 'You know nothing,' he said from his split lips.

'Oh but I do.' Endellion leaned in close, her words little more than a whisper. 'I know how torn you are. How conflicted with love

266

and hate. You would give everything to save her. And failing that, you would give everything to kill *him*.'

He looked at her then, his eyes burning through the darkness. 'Have you just come here to mock me?'

She smiled back at him. 'Perhaps I have. Or perhaps I have come here to end your misery.'

'Then get on with it,' he said.

Endellion smiled at that. It was much more entertaining when they resisted. That little spark of defiance in the face of despair.

She ran her finger down one side of his face, collecting a clump of congealed blood.

'What reason would I have to kill you? When I would much rather use you.'

River looked back to the city. 'I will not be used as your toy, Elharim.'

'No? Not even if it meant saving her?'

He looked at her suspiciously. 'You would never—'

'The temple,' Endellion said, pointing towards Steelhaven. 'That will be your city's last defensible position. That is where he will find her, and that is where he will take her head.' She stared deep into his eyes. 'Unless you can stop him.'

His look of suspicion drained to be replaced by disbelief. 'Why? Why would you . . .'

Endellion stepped back and drew her blade in one swift motion. Four deft cuts and he was freed from his bonds. He dropped to the ground and she wondered if he would even be able to stand, let alone fight. As he rose to his feet, eyes glaring with hate, she had her answer.

The sword in her hand was lowered at her side. Endellion hoped he would have the sense not to attack. What a waste that would have been.

'You can avenge yourself on me . . . or you can save her.'

No sooner had the words come from her lips than he ran. Endellion was impressed by his vigour – an energy born of urgency . . . of love.

She watched him disappear in the shadows to the south, wondering if he would reach his queen in time. Wondering if

Amon Tugha would kill her first. She didn't wonder for long before realising she didn't really care.

Without a second glance back, Endellion turned to the north and started to walk.

# FORTY-THREE

The Khurtas were flinging themselves against the wooden barricade but the defences had held so far. Regulus roared his defiance as another wave came charging through the open gateway. Janto stood silent by his side, armour drenched in blood, axes dripping gore despite the rain washing them all from head to toe. Steam plumed with every breath in the cold night, but Regulus could not feel the chill. His labours kept him hot, as though he were standing on the plain, the sun high above him, warming him to the quick.

As the Khurtas charged towards them the sound was deafening. Every wave came as though it were the first, as though thousands before them hadn't already come rushing to be slain. With every attack, though, the defenders dwindled – Janto and Regulus were resolute but around them the Coldlander numbers had grown fewer and fewer. To Regulus' right stood a red warrior, the plates of his armour intertwined with a pattern of thorns. Regulus did not know his name, had not even spoken a word to him, but already he admired the man's fury in battle. The rest he did not remember, so enrapt was he in his work. And it was bloody work indeed. Work he was born for.

His black blade struck down as a Khurta raced up the bodies of his kinsmen piled against the barricade. The head split, the body fell but there were more behind. There were always more. Janto took a head, then another, silent in his black armour. Regulus had long since lost his helm, but part of him was glad of it. Let the Khurtas come, let them see his face, let them watch his fury as he slaughtered them by the dozen.

This time the Khurtic attack seemed to end as quickly as it had begun. Regulus watched, staying on his guard, as the survivors of the assault retreated.

Someone laughed further along the barricade as the defenders started to relax, thinking they had won yet another victory. Janto and the red-clad knight to either side of Regulus still stood vigilant. It was obvious the Khurtas were far from beaten.

There was fire from beyond the gate. Regulus could see it through the rain, bright burning brands raised high. A bellow rang out in the night, deep and resonant from the belly of a beast. The sound of stampeding hooves built to a rumble before the barricade beneath began to shake.

'Steel yourselves!' yelled the red knight.

Janto roared. His cry was met with another bellow as a herd of massive creatures rushed through the open gateway. They resembled huge beasts from the plains of Equ'un, but these were no docile grazing animals – they had tusks, curved and sharpened to points, their hide furred, their hooves clawed and churning up the soft ground beneath their feet.

There was a cry of woe as someone fled in the face of such terror, but Regulus stepped forward, eyes fixed on the charging herd.

The beasts trampled the bodies of the Khurtas strewn about the entranceway, their eyes wide in anger and terror as they were driven on by the fires behind them. The first one smashed into the barricade, throwing wood and stone and men all about.

Archers ran to the fore, firing randomly at the beasts, but the arrows barely seemed to slow them. Regulus stood firm as one of the monsters charged his way. It snorted its anger, vapour shooting from its wide nostrils as Regulus and Janto crouched low, bracing themselves against the impact. The beast hit the barricade, rocking it back but not splitting it apart. With a growl of rage the creature backed away, shaking its head before rushing in again.

Janto roared, leaping from the top of the barricade and plunging an axe into its hide. Regulus was not to be outdone, bounding forward, his sword skewering the beast's neck.

As it fell, both Zatani rolled clear. Regulus barely had time to dodge the charge of another creature before it bowled into the barricade, smashing its way through. When he found his feet, Janto was standing beside him, breath still coming in deep pants from behind his helmet, rain tamping off his armour.

The sound of the Khurtas rushing towards the gate in the wake of their beasts was like the distant drum of a waterfall crashing down. Regulus ignored it; he was too intent on Janto's blue eyes regarding him from within that dark helm.

Regulus nodded. He knew the Sho'tana warrior had made his decision. There was no loyalty left between them. Despite the enemies that would pour through the undefended gate, Janto was to have his day.

'Now?' Regulus said.

'What better time?' Janto replied.

Regulus roared, leaping forward, his black blade slashing left to right. Janto was forced to back away, his axes barely coming up in time to block the onslaught.

The Khurtas burst through the gate. All around them the Coldlanders were shouting to *form up* and *defend the way*, but Regulus only saw Janto.

The Sho'tana parried a swing of Regulus' sword, locking the blade between his axes. They stared at one another as the Khurtas swarmed through the gate.

'We will die here,' said Regulus.

'One of us will,' Janto replied, shoving Regulus back and spinning to hack down a charging Khurta. Regulus' sword spun twice in quick succession, eviscerating two of the savages, and he barely had time to turn and parry Janto's axe as it struck in once more.

From the corner of his eye he could see the defenders were being overwhelmed by the sheer numbers in the Khurtic horde, but Regulus had more immediate dangers to consider.

'This must wait,' he said. 'You'll see us both dead.'

'Isn't that what you wanted?' Janto said. 'A glorious end? Like the one you gifted to each of the warriors who followed you from Equ'un?'

Regulus felt a shot of anger, growling as he pushed Janto back. They both stood and faced one another as the battle raged around them.

'They each made their choice. They each died as a warrior of the Gor'tana should.'

'And yet you still live,' Janto's voice sounded hollow and cold from within his helm, like a ghost's. 'But you will sacrifice no more to your cause.'

He made to race forward, but before he could even bring his axes to bear there was a howl from within the city, beyond what remained of the barricade. It was no human voice, no mortal could have made such a sound, and it almost turned the blood in Regulus' veins to ice.

Janto seemed to forget his attack, staring to the south from where the noise had come. Likewise the battle around them froze in time when that first howl was followed by a second.

As the warring factions stood transfixed, the barricade burst apart. At first Regulus thought the animals of the Khurtas were attacking again, but these were no beasts of burden.

Though these things bore the bodies of men they were twisted and misshapen, their limbs elongated and ending in talons to rival any Aeslanti. Their heads were likewise huge, their lower jaws distended to house their massive fangs. Black eyes were sunken deep into each head, staring out balefully, full of hate and a thirst for slaughter.

The creatures fell upon the Khurtas with a ravenous hunger, though many of the defenders were likewise caught in the onslaught. They howled as they slew, tearing heads and arms from shoulders, rending with claws, biting the faces off their victims. Regulus stared in awe at the level of carnage until a shadow fell over him. He looked up to see one of the creatures bearing down, slaver and blood dripping from a black maw.

But Regulus did not falter. If this was to be his end he would meet it as a son of the Gor'tana.

With a roar he leapt forward, black blade sweeping in. The

creature moved with preternatural speed, ducking his blade and batting him aside as though he were made of straw. Regulus landed hard, rolling with the impact and rising to his feet, just as the beast was on him. His sword came up ready, impaling the fiend's chest. It screamed at him as black blood spewed from the wound. Regulus could not resist, bellowing back from the bottom of his lungs as the creature took hold of his wrist, pulling itself towards him along the blade, ready to take a bite with those infernal jaws.

In a plume of dark cruor its head spun from its body. Janto stood behind the beast, his twin axes still dripping. Regulus stumbled back as the beast fell, his sword still buried in its chest, and Janto came on, glaring down from behind his helm. It seemed Regulus' saviour had only rescued him to satisfy his own need for blood.

Regulus stood tall, ready for the final blow that would end his life.

With a hellish scream, two more of the fiendish beasts bowled into Janto. He raised an axe, hacking into one of them as the second tore his breastplate asunder with its talons. The Sho'tana roared as he was dragged away into the melee, his axes rising and falling in a desperate flurry as the monsters ripped with their claws and bit into the black steel plate that encased him.

With Janto gone, Regulus stumbled away from the battle, looking around for his sword; though he knew that in the fray it was hopeless he would find it. The defenders of Steelhaven were in full rout now, and the hellish creatures that had attacked seemed to be concentrating their fury on the Khurtas.

As he moved away from the slaughter Regulus caught sight of red armour through the dark and rain. The knight who had stood so resolute beside him was prone, struggling to crawl away from the battle.

Without a word Regulus helped him up. If he were not to gain glory in battle this day, then he could at least help a fallen warrior. As the battle raged on, Regulus guided the knight to safety.

# FORTY-FOUR

Arun was always a greedy boy. His mother had often chastised him for being so. As a child he always wanted more on his plate, always wanted to play with everyone else's toys, always yearned for the things he couldn't have. Arun had never been the sweetest or prettiest of boys, and so to get these things he'd had to think of ways that didn't involve a pleasant smile or a kind word. He'd learned fast that sleight of hand and subterfuge were all well and good, until you were caught. And so it hadn't taken him very many beatings with the birch branch to learn how not to get caught.

Never let anyone know what you're thinking. That had always been his tenet. Keep your own counsel, don't appear a threat, smile in all the right places no matter how ugly the smile. These simple rules had seen him go a long way. Had seen him rise from the son of a cooper to take his place in the palace of Skyhelm. To become one of King Cael's most trusted aides. It had been a long road, but one he had committed to.

And if nothing else, Arun Durket was a committed man.

Commitment could only bring a man so far, though, and Chancellor Durket, as he had become, found himself presented with many fortunate opportunities. Indeed, fortune had smiled upon him with its bounteous offerings many times, but only a man of true vision would have the stomach to grasp those opportunities and make them blossom.

When he had been given the opportunity to seize yet more power by the agents of Amon Tugha he had grasped it like the neck of a viper and held on tight. He had stuck with it despite the considerable dangers to his wellbeing, because he realised if he was ever to rise from beneath the shadow of the Crown, of the rightful rulers of Steelhaven and the Free States, he could only do so through betrayal.

*Betrayal.* Such a nasty word. Durket had never been afraid of it, though, not as other men were. Braver men. No one survived a coup or an attempted murder by being courageous or loyal. And if Chancellor Durket knew one thing it was how to survive.

Not that survival had been easy or his plans and schemes run smooth. The passing weeks and months and years had seen his path strewn with cow shit from Arlor's very own divine herd.

Recently, Kaira Stormfall had been the main thorn in his side, protecting the queen at every turn. Then the arrival of Azai Dravos with his offer of marriage. Durket had done his best to appease the man but he had been ever so persuasive. On that occasion Kaira had solved his problem for him, but not before Dravos had used his magicks.

*Magicks that haunt you even now. Darkness that threatens to consume your every waking hour.*

The aftermath of witnessing Azai Dravos and his fell sorcery had indeed taken its toll. When Kaira had confronted Durket outside the treasury his act at insanity had been no mere mummer's play. Dravos had left an indelible mark – *the nightmares, the voices* – but Durket had faced adversity before and he was damned if he would give in to it now. Not when he was so close.

Kaira had accused him of theft, and that much was true, at least. But he was not fleeing the palace with money from the coffers; he was merely taking it to pay Rogan and his Inquisition agents who had been so instrumental in ensuring his schemes were seen through to fruition. Better that she thought him the common thief. Had she thought him guilty of treason then he would be dead already.

Durket made his way down through the palace. With any luck the archer he had sent to the western extent of the city would have sent the signal without incident. Hopefully he was more capable than Durket's other collaborators.

Leon Magrida had proven to be incompetent beyond words. But then he had been glamoured by Elharim magicks in order to guarantee his loyalty. That in itself had made him unpredictable. In the end he had succumbed to the madness of it all, but at least Durket's involvement had remained a secret.

Rogan had also proven difficult to the end. It had taken the promise of considerable riches to turn him. But at least Rogan had already served his purpose. He had been the one to persuade the Matron Mother to keep her Shieldmaidens in check within the Temple of Autumn. It had been a job he was uniquely suited to. Besides, when all this was over and Amon Tugha gone, Durket would need someone suitable to act as regent. Rogan would have to be that someone. There was no way Durket was about to peek out from behind his curtain and put himself in the frame. Staying in the background had served him well enough so far. Why change now?

Durket passed a window. In the distance he could just see over the western wall. Beyond it would be Khurtas hard at work in the Old City, burrowing underground. They should have reached the entrance by now. There were forgotten tunnels into the city of Steelhaven, secret ways that only Durket knew of. Those secret ways would see an end to all this.

He walked into the lower chapel, where years before the Old Gods had been worshipped before the veneration of Arlor and Vorena. This place was ancient, older even than the Temple of Autumn.

The thought of that brought a smile to his face. The Temple of Autumn was the key to all this. It was where he had planted his earliest seed. Where the corruption within its organisation had allowed Durket to weave his plans. It was where the queen would meet her end.

He felt no guilt at that – she had always despised him and he knew it. She was a child – weak, inexperienced. This had all been inevitable.

Durket moved to a sconce in the wall, removing one of the

torches and twisting the stanchion. There was a click of stone on stone, a grinding of gears as three slabs on the floor twisted out of place revealing a staircase winding downwards. Stale air billowed from the dark and Durket took a breath. This was it, his big gamble. He was bargaining his life on this, trusting to the word of his kingdom's enemy. But with the greatest risk came the greatest reward.

He held the torch before him to light the way as he gingerly walked down. The stairs wound to a passage at the bottom, wide enough so that five men could walk abreast. As Durket moved along it the torch lit up ancient murals on the walls; scenes of age-old heroes battling daemons, forgotten kings, fabled swords and suchlike. Durket had never put much store by legends but he knew daemons were real enough. There was one waiting for him at the end of this passage.

*And there are the ones in your mind, Arun. The ones left there by Dravos. Horas is watching you always . . .*

Durket shook his head, a bead of sweat running down his face as he did so. At the end of the corridor stood a massive door. Beside it a wheel, rusted and crusted with dirt and dust. He laid the torch down, staring at the wheel. This was a job for a much stronger man. Perhaps he should have brought someone with him . . . but then again perhaps not. There were already enough people who knew his aims and goals. Too many people with whom he had shared so much. This was his task and his alone.

He laid the torch on the dusty ground and grasped the wheel. As he suspected, it would not turn immediately as he applied more and more pressure. The sharp edges of the rusted metal dug into his palms and he gritted his teeth against the pain. The single bead of sweat on his brow was joined by a host of others as he strained, a high-pitched sound issuing from inside him as he exerted himself. Just as he thought he would have to give up, the wheel moved by an inch. Buoyed by his progress, Durket strained against the wheel once more, the noise from inside him turning from squeal to grunt to roar. As he screamed at the top of his lungs the wheel turned and the doors at the end of the corridor began to open.

Cold air rushed through the gap, filling the tunnel. Durket felt the moisture on his brow go cold as the wheel seemed to loosen. Vigorously he turned it, encouraged as the doors widened revealing the chill blackness beyond.

When his labours were over and the door stood wide, Durket picked up the torch and stood waiting. His breath came heavy as he stared into the dark. There was no sign of anyone beyond the doorway and he began to wonder if the Khurtas had seen his signal. Perhaps his archer had failed, or been killed before he could fire his burning arrow. Perhaps the diggers had not been vigorous enough in their work and needed more time. They had, after all, been given the task of unearthing a passageway from the Old City not revealed for centuries.

Just as he began to think his efforts had been for nothing, eyes suddenly peered at him from the shadows. Two pools of red coming closer as he watched. Then a second pair.

Durket began to shake. He had expected to be afraid, but he had not anticipated this.

The eyes came closer, moving like disembodied specks of fire until they reached the threshold of the doorway. They stopped, regarding him from the dark for untold moments. Then there was a growl, a noise that filled him with dread. It was followed by a clawed foot stepping out into the torchlight. A head; a hound's head, huge and feral, appeared from the dark, glaring at him all the while. Its twin followed, the two huge dogs moving towards him with measured care.

He could feel his legs shaking, his lip quivering, but he did not move. Arun Durket was not a brave man but still he stood as those beasts advanced on him. Was he paralysed with fear? Or was this the fabled magicks of the Elharim he had heard so much about? Whatever the reason, he did not move as one of the hounds stalked right up to him, nose twitching, throat emitting its low growl all the while.

It sniffed at his leg, snout pulling back to reveal huge teeth that could have torn the head from his shoulders with ease.

'Sul!'

The voice echoed from beyond the doorway and Durket flinched, making a pitiful sound as he did so. To his relief the hound backed off, keeping its eyes on him all the while, but Durket was no longer concerned with animals. There was a creature much more terrible to be feared.

Amon Tugha walked from the dark, his eyes shining gold, brighter than the red of his war hounds. He regarded Durket as a butcher might look at a slab of meat. The huge spear he carried across one shoulder looked keen enough to slice Durket in two. All of a sudden having his throat ripped out didn't seem such a fearsome prospect.

More figures moved from the dark. Khurtas, painted and scarred, their bodies lean, their weapons drawn. They filed past Durket on either side, ignoring the Chancellor as though he weren't there. All he could do was stare up into those golden eyes, too fearful to move or make a sound.

Amon Tugha said no words, merely waited for his warriors to stalk up the passage towards the chapel before he himself moved on, his hounds following in his wake.

Arun Durket was left alone in the cold tunnel, the torch sputtering pitifully in the dark. It took him some time to realise that warm piss was running down his leg.

# FORTY-FIVE

They hunkered behind the barricade as the rain fell. Merrick kept his head down, sheltering within his helmet, watching through the breach in the wall for any sign of the enemy. So far they had been lucky – the main Khurtic attack had centred on the Stone Gate to the east and the River Gate to the west. Very few Khurtas had appeared from the dark. For the most part Steelhaven's archers had managed to deter any attack on the breach with volley fire, and the piles of rubble that were spread across the foot of the curtain wall were covered in dead savages.

Merrick had to admit, he was growing impatient with the waiting. As though the prospect of being attacked was worse than someone actually trying to cut his head off. It was clear his father shared his anxiety.

Tannick stalked up and down the defensive line, grumbling to himself as he did so. No one dared question him as he tried his best to quell a rage that yearned to be unleashed on the enemy. For their part, the Wyvern Guard stood resolute, awaiting their chance, eager for the kill. Their attitude wasn't shared. As much as the rest of the defenders had acted bravely over the past days, they looked tired now. It was as though every man could sense the end was near, and it was most likely not going to be a good end. The only man who didn't seem affected by the atmosphere of gloom was the one they called the Black Helm. He had come to join them some time in the night, his body soaked from the rain, his clothes stained with blood. He seemed more animal than man, and Merrick was only thankful he was on the same side.

There was noise to the east. Another attack. Merrick couldn't see through the rain and the dark but he was sure he could hear the braying of animals. Every man looked across, wondering if this would be the time the Khurtas broke through. Even Tannick stopped his pacing, glaring over towards the Stone Gate, clearly desperate to be a part of the fight.

Then there came noise from the west, towards the River Gate. The Khurtas were attacking again, sending the last of their siege engines and ladders at the wall. Somewhere over there was the queen, come to the fore to marshal her bannermen. He could only hope she was up to the task.

Merrick looked back through the breach, into that black yawning gap, and knew the Khurtas were waiting for them. The tension across the line only grew as the noise of battle carried across the wall. It didn't sound like things were going well for the city's defenders as the roaring grew louder. Men all around were praying, knowing that whether they would live or not was in the hands of the gods, but Tannick Ryder was not a man to let the gods decide his fate.

The Lord Marshal stepped forward across the barricade, staring through the breach. Then he turned.

'Wyvern Guard,' Tannick shouted. 'The enemy waits, picking their moment to attack. I will not allow them such a luxury.' He drew his sword, the *Bludsdottr*, and held the massive blade easily in one hand. 'We choose our own fate. We choose how we die – not cowering behind a barricade waiting to be overrun, but on the field, with steel in our hands and a curse on our lips.' Some of the Wyvern Guard moved forward now, and Merrick couldn't stop himself, caught up in the bloodlust that suddenly seemed to grip them. 'Remember what I've taught you. Every last man here is a heartless bastard fed on blood and steel. My sons and brothers both.' Some of the Wyvern Guard cheered, drawing their blades. Tannick was staring straight at Merrick now, a mad smile on the corner of his lips.

With that the old man turned and began to run. Without a word or an order the Wyvern Guard followed, Merrick running as fast as any of them straight at the breach. They charged over the rubble, leaping through to the other side of the broken wall. Merrick's breath came in a flurry of mist as the rain continued to beat down. His feet churned up the soft earth and for a moment, with the light of the city behind, he was plunged into blackness. Then he saw them – the entire Khurtic army standing in the rain, waiting silently for their order to attack.

When he had charged them on horseback it had been suicidal. He had chased Cormach Whoreson into the enemy's maw, but at least there had still been a chance he would survive, one glimmer of hope that he'd make it back alive.

Now he knew that chance was gone. And for the first time he didn't care.

Every man died, he knew that now. All his life he'd been avoiding it, staying one step ahead of the Lord of Crows. Now he knew he was going to die, a horde of Khurtas would see to that, but all he wanted was to give them a taste of steel before he went.

Merrick felt his heart beating faster, a grin coming to his mouth as he ran alongside the rest of the Wyvern Guard. He flushed with pride at being beside these men – men who had become his brothers. At being beside his father, a man he had hated all his life but who he now followed to his death.

This was what it had all been for. This was where his life had led and he was glad of it.

Tannick hit the Khurtic line, his massive blade hacking the first of the enemy almost in two. Then, in a bronze wedge, what remained of the Wyvern Guard fell on the Khurtas. Shields rang discordantly as they caught the enemy blades, smashing into the line of invaders with unkempt fury.

Shouts went up from amidst the Khurtic ranks, their battle cries rising above the sound of clashing weapons. Merrick barely heard as he looked for his first foe. His blade came down, slicing through the rain, slicing through the top of a wooden shield, slicing into a Khurta's neck. He screamed, unleashing his rage, every lesson he had learned in the Collegium of House Tarnath now gone, to be replaced with a savagery all his own. He heeded his father's words well. He had not grown up in the harsh mountains but tonight he was every inch a heartless bastard like his brother knights.

After their initial rush the Wyvern Guard formed up a shield wall, locking together with unspoken discipline. The Khurtas battered at the circle of steel, moving to surround them, and in no time they were being assailed from all sides. Merrick desperately parried the flailing attacks, his blade swift to counter as he stood shoulder to shoulder with Cormach and his father. For his part, the Whoreson moved swifter and stronger than anything Merrick had ever seen, in his element, a true beast of war. Tannick swung the *Bludsdottr* with a fury, laying low any Khurtas that dared to attack.

The Wyvern Guard were in a tight circle now, surrounded by deafening screams and wicked blades. It was hopeless, they would never survive this, but Merrick Ryder felt a joy he had never known. At the point of his death, for the first time, he was truly alive.

Something hissed past Merrick's head, and with a grunt his father fell to one knee. A Khurta ran from the horde and, before Merrick could intercept, his sword struck forward. Half the blade sank between Tannick's spaulder and breastplate. No sooner was the blow struck than the old man roared, his mighty sword coming up to impale his attacker.

'The Lord Marshal,' someone shouted, as Tannick foundered, all vigour gone from his body.

Merrick grabbed one of his father's arms, Cormach the other, and they dragged him away from the Khurtic onslaught. The shield wall was hastily re-formed around them, the fight raging on as Merrick cradled the old man in his arms.

He removed his father's helm, confused to see Tannick smiling through a blood-rimmed mouth. They looked at each other, the sound of the battle seeming to fade in Merrick's head. He opened his mouth to speak but had no idea what to say.

'Do you see now, boy?' said Tannick. Merrick had no idea if he did see or not. 'It's your turn now.' Tannick thrust the *Bludsdottr* towards him. 'Take it. It's yours.'

Merrick looked down at the blade and shook his head. 'I can't.'

'You can. It's yours. It was always meant to be yours. These men were always meant to be yours.'

Merrick looked up at Cormach. The Whoreson simply stared back, offering no words of advice, though Merrick knew he'd never get any from this bastard.

The blade looked big and heavy but it wasn't its unwieldiness that filled Merrick with doubt. It symbolised the heart of the Wyvern Guard, only to be wielded by the Lord Marshal. Merrick was no leader of men; he had no right to it. The Wyvern Guard would never follow him. Not these warriors, tempered in battle and hate. Who was he but a drunken fop? How could he ever hope to lead knights?

'I can't,' Merrick said again. 'I'm not the man you want me to be. I never will be.'

'For fuck's sake!' Cormach said, wresting the sword from Tannick's weak grip. 'I'll fucking do it.'

Merrick looked up just as the shield wall broke. Three Khurtas burst through the defence, leaping over the corpses of fallen Wyvern Guard.

Cormach lifted the sword but stumbled as he did so. All his prowess seemed to leave him as he tried to swing the huge blade and he missed the first Khurta. The second hacked in as Cormach almost fell, the sword seeming to weigh him down as though he was lifting a tree trunk. An axe glanced off his arm and he dodged back, dropping the *Bludsdottr* to the ground. Jared rushed forward, doing his best to divert the assault, but he was outmatched by the three assailants and it was all he could do to stay on his feet.

Merrick stared down at the sword. His father was unable to speak now, his eyes staring, imploring. The *Bludsdottr* lay there, huge and cumbersome.

He could hear screaming. The last stand of the Wyvern Guard failing fast now its Lord Marshal was mortally wounded. Merrick stood amidst the confusion. Stepping towards the sword as the battle raged. Men fought and died, the rain pounding down all around them as he stopped and knelt, his hand closing around the handle . . .

*The grip is bigger than any sword you have held but fits in your palm like it was made for you . . . because it was made for you. When the Bludsdottr was forged by Arlor himself it was gifted to a line of heroes – a line of kings – and now, after the centuries have passed and it has served men in battle for all that time, it is finally yours to wield.*

Merrick lifted the blade as though it weighed nothing. Battle went on all around him but he was calm within the seething tempest.

*Your blood, and the blood of your ancestors has been spilled in defence of this realm for more than a thousand years and this sword has served them all. It is yours and yours alone. It is part of you; your heart and your soul.*

A body came screaming through the rain, an axe raised high. Merrick barely noticed it, but the *Bludsdottr* spun in his one hand, twisting through the rain as drops bounced off the blade. It cut the Khurta in half, his blood spattering Merrick's bronze-armoured body.

*It will serve you unto death, and afterwards it will serve the blood of your blood until the end of time.*

No sooner had the first Khurta fallen than a second came, then a third. Merrick grasped the sword with two hands, feeling his blood course, pumping in his chest, thrumming in his ears. The blade spun again, arcing through the air, severing a head, then a leg.

The Wyvern Guard rallied, falling back to stand beside Merrick who stared out from a bloody face. The Khurtas stood aghast, wary now as Merrick looked back at them with clarity. His fugue was over, the sword in his hand having cast its spell. He knew its worth . . . he knew *his* worth.

But no number of magick swords would save what remained of the Wyvern Guard from the thousands arrayed against them.

Merrick smiled as they stood before the enemy. He wanted to speak, to spout some litany worthy of a hero, but for once he had no words. There was no way even he would fuck up this moment by opening his mouth. This time was sacred, he knew that now. To die with these men was an honour even he could not spurn.

Before Merrick could lead their final charge a howl cut the air. A cry of death that froze every man to the spot.

From the city came a swarm of daemons, spewing through the breach, out of the city like all the hells had just been opened.

As it came for them, Merrick Ryder raised his father's blade and laughed.

# FORTY-SIX

From her vantage point on the bastion of the River Gate, Janessa watched again as the Khurtas attacked. She'd lost count of the number of men she'd seen slaughtered, the number of Khurtas cut down by volley fire. And still she watched.

Through the rain she watched as brave men died. She watched as the Khurtas attacked again and again. She watched as they flung themselves at the Steelhaven phalanx. Janessa Mastragall watched until she could watch no longer.

Now was the time to act. Now was the time to fight. All else had to be forgotten – all her pain and grief. All her past doubts. Even River, who she had last seen held prisoner by her most hated enemy. It all had to be forgotten as she led Steelhaven against its unstoppable foe.

A siege tower moved inexorably into view, peppered with arrows, looking like it had been hacked from a mountain of steel. There were barely half a dozen men to stand against it, but still they stood, ready to die to defend the city. Her city.

Janessa's heels kicked her horse's flanks as she loosed the reins. The Helsbayn rang from its scabbard as she galloped along the wall. Kaira cried something in her wake but Janessa paid it no mind. Men moved from her path in panic and arrows hissed past her bare head as she made her way towards the siege tower. The ramp fell with a metallic clank just as she reached it and the Khurtas within were unleashed, howling at the night.

The Helsbayn sang its reply.

Janessa felt the excitement of her first kill as the blade took a head from its shoulders. The thrill of that one small victory. A hunger began to burn as she swung again, taking another Khurtic life. Her steed bucked and snorted, its bulk knocking three of the enemy from the ramp. Janessa was screaming now, adding her own battle cry to the dirge. Blood splashed her armour and chin, matting the curls of her hair. She had no idea if any of it was hers but it mattered little to her now.

She turned to see Kaira watching from the saddle of her own horse, the sword in her hand slick with blood. Her eyes were wide with disbelief, but there was also pride. She said nothing, she didn't need to. Janessa merely gave her a nod, which Kaira returned, and that one gesture meant everything; more than any words could ever convey.

*You are a warrior queen now.*

Janessa turned her attention back to the battle. All along the wall she could see the Khurtas swarming to attack. Even she knew that every man who stood against them would be slain if she did nothing.

She spurred her horse, riding it along the walkway, shouting at the top of her voice for her men to rally, to hearken to her call. Janessa held the Helsbayn aloft as she rode and saw every eye turn to her. As she rode past one of the wall's bastions she plucked a flag bearing the Steelhaven coat of arms and raised it up. The flag was drenched from the rain and heavy in her grip but she held it out for all to see the crossed sword and crown emblazoned upon it.

'Rally to the square,' she cried. 'Follow me.'

Janessa rode back down the stairway, her fleet horse managing to stay sure of foot on the slick surface. The open space had few defensible positions but at least her soldiers could form ranks. The Khurtas would be channelled, their numbers less overwhelming in the confines of the square.

As soon as she reached the bottom of the stairs Kaira and Captain Garret were by her side. Kaira's destrier snorted, sensing battle was coming.

'This is madness,' said Garret. 'We have to get you away from here. You have to retreat to '

287

'I won't leave them,' Janessa said, as men flocked all around, milling in the square awaiting their orders.

Kaira began forming the defenders into ranks, ordering an upturned cart be made into a meagre barricade and that archers take positions to the rear.

'Your safety is paramount,' said Garret more forcefully. 'I cannot protect you if this is what you insist on.'

'Then don't protect me,' Janessa replied. 'Protect my city.'

It was not an order, which she knew he would obey without question, but a plea.

Garret stared at her, the rain soaking through his hair and beard. The days of fighting had left him looking smaller somehow, his face matted with dried blood from half a dozen wounds.

'Always, Majesty,' he replied.

Janessa glanced back towards the battlements. Already the Khurtas had breached the wall, flooding over it, the noise of their arrival rising above the pounding of the rain on the square.

She urged her horse forward, still holding the flag in her hand, raising it aloft.

'Men of Steelhaven!' she cried. 'I don't ask that you fight for your city and never that you fight for me. Only that you fight *with* me this one last time.'

There was a cry from every man. A cry that filled Janessa with pride. For a fleeting moment she only wished that her father had been here to see this, to see her one last stand. But he was not here. There was only her. Queen Janessa Mastragall. Sovereign of Steelhaven and the Free States. Protector of Teutonia.

The Khurtas had reached the bottom of the wall now and were charging towards the square. Janessa spurred her horse, drawing the Helsbayn from its scabbard once more and riding forward. There was a cry on her lips, something feral, something from the dark empty pit inside her. Kaira spurred up beside her, as did Garret and half a dozen Sentinels – all that remained of her retinue. They smashed into the Khurtas like an axe hitting rotting wood, splintering the enemy charge. The Helsbayn hummed through the air, delivering Janessa's fury.

As they fought there was a thunderous smash. Janessa pulled

back on her reins, her horse rearing as in the distance she saw the Tower of Magisters had been struck by a massive boulder. The ancient stone at its base suddenly gave way, the tower lurching back violently. It toppled, crushing rooftops and houses beneath its vastness, but Janessa had no time to lament the loss as the battle still raged around her.

Arrows whistled overhead in both directions whilst the rain beat down relentlessly. Janessa's red curls were plastered to her head, the rain running in rivulets within her armour, but it did not weigh her down or hinder her as she swung that sacred blade.

Something struck the haft of the flag she held, jarring it from her grip, and it fell amidst the press of Khurtas. She parried a swing of a sword, raising the Helsbayn to counter when her horse stumbled beneath her. With a squeal of anguish the stallion collapsed to the ground, Janessa crying out in anger and frustration as she fell. The impact jolted the sword from her grip, her head hitting the cobbled ground. Her vision swam as Janessa made to stand but her leg was pinned beneath the dead animal. Panic gripped her as she realised she was helpless.

The melee continued to rage all around as the Sentinels did their best to protect her, but she was held fast. The Helsbayn was just beyond her grip, tantalisingly close as she reached with outstretched fingers.

Janessa looked up in time to see the sneering face of a Khurta bearing down on her but his expression twisted from anger to agony as a sword blade pierced his chest. Garret withdrew the blade with practised ease, reaching for her as the Khurta fell. She gripped his arm, crying out as he dragged her from beneath the horse, her leg numb from being crushed beneath its weight. She still had the presence of mind to grasp the Helsbayn as Garret helped her to her feet, despite the pain. In an instant Kaira was also at their side, her own horse forgotten.

'Get her out of here,' snarled Garret. 'To the temple.'

Kaira nodded, dragging Janessa away from the battle as her Sentinels and bannermen blocked the Khurtic assault. She was about to protest but the pain in her leg stifled any objections. As they retreated Garret turned back to face the Khurtas, his sword held high as he proclaimed his loyalty to the Crown for all to hear. She could only stare at Garret – brave, loyal Garret – as he was consumed within the mass of savages, his blade still swinging.

Janessa held onto Kaira as they backed away from the fighting. 'Retreat!' Kaira barked to the rest of the men, cowering behind their barricade. 'Into the city, hide yourselves!'

Some of them ran immediately, needing no further encouragement, but some raced forward, helping Kaira lift Janessa to her feet.

Her leg throbbed, a stabbing pain shooting through her knee with every step, but still Janessa moved. She had wanted to fight the Khurtas to the end, but now that seemed like madness. This whole thing was madness. In the distance something brayed to the night, like an angry herd of bulls had been unleashed upon the city, only adding to the insanity.

The Khurtas were rushing forward now, their fury unrestrained, cutting down anything in their path. Kaira did her best to help Janessa move south, away from the carnage, but with her leg the way it was she knew they'd never get far.

Two Khurtas burst from the pack, charging forward with blades raised. Janessa pushed herself away from Kaira, stumbling slightly but still finding her feet. She raised the Helsbayn as Kaira had taught her, holding it poised to strike. It felt good in her hand, it felt ready to kill.

A shadow dropped from the building next to them, pouncing on the two Khurtas like a leopard on its prey. Janessa watched in horror as the beast caught one of the savage's heads in its mouth, gripping the other by the throat. With a snap of its jaws the head came free. A squeeze of talons and the throat was ripped out. For a moment it took the time to feast, tearing flesh from its victims with abandon, and all Janessa could do was watch in horror. Then the beast's black eyes looked about as it sniffed the air.

Janessa felt Kaira's grip on her arm, pulling her back, and slowly they moved away until the monster was out of sight.

'What was that?' Janessa asked, her heart thumping in her chest, the hand that did not hold the Helsbayn shaking uncontrollably.

'I have no idea,' said Kaira. 'But we can only hope it hates the Khurtas more than it hates us. Now come, I must get you to safety.'

'Where are we going?

'The Temple of Autumn. It is our last line of defence,' said Kaira as they stumbled south through the deserted streets.

Janessa saved her breath, moving as quickly as she could and biting her lip against the pain in her leg.

The sky was lightening. She could only hope that when the new day dawned there would still be a city to defend.

# FORTY-SEVEN

He had no idea why the Elharim woman had set him free, but River was not about to waste time thinking on it. All that mattered was finding Jay, but first he had to survive long enough.

The Khurtas stood before him on the plain in their thousands but their focus was on the city. River was stripped to the waist, his face a mass of bruises and blood; it would not be difficult to go unseen amongst this savage horde.

There was a huge breach in the wall and Khurtas stood before it, awaiting the order to attack. It would be impossible to enter there. To the west the Khurtas were assaulting the wall in a vast mass of bodies but to the east River could see the giant gate had been smashed in, the ram that had done its work now discarded. Through the rain, in the light of a thousand sputtering torches, River saw the Khurtas were urging on their war beasts, whipping them into a frenzy.

He ran towards them, passing waiting warriors, patient to take their turn in the slaughter. River didn't care now if they recognised him, this was no time for caution.

As he drew closer he could see the beasts were chained, their handlers burning their flanks, whipping their hides. The creatures cried out in fear and pain, thrashing against their bonds. Then, as one, the chains were struck, a chorus of clashing steel ringing out above the sound of thumping rain. The beasts began their stampede, rushing forward towards the open gateway, corralled by fire-wielding Khurtas.

River sprinted after them as the Khurtas charged in the wake of the rampaging beasts. All around him the flood of bodies ran for the gate but not one of them tried to stop him, not one was concerned with yet another madman sprinting after a herd of feral monsters.

He passed beneath the gateway, coming out into the city and seeing a smashed barricade ahead. Warriors were fighting valiantly, despite what the stampede had done to their defences. For a moment River felt a pang of sorrow that he could not join them, could not take up arms in defence of Steelhaven. It had, after all, been his home. He had lived amongst these people all his life, but it was clear now the city was lost. There was little one man could do to save it. There was only one life he was determined to save. And if he was unable to save her, then there was yet one life he was determined to end.

River sprinted across to a gap in the barricade as Khurtas flocked all around him. The ground was scattered with detritus and River scanned the battleground for any sign of a weapon. A dagger lay discarded nearby and he stooped to pick it up, barely breaking his stride. No sooner did he have the weapon in his grasp than he stopped in his tracks.

There was something in the dark shadow of a nearby building. What gave it away he couldn't tell but even from this distance he could sense it was fetid, evil.

A screech rose above the city and it struck River deep, almost chilling the blood in his veins. From the shadows stalked a beast neither human nor animal. It glared at him with dead corpse's eyes and for the first time in an age River knew fear.

Instinct made him move, his legs pumping fast along the ground. He knew the creature would give chase if he ran but there was no way he was about to stand and wait for death to take him.

The nearest street was empty, darkness consuming it as he ran, as though he were sprinting into the hells themselves. A stairway to his left led upwards and he dashed towards it, taking the stairs four at a time. If he could make the rooftops, his familiar domain, perhaps he would stand more of a chance against this creature.

Reaching the top of the stairs he vaulted onto the rooftop. The rain made the tiles slick, and his usual sure-footedness seemed to flee him as he slipped across the roof. A quick glance back revealed the creature was indeed in pursuit, its brow furrowed in rage, teeth dripping with ichor. Its limbs were impossibly long and it made for him on all fours.

River turned back to the south, making the roof edge and leaping through the dark. He landed badly, slipping across the roof of the next building, but he was back on his feet immediately. He sprinted on blindly, hearing the thump and crack of the beast landing on the roof behind him.

As he ran, a tile betrayed him underfoot, cracking beneath his weight, and River went stumbling, sliding to the edge of the roof but managing to stop himself before he tumbled into the darkness below. He glared down into the black, knowing there was no escape that way. Glancing back he saw the creature was stalking him more carefully now, its talons scraping on the tiled roof. River dragged himself to his feet, brandishing the dagger which looked as though it would be useless against this beast.

*Your time is over. There is nothing you can do against such a fell creature. You have failed her.*

As the beast made to pounce the tiles beneath its feet gave way. Its flank disappeared as the roof collapsed, talons scraping for purchase but finding none on the greasy surface. It fell into the building, and River took a deep breath in relief. Giving himself three strides' grace he ran to the roof edge and leapt again, landing on the next roof and making his way towards the palace.

His route was a familiar one; he had taken it many times, but never with a heart so heavy. The Khurtas had breached the wall and now there were beasts from the hells abroad, unleashed by the gods knew what. Jay was in more danger than ever if he could not protect her.

By the time he reached the palace screams of woe and violence were echoing across the city like the knell of death. It seemed Steelhaven was damned and he along with it.

The gates to Skyhelm lay open, and the place looked deserted. River ran inside, across the gardens with abandon where previously he had taken such pains to remain hidden. The main doors were ajar, and he pushed them open before rushing inside. Lanterns flickered within and he paused, listening for any sound, but he heard none.

He ran up the main stairway, past a dozen empty rooms, through chambers and hallways until he eventually reached a massive room where he stopped. There was a stone throne at one end, and sitting upon it was a man, robed and hooded, his head cradled in one hand.

River made his way across the hall, not even trying to hide his presence. If the man heard him he gave no reaction.

'Where is she?' River asked as he reached the bottom of the stairs that led up to the throne.

The man looked up, tears in his eyes but a smile on his face.

'Where's who?' he answered, as though he didn't care.

'Your queen,' said River. 'Queen Janessa.'

The man shook his head, his tears still flowing, his smile growing wider. 'What the fuck does it matter where she is? Dead, in all likelihood, just like the rest of us.'

River drew his dagger, pressing it to the man's throat. He seemed little concerned that he might be about to die.

'Where?' River said, pressing the blade against flesh and drawing blood.

The man giggled. 'I was a powerful man in this city once. I was respected. And I did my duty to the Crown . . . to my king. What am I now?'

'You're dead if you don't tell me where she is.' River twisted the knife, pressing the point into the man's chin and drawing another bead of crimson.

'All right,' he struggled to say. 'She's at the temple. The Temple of Autumn. That's where I was told to send her. That's where I ensured would be the last safe place in this city.' River released the man, turning to leave. 'But you won't save her. It's a trap.' He dabbed at the blood at his neck with the sleeve of his robe, staring down forlornly.

'What do you mean?' asked River.

'It was all a ruse. Durket had planned it all along. She thinks it's safe but it's not. Now he knows where to find her. And they won't protect her.'

River wanted to ask who this Durket was and who it was that wouldn't protect her, but a cry from outside the palace reminded him that time was not on his side.

He ran from the throne room. Ran from the palace and the Crown District. Ran south and east across the city. Ran towards those two statues of ancient gods that still stood staring so proudly, he towards the north and she towards the sea. As he rounded a corner taking a tree-lined avenue, the temple almost within reach, he saw them.

Khurtas were moving with impetus, their destination clear. And at their head strode Amon Tugha, walking the streets of Steelhaven as though he already owned them.

River would show the warlord he had not conquered this city yet.

He sprinted towards the rear of the war party, but he was not within a hundred yards before one of Amon Tugha's hounds yelped, turning towards him and snarling. The giant Elharim turned at its yapping, a smile crossing his face as he saw River down the street. The Khurtas turned to face him but Amon Tugha beckoned them onward. Instead of unleashing his men, he spoke two words to his hounds. They obeyed immediately, racing down the street towards River, eyes wide with hunger.

He thought about fleeing, about evading these vicious beasts, but there was no time. If he ran and managed to evade the hounds Amon Tugha might well have found Jay before he had a chance to protect her.

River moved forward to attack, seeing Amon and the Khurtas disappear towards the temple. Desperately he met the first of the hounds, his knife flashing through the rain. The hound dodged, snapping at his outstretched arm and taking a strip of flesh with it. The second was upon him in an instant and River grasped its ear as it made to bite his throat.

The creature was incredibly strong, bearing him to the ground, and River lost his grip on the knife. From the corner of his eye he could see the second hound had turned, moving forward to join its brother.

River screamed in defiance. He knew he had no chance now. All he could do was cry his last to the dark skies.

The ghoul landed with a screech, its claws digging into the approaching hound before it could begin its attack. There was a yelp. A flurry of fangs and talons and fur. The undead beast must have pursued River halfway across the city, following his scent better than any hunting dog.

Still in River's grip the first hound barked, desperate to aid its brother. He released his hold on its ears, allowing it to rush into the fray.

River rose unsteadily to his feet, feeling pain in his chest where the hound had raked him with its claws. The two dogs tore at the ghoul, rending with their jaws, but the beast seemed to wear the attacks with indifference, returning every strike with a gash of dripping talons.

He did not wait to see the outcome. Amon Tugha was most likely at the palace already.

As he sprinted down the street towards the Temple of Autumn, with the sun rising on the eastern horizon, the rain suddenly stopped.

# FORTY-EIGHT

The rain beat down, unrelenting, as they splashed through the sodden streets. Kaira carried Janessa as best she could, the queen trying desperately to keep the pace, but her leg had been all but crushed beneath her steed and she could do little more than stumble unaided.

There was only one place to go. The Temple of Autumn was the last bastion in the city. Steelhaven was about to be overrun, something evil had been unleashed and if there was to be a last stand then Kaira's former home was the only place it could be. There was some kind of poetry to it. A kind of logic that it should end there for her. But then none of this had ever been destined to end well.

By the time the temple came in sight they were both breathing heavily. Janessa still clung onto the Helsbayn as though her life depended on it, and there was every chance it would.

As they limped towards the main gate Kaira glanced upwards. The light of dawn was turning the sky from black to grey, and as she looked up the rain suddenly stopped, the sound of its relentless pounding ceasing like the end of a choral piece.

Up ahead they could see the gates to the Temple of Autumn lay ajar. Sanctuary was but a few feet away. The pair stumbled up the steps, Janessa almost collapsing as they did so, but Kaira was not about to let go, not about to give up now they were so close.

When they reached the summit, Kaira shouldered the gates

open wondering if there would be anyone here to greet them. When she dragged Janessa inside she stopped, staring about the austere courtyard.

Shieldmaidens lined the yard, standing in ranks, spears and shields held at the ready. Their leader, the Exarch, stood before them, her face hidden behind a full helm. Beyond them Kaira could see the Daughters of Arlor were waiting too, heads covered by their white veils. None of them moved as Kaira and Janessa crossed the threshold and entered the temple.

'Close the gates,' Kaira said, still grasping Janessa, who was panting in her arms.

At first nothing. Then a figure from the rear stepped forward. Kaira recognised her instantly despite the veil that covered her face. The Matron Mother's stooped gait was unmistakable as she walked to within ten feet of Kaira and the queen, and pulled back her shroud.

'This temple exacts the will of Arlor and Vorena,' said the old woman. 'Of course you are welcome, Majesty.' For a moment the Matron Mother regarded Kaira with a look somewhere near pity. 'Close the gates,' she finished.

Two Shieldmaidens moved to secure the gates to the temple, but before they could do so another warrior stepped forward, moving towards the Matron Mother.

'Wait.' It was Samina, her chin raised, her eyes defiant. 'This temple does serve the will of Vorena. But it offers no sanctuary to you.' She stared at Janessa.

'What is this heresy?' said the Matron Mother. 'Have you gone mad?'

'Mad?' Samina replied. 'I have only been blindfolded, like a goat taken to slaughter. I was a fool when I allowed this place to be desecrated by the High Abbot. We have all been fools to allow our order to be used by kings and lords and priests for centuries. Now is our chance to rise.'

The Matron Mother turned on Samina. 'Know your place,' she said, pointing back to the Exarch, who looked shocked. 'Obey and you will—'

Samina's sword flashed from its scabbard in a blur, slicing the Matron Mother's neck in a red arc. The Daughters of Arlor were screaming in a blood-chilling chorus before the old woman hit the ground.

'What have you done?' demanded the Exarch.

Kaira could only stare in horror at her sister's crime, barely able to comprehend what was happening.

'I have done what you should have done years ago,' Samina said to the Exarch. 'I have sought to free this temple from the base corruption it has suffered at the hands of others. Now *we* will control what happens here.'

'You've gone insane.' The Exarch drew her own weapon, stepping forward as Samina held her arms wide in greeting. Before the Exarch could move more than five paces, two Shieldmaidens rushed her, their spears thrusting through her breastplate.

Across the courtyard, Kaira could only watch as two Shieldmaidens attacked one another. Then more, as a battle between her former sisters sprang into life from nothing.

This was madness. Part of her mind told her this could not be happening, but it was clear a plot had been laid here, a plot that had nurtured itself for months if not years.

Samina turned back to Kaira. 'You can join us. You can return to us,' she said. 'All you have to do is give her up.' She pointed at Janessa.

Kaira shook her head, backing away. 'Never.'

She turned, wondering if they would be able to flee this place before Samina could stop them, but what she saw advancing up the steps to the temple stopped her.

Khurtas, brutal and hungry, stalked towards the temple with murder in their eyes. And at their rear, bearing all his arrogance, came Amon Tugha.

This had been a trap. The Temple of Autumn was not a sanctuary but a tomb, and Kaira had brought her queen right here.

There was no time to curse herself for her folly. She turned back to Samina, hefting her blade. Before she could rush to attack, two Shieldmaidens came at Samina and she was forced to defend herself. In the confusion, Kaira grasped the queen and bundled her across the courtyard.

Shieldmaidens fought all around as the Daughters of Arlor fled the violence screaming. Sisters who had lived with one another for years were now slaughtering each other. There was no time for lamentation, though; the only thing on Kaira's mind was escape.

Janessa did her best to keep up; both women were mindful of the danger, neither needing to speak. There would be no rescue now. They had to flee or die.

Kaira led them from the courtyard, through a corridor to stairs leading to the cliff edge. They came out on the temple's upper tier – a sheer wall of yellow rock that looked out on the Midral Sea. The sun was rising now, spreading amber light on the stark green waters. Kaira could see a boat moving past in the distance. It could have taken them to a hundred destinations, any one of them safer than here, but the drop to the seas below would have killed them both; it may as well have been a thousand miles away. She pressed on, moving along the wall, knowing that there was nowhere else to go. Knowing that she was merely choosing where they'd die.

'Wait,' said Janessa.

'We have to keep going,' Kaira replied, unable to hide the desperation in her voice.

'Enough . . . you've done enough.'

Kaira stopped, staring at the exhausted girl in her arms as she still clung to that sword, that legacy she had been burdened with. A girl who had stood tall to every challenge asked of her, who had offered herself as sacrifice to save a doomed city.

'Then we'll rest awhile,' said Kaira, leaning the girl against the foot of Vorena's statue.

If only there truly was time for rest. If only . . .

Kaira turned, knowing he would be there. Amon Tugha stood watching as the sound of battle rang up from the courtyard where Shieldmaiden fought Shieldmaiden and Khurta alike. Where blood was being spilled in what should have been a sacred place of sanctuary.

'I could have spared you all this,' he said walking forward. 'I could have made all this suffering and death mercifully swift. But no, you southrons are stubborn, I see that now. It will make the centuries to come challenging. Subjugating you will be difficult . . . but not uninteresting. Eventually I will bring you people to heel.'

Kaira stepped forward to meet him, taking up a defensive stance, raising her sword to head height. 'Then start with me.'

Amon Tugha smiled, raising his massive spear in salute. Then he rushed at her. His weapon hummed through the air as though tearing a slice from the dawn sky. Kaira ducked, spinning, swinging for all she was worth, hoping against hope that perhaps one lucky . . .

The Elharim parried her blow, their weapons clashing, the impact jarring up Kaira's arm. She screamed, furious at her powerlessness against this man. Her skill would never beat him, her goddess was not about to come down from the skies, but maybe if . . .

He dodged her blow, hacking down, striking the sword from her hand, turning his blow in mid strike and hacking the spearhead into her thigh. Kaira screamed in rage and pain for the briefest moment before the warlord swung the haft of his weapon into her face, a hammer blow that smashed into her cheek, throwing her to the ground.

Amon Tugha spared no time to gloat – his prize was waiting. Through blurred vision Kaira could only watch as he turned to Janessa, and in turn the girl limped to face him. She showed no fear, her father's sword in her hand, ready for the death this monster would give her.

Kaira tried to speak, but her face wouldn't form the words as blood dripped from her mouth and nose onto the ground. When she couldn't rise to her feet she tried to claw her way towards him but it felt like she was swimming against the mightiest current.

Amon Tugha stopped before Janessa, speaking to her for one last time, but Kaira couldn't hear the words. The queen simply stared back at the giant Elharim, defiant to the last.

The warlord raised his blade.

The Helsbayn shook in Janessa's hand. Despite her fatigue, despite her crippled leg, she stepped forward with uncanny speed, the sword thrusting like an arrow from a bow, piercing Amon Tugha's body. He grimaced, his face contorting in rage at her unexpected attack, and he staggered backwards, but not before delivering a thrust of his own, the point of his spear cutting through Janessa's breastplate.

Kaira screamed as the Elharim pulled his weapon free and the queen fell to her knees, all the vigour, all the defiance now gone from her. Amon Tugha took another step back, grasping the blade of the Helsbayn and pulling it from his body, blood spouting from the wound in a red river. He stared at the blade as though shocked that it had pierced his flesh, then flung it aside, where it bounced once before spinning from the wall and into the sea far below.

As he stepped towards where Janessa knelt, Kaira felt herself screaming, but in her malaise she couldn't form any words. Still she crawled, still she fought her way towards him though there was nothing she could do now to stop him.

Amon Tugha raised his spear one last time.

A figure sprinted past, stripped to the waist, his body lean, powerful. He leapt, arm raised high. Before the warlord could make his killing blow the man, one side of his face a mass of criss-cross scars, plunged a dagger into his neck. The Elharim dropped his spear, stumbling on his mighty legs as the lone attacker grasped the warlord's spiked hair and stabbed the knife in again and again.

Kaira could only watch as the Elharim staggered, blood spurting from the wounds in his throat that not even his massive hands could stem. He stared wildly, disbelief written large in those golden eyes as his attacker clung fast to him, pulling him away from Janessa. For the briefest moment Amon Tugha fixed those eyes on Kaira, one last look of confusion. Then he and his attacker were gone, toppling back over the wall, following the Helsbayn into the Midral Sea far below.

Kaira crawled to Janessa, who now knelt silently, her head of red curls bowed forward. Every yard was agony, but Kaira fought back the pain, fought back her tears. When finally she reached her queen she held out a hand, unable to speak. Janessa collapsed against her, resting her head on Kaira's shoulder.

The sun had come up now, bathing them in a light by which Kaira could see she was too late. Janessa was gone.

At the foot of Vorena's statue, Kaira held her queen close until the light of the morning seemed to fade. Until the shadow of exhaustion took her . . .

# FORTY-NINE

'Hake?' he shouted, his voice echoing around the battlefield above the distant sound of fighting, of snarling beasts, of dying men. 'Where are you?' Nobul could hear a hint of desperation in his own voice, but he'd lost Hake in the confusion of battle. He hadn't wanted to admit it until now but he needed that old man.

There was no one else left alive at the breach – they'd run or died. When those monsters had come from the dark the rout had been complete. Only Nobul was left standing, but where in the hells was bloody Hake?

He stumbled down from the smashed barricade, feeling his shoulder and knee and back jarring with every step. His clothes were sodden but thank fuck the rain had stopped. The sun was rising over the wall but there was still barely any light down in the shadows.

Nobul gritted his teeth against the pain.

*Not yet. Don't give in to it yet, you're not finished. Not by a long way. There's more to be done, more killing to be had before you fall, Nobul Jacks.*

The hammer was heavy in his hand. So heavy he could have happily let go of it, let it drop to the ground and never picked it up again. His breath came thick and laboured, casting a mist into the damp dawn air.

*Or maybe you are finished. Maybe it's time to lie down in the mud and the rubble and call it a day.*

A Khurta came screaming at him through the breach, just like his brethren had come before him. This one didn't have a face twisted with rage, though – this one had a face marred with terror, like it was running from the hells. Still Nobul raised his arm to attack and tensed, planting his feet, swinging that hammer again. The impact rang through his every fibre as he almost took the bastard's head off, silencing his scream of fear.

The body fell in a crumpled heap as Nobul staggered back.

'Hake?' he shouted again.

Hake didn't come.

Someone else did.

They came walking through that gap in the wall all slow and measured. Not screaming like maddened killers, but stalking like hunters. The Khurtas gave him a wide berth, moving round him like he'd kill them if they got too close. And he would, he'd kill them like he killed all the rest.

He should have rushed one of them, not given them the chance to get him enclosed, but Nobul was tired. Oh so tired. The time for rushing had passed. Let them come to him; he'd show them he was no wounded animal ready for the slaughter.

There were six in all, each pair of eyes staring at him intently, every weapon held at the ready. They stopped and glared through the cold as the last of them walked through the breach. His weapons weren't drawn, sword and axe hung loose at his sides, hands resting on them. He stood there for a while, eyeing Nobul with interest . . . respect even.

The helmet felt heavy on his head now, weighing him down like he'd forged it from a block of granite, not black iron. Nobul lifted it from his head and let it drop to the ground with a dull clank. Let them look at his face – his beaten, bloody face. Let them see his eyes. That would let them know, without a word, what they were about to get into.

Nobul squeezed the handle of his hammer one last time, taking solace in it. Then the leader spoke a word in their filthy alien language and they were at him.

He picked his target. They were rushing him as one and they'd most likely take him down, but he'd at least drag one of them along to the hells. They didn't make a sound as they came, which was more unnerving than if they'd come screaming, but Nobul was past being unnerved.

He swung at the one straight in front, but the bastard planted his foot, halting his attack and leaning back from the swing. Nobul cursed, expecting to feel the impact of a blade, the pain of his flesh splitting, but it didn't come. Instead two Khurtas bowled into him, knocking him off balance, and they all went down into the rubble. One of them had hold of his arm, another around his neck. His hammer arm was free, though, which was all he needed.

He planted his knee on a Khurta's neck, slamming his hammer down. It crumpled the side of the Khurta's skull and he went limp. They were shouting now in their weird tongue, as though coordinating their attack. The five of them jumped on him at once and he writhed, shrugging two of them off. His other hand got free and he grasped one by the throat, squeezing for all his might. Nobul roared, raising his hammer, but something snared his wrist, tightening. A rope. One of the Khurtas was on the other end of it, pulling for all he was worth. Nobul snarled in pain but he couldn't hold onto his hammer. As it dropped from his grip he grasped the rope instead and pulled, dragging the Khurta towards him a pace.

'Come on, bastards!' he screamed, lifting the Khurta he held by the throat. The man struggled in the air for a moment before Nobul slammed him down head first amongst the rubble, cracking his skull.

'I'll kill all you fuckers!'

They were on him again.

He butted one of them, shattering his nose, but this Khurta was determined enough to keep hold.

They all breathed heavily, locked in a wrestling match, four on one. Nobul staggered, feeling his strength ebb. One of them could easily have pulled a blade, stuck it in his ribs and ended all of this, but they didn't.

Under their weight Nobul fell to his knees. His breath came in strangled gasps and in front he could see the Khurta with the sword and axe, walking all casual, watching on like this was sport for him.

'Bastards! Fucking bastards,' screamed Nobul, his voice hoarse as he tried to spit his defiance.

A rope came over his head, not quite reaching his neck, and he caught it in his teeth, biting down, growling like an animal. More ropes were flung about him, securing his arms, and he could feel them binding his hands behind.

Nobul bit down on that rope, still roaring from his throat. Screaming at that lone Khurta as he stood watching, a smile slowly creeping up his face.

He stepped forward as more rope was tied around Nobul's beaten body. Then he spoke – words that were soft and slow for a Khurta. Words that spoke Nobul's defeat louder than the roar of battle or the feel of a knife to the throat.

Then black.

# FIFTY

The roof of the Chapel of Ghouls provided the perfect vantage point from which to view the city. On any other day Waylian would have appreciated it. Revelled in it. Not now, though. What he could see filled him with dread. A horror he had never felt before, even with everything he had been through.

It was better than what lay on the roof, though.

Behind him his mistress was dead, her body already blackened by the unholy canker she had allowed Bram to infect her with. But her plan had worked.

As the rain poured, the Khurtas had come again, swarming over the walls and through the smashed Stone Gate. The ghouls had met them with all their fury. From the top of the chapel Waylian had been able to see the carnage, their hunger for slaughter, the torn and wasted bodies they left behind. It was for good reason they had been imprisoned for so long – nothing could stand against them.

As the sun came up and the rains halted it seemed the Khurtas had been routed, unable to withstand the feral hunger of the ghouls. They had done enough. It was time for them to return to their prison.

Waylian turned to Bram, whose head was bowed, face hidden by the mass of sodden black hair. He did his best not to glance at Gelredida, whose body lay prone on the roof of the chapel.

'Call them back,' Waylian said, as a scream rose from over the city. It was accompanied by an unearthly howl from the depths of the hells itself, reminding him that he needed to act with urgency before the creatures destroyed what remained of Steelhaven.

Bram slowly looked up through his matted hair. Waylian felt his heart stutter as he saw those eyes, blacker than the deepest pit, glaring at him. Though Bram's hands were still secured in iron manacles it did little to reassure Waylian that he was safe.

'Why?' asked Bram, the hint of a smile on his face.

Waylian took a threatening step forward, or at least as threatening as he could muster.

'This has to end. You've done enough.'

Bram shook his head. 'No, Grimmy. I haven't done enough by a long sight. I haven't done enough until this city is flattened and the heads of the dead are piled and rotting higher than the palace of Skyhelm.'

'You can't,' said Waylian, half pleading, half demanding.

'And who's going to fucking stop me, Grimmy? You?'

'If I have to,' answered Waylian, taking another step across the roof.

Rembram Thule laughed through his yellowing teeth. His manacles jangled as he pulled something from the sleeve of his tattered robe and Waylian stopped when he saw it was the iron dagger he'd used to sacrifice Magistra Gelredida.

'You've got brave in your old age, Grimmy.' He spun the knife in the air, catching it deftly by the handle. 'Not that whimpering little puppy you were when I first found you.'

'I've been through a lot,' said Waylian. 'And I'm not scared of you.' His words might have had more impetus if his voice hadn't cracked while he was saying them.

Bram laughed again. 'What do you think you're going to achieve? This city is doomed anyway, look around you.' He pointed with his knife at the destruction evident in all directions. 'Let it crumble. Then we can build it anew, in our own image, Grimmy. Imagine that.'

'What? You think I'm just going to join you?'

'Yeah, why not? I know we've had our disagreements in the past, and we did try to kill one another, but why let a little thing like that get in the way of ruling a kingdom? Think about it; the old order is dead. We are the new, Grimm. You and me.'

Waylian shook his head, eyeing the knife in Bram's hand. 'You're insane.'

'Now, now,' said Bram with a frown. 'There's no need to be rude.'

'You are insane.' Waylian could feel the rage bubbling up inside once more. 'You've always been mad. I thought you were just arrogant and selfish at first but no – you're a fucking lunatic.'

'Be careful Gr—'

'It's not as if there's any hiding it now, is there? You're absolutely barking. Look at you! Rule a kingdom? You couldn't rule a fucking privy!'

'I'm not fucking mad!' Bram yelled, rushing across the rooftop.

Waylian let him come, watching as he held the dagger high in his hands, measuring every step as his feet splashed across the soaked roof. Bram screamed as he came, eyes of black, skin pallid and waxy like he was half ghoul himself.

When he was within reach Waylian kicked out, one swift boot to the bollocks. He was relieved when he struck home and Bram collapsed, his cry of rage rising a couple of octaves. The knife went spinning from his hand and Waylian pressed in, leaping on top of Bram as he fell.

'Call them off, Bram,' shouted Waylian, grabbing him by the lapels of his robe and slamming him back to the tiled roof. 'Call them off!'

He slammed Bram down again, smashing his head against the rooftop.

'Fuck you,' Bram answered, punching out with his manacled hands and catching Waylian under the chin.

Blood spurted into his mouth as Waylian was thrust backwards, falling from Bram and splashing in a puddle on the roof. As he foundered, Bram stood up, glaring down with black eyes.

'I'll destroy this fucking city,' Bram said, black smoke emanating from his hands as they began to elongate, talons springing from their tips. 'But first I'll destroy you like I should have done last time.'

Waylian could taste the copper tang of blood on his lips, his head spun, but still he managed to focus on Bram. In the air his former friend was tracing a sigil with those black talons, magicks of the most dark and evil nature. Waylian could feel something stirring from beyond the Veil, could sense whatever it was would consume him utterly, perhaps even eat his soul.

It would not happen. He would not let it.

He slapped a hand on the shallow wall that ran around the roof, staring through his muddled sight as he dragged himself to his feet. Bram opened his mouth to speak, to unleash all the hells, but he was not quick enough.

Waylian uttered a word.

In that instant he understood it all. He tapped the Veil, feeling the planes of magick that hid in the shadow of the plane of men. It was terrifying and beautiful all at once, birth and death, elation and agony. And Waylian Grimm embraced it; let himself flow beyond and within it like he had been born to the task.

A voice from deep within issued forth, a command he could not comprehend, and Bram screamed, high-pitched and deafening, as his left eye exploded from his head in a shower of crimson gore. He clapped a clawed hand to his face and, still whining, he staggered to the edge of the rooftop, the backs of his knees catching on the wall behind him. Bram reached out, but with manacled hands he could not stop himself as he was tipped back off the roof of the chapel.

Waylian didn't rush to see what had happened. There was no time left to check if Bram was dead. He half stumbled, half crawled to the centre of the rooftop where lay the sacrificial dagger. Grasping it in both hands, feeling the iron unnaturally cold to his touch, he closed his eyes, gritting his teeth . . .

*The beast had a thousand eyes. With them he could see every street and alley in the city, could see the dead as they lay amidst the carnage, see the fleeing masses as they were hunted down and slain. The beast lay fat over the land, spreading its girth from the apex where Waylian stood. From the prison whence it had been released. Unleashed to hunt and kill as it had done so many aeons ago.*

No more.

Waylian drew it in. Breathing deep and pulling back the beast.

*It protested – it mewled and it whined and it clawed at the ground, desperate to remain free.*

He could not allow that . . .

Waylian knelt atop the Chapel of Ghouls, gripping tight to that dagger, his lips moving silently as he recited ancient and forbidden litanies he would never remember in any waking moment, nor would ever want to.

Monsters that should never have been allowed to roam the lands of men were dragged back to their eternal prison.

And the city screamed.

# FIFTY-ONE

The tunnels seemed like they'd collapse at any minute. And the howling. Rag almost felt the need to press her hands over her ears as she sprinted through the darkness but she couldn't, she daren't let go of Tidge's hand for an instant in case she lost him in the black.

Despite the rumbling from above and the screaming that seemed to echo down every passage, she could still hear them coming after her. Shouting for her to stop, and telling her what a bitch and a little whore she was. Rag had never understood that – how blokes would always demand you stopped by shouting insults. Surely if they wanted her to stop they should try being fucking nice.

They ran out into a massive cavern, crates and caskets piled high along one side with all sorts of other dusty crap. There didn't look like there was a tunnel leading out.

'What the fuck do we do now?' asked Tidge in his bravest shit scared voice.

'I'm thinking,' said Rag, glancing round the cavern just as there was a rumble that dislodged a load of dirt from the ceiling.

*You need to think harder, girl, or you're both gonna die down here.*

There was the scrape of a boot on the floor behind her. Rag spun to see that Greencoat standing there in the entryway, knife in hand.

'Enough bloody running. Now you both get cut,' said the Greencoat, taking a step forward.

Rag shoved Tidge behind her, backing off further into the cavern, but she knew there was nowhere to go, nowhere to hide.

'You don't have to do this,' she said, having run out of sensible stuff to say. 'You could just let us go. City's gone to shit anyway, what does it matter now?'

'It matters to me,' said the Greencoat, as a massive clod of earth hit the ground behind him. 'And it matters to Bastian. You fucked things up for him and now you're gonna pay for it.'

Rag backed up further, feeling Tidge tighten his grip on her hand. Behind the Greencoat another clump of earth fell down from the ceiling, splattering on the damp floor.

He'd walked out into the lantern light now and Rag could see a big old smile on his face. The blade of that knife glinted and she knew this wouldn't be quick. Rag had known men like this all her life, men who took pleasure in other people's pain. She'd known to avoid them at all costs, but it didn't seem like she had that option now. Maybe if she gave herself up willingly it'd give Tidge enough time to escape . . .

There was another thud behind the Greencoat, but this time it weren't no sod of earth that came from the ceiling. It was huge, limbs impossibly thin, head impossibly big. Rag opened her mouth to scream but nothing came out.

The Greencoat was almost on her, but the thing came on faster, moving across the cavern floor like a gigantic spider. Tidge made a noise, a strangled gasp in his throat, and the Greencoat's smile widened – thinking it was him that was doing the scaring. By the time he realised his mistake it was too late.

The creature snapped its head forward, jaws closing on the Greencoat's shoulder. He had time to open his eyes all wide-eyed and shocked before blood spurted out all over his face and jacket.

Rag weren't about to hang around and see what happened next. She grabbed onto Tidge's hand and ran like fuck, past where the feeding was going on and back down the tunnel. The Greencoat had the notion to scream as she ran off, but it was doubtful it would do him any good. There was a tearing sound just as Rag dragged Tidge out of that room and the screaming stopped.

Her heart was pounding now, her breath coming short and sharp as her feet clapped down the tunnel. To his credit Tidge didn't make a fuss nor ask no questions – he ran right alongside her like his life depended on it. And there weren't much fucking doubt his life did depend on it.

She was running blind now. Any chance she'd had of remembering which tunnel led where was gone. Best they could do was try and avoid the howling, especially since she'd just seen what was on the other end of it.

So desperate was she to escape that she didn't give a shit what waited for them down the tunnels or in the little caves they came out in. Didn't slow as she ran out into a bright-lit chamber. Didn't see Bastian waiting for her or the big old blade in his hand.

Luckily her reactions were still quick enough, so she ducked in time before he could cut her head off.

Rag stumbled, falling to the floor, skinning her knees and her palms. Tidge tried his best to pull her to her feet as Bastian came at them.

'You've fucked it,' he said, pressing that knife to her throat and entwining his bony fingers in her hair. 'You fucked it all.'

Tidge struck out, hitting Bastian in the side of his big skeleton's head, but he didn't even flinch, just swept Tidge off his feet with the back of his hand.

'We have to run,' Rag said desperately. 'Believe me, we have to run.'

Bastian smiled, teeth like gravestones, breath like a sewer. 'Oh, I will be running. Just as soon as I've—'

A howl long and loud and all too close stopped him before he could finish. Bastian looked over his shoulder, doubt creeping onto his face.

'We told you,' said Tidge, standing there rubbing his cheek.

Bastian took a step back and Rag was sure she could see the hand holding his knife shaking. She could understand how he felt; she was shaking so hard she might just as well have been caught naked in winter snows.

A shadow fell across the entrance to the room and it seemed to leach the light from the surrounding lanterns. An arm reached from the shadows, long and pale, tipped with black claws that sank into the earth.

Rag looked at Tidge, signalling for him to come close. He moved towards her and they both backed away. Behind them the cavern rose up into the dark and they began to crawl. Bastian just stood there, watching as that creature clawed its way from the black.

'What the fuck?' said Bastian, having the smarts to back up now. He might have been the head of the Guild with the power to have anyone he wanted murdered with a word, but there was no way he was messing with this thing.

Still the creature came on, sliding from the shadows on all fours. Rag could see another of the things behind it, clawing its way into the room, clinging to the wall like a cockroach.

She had made it up the rise now but there was nowhere else to go, just a tiny little inlet to a tunnel beyond, maybe big enough for Tidge to fit through but Rag had no chance. She glanced back down again as she heard Bastian say one word . . .

'Dead!'

He was staring straight at her.

As Bastian ran towards her, knife held up, the beasts that were stalking him ran too. He stumbled up the rise to the back of the cavern and Rag desperately shoved Tidge through the gap in the rock wall. He turned when he was through, holding his hand out to her, but Rag knew there was no way she'd fit.

She turned back in time to see Bastian bearing down. He grabbed her by the ankle, dragging her towards him, and that knife came down. Rag tried to hold his arm back but he was too strong, the blade biting into her cheek. She screamed, kicked out, flailed, fighting for her life but it was useless.

'Fucking dead,' said Bastian.

Rotten fingers pressed their black talons into his cheek as the cavern rumbled. Bastian's eyes went wide as the flesh burst, tearing from his face. He gasped, the sharp outtake of breath rising hideously into a scream of agony. Rag watched in horror as the beast dragged Bastian's face off, blood oozing as the bone and muscle was unveiled beneath.

Bastian was screaming continuously, high and long as the two creatures dragged him back down the ridge. Rag couldn't pull her eyes away, couldn't close them as she saw him being torn to bits.

One dragged his arm from its socket, the other biting down hard on his lower jaw, ripping it from his torn face.

As Rag watched, a third beast moved into the cavern from the dark, sniffing the other two as they feasted. Then it smelled the air, black eyes gazing around the cavern until they fell on Rag. It hissed, and she scrambled backwards, but there weren't nowhere else to run to. Tidge reached out from the tunnel, grabbing her shirt to pull her in, but there was no way through for her.

'You have to go,' she said as the creature clawed its way towards her, hunger in its black eyes.

'I ain't going nowhere,' he replied.

She turned to him, looking at his little dirty tear-streaked face to demand he go, when the entire cavern rumbled again. This time some masonry fell from the roof, smashing down to the ground and shattering. One of the things feasting on Bastian lifted its head, then howled so loud Rag had to clap her hands over her ears.

Like an invisible hand had taken hold of it, the creature slid across the cavern floor towards the entranceway. It howled, clawing at the ground for purchase, but there was nothing to grab. As the cavern rumbled again it disappeared through the tunnel, screaming its defiance.

Rag stared in disbelief as the second beast was also dragged away screaming, as though some divine wind had blown it from the cavern. The third creature stared at her, still moving its way up the ridge. It was almost within reach now, staring and snarling and clawing its way closer. Then it slid back down the rise, its claws leaving ridges in the stone. One last snarl and it was dragged through the air and across the cavern to disappear with a defiant roar.

The rumbling continued, more of the ceiling dropping free as the cave began to collapse. Rag turned to see part of the rock barring her way to Tidge and the tunnel beyond had been dislodged.

'Let's get the fuck out of here!' she cried, crawling inside as Tidge moved through the little tunnel.

It was dark and wet inside, and Rag followed Tidge's arse as he struggled through the blackness. The rumbling never stopped and at any moment Rag expected the tunnel to collapse, enclosing them in a tomb till the end of time. She breathed out, holding back her tears, when she saw there was light from ahead.

*About time a bit of luck went your way, Rag. Best not get used to it though.*

Desperately they scrabbled forward through the tunnel until eventually they both fell into the street through a little drainage outlet. It was light now, the rain stopped and everything eerily silent. She recognised the street they were on, but she couldn't remember when she'd ever seen it so quiet.

Rag looked down at Tidge and his filthy little face. 'You all right?'

'Do I fucking look all right?' he answered.

Rag let out a little laugh. 'You look like I feel,' she said, licking her thumb to wipe some of the dirt from his face, then reconsidering. There was far too much shit for one thumb to wipe. Tidge would need a bath after all this, and she knew he'd rather have faced another of those evil bastard creatures than be given that news.

On the walk back to the tavern the streets didn't get any louder. The Khurtas didn't come screaming through looking for people to kill and rape. No one stopped them as they walked up the street, bold as brass. For the first time in days the sound of battle didn't echo over the rooftops.

When she stepped into the tavern she expected it to be empty since she'd ordered them all to hide. What she saw made her stop dead, panic gripping her stomach.

Essen, Shirl and Harkas were sat at a table. Surrounding them were other lads – lads from the Guild, from other crews, from Bastian's retinue and half a dozen other gangs she'd seen before. They were all arguing, the noise cutting through the silence of the tavern and ruining what might otherwise have been a fairly pleasant morning.

None of them knew what to do, where to go, who to see about what was next. Rag had a notion they weren't gonna get no joy any time soon, since Bastian was a half-eaten lump of flesh and bone.

*It's now or never, Rag. Cut and run or step the fuck up.*

She glanced at Harkas. At Shirl and Essen. At Migs and Chirpy, who ran forward when they saw Tidge alive and well.

*Fuck it, you'll probably only get one crack at this anyway.*

Rag climbed up onto the bar and grabbed the old tavern bell. She'd never heard it rung – no one had ever needed to before – but she grabbed the rope anyway and smashed the clapper against the bell.

The tavern fell silent, all eyes on her.

'Bastian's dead,' she announced. Immediately the place went up again, lads bickering, panicking and the like. Rag rang that bell one more time, this time longer and louder, making sure she had everyone's attention.

Then she smiled.

It was the smile she'd given Friedrik, the smile she'd given Harkas and Bastian. A smile that had kept her alive when she should, by all rights, have been a corpse in the ground. A smile she knew she'd have to start using pretty often from now on.

'Don't worry yourselves, lads,' she said. 'I've got an idea . . .'

# FIFTY-TWO

He'd found a discarded cloak in the wreckage of the battle-field, which now flapped around him in the stiff morning breeze. Regulus could smell blood in his nostrils, the rotting dead, dying embers. Sorrow. In all his dreams of glorious victory, this had been in none of them.

The enemy was gone at least, fled north from where they had come. The fell beasts that had risen to attack them had also gone back to the pit, dragged back to Hel by sorceries beyond Regulus' understanding. Word had also reached him that the great warlord Amon Tugha was dead, but then so was the city's valiant queen.

They were not the only ones. The dead lay all around. It was as though the city harboured more corpses than those left to tend them. Here and there a funeral pyre had been built and in the distance, to the north of the city, Regulus could see graves being dug.

As for the city – where before had stood unparalleled magnifi-cence, now stood a shell. Burned and crumbling edifices. Fallen monuments. This place was a giant cairn, silent and brooding in its victory. Regulus knew he had no place here, if he ever had in the first place.

There was only one thing he had to do before he left. A debt he was determined to pay.

He walked down from the battlements to the huge breach in the wall. The dead lay scattered all about here. Regulus wondered if anyone would even remember their names. There were names he would never forget – Kazul, Hagama, Leandran, Akkula. His warriors. Men he had lived beside, grown beside, and who had ultimately died for the glory of the Gor'tana.

Should it have been he who died in their place? Would it not have been more fitting for him to fall in battle alongside them? That shame would shape itself in its own way. Time would tell if the guilt of their deaths, and of his survival, would weigh on him. For now Regulus had to look to the living.

Beneath the rubble the soft earth was churned up all around. The rain the night before had made it all but impossible to discern any tracks in the mud. Still Regulus walked the battleground, his eyes scanning for a sign, his nose keen to the scent he was searching for. Before long he found it lying discarded; dented and useless in the dirt.

Regulus knelt and picked up the black helm, turning it over in his hands. He glanced about, scanning the bodies that lay fallen all around, but of Nobul Jacks' corpse there was no trace. As he searched he saw there was something else, nearer to the breach in the wall. Regulus dropped the helmet and moved towards it. Half buried in the soft earth was the hammer, lying there like some ancient weapon lost for a hundred years. He grasped the handle and wrenched it from the ground, wiping away the dirt to reveal the intricate carving on shaft and head.

Nobul Jacks was not here. Perhaps he was dead . . . somewhere . . . but not on this field.

Regulus looked to the north. The life debt of the Zatani was a holy vow, an ancient pledge that could not be broken. Nobul Jacks may well have perished, but Regulus Gor's debt to him would not be satisfied until he knew for sure.

Securing the hammer within his cloak, Regulus stepped through the breach, out onto the devastated plain north of Steelhaven, and began his search.

# FIFTY-THREE

It was a big old fire, that was for sure. Merrick had never seen its like – the Wyvern Guard had given the old boy the best send-off they could have.

The Lord Marshal lay in full armour, but without his magnificent winged helm. Jared held onto that under one arm as he watched with tears in his eyes. He also held onto the *Bludsdottr*, the sword Merrick's father had forced him to take during the last battle.

Most of the previous night had gone by in a haze. Merrick remembered taking up the weapon, remembered the Khurtas, remembered the ghouls. After that he had no idea what happened until they'd had to prise the sword from his hands while he screamed blue murder at the sky. His armour was still covered in gore, but cleaning it didn't seem to matter right now.

When he'd heard about Janessa his heart had sunk. Merrick had almost died to save her once, but perhaps it had been destined to end this way from the start. The girl had been doomed, that much was clear now, but Merrick was determined not to cry about it.

*Because you're a changed man, Ryder. Made from mountain rock – all iron and blood and the rest of that shit your father spewed. You're beginning to believe his lies almost as surely as you've grown to believe your own.*

The stench from a hundred fires was beginning to turn Merrick's stomach. Burning pork, though none of it he'd want to eat. Didn't stop the gurgling inside, though. It reminded him he was hungry, though he had no intention of eating anything until he was bloody miles away from here.

Still, he supposed he'd have to stand and watch as they burned the rest of their dead. Of the three hundred men who'd come down from the Kriega Mountains, now remained only thirty-seven. They stood in silence, no more boisterous talk, all solemn observance as they watched their dead burn. It had been a hard-won victory, but a victory nonetheless, though none of them felt like celebrating, Merrick least of all.

As the day wore on and the fires died, Jared gathered them all in one of the Northgate squares. Earlier in the day it had been piled high with bodies but the burial teams had done their jobs efficiently enough that it was almost empty. The thirty-seven Wyvern Guard stood awaiting the word of the Lord Marshal's second as he clutched that sword and that mighty helm.

'Our day is won, boys,' said Jared, with little joy in his voice. 'It's what we were born for, and there's something to be proud of in what we've done. Might not feel like it now, but that's the truth.' Merrick could see some of the lads nodding their agreement, others just staring, faces still covered in blood and dirt. 'We'll be on our way back north soon enough to wait for the next call. Might not be for years, some of you might be old men by the time we're needed again. But before we go there's a decision to be made. One that can't wait.'

A sudden wind blew up around them, a cold gust rolling in off the sea, and Merrick felt it chill him to the bone. None of the other lads gave a sign it affected them, so he was damned if he'd do any different.

Jared passed the helm to one of the other lads and took the *Bludsdottr* in two hands.

'You all know this blade,' he said. 'You all knew the man that wielded it. This sword was his by rights, passed down through his bloodline for over a thousand years. It's the blade of our order, wielded by our Lord Marshal. And last night it showed us who would take Tannick's place.'

Merrick swallowed hard. He could sense what was coming and it didn't feel a bit bloody right.

'No,' said Cormach quietly, his word echoing Merrick's thoughts.

'Only one man can wield the blade,' Jared continued. 'Only one man has the right. That man stands right there.' He pointed at Merrick, and the rest of the Wyvern Guard moved aside, giving him some space so they could all see.

'This can't be happening,' said Cormach, though none of the other lads paid him any mind.

'But we'll do this by the old ways,' said Jared. 'It's not just my word we'll go by. All those in favour, say "aye".'

The first three lads said it together, no hesitation. Then they went along the row of Wyvern Guard, one after the other, none of them showing any doubt, all of them looking straight at Merrick as they said 'aye'.

Merrick wanted to tell them to wait. That maybe he wasn't the right one for this. That he wasn't worthy – all he could do was lift a sword, not lead a band of warriors – but none of them seemed to want to hear it.

They'd gone along the row now, and Jared walked up to him, eyes bright despite the filth that surrounded them.

'Lord Marshal,' he said, and took to his knee, holding up that huge sword and presenting it like Merrick was some kind of prince. Merrick took the blade, still barely able to believe something so big weighed so little.

As soon as Jared went down, the rest of the Wyvern Guard followed his lead, each one dropping to his knee, head bowed towards Merrick. All but one of them.

'This is fucking bullshit!' shouted Cormach Whoreson. 'Not him. It can't be fucking him.'

'Mind your mouth, Whoreson. This is the new Lord Marshal,' said Jared.

'Fuck you, old cunt,' Cormach spat. 'He's not my fucking Lord Marshal. I'll not follow this prick anywhere.'

'The decision's been made.'

'Not by me it fucking hasn't.'

'Makes no odds,' said Jared, rising to his feet. 'You're a man of the Wyvern Guard. You're bound to it.'

'Like fuck I am,' Cormach shouted, tearing off his helmet and flinging it to the ground, where it bounced with a hollow clang before rolling off across the square.

'Whoreson—'

'Fuck you and fuck this,' said Cormach staring at Jared, not backing an inch. 'I'll not follow that arsehole anywhere.' He jabbed a finger at Merrick. 'I've had enough of all this shit anyway. I'm done.'

With that he turned, ripping the dishevelled white fur cloak from around his shoulders.

'You're going nowhere, lad,' Jared shouted. 'You don't just walk away from the Wyvern Guard.'

Cormach stopped but didn't turn around, gripping his fur cloak in one hand, the other hovering over the hilt of his sword.

'And who the fuck's going to stop me, old man?'

He waited for someone to tell him, but neither Jared nor the rest of the Wyvern Guard were about to tell Cormach Whoreson what to do. Merrick was damned sure he wouldn't be the one, Lord Marshal or not.

When there was no reply, Cormach walked the rest of the way across the square, only pausing to fling his fur cloak into one of the waning funeral pyres before disappearing.

Once he'd gone, Jared turned back to Merrick expectantly.

*They want you to make a speech. They want you to lead them. Good luck with that, Ryder.*

Merrick glanced down at the *Bludsdottr*, as though it might fill him with inspiration. That he might open his mouth and give a rousing speech about the future of the Wyvern Guard and how this was only the first of many glorious victories. How word would spread of their legendary prowess in battle and how they would unite the Free States and make it a better place for all the little children.

'Gather your equipment and prepare the horses for the journey,' Merrick said.

Some of the lads looked at each other for a moment, wondering if that was it, before moving to obey. Merrick was relieved at that. He'd half expected to start giving orders and be told to fuck right off, but it looked like they were taking notice of him . . . at least for now.

As the remaining Wyvern Guard went about their preparations, Merrick noted a figure approaching from across the square. He recognised the man even from a distance, his walk so slippery Merrick expected him to leave a trail.

Seneschal Rogan came to stand beside Merrick as he buckled on his sword.

'Congratulations on your appointment, Lord Marshal,' said Rogan, with a smile dripping with insincerity. There was a fresh cut on his neck that had barely begun to heal over, though how he had managed to see any action was a mystery.

'What do you want, Rogan?' asked Merrick, in no mood for the Seneschal's veiled compliments.

Rogan let out a sigh, as though even he were bored of the pretence. 'I merely wondered when you and your men were leaving and whether there was anything I could do to make your journey more . . . fleet.'

'We'll be going as soon as we're ready. Before sundown, I would imagine.'

'And the queen? You will be paying your respects before you leave?'

Merrick shook his head. 'Our respects will do her no good now.'

'Indeed,' said Rogan, and for the queerest of moments Merrick thought he heard a hint of sorrow in the man's voice. 'Rest assured, in your absence the city will be in safe hands.'

'I'm sure,' said Merrick. 'With the end of the Mastragall line I guess that makes you regent, doesn't it?'

'Quite,' said Rogan, his eyes twitching as he said so. 'A duty you can be sure I will fulfil with the utmost thoroughness.'

'I bet you will,' Merrick replied, fast losing patience. 'What of the Sentinels? What of the Knights of the Blood? Do you still control them?'

'The Knights of the Blood have refused to show fealty to a regent in the absence of a monarch. They served the Mastragalls, not Steelhaven. As a consequence they are now little more than just another Free Company.'

'And the Sentinels?'

'Alas, no more. Wiped out in defence of the queen and the city.'

Merrick felt his heart grow heavy. 'But there was one survivor. Your former colleague Kaira Stormfall yet lives . . . for now.'

'For now?'

'She may well have proven troublesome in the last day's fighting. There are rumours she turned traitor. Led the queen into the ambush that saw her murdered at the hands of Amon Tugha. When she is well enough she will stand trial for treason.'

'No,' said Merrick, fighting to control his emotions. 'She couldn't have. She loved Janessa like a sister. She would never have betrayed her.'

'That is not for me to determine, I'm afraid,' said Rogan.

Merrick turned on the man, staring deep into his eyes. He found himself gripping the hilt of the *Bludsdottr*, drawing strength from it, even though the weapon remained sheathed. For all Rogan's arrogance, for all his self-assuredness, Merrick saw doubt cloud his usually confident expression.

'No,' he said. 'There will be no trial. Let me tell you what's going to happen . . .'

# FIFTY-FOUR

Something cold touched her forehead, moisture dripping down her temple and into her hair. Kaira's hand flashed out, grasping a wrist. She heard a gasp of pain before she opened her eyes and squinted in the daylight that glared through an open window.

As her eyes adjusted to the light she saw the sparse details of a room, more a cell than a bedchamber. She was holding tight to a thin arm, squeezing hard, and when she could finally see she realised it was one of the Daughters, her hand still grasping the damp cloth she had used to dab at Kaira's brow.

She let go and the girl stumbled back. The Daughter of Arlor's face was veiled but her fear was obvious. Kaira opened her mouth to speak, to tell the girl she was in no danger, but her throat was so parched no words would come. By the time she had cleared her throat enough to speak, the Daughter of Arlor had fled into the corridor.

As she tried to slide her legs over the edge of the bed Kaira winced. She saw her left thigh was heavily bandaged, the pain of it stinging intensely. Memories of battle flooded her mind. Of Amon Tugha, of Janessa . . . cradling a head of red curls until the welcome dark of unconsciousness took her.

Gritting her teeth, Kaira forced herself to sit. She gripped the edge of the bed as tightly as she was able, taking the pain, swallowing it up along with her grief.

'You live.'

Kaira looked up at the voice, feeling something burning inside. Samina stood watching from the doorway, her expression giving away nothing of her emotions.

'And yet I'm not sure why,' Kaira replied. 'Did you want the pleasure of killing me yourself?'

Samina smiled and shook her head. 'Why would I want to kill you? We are sisters, after all.'

'We are sisters no longer. You have betrayed our city. Our queen. You turned your back on everything we stood for . . .'

'Everything we stood for was a lie. You know that, Kaira. Why else would you have walked away from this place when you were welcomed back so readily? The Temple of Autumn had to be born again. Raised anew. And it had to be done in the blood of those who allowed it to become so diseased. The Matron Mother. The Exarch.'

Kaira shook her head. 'Whose words are these? Are they the words of Amon Tugha?'

Samina threw her head back and laughed. 'You think this was all about him? You think we gave a damn about the Elharim and his crusade? This was about us. About our order. About making it pure once more. Amon Tugha was a means to an end. Had he not died at the queen's hand then it would have been someone else's.'

'You're a fool,' said Kaira, rising unsteadily to her feet, feeling the hot sweat of fever sticking her shirt to her back.

'Am I? Who stands victorious, sister? Who lives when so many are dead? The Khurtas are fled. The warlord is perished and our queen is no more. A new order beckons.'

Kaira felt her gut tighten at the words. Janessa was dead. She had failed.

'Forgive me,' Samina continued, taking a step forward. 'I knew you were close. Her death was unfortunate . . . but necessary.'

Kaira held up a hand to stop Samina coming any closer. Her breath came quick between her gritted teeth as she bit back her anger.

'Necessary? She was your queen.'

'And she was weak. A child. She would never have held the Free States together.'

'And who will do it now? You?'

329

'I will be amongst those who will strive to keep the provinces united. You could be too, Kaira. You can still join us. You can still save the city, the kingdom.'

'And if I refuse? I'll be killed, executed as a traitor?'

Samina shook her head. 'That was never the fate I would have chosen for you, sister, but there were those who would have forced the issue. It appears they have since had a change of heart, though. If you will not join us, you are free to leave.' She stepped aside from the doorway.

Kaira limped forward, taking the pain in her thigh, feeling the freshly stitched wound protest with every step. As she reached the doorway she paused, offering Samina a sidelong glance. In that moment she would have given anything for her armour, for a weapon. Wounded as she was they would most likely have served her little, but at least she would have been able to make one last show of defiance.

As though she could sense it, Samina took a further step back out of Kaira's reach, her hand never straying far from the hilt of the sword at her hip.

Without a word, Kaira limped through the doorway and out of the temple. Bodies lined the great courtyard, Daughters of Arlor kneeling beside them, whispering the last rites. Kaira couldn't bring herself to look, knowing there were sisters she had known and loved amongst their number. There was nothing she could do now, unless she wanted to add herself to the list of dead.

The wound in her leg continued to burn as she made her way out of the main gates and proceeded north through the city. There was an eerie quiet cast over the streets now. Burned and smashed buildings sat in sorrowful silence as she walked past. Here and there dishevelled souls were scraping through the wreckage of their former homes in a vain attempt to reconstruct their lives. Kaira wished them well; though she was sure they would ultimately see the folly of it.

When she had limped halfway across the city she stopped. Ahead she could see a sorry procession making its way into the Crown District. Kaira could only guess what it was – the grieving masses come to bid goodbye to their queen. To see her lying in state for the last time. They filed in through the gates of the district, some weeping openly, others simply staring at the ground, all hope fled from them.

Kaira knew she should have joined them, should have said her goodbyes, should have begged Janessa's forgiveness. But what good would it do? The girl was dead and no amount of mournful pleading would bring her back.

She moved on, feeling weariness piling onto her shoulders with every laboured step, but she could not stop. This place was cloying, strangling her, and she would only be free of that feeling once she was out of the city. There was nothing left for her here, no friends, no duty. It was clear now she had been abandoned, even by Vorena herself.

Kaira Stormfall owed nothing to this city, not any more. It had taken everything from her.

By the time she reached the Lych Gate she could hardly walk, but Kaira would not be stopped. Horses milled around the courtyard before the gate and a group of men looked set to leave. As she reached them she recognised a number of faces – the Wyvern Guard – unarmoured, swords and shields tied to their saddles, making ready to return to the Kriega Mountains. They looked odd without their battledress; like any normal band of travellers, if a little broader in the shoulder and arm. When her eye fell on the welcome face of Merrick Ryder, Kaira could barely hold back her tears.

He saw her watching him, offering a smile before walking towards her.

'You are wounded?' he asked.

'I'll live,' she replied.

He nodded, a regretful look falling over him. 'Look, I'm sorry about—'

'Don't,' she said, fighting to stay in control. Her pain and grief were threatening to spill over and were she shown sympathy, especially from Merrick, she thought she might break.

'Come to see us off then?' Merrick said, and Kaira was thankful for him changing the subject.

'No,' she replied. 'I am leaving. There is nothing for me here now.'

'I can understand that,' he said, glancing up at the ruins that used to be Steelhaven. 'You could always come with us. We could use a good sword.'

Kaira smiled but shook her head. 'No. I have served enough for one lifetime. It has brought me only sorrow.'

'Of course,' said Merrick. Behind him the rest of the men were mounting up. 'If you change your mind, go to Silverwall. I'm told if you find a man called Crozius Bowe he'll be able to put you in contact with us. He's been our agent in the city for decades, so you know you can trust him.'

Kaira gave him a nod of thanks, offering her hand. Merrick took it in both of his, squeezing it warmly. Without another word he turned and mounted his horse.

'All right,' he shouted, his voice echoing around the courtyard. 'Let's get out of here.'

With that the Wyvern Guard filed out of the Lych Gate as Kaira stood and watched them go. Merrick was at the rear and he turned for one last glance, a last smile from the corner of his handsome mouth, before disappearing through the gate.

When they had gone, Kaira limped towards the gate herself, pausing at it, staring out east onto the long road that led from it. There was emptiness out in the Free States. No one she knew or cared about. Without turning to look she knew there was even less behind her.

She had nothing and no one. No duty, no monarch. Perhaps even her goddess had abandoned her. What would she do if she left the city but wander?

Perhaps she should remain here. Perhaps Samina's offer was her only remaining option. If she stayed at least she could serve. At least she could try and do some good for the city and the kingdom.

Or perhaps Kaira Stormfall had done enough.

Gritting her teeth against the pain, she walked through the gate and took the road eastward.

# FIFTY-FIVE

aylian stood amidst the ruins. The top half of the Tower of Magisters was still mostly intact, laid out across Northgate like the head of some vast wyrm. Entire streets had been crushed beneath its fall. The base was only rubble; a mess of immense stones and timber. The symbolism was not lost on Waylian – along with the death of the tower had also come the death of the Caste. The magisters of Steelhaven were no more. All that remained was a disparate group of casters with scarcely the strength or resources to rebuild a shed.

Drennan Folds had died on the final night, a single arrow piercing his eye – whether the blue or the white Waylian had no idea. Likewise Crannock Marghil had fallen during the night, though details of his demise were not forthcoming. The Raven Knights had been all but wiped out; a handful even now searched through the wreckage of the tower, for what Waylian had no clue. He almost smiled as he watched them – ravens picking through the detritus of battle.

Waylian moved away from the dead tower. All he could wonder was, what next? The queen was dead, the city wounded, perhaps beyond recovery. Where was his place now?

*You could always go back to Groffham. Back to your mother and father. Back to the safety of anonymity. Back to the quiet security of an ordinary life. You are beholden to no one now. There is no Red Witch to taunt you any more.*

He felt the sudden wrench of his gut at the thought of her. Gelredida had been a constant bane, and treated him no better than a dog. And in the end she had sacrificed herself to rescue the city, putting ultimate trust in him to save Steelhaven if her gamble turned out to be folly.

*And you did not let her down, Grimm. You lived up to every task. You made her proud.*

Waylian smiled. He knew it was odd, standing amidst the dust and rubble of a city destroyed, smiling to himself like a bloody loon. But there was still victory in this devastation. They had won. They had defeated their enemy despite the cost and the Free States would endure. The people of this city would rise again, no matter what they had suffered. The only question was whether Waylian would stay here to help.

The remnants of the city's Caste sat in what used to be the gardens that surrounded the base of the Tower of Magisters. Waylian walked past an old man mumbling to himself, his robe burned and tattered, though the flesh beneath seemed undamaged. He ignored Waylian as he chuntered to himself, seemingly trying to solve a flood of equations as they ran through his head. Whether he'd been of sound mind before the siege, or if his efforts in repelling the Khurtas had driven him insane, was impossible to tell.

A group of apprentices sat on a stone bench some yards away. A young boy gently wept on the lap of the girl next to him. Both were flanked by older, yet no less traumatised youths, who sat staring blankly at the crushed and singed foliage that lay strewn around them. Waylian was sure he recognised them, but not well enough to strike up a conversation. Besides, they looked as though they were best left to their own devices.

Here and there magisters tended to one another, rubbing salves into wounds or bandaging limbs. None of them used any magick, as though the efforts of the last days had expended all their energies. More likely the consequences of tapping the Veil so rigorously over the past days were yet to manifest. Any further use of the Art would likely have dire effects. Everyone was fearful of what the ultimate consequences might be and Waylian could hardly blame them. After what he had felt and experienced on the roof of the Chapel of

Ghouls he doubted he would ever want to dabble in the Arts again. Only time would test his courage.

A figure came to stand beside Waylian as he watched the sad scene, heralded by the crunch of gravel beneath shoes. Aldrich Mundy adjusted his spectacles, one lens cracked, the frame bent awkwardly. Waylian expected him to speak in his usual babble of verbosity, but Mundy didn't say a word, as though even he recognised the need for solemn silence. It wasn't long before Waylian could stand the discomfort no longer.

'What now, do you think?' he asked, preferring Aldrich's doubtlessly obtuse opinion to his silence.

'Now we rebuild,' Mundy replied.

Waylian waited for more, but there was nothing. Aldrich just stared at the gathered magisters with an expression Waylian couldn't read.

Perhaps Aldrich was right. Perhaps this was a time to rebuild. To make the tower anew, to forge the Caste in a fresh image. Waylian began to believe that was something he might be able to stay and help with, but when he saw who was approaching down a gravel path to the east, he suddenly changed his mind.

Lucen Kalvor walked towards the clearing flanked by two Raven Knights. As the last surviving Archmaster he was the surrogate head of the magisters. It was still unclear whether he knew about Waylian's part in his blackmail. Perhaps he had no idea. Perhaps he was biding his time before he sought vengeance. As the Archmaster approached, Waylian knew he'd be a fool to stay and find out.

Kalvor stood amidst the burned topiary, flanked by his honour guard, and considered the sorry collection of magisters surrounding him.

'Ladies and gentlemen,' he said. 'Friends.' At that word his eyes locked on Waylian. It was obvious from that look he was not, nor ever would be, a friend to Waylian Grimm. Perhaps, despite all the work there was to do, this was the time for Waylian to bow out gracefully.

As Kalvor addressed his remaining magisters, telling them what the future had in store, Waylian slipped from the gardens, making his way north through the city.

It was obvious there was little here for him now, but was he ready to return to the relative safety of Groffham?

*Don't be ridiculous, Grimm. You were never going to do that in a million years. Gelredida saw something in you; it would be an insult to her memory for you to waste it.*

Waylian smiled as he made his way north. There was a world out there, a kingdom that might be about to sink into turmoil. The Free States would need all the heroes it could get.

Besides, Rembram Thule might be out there somewhere, scheming his schemes of domination. There had been no body, smashed and broken, at the base of the Chapel of Ghouls. It was more likely he had escaped death once again and now roamed free, ready to bring about the end of days.

And who else would stop him if not Waylian Grimm?

# EPILOGUE

The city had burned for almost a week. Seth watched the smoke rising beyond the eastern horizon, slowly fading as the days went by until there was nothing left but a clear blue winter sky. No one would ever have known the siege of Steelhaven had even happened.

But Seth knew.

He had wept for those poor souls lost to the Khurtas. Said prayers to Arlor for the heroes that defended the city so valiantly. And the queen . . . his queen . . .

What would befall them now she was gone? Now the line of the Mastragalls, which had united the provinces in the first place, was gone? Already there were rumblings from Braega and Stelmorn. Talk of the union of Free States collapsing. That would mean war, Seth knew beyond doubt. Nobles would vie for power and the men and women under their yoke would suffer for it.

Seth could only be thankful he was in a trade that would be much sought after in the months and years to come. He might be old but he was still firm in the arm, and the fire in his forge hadn't gone out in thirty some years.

He had been a blacksmith all his life, and his father before him. He had a daughter of his own but she had left many years before, yearning for a life less harsh than the one he could provide for her.

He didn't blame her for that, and since Seth's wife passed he had been content to work his forge alone.

The old man glanced through the window of his small cottage, once again thankful for the pane of glass, the only one in his home, that kept out the winter cold. His forge sat across the Great East Road from the cottage and beyond that was the Midral Sea. How much work would he be called upon to perform within its confines in the coming time of strife? How many shoes would he hammer to hooves, how many swords would he sharpen in the coming years of conflict? The thought almost made him hear the ringing of hammer on steel in his head.

Or was it only in his head?

Seth frowned, stepping closer to the window, straining his failing ears. Another ring, dull but still unmistakable. Seth opened his front door, taking a step outside into the crisp air, feeling the crunch of morning frost beneath his boot. He paused, wondering if his ears were deceiving him, but no. There it was again, the clank of metal coming from his forge.

He reached back inside his cottage, grabbing the axe that sat beside his door. As he quickly made his way across the road, his heart began to thump the harder, his grip tightening on the wooden handle. He'd only ever chopped wood with this axe, never in his life had he had reason to raise a weapon in anger, but he'd bloody well do it if need be. Seth might be getting on in years but he was still fit, still able to look after what was his.

Another clang of metal echoed within the forge as he reached the door, this time accompanied by a muffled curse. Seth reached for the handle of the door and noticed that his hand was shaking. For a brief moment he tried to tell himself it was because of the morning cold, but the old man had never been one to lie to himself. He knew he was scared. Better to admit it than try and pretend he had ever been a brave man.

The door swung open silently. Seth felt the last of the forge's heat blow in his face as he did so. Embers still burned in the fire, casting a dull glow within the building. As quietly as he could, Seth stepped inside, grasping the axe with two hands. He peered through the gloom, staring across the forge towards his anvil.

A gaunt figure stood beside it, Seth's hammer gripped in his hand. In the other he held a chisel, pointing it awkwardly at the chains that bound his wrists. Vainly the figure tried to strike the head of the chisel, but the chains that restrained him made it almost impossible. The best he could do was tap weakly, but not so weak that the sound did not echo around the small room.

The figure cursed, and Seth could see raw and livid welts around those manacled wrists as though they had been bound in irons for weeks.

'For fuck's sake,' sighed the bedraggled intruder, lifting his head forlornly.

Beneath a tangle of dark hair and wispy beard, Seth saw a young face, handsome yet marred by care. One eye was covered by a makeshift patch; a piece of cloth torn from his filthy robe. Blood had run and dried beneath the patch, staining the young man's cheek with black.

'What are you doing there?' demanded Seth, though it was obvious for all to see what the youth was doing.

With another sigh, the intruder looked across the forge at Seth. Then slowly, as though Seth were some kind of old friend, he smiled.

It was a cold smile, a smile of death. Seth could feel it right in his heart. At that moment he knew this boy was dangerous, but despite his fear, despite the shaking in his knees and the cold dread that seeped into his bones, Seth knew he couldn't run.

'I appear to be making a fool of myself with these chains, Seth,' said the lad.

It took two heartbeats before Seth realised there was no way the young man could have known his name.

'How did you—'

'It doesn't matter,' he said, shaking his head as though already tired with their whole conversation. 'All that matters is I need these chains gone. And you're going to help me get rid of them.'

Despite his fear, Seth tightened his grip on the axe. He wasn't about to be ordered about in his own forge. Whoever this lad was he couldn't just expect Seth to do his bidding. Besides, someone had put those chains on him for a reason. Seth would be foolish to take them off without so much as a 'by your leave'.

'I . . . I'll do as I damn well please,' said Seth. 'I'm the one with the bloody axe.'

The lad sighed again. 'Indeed you are, Seth. But that's not the only weapon in the room.' Seth glanced at the hammer in the lad's hand, but he knew that wasn't what he meant. There was something not right about this boy and Seth knew he had to be wary – his life might well depend on it. 'Knowledge is as powerful a weapon as any blade. And I have knowledge, Seth. I know about your daughter in Fleetholme. I know about her children, Dorry and Karl. I know how they'll all die. I know their last words.'

Seth felt the forge grow colder as the lad spoke. It chilled him to his very soul. He felt his fingers freeze as they gripped that axe and he knew it would never do him any good. It was obvious now – this boy was doom. For the first time Seth wished he'd been a much more pious man. He could only hope Arlor was watching over him.

'Don't hurt them,' he said. He knew it was pitiful and stupid. That he had no bargaining power here, but he had to say it all the same.

The lad smiled again. 'Get me out of these, Seth,' he said, laying the hammer and chisel down on the anvil.

Seth felt the axe drop from his grip. He hadn't made a conscious decision to let it go, but still it fell from his numb fingers. He walked forward, feeling a cold tear trace a line down his cheek. As he picked up the hammer and chisel he felt the sudden wrongness of what he was doing – as though he had a brief opportunity to do something good, do something right for the Free States, for the world. If he took the hammer and smashed this boy's head to offal he would save countless lives and if he died in the process it would all be worth it.

Instead, Seth braced the edge of one cuff against his anvil. It was secured by a double bolt at the rim. Seth raised his hammer and struck one clear, then again to remove the other. The iron fell from one of the lad's wrists and with another smile – that cold, dead smile – he placed his other cuff on the anvil. Two more strokes, two more bolts, and the boy was free.

He stared at his ruined wrists for some moments, as though

breathing in his new-found freedom. All Seth could do was stand there with the tools of his trade in his hands, knowing it was probably the last time he would ever use them.

'Thank you, Seth,' said the lad, looking up at the old man with his one eye.

Seth saw only darkness in that eye. Saw the death of everything. Saw the end of the world.

'Are you going to kill me now?' the old man asked.

The lad paused, as though considering it. Then he laughed, long and loud, harder than any joke should have made any man laugh.

'Seth, I like you,' he said. 'And rest assured, you're going to live.' All the humour drained from his face, all warmth seeped from every gap in the walls and the light seemed to dim. The lad leaned in and Seth could smell his fetid stench as he whispered. 'But you'll wish I'd killed you. When you see what's coming, Seth, you'll wish I'd torn the flesh from your bones and left the rest out for the gulls to peck on.'

Seth felt a second tear roll down his cheek.

The lad was smiling again now. Smiling as he moved by, walking on thin bare legs. He paused at the door for a second, breathing deep of the cold morning air.

'And when the world is crying out in pain,' he said. 'When a thousand thousand souls are screaming for mercy. You can tell them it was Rembram Thule who brought this whole stinking mess down on them.' He turned to Seth, showing his yellow teeth in a wry smile. 'And you were the one that helped me do it.'

With that he was gone through the door, leaving nothing but cold dread behind him.

Seth stared after, the open door letting in the cold for a long while.

That day, for the first time in thirty some years, the fire in his forge died.